Low, In The Valley

Dave Felholder

To Annie
I can't think of
anywhere else I'd rather be...

While we seek mirth and beauty, music light and gay,
There are frail forms fainting at the door;
Though their voices are silent, their pleading looks say,
Oh, hard times come again no more.

Hard Times, Come Again No More - Stephen C. Foster

CHAPTER ONE
For A Morgan Silver

Charleston, West Virginia - 1887

I saw a gorilla once.

It's a funny thing I guess. The things you think about when you're on the edge of dying. Up until then, I'd forgotten about that gorilla. But, the man lying on top of me, pressing my face into the dirt must have have done something to jolt my memory back to that day.

They'd brought the beast to Charleston all the way from the deep jungles of Africa in one of those traveling circuses. The kind that slowly moved along in those long trains desperate to earn some coin in whichever backwater town they stopped in. The stop this time happened to be outside Charleston, the city I called home. Like most cities, nothing came free in Charleston, not even gorilla poking sticks.

They kept that gorilla cramped in a small cage outside the city for everyone to see and prod with their little pokin' sticks that you could purchase for an Indian Head of course, if you were so inclined to poke a gorilla. There were other tents as well, caging a variety of other wild creatures from equally exotic locations as this gorilla, but there was just something about him that held appeal. Everyone needed to see him. Everyone needed to poke him. He was beaten, he was defeated and he sat and took those pokes as any caged creature would, with a sad dignity, grinning. Take no offense on the account of the gorilla, I'm sure he was lovely, I just never had the chance to get to know that particular one on a personal level is all.

That gorilla wasn't mad at me for putting him in that cage no more than the man on top of me was mad at me for stepping too close to the Cairns. No, he was just mad for being where he was, getting poked with a stick until his mind broke. The man sprawled out on top of me was mad for a different reason beyond a broken mind, though he had that as well. The man was mad because he had the darkness of the Cairns inside him and like that gorilla there was just nothing left of him worth reasoning with. And, I couldn't fault either one. It was just in their nature to hate the things that tortured them.

Everything had gone wrong, which was where I found myself often, on the wrong side of everything. But I will say, lying on my stomach in the middle of that brick road gazing into the darkness of the Cairns with my corset barely containing me and my dress hiked up around my waist about to be crushed alive by the considerable girth of a gorilla-sized Cairnborn man was exactly how I would describe things as going wrong.

As I lay there, pretending to be dead, I felt the Cairnborn's cold, clammy hand creep down toward the small of my back, clawed fingernails tearing at my corset looking to explore my southernly regions.

I really was trying not to piss myself, sincerely, I should have stopped to squat in an alley before walking all the way east down Quarrier St to the Cairns. Could have made a stop along the way in a hundred different places. But, a nickel is a nickel as they say; though this job was worth more than that. Worth more than two nickels even, hell maybe even a whole Morgan. We would have to see. My point being, I needed to pee and how embarrassing it would be for anyone that found me. Guess it wouldn't really matter to me after I'm dead, but I did secretly hope this man would drag me further into the Cairns when he was finished exploring under my dress and leave me far from the eyes of anyone to find. Shouldn't have swallowed so much ale before coming over, but hey, sometimes I needed the extra liquid push to get a job done.

I do tend to ramble about unimportant things when I'm nervous. I apologize.

The most important thing you should know about me is I would do *anything* for coin.

It was my job after all, to *do* anything. I never had much of a taste for belly-tickling every night or being leg-up on an alley wall like a lot of tit-bits around my age, though I did try it for a couple years back. I didn't care for the clientèle. Old men with limp dicks and even worse things congregating on and around their livery bodies. Occasionally, a younger man may shy his way toward me and I would teach him a few things to take back to his *inamorata*, but in the end those lads would always search me out again having grown bored with their own one-trick-fillies at home. I was younger then and still learning all of my life's lessons well before I had truly become into being womanly, but it was boring for me. Trivial. The same ins and outs, day after day after long nights in Washmaid Row earning that coin. The scenery rarely changed.

Having humbled the rest of the *nymphs du prairies* all around Washmaid Row, earning every single small amount of coin I possibly could, I discovered I did have a minor bit of respect for myself mixed with an equal amount of wicked depravity which earned me quite a reputation. So I went from servicing the lads in the brothels to servicing them to my own higher standards in my own time. A *selvedge* in a town of *bumblebunches* just looking for my own way. The other girls hated when I called them that.

I made it a point to better myself and to better my patrons since my early shackled-limb nights on Washmaid Row. They were slightly less perverse - maybe more so in a *specific* kind of perverse way - heavier handed with the silver and a lot more hands-on direction than before but that worked for me. It's all about who you know and *knowing* who you do and doing who you know. That was confusing for me as well, but it's what I lived by back then and still live by to this day so don't worry.

But, you're not reading this because I'm a brave person. You're reading because I'm a fool.

So there I was, hands tied, face down at the edge of something I had no right being at the edge of. Death. Going to the Harvest.

I looked back over my shoulder in awe at the Cairnborn on top of me. Just like that gorilla, he was an absolute beast. Maybe the biggest man I'd come across in all my years spent measuring the size of men. I tried to wiggle free, but it didn't help that my hands were tied behind my back and the large man from the Cairns was pinning me down with his legs. Trying to take a full breath was impossible with him on me, crushing me. I wanted to close my eyes.

With a quick twist of my hips I managed to roll myself over, lining up my face with his. It was hard to make out in the absence of lantern on such a dark night, and being this close to the Cairns, everything lay cast in heavier shadow, but I'm pretty sure the man grinned.

My mind went back to the gorilla in the cage again. If you're wondering if I stood all day in line to poke that gorilla, yes I did. Of course I did. He was a giant. A giant among apes. It was in my nature after all, to poke at something until it broke.

The shirtless man - lying off to the side in the alley not far from the Cairnborn and myself - hired me out for some nefarious activity not worth going into here. Tied my hands behind my back, then left me out there before he went and lost his head. That being, his head taken, ruthlessly, by the Cairnborn sitting on me. Quickly twisted it off like a damned supper-chicken. Crack and painless. I realize that describing this poor sod as shirtless first was probably not as effective as headless, but I like to save the drama. I also didn't get payment for our wickedness ahead of time and I'm not one to clean the dead of their dollars, even if they do owe me. Blood has a way of soaking into money by more than just what's washed off from the surface.

Pockets, is what I'd taken to calling this new patron of mine in all the thirty-seven minutes I'd known him. I didn't know his real name, doesn't matter I reckon. All I cared about was how deep his *pockets* were and how much coin he'd toss me when we finished. See how I got that nickname now? Yeah, you're getting it, I'm also brilliantly witty. No limit to my wit. Or, so my Mama always said. I get that from her, left quite an impression on me. The other things I got from my Dad. That being my handsome looks and my devilish sense of turpitude. Things men are willing to pay good nickels for. If Pockets said bend over backward and he threw me enough Morgan silver, I'd ask if he'd like me to kiss my own heels. I'm that flexible. Another gift from Dad, or so Mama said.

Everyone knows you don't get this close to the Cairns, a dark and deep block of city streets tucked away east and south in our fair, sweet Charleston. You stayed back far as you could, at least to Brooks St, Broad if you could help it; certainly didn't want to find yourself on Morris or you were in the thick of it by then. Something not so pleasant held those Cairns streets in utter blackness we called the Keening, thick and black as the burning coal from the mountains and one would do well to avoid. Look into the Cairns long enough you'd see things moving along with the foggy Keening as it floated and rose among the decrepit houses and grassy covered old stone streets. Shadows became shapes became ghosts. You'd have to be the holiest (or dumbest) of men to step inside that haunted place and not soil your trousers. Poor Pockets found that out quickly in our duplicitous game of *dare* and he didn't even go all the way inside. Just lingered around the outness of it. He didn't realize his mistake either of course, unless heads can still ponder when they are rolling free from their bodies.

The Cairnborn man straddling me *was* a beast of sorts. What *sorts,* I had not a guess. Not a gorilla, I know that. He was forgotten by regular civilization, lost and living in the shadows and tall stones of the foul place. His teeth were cracked like a rock-eaters' and loose pale skin sagged around his cheeks and eyes. My knees tucked against my chest were the only things holding him at bay. I wasn't strong enough to push him off, I had the sense he wanted to bite into my flesh.

Cairnborn never ventured out into the city but tempt the fate of the Cairns, as Pockets and I did, and it will draw one or two of them close to the edge. As kids we were told not to venture into the Cairns.

> *Far do the Keening reach from Cairns' deep*
> *Deep does the dark cry under children's feet*
> *O' weep, O' weep*
> *Don't you weep for me*
> *Fallen O' worm of Autumn*
> *Keep your tears from me*
> *For Ay'll see you at the waters' bottom*
> *An' under the earth I sleep for thee.*

We were told it was to keep us safe. I said otherwise. Pockets didn't have much of a thought whether it was or wasn't safe. He wanted to go there just as much as I did. Said he was bored, and willing to pay for my misdeeds. Our misdeeds.

The Cairnborn man coughed and hacked in my face.

"You have no manners, sir," I said to the sow-faced, heavy-weighted, bulge of a man. He pressed further on, hot drool dripping from his mouth to mine. Tasted like goat milk gone two weeks past sour. I turned my head and spat. Not a fan of milk. Not even really a fan of goats.

I heard frantic murmuring behind me; I looked back, still keeping the brutish man at bay with my knees. Solemn, shadowy figures lurked on the edges of the Cairns, dodging in and out of the teeming Keening, too scared to follow their companion into the city. Some of the figures rose tall and then retreated with the Keening like animals caught; some stood as dark statues, watching and anticipating. I would not be a meal for these starving bastards. I would not be dragged into the Cairns.

I was in quite a pickle.

"Burrow, if you're there, I could use a little help," I whispered to my own hallowed providence of timidness, or Hallowfulk, you could call her if you were pressed for time.

The last of my breath caught in my throat as the Cairnborn squeezed his cold hands around my neck.

I closed my eyes. It was hard to breathe.

I wanted to sleep. I wanted to keep my eyes shut and slip back into the sweet nothingness of the Harvest.

A harrowing cry called from the Cairns, jolting me, followed by a baying of hounds. The Cairnborn sprang to his feet, releasing me. I took as deep a breath as I could, painful, not knowing if it would be taken again. His hands grabbed my hair, tugging me along and since I didn't want to lose my locks I shuffled with him as he dragged me finally into the Cairns. Once past the dark border, he released my hair and let me fall to the ground. My head hit the brick hard.

Wooden buildings, dark and old, stood like felled forest pine lining the moss-slick cobblestone roads. Windows were boarded, no breeze blew through the black alleys.

Figures shifted in the thick of the Keening as it flow closer to me like an eager bride. I felt the coldness from the Keening shivering into me like a depression. Starting at my legs, through my tights. Up my thighs and dress. My corset, then my shoulders. I felt a heavy depression weighing on me like a blanket of sod in a grave.

Maybe it was due to being dragged across cobblestone, or maybe it was a small blessing given from

Burrow, but I felt the rope bindings around my wrist loosen. I slid my hands free, but remain on my knees and holding still as a virgin before her betrothed, I shivered.

The man no longer had a taste for me as he watched the growing shadow figures around him. The shapes moved in closer and he hissed at them like an animal. I fingered Sparrow, the small knife I kept at the dimples of my back, then slowly stood, rising to face what seemed my inevitable doom. Everywhere around me, bodies from the depths of the Cairns crept in as the Keening rose higher.

I held Sparrow up, letting them see her, though I knew damned well it would do no good. If it were to be knife work, I'd have to step in close. Sparrow had a slight curve to her, for slashing more so than stabbing. Slashing is easier, less messy. Stabbing is nasty business on account of pulling the blade back out, tends to stick if you hit bone. But, these things, these Cairnborn didn't have the mind to think about things like that. Getting stabbed or slashed. Not like you or I would when faced with a bloodied, desperate girl with a knife.

I wasn't going to die without a fight.

I wasn't going to be a victim of my own foolishness.

I felt a flash of light. *Felt*. It was that bright. I held my fingers to my eyes, blocking the light and the heat as it pushed me back a step.

A man stepped forward out of the bursting light from within the further depths of the Cairns.

Like a burning lighthouse in the sea of night more men appeared from the darkness and the Cairnborn vanished, hissing and angry at the new visitors.

One of the Deluge stepped forward; a middle aged man, deep set cold-water blue eyes and cropped black hair bleeding down to his bearded jaw. The light that had been irradiating from him was fading to a soft glow.

He spoke. "Conley Mahren, come with us."

I recognized the man as Anrose, Second Chancil of the Church of the Deluge and one of the few men I did *not* want to find me there. I went with them with no argument. The Deluge I could deal with, I have before many, many times. Being alone in the Cairns, however, I had no stomach for that.

It was an obvious choice to me.

CHAPTER TWO

The Glorious Revolution Of Spain

I'll start again by telling you of Queen Isabella II and how a single bottle of wine she'd been rather fond during her stay in *Chateau de Pau* had found its way to cross the Atlantic into my glass, and there severely altering the trajectory of my life. I mention this, because in hindsight *and* in theory, this is all the wine's fault.

"You slipped into something more comfortable," I said, watching Anrose. The Deluge wasn't laughing. It wasn't that funny anyway, I understood that, but the ice needed breaking. I was also regarding the Deluge shift I was allowed to change into - comfortable yes - styled in a way that spoke to modesty. I was also given fresh underclothes - a short chemise and drawers with some nice wool leggings, though I wished for silk. They even offered me a chance to clean myself in a warm bath. All in all it wasn't a bad trade for being dragged here.

Anrose kept no attempt at modesty when we first arrived in his room; unbuckling a chainmail gorget from around his neck, followed by a black surcoat made of tightly woven wool with the white open palms of Low the Kind sewn at the chest.

Anrose kept his steel born eyes on me as he pulled his cassock over his head, an indication of his high rank among the Deluge. Barring his overall imposing stature, it was hard to take this man as a threat as he stood before me wearing only his stark white union suit. He crossed the room to hang the wool surcoat on a hook, then placed the gorget on top a chest-of-drawers. Finally, he looked back at me.

I thought about asking if he brought me here to transgress or if this was only for show, but I held my tongue. Of course I couldn't hold my tongue still for long. Another skill of mine.

"Do you care if I lie down a bit? In that cozy looking bed?" I offered him a crook of a smile as I spoke. "I'm a little more accustomed to less accommodating manners much deeper in the bowels of this fortress. Is it satin? Looks expensive."

One of his eyebrows raised in that kind of "who even are you" look when someone oversteps their place. I'm sure you've seen it before. The kind of look telling you to still your tongue, no time for jokes, no time for small talk, this is all business.

A young girl with dark hair and blue eyes stood at the edge of the room, holding a bottle of dark red wine (yeah, that bottle. Queen Isabella's). She puffed a breath of laughter out of her nose, then grew silent again when Anrose glared at her.

Normally when I'm *invited* to the Cistern I'm taken directly to the below rooms, where all the other regular folk *wait* to be reminded of their wrongs. I was quite familiar with the Cistern, a glorious building raised to the testament of Low the Kind.

The Cistern was a round, five-story, black stone tower built on the banks where the Kanawha and Elk Rivers met. The first floors of the Cistern were empty except for a two-story deep pool of water, called the Basin. It was the holy water of Low the Kind, untouched by anyone except the few Deluge assigned to maintain it. Get caught dipping your unholy ass in that water, you'd be hanged the same day.

Simple barracks for the Deluge and rooms for classes - worship, military strategy, etiquette and so on - were on the floor above the Basin. Under the Basin in the basement (or, the below rooms we called them) were for the ne'er-do-wells like myself when brought in for higher learning.

On the top floors were the nicer rooms for the more senior members, like my friend Anrose here. Second Chancil. His room was lavish. Paintings of prior Chancil stood watching like carrion birds along almost every wall, leaving little room for more. A large fireplace sat quietly burning in one corner, above it several rifles ranging in vintage from the Rifled Musket kind made in Springfield to the more modern lever-action Winchesters - the weapon of choice for the followers of Low.

Anrose noticed me looking at the rifles. "How long has it been since you held one?" he asked.

"I don't reckon ever," I answered. "I was only twelve when the war ended and your lot took the guns when no one was looking." Go ahead and ask anyone, the Deluge ruled Charleston and the Parish with their rifles, like it or not and the U.S. Army didn't give a shit, they were too busy tidying up after the Reconstruction Act was finally worked out.

I wanted to hold that Springfield, I hadn't seen such a thing in years.

But, I changed the subject. "The light in the Cairns. What was it?"

"Simple trick to scare away those born there," Anrose said. He sat with one leg crossed over the other in a simple wooden chair across from where I sat. It creaked when he leaned back. My chair was nicer, padded with velvet; the only furniture in the room, other than the comfortable looking bed.

A gold and silver rug warmed the cold stone of the floor; it's embroidery looking from the regions somewhere around Western Anatolia. Rugs and wine, the Turks traded them out like a Farrowyard whore; different than a Washmaid girl, and if I have to tell you the difference between those strumpets, then you've clearly never been to Farrowyard. Best to find a quick bath after that tumble.

We sat in a long silence staring at one another. It was almost too much for me to bear. The thick mid-summer humidity settling into the room from the open window was also unbearable.

"Faith," Anrose added to the silence and the creaking chair. My face must have told him I wasn't understanding. "To frighten away the Cairnborn. It's effective, for now," he said.

I kept my eyes locked with Anrose's. I was getting bored of this room.

"Have you brought me here to be a sacrifice? Or, hang me just for living?" I asked.

No response.

"You brought me here for a reason, right? What do you want?" I looked from him to the satin bed and back at him again.

He shook his head *no*. "Silence would make me content," he said.

Fine, silence it was.

I heard the uncomfortable shifting of the dark haired girl holding the wine as she endured the silence with us. It must have been tough on her to deal with the stubbornness of the two of us.

"You can-" I started to say, but Anrose cut me off.

"Please don't speak to her," he said.

So I didn't, I chose to ignore her for the rest of the time. Hard to do, as pretty as she was. Wasted here. Youth and beauty go a long way and earn a lot of coin in Washmaid.

We waited for what seemed like hours in this game of shifty eye contact until finally the bedroom door swung open.

High Chancil L'fowl shuffled in. He was much older than Anrose, kept his hair in tradition of the Deluge, cut cropped to his scalp, thick white sideburns leading into a chinstrap of a thin white beard. His furious eyebrows bounced back and forth below a wrinkled brow with every shuffle he made toward us until finally he stopped behind Anrose.

Anrose stood and let L'fowl sit. Baffling they would allow me to have the better seat in the room. I rubbed the velvet with the palm of my hand to remind myself of my current comforts before they were taken.

"Conley, you came," L'fowl said. He coughed into a rag. His eyes moved quickly around the room.

"Did I have a choice?" I asked.

"No." Anrose replied from the side of the room where he lurked.

"Listen, whatever I've done this time, I'm sorry. Again," I started. "I didn't know she was promised to someone."

"No, girl. Listen now, quickly," L'fowl said. He had a manic urgent way, moving around the room. Shuffling papers here and there on the desk.

"I'm listening as quick as I can. Pockets, err what ever his real name was, paid me so you know, before you go off to scolding me. Actually he didn't pay me. I should have taken the coin first. My mistake. He *was* going to pay me for-"

"Pockets, is that what you called him? How delightful. Pockets - " L'fowl was saying.

"Owen is…*was* still a member of the Deluge. Though he was starting to go astray in some of his dealings with the flesh," Anrose said, he spoke over L'fowl from the edge of the room. "But, whatever was between the two of you tonight is now why you are here. We knew of your dealings with Owen, and where it would lead you and where to find you. A matter has come up and we need someone of your…"

I stopped him, then looked from L'fowl to Anrose. "See…you said you didn't bring me here to you know…you know. I would say it but I don't want to soil those virgin ears of yours." That earned me a wicked look from the bearded warrior and another nose scoff from the wine girl that I was suppose to be ignoring.

L'fowl chuckled in a way that slightly shook his eyebrows, then grew serious again, drawing my attention back toward him by coughing. "Conley-" he started.

Anrose went to the door and whistled short and quick down the hallway, stopping L'fowl from speaking. A young man looking to be in his early twenties walked in.

"Samuel, do you know her?" Anrose asked the young man, he nodded toward me.

The young man only shook his head "no".

"No, I don't suppose you would, considering. All the same," Anrose moved around Samuel, looking over him like a prize. "Samuel, this is Conley Mahren."

Again, L'fowl tried to interject himself but was cut short by Anrose holding his hand up. L'fowl was old, and the High Chancil, but clearly Anrose was the one to be commanding this room.

I bore my eyes on Samuel. Good looking lad and he'd not adopted the cropped-short hair style of the Deluge just yet, thankfully, keeping his hair messy but not unclean, or ratty. Likely on purpose that way, to separate his youth from the rest of the aging Deluge. With all that, what lured me into him were his eyes. They were gentle. Still untainted by the dredging of the Deluge's strict way of living. There was still a life in them, still hope.

"Conley," Anrose began, "Knowing your *reputation…*"

L'fowl was overtaken by a coughing fit, but settled it soon with a stern look from Anrose. A line of drool ran from his mouth and he covered it with his rag as he tried to speak, coughing again just a bit, turning his face red to hold it in. "Forgive me, I am old," L'fowl whispered. "And, only a fool."

"As I was saying. Samuel has been raised since birth to be the most pure of us all, an ender to the darkness if given the chance. He is completely untouched. High Chancil L'fowl saw to his upbringing since birth."

"You want me to take him into the Cairns?" I guessed. Why not? It was a good guess considering they stalked me to the edge and brought me all the way back here to their fancy bedroom with a nice big comfy looking bed.

"Nothing like that. As I said, he is pure," Anrose paused. He looked at Samuel.

L'fowl stepped forward, "Second Chancil, I can't-"

Anrose held that damned hand up again to silence the

older man. "Please give us the room High Chancil. You've done your duty for this night and I thank you. It's time for you to retire to your chambers."

"I'm not tired," L'fowl let out a deep sigh. "We've been diligent since his birth to make sure he would be the one to end that…that thing. All of the boys I've raised are gone! He is the last-"

"Enough." Anrose opened the bedroom door and motioned for L'fowl to leave. He was gentle with him, like a son would be with an elderly father.

"We agreed this boy would be the one. Please, not this way…you're making a mistake Anrose," L'fowl pressed.

When it was only the three of us, Anrose continued, "I don't really care how you do this. I'm sure someone of your *aptitude* can muster something. Some reason. Nothing fancy. He has no experience in the matters of the carnal."

"But, don't you people want the Cairns sanctified or something?" I asked. I was beginning to feel like I didn't have a say in this matter before me. Nor did Samuel.

"Some things are better left unasked. But, I'll give you this much; L'fowl has lost his way in preserving what we Deluge have worked so hard for. Peace through Low, above all things. Now, I would of course make this very worth your time if you kept this all between you and Samuel." He tossed me something. It caught a gleam from the sun peering the window.

I caught the silver Morgan with the deftness of Halfway Criley, which was to say I dropped it. They didn't call him Halfway because he was born with only had one arm, that's another story, Burrow bless his mother. I bent and picked up the coin, fingering the stamp of the eagle on one of its sides; the profile of our Lady Liberty with flowers in her hair carved on the other. It was real all right. Newly pressed and mint.

"There's a lot more when the deed is done." Anrose walked toward the door, "I shall have the wine poured for you." He shut the door behind him, leaving Samuel and I alone in the room with only the nice linen bed.

"Lots of wine," I smiled as I looked at the nervous boy standing across the room.

Everything was about to change.

"I can go if you ask me, or I can stay and we can figure this out. I know three ways out of here." I really didn't. I'm sure I could figure it out.

"I'm afraid it's not that easy. Low the Kind is here, watching us." Something moved in the shadowed corner of the room. A figure. I couldn't focus on it.

Samuel was right, Low the Kind was here and he was watching.

Getting into the purse of the Deluge was as stupid as it was lucrative. I wanted to say no, but my mama didn't raise a quitter and while I did consider myself lately more of a hobbyist in the matters of rattlin' headboards, coin is coin, and the Deluge had plenty of that. I've done so much worse in far worse places than a fine linen bed in a well-lit room with a boy as pure as he and all his consecrated, firm body.

Samuel slowly sipped at the glass of Queen Isabella's wine, dark and red, heavy like the air in the room, but just as sweet as the lad's smile.

I should pause and tell you that I probably would have done this for free had the setting been anywhere but the Cistern - as I've mentioned I am still one for entertaining hobbies - given Samuel's eagerness. He was nervous, it wasn't hard to see. We talked and sipped that sweet wine for a while after Anrose left the room. Samuel told me of his being raised in the Cistern alone, not allowed to leave the fortress. They kept him pure and away from the streets and of our sinners. They fed him fruit from trees grown in the gardens of the Cistern, as pure as he. White goat's milk when he was a babe, then pure spring water bucketed in from the mountains of the Allegheny; not an easy walk out of Charleston. I was the first woman he spoke to; he had seen them before, *of course*, he was sure to mention with pride as some sort of achievement. Proud and pure he was. And impossibly kind. He allowed me to lead the way in our indecent duties.

I removed my shift - pulling it up over my head slowly at first to give Samuel a little something to look forward to. I felt the presence of Low in the room growing. Spiteful. Jealous. Hateful. I felt if I hadn't gone through with this, it would be a curse to Samuel and me. I certainly do have a sense of self preservation, and if that can be honored with a quick tumble, then so be it. I held my silver coin in one hand and tried to enjoy what came.

"What's your last name, Samuel?" I asked, already at

a loss for small talk and sensing he was beginning to get the nervous shivers. He nodded.

"I don't reckon I have one," he returned, watching as I rolled down one leg of my wool leggings. "Why?"

"Don't reckon it matters."

We got wine drunk, fumbling around with what clothes remained then climbed into that nice linen bed.

I faced away from the lad, lying flat on my stomach to feel the linens; it wasn't everyday I was allowed to bed in something as nice and soft as this after all, so why not enjoy? I couldn't look Samuel in the eye anyway, it didn't feel right with what watched from the corner of the room. Low be damned, the *peeping bastard* they should call him. Samuel took me that way, setting to task to appease the Second Chancil's request with a sense of duty as I watched the thing in the dark corner of the room watching me.

The standard of my depravity couldn't possibly go any lower. You'll see. It was all up from there.

I was full of wickedness and that's why I was there, just like that one random bottle of wine purchased in *Chateau de Pau* by Queen Isabella II. Two things, from across the world brought together by happenstance and a little bit of violence and depravity. Had Queen Isabella known her bottle of wine would set my life on course to destroy everything I love? Of course not, don't be a fool. It's was only a bottle of wine. A catalyst for excuses and all rather silly.

And, yeah, that silver coin certainly helped.

CHAPTER THREE
Black Abby

"Burrow help me that was…*odd* right? That bastard Low watching us as he did. He was there right? I felt him. Did you feel him? Physically feel him? I think he touched me at one point. Someone grabbed cheek and I definitely know where your hands were and were not." I looked over at Samuel, lying on his back staring at the ceiling, counting the bright beams of moonlight coming in from the window with a silent mouth.

"You defile Low, like you defiled me," he breathed heavy, exhausted.

"Nothing a little hot water can't wash off, partner." I rolled from under the linen covers and retrieved my chemise, slipping my legs through the top and pulling the straps to my shoulders. I left the drawers on the floor, I was never fond of wearing that type of underclothes, they cinched around my belly a little too tight for my taste. The chemise was nice though, and fit short enough under the shift it went unseen so I decided it was mine and had no intentions of giving back.

"It was only my purity you ruined." Samuel followed suit, keeping his eyes away from mine.

"You were very…eager after that wine got your blood flowing through you. Good stuff. I'll have to thank Anrose later."

"My purity…"

"Should I go? I should probably go right?" I was finished dressing after have slipped the shift over my head, making it safe for Samuel to spare his eyes on me once again. "I feel like this pillow talk couldn't possibly go any better than it's heading."

He sat on the velvet chair. "Don't forget the rest of your payment owed. I'm sure you'll want that for the things you did." Samuel moved over to the open window and began to whisper to himself.

"What's that then?" I asked.

"I'm asking Low to forgive me," Samuel said, not turning back from the window.

"Forgive you for what? Does it have to do with the prayers you were only moments ago muttering to my under carriage?"

I could see the back of his neck grow a fair shade of red.

"I'm sorry that's unfair of me," I admitted.

Samuel continued his *chanting*. It seemed he was determined to win back his purity through pure will with words alone. Realizing he was through with me and not willing to overstay my welcome, I shook the bed from my hair and sulked toward the bedroom door. This part was always a little awkward.

Before I even had the chance to finger the door handle it burst open, banging against the wall and giving me quite a fright. Samuel made a small "yelp" sound and finally broke from his cursing of the moon.

A bloodied L'fowl stumbled in, belly cut from stern to bow; red seeped through his tight fingers as he tried to hold his life-blood in. It wasn't working, a river that's impossible to dam.

L'fowl could barely stand. He couldn't do much of anything except leak a little from his eyes and a lot from his gut. He wouldn't last long, seconds maybe.

L'fowl grabbed my arms and as gently as I could, I set him on the ground by the door. I poked my head through the threshold and squinted down the lantern-lit hallway, both ways. Something was there in the shadows, slowly moving toward the bedroom. It shuffled disjointed, crooked. It came faster, then I pulled my head back into the room quick.

L'fowl gurgled as I returned to him. I had to leave him on the ground to bleed out. He reached for my hand and through tight teeth he whispered, "Below the Cistern…the Stone of San'ctu…under the…Basin, under the earth, a terrible thing…whispering. Always whispering. Reach…" Sometimes you look back at the pieces you were given early and realize you were a fool to not realize it then what was offered.

L'fowl coughed, dark blood bubbling out of his mouth as his life was escaping him.

I looked up toward the door, nothing yet. Then I eyed the room. No more time.

I grabbed Samuel and forced him in a closet, knocking over the velvet chair in my retreat.

The closet was small, too small for two adults to squeeze into without feeling the pulse and heat throughout each other's bodies. Only a knuckle of cassocks hanged inside next to one surcoat - a spare, I assumed - along with a nice pair of boots and a small picture of a black haired, blue eyed young lady on the inner wall by the door, so no one would see unless you're looking out. His wine girl? Oh, Anrose, you devil.

Samuel's breath was hot on my neck, not the nice way. I could taste the sweat and heat coming from him. I put my arms around him and pulled him closer to free ourselves from the awkward air between and add a little more space around us to keep from bumping the closet walls.

I bent as best I could and looked through a small crack between wall and door. The thing from the hall was in the room, standing over L'fowl. The old man stopped moving completely.

Full moon light illuminated the thing in the room standing over L'fowl.

Black Abby.

One of my…*personalities* if you will.

I have a patron - Lady Tabitha, but not much is worth mentioning about her here now other than she occasionally pays me decent silver to appear as Black Abby and hunt her through the streets of Harklow Down. Easy job, no one gets hurt, I don't have to take anything off. Just sulk through the streets in a simple game of *hide-n-find*. She loved it, I loved it. We all loved it.

This thing even had *my* mask. I got bored one night around camp with some lads and I lashed some twigs that I'd gathered together into a woodsy cult-like thing; cut out the eye holes and everything, with the intention of scaring them. Well, it worked I could say as much, never saw one of those lads again in my life as he damned pissed his pants and likely went to die of embarrassment. The mask this Abby wore was no replica, it was my own. I could easily tell because I'd done such a piss-poor job none of the twigs were even, some poked up higher than others on the right side of the mask and I tied a black bird feather to the smallest stick, as so it wouldn't feel inferior to the others.

This fake Abby moved toward the closet where Samuel and I hid, holding our collective breaths, but trembling still. I felt Samuel's Winchester poking through to my stomach. Luckily it was one of the first things he put on, before getting all the way dressed. These Deluge boys were hard pressed to depart from their beloved rifles and tended to hang them at their sides in a long sheath to mimic the damned Crusaders they worshiped so much. If they could get away with carrying long swords, I'm sure they would.

Black Abby stood at the closet door. I wasn't about

to wait for this fake Abby to murder us in such a coffin of a closet. I put my hand around the stock of Samuel's Winchester and started to pull it, but the fool's hand stopped me. He was shaking his head *no*. Something worth mentioning is how the Deluge are very private about who handles their rifles. I would go as far to say it's usually just the owner and for good reason, not just anyone was allowed to handle the weapons, hell I'd never even handled one, let alone shot it. I'd been shot at, but being shot at is quiet different than shooting. Complete opposites in fact.

Sparrow would have to do. I kicked the closet door as hard as I could, sending Abby back several steps tripping over the fallen chair. Before he could recover I was on him, dagger in hand, ready to avenge the poor L'fowl for his life.

Abby bucked, shimmied out from under me, then kicked me like an unwanted child. He drew twin daggers of his own. A knife fight it would be then, except I was out daggered by one. I stepped in quick to try to ham him across his leg, but he came forward with a knee and caught me in the stomach. I felt like tossing vomup all over the beautiful Turkish rug. Abby lunged forward again and kicked me with the flat of his foot, sending me to land on my back, hard. I lay for a breath, looking at the ceiling. Abby's twig mask slowly rose in my blurry vision. He was straddling me.

Three things crossed me.

First, where the hell was Samuel?

Second, was that sweet cinnamon I smelled?

And, third, fuck Samuel. Shoot the bastard.

I used the same maneuver I used moments ago when I

was staring at the moon from my back under Samuel. Always catches the lads off guard when I do the twist, gets me where *I* want to be. Elbows over ass, I was on my knees and donkey-kicked Black Abby back and away from me. In a brief moment I had to decide what to do. Stay and fight, or…?

I choose the window and ran. Samuel was on his own.

First I asked my Burrow to at least grant me the deepest part of the moat below, not the rocky part. I placed my foot on the window's ledge and leaped without looking back. It was dark as sin outside in the mid of air.

I was dropped in a shock of cold, nasty water. As I floated on my back looking up at the pregnant, full moon I had only one question on my mind.

What the fuck?

CHAPTER FOUR
The Perky Daughter

I walked wet and shivering through the streets of Charleston pondering on where to sulk. I couldn't go home, not just yet. If the impostor Black Abby was able to follow me I wouldn't want to give him an open invite to where I lay my head at night. I did long for a bed at this point, one for sleeping.

It didn't take long floating in the pond for me to come to my senses and get away from the Cistern. Nothing followed me out that high window into the night and as far as I could tell, nothing followed me still except wet slopping foot prints from my drenched shift. My boots would still be in Anrose's room, they were not that great anyway. Hard-boiled leather, leaving blisters on my heels. I would get another pair, maybe soft doe-skin. That would be nice, wouldn't it?

I felt the heavy silver coin from a sour job done slipping further down into my wool leggings. Still there. I pulled it out and tossed it up, flipping it. Dirty money. I didn't want it. I wanted to get this night past me as quick as forgetting. A single piece of silver wouldn't get me all I wanted, but if I was lucky I could snuggle up to someone buying and get a few rounds of bourbon down before they realized I was only for taking, not giving.

So that night, under the fat, summer moon I plodded my wet ass across town to Washmaid Row, a tiny row of narrow streets tucked off Laidly St, not far from the State House, which was convenient for government officials. You'd be hard pressed to find it on a map. Washmaid was my old side-step to avoid being alone and the best place to find a friend.

The best place to find a friend along Washmaid Row was a well-lit, well-established brothel called The Perky Daughter, named ages ago by a father who didn't quite grasp the meaning. One, he didn't have *a* daughter, and two; he only wanted to offer visitors to Washmaid Row a place to get their minds off life as they paid too much for Kentucky Bourbon, which he had plenty of and not the cheap stuff sold in wholesale either, directly from the distillery these ones were. He truly had no intention of selling a side of cunny to go along with the bourbon and ale-steak pie cooked up in the back. This is where the *perkiness* came in. Now, I did say he didn't have *a* daughter, but the truth was he had seven, yes seven, only one of which was actually *perky* (I truly hate that word…perky, leaves a bad taste in my mouth), the other six were quite gamely, but could ruffle up a man's feathers just enough to keep them coming. The perkiest of his loved daughters was the first to try her hand at earning some extra coin between serving whiskey and pie. I won't go into full account of the things she did - as I'm sure you have an imagination as vivid as mine - hidden away from the eyes of her father, but let's just say business really picked up for the old lad, and soon he couldn't serve pie fast enough. The other sisters soon followed and not long after that, they commissioned a woodcarver to whittle them a nice little sign to hang out front, replacing the traditional slab of wood in the shape of a mug, with the silhouette of The Perky Daughter. This was years ago of course, and Washmaid Row became more than just a district to get your clothes cleaned and hemmed, it became a place to get your jollies wringed. These sisters are what we referred to as *Pettiwaist*, girls in Washmaid that stick to one place and are paid by the establishment that hires them on, in this case, The Perky Daughter. A nights worth of coin was gathered up by the original, business-savvy sister and divvied up equally amongst her siblings. Typically they all make the same amount of coin.

More and more places popped up around Washmaid Row. The Eager Wife, Undertable, Whiskey First, Bearmaiden, Pleasant Bottom, Papa's Good Seat, The Bend-Me-Over (let's not talk about that one, it belonged over in the Farrowyard and hardly worth a coin unless you liked it as straight forward as they served) all opened within months of The Perky Daughter.

What I'm not telling you is, for a place as nefarious sounding as Washmaid Row, due to the picture I'm painting for you, is that it's a safe place to be and a lucrative place to earn some coin and get an education. A real education. Other than the brothels, the district was chock-full of houses of education. Real ones, where young ladies could learn to manage their finances, the way of numbers, histories and sciences, all funded thanks to the Guilds of the Washmaids. Some of the most educated women came from here. Including myself if you don't mind. Hard to see that now due to what you know of me so far.

The Perky Daughter was busy that night; as it usually was. The guitarist, a large man named Tubwater, was on a small wooden stage sat in the corner of the saloon fingering with his catgut about to play. *Beautiful Dreamer*, one of my favorites, and Tubwater's low and rich voice was very sweet to my ears.

Men and women gathered in droves, moving like slow water around high-tables of wines and ale. The bourbon drinking was kept solely to the bar; a long, imported piece of dark oak, stained and polished to clash against the painted white shiplap walls behind it. Behind the bar were rows and rows of neat bottles of bourbon sitting on shelves, mostly from the Kentucky area with a few whiskeys imported in from overseas. Ireland, Scotland, even Japan I reckoned and more in the cellar down a long flight of stairs. The bar stood like a lighthouse for bourbon drinkers visiting

The Perky Daughter, a place you could nuzzle up to and a place away from the waves of people moving in and out seeking things more than a quick burn of the throat.

I pulled a stool out and sat, my leggings were still holding to their water from the moat and made a *plosh* sound as I leaned forward to signal the barkeep. He came over. A bushy man with a wiggly mustache. Sterling was his name. I knew him well.

"Sterling," I said. "Do you know if Keefie is working tonight?" I asked. Sterling slid me a bourbon without me asking, poured from a clear glass bottle. That's the reason you visit a bourbon bar, to drink bourbon isn't it?

"Went home already," his mustache shimmied above his lip. "Earned her coin, came over here and spent that coin, then headed out. Left not but an hour ago."

I squeezed my wet hair slightly clear enough away from his bar as to not get it wet.

He laughed, "Obviously you've been out working as well. Rough night?" he asked.

"Took a dive out a window, but yes water is wet and here I am too," I looked around the main room of The Perky Daughter for any familiar faces, or even an unfamiliar one worth scooting up to. Everyone seemed so boring after that night. I looked back at Sterling, "I'll clean this up don't worry," I said, motioning toward the puddle at my feet.

"I'm not, never am," somehow his mustache managed to wink and he slid me a second and third shot of the amber bourbon.

"To Augustus, Burrow rest his soul," I said as I

downed both, back to back and savored the throat burn after. I put my single coin on Sterling's bar, hoping it would buy me in for the night. Oh the shame I almost felt drinking away that Morgan for my deeds with that young Samuel lad. Dirty, dirty money. Low *bless* him as well and his cowardly closet hiding. Burrow *bless* him and shove the whole of his own Winchester up his arse to the hot, smoking barrel. Burrow would never do that of course, silly of me to ask her. "Saw an important man get kil-"

A thin hand appeared on my shoulder. I felt a second, equally small hand fish around at the hem of my shift.

"Getting frisky are we, Tapper?" I didn't even need to turn to look. I spotted him slying up behind me reflected in the caramel, liquid mirror of my forth bourbon. Down she went. "No pockets," I laughed.

"Just checking," said Tapper. "No pockets." He sat on the stool next to mine and tapped the bar. "She's buying," to Sterling.

"To Hell she is. She's no more than you do," Sterling said as he poured Tapper a shot of the wholesale, watered-down tangle-leg stuff from below the counter - which probably made a journey half way around the States from Kentucky before ending up here, getting loaded with water and prune juice. May as well just serve the lad moonshine and call it a night.

"I saw the silver," Tapper said. "Should buy more than this dishwater wash."

"Checking for what?" I asked, glancing at the young man, inviting the conversation back to me. He was cleanly shaved, usually was. Could be that he just didn't grow a beard yet on account of his age.

"If you've had enough drink to slow your judgment."

"Usually when a lad grabs cheek like that he's paid me first, or at least a round," I smiled.

Tapper wasn't good looking. Smooth skin yes, but it didn't help much. His eyes bulged from their sockets and his lips were a little too full for his skinny face. I'm also not sure the mop he kept on his head would pass for hair in the dirtiest of places, such as the Farrowyard. I'm not joking when I say don't go there, it's not worth your coin. Or, the itch you'll walk out of there with after.

Of course Tapper wasn't going to buy me a drink, that's not why he cozied up to me. He had a job, I'm sure of it. But, it was late. Saturday would be fading into a pure Sunday within the hours and I tried not to work on Sunday, no one did. Except for the Deluge. The Deluge work everyday.

It was late and I longed for my own bed. I thought about it again. It was probably safe to go home and if it wasn't, well then fuck me I guess.

"Seen Keefie?" I asked Tapper.

"You working tonight?" Tapper changed the subject, not like he knew where Keefie was.

"Already done, bruised everything on me toe-to-tit for that drink you just swallowed."

"Rough one?"

"Weird one, best to forget it. And trying I am." I could finally feel the bourbon working its warmth on my guts.

"Listen, Tapper, take me home, okay?"

"I don't have any coin," he laughed. "We already established that."

"No, shh listen. Listen. Ugh, you're a silly lad. I need to find work, something a little lighter than usual, but not tonight. Find me something, but first tuck me in, then find me where you find me." I placed my head on the dark oak bar and closed my eyes. Four bourbons just about did it. I let the bourbon take me to the dark and felt myself being lifted. I'm not heavy.

Yup, the whiskey had me spinning.

I was working on an empty stomach, okay?

CHAPTER FIVE

Brightly-Haired Rye O'Keefe

Tapper owed me a nickel. At least one.

As much as I appreciate him bringing me home, taking my wet pond clothes off and slipping me through my night-shirt; he got more than he payed for with that *extra* bit of help, which was nothing. He paid nothing. I'll consider him in my debt. I trusted the lad though to do what I asked and nothing more. Young of age, high of morals. Not the morals that would stop him from stealing, but other ones. Important ones.

Plus Keefie was there.

Rye O'Keefe. I called her Keefie right off. Even before we both were old enough to run with the Rinmnir Gypsies over in the Shake looking for something to do and earn some coin in the meantime. The Rinmnir lads were nice enough fellas.

We found one another after her Da used her for leverage in a side of Two-Bone gambling in Farrowyard, hustling her away for a chance at something better for himself. Couldn't even tell you how to play the game. All that matters was he lost. Keefie never saw him again anyway. The only thing he left her was his name, so she kept it. She never even had a chance to meet her Ma as an adult before her Da stole her away and brought her to the States.

I felt her shifting under the covers next to me, she was just waking up, as was I, with a jaunty headache for sure. Judging from the high sun on this wickedly bright Sunday, I managed to steal at least a handful of hours of sleep.

Her leg slid over mine and she pulled it back, realizing I was there. She sat up, letting her night-shirt fall from her shoulder. She shivered and squinted at me, taking every unwashed and pond *water-d* bit of me in, then relaxed when she saw it was only I. Her wrinkled-faced gaze hesitated on my hair and reaching my hand up, I soon found bits of water weeds and lily things mingling amongst my loose curls.

My hair held more honey than her pale-smoke blonde, which suited her fine. Her Da was - before he stole her away - from Ireland, but she was born somewhere in the mountains in Germany to a local woman where they grew them cold and bloodless, though she bled warm and red like all of us. All I'm saying is she was very pale, but not in that sick, feverish way. Freckles also sprinkled like spit tobacco on a white wall all over her entire body, gathering mostly around her nose, cheeks and shoulders. Yes, she was Burrow-damned adorable if I'm doing her justice in my telling.

That pale-smoke blonde fell wavy, slightly passed her freckled collarbone from the Albert helmet she was currently wearing. Which is just a fancy silver dragoon helmet from the Royal Horse Guards with a red plume standing half-erect at the top. Think British Military, Royalty and all that mess we don't have to deal with here in the States anymore. If King Edward VII could love them, then so could regular Rye O'Keefe from the chilly north.

Keefie must have passed out mid change getting ready for bed since she still wore other ornate pieces of silver armor likely from whatever royal household lad she'd fetched em from. And, how she slept as such with all the poky bits, I have no idea.

Wiping drool from the crook of her mouth, she smiled. She rolled over me out of the bed, scooting a few more discarded armor pieces away on the floor with her feet and stood, stealing herself a breath. All while the room and my head were still spinning. Keefie loved the armor and uniforms. She was a collector of old weapons and other pieces she'd take as, what she called, "souvenirs from her lovers," but I knew them as *payment* for when a lad couldn't pony up enough coin for her services. They could always fill in what ever gaps from their uniforms they'd offered up to her when they went back home.

Keefie made no "good mornings" other than a *huff*.

I kept a full length polished mirror in my room, where

she was standing, surveying herself. She held the allure of something sweet and innocent concealed under the hard edges of a uniform made harsh for war. It was a perfect mix and she dripped with appeal making it an easy choice for the picky patrons of Washmaid Row. She was the perfect princess of the brothel Bearmaiden. She was the only girl that worked there, a *Highcollar*, and all Bearmaiden needed to draw in the crowds. None of that mattered through, her face was pretty enough to earn a coin where ever she wanted, but it was Bearmaiden she called her second home.

Bearmaiden earned its name from this freckly Irish-German girl when she showed up one late night wearing nothing but her curves (which we assumed she inherited from her Ma, because her Da was shaped like a board, much like mine. She was lucky in that respect.) and a black bear fur *and* a little bit of modesty concealed with some well placed bear paws. The house - formally known as The Knotty Bottom - took a collective, long held breath when she walked in. By the time the few visiting patrons sighed again the owner was signing Keefie on as the new, wild darling from the north. He sent every single one of the other girls home that night sealing Keefie's position as *Highcollar* for years to come.

The Bearmaiden, a play on words if you don't mind, was born. Keefie was settled there, earning a place to drink and eat and call her own and a few extra knuckles of coin when the patrons felt like being generous; even just to see her. It was all at my suggestion, I knew she could use what the mountains gave her for something other than waking up early every morning to bake sweet buns for the tradesmen in Hawker Square. No coin in that. She was too content. Too bored and the sweet buns were starting to soften her in places men might enjoy, so one night I said, "Let's take this old bear rug and go earn some decent, honest coin." She agreed and we did. Bearmaiden.

I moved next to her in the mirror. All grubby with pond life and stink and leeches (I found out about those later). Night and day the two of us - for the moment anyhow - as we stood eyeing back and forth trying to hide grins.

I wasn't much to look at, I think, maybe, by now you have a good sense of Conley Mahren, expert and *hobbyist* in all things carnal in the Washmaids. I stood only a little taller than Keefie and I got my looks from my dad. I kept my hair below my jaw but above my shoulders, sometimes it was wavy, sometimes it was curly, sometimes it was an absolute mess depending on the humidity. Honey blonde it was, as above so below, as if it were dipped right away from the bees. If you knuckled me some coin I could show you. I had a constellation of freckles under my eyes that women always pointed out, men barely noticed. Naw, I don't reckon I was much to look at, not standing next to Keefie. Away from her I was marigold; next to her I was a daffodil. Still fun to blow in the wind.

Keefie pulled the calvary helmet away from her head. Her eyes were as blue catching the sun's light as the button sitting mid-breast against the stained pond water white of my chemise.

A moment of quiet and she finally grinned wide and

we both laughed at how ridiculous I smelled.

We spent the next hour getting ready for the Folks Emery bare-knuckle fight happening later in the evening, just before sunset, so we had time to dwell. I splash-bathed off the nasty of the pond in a gutter running parallel to our street on down to the Kanawha River - yes, we had a bath, but heating the water was excruciating and I don't know if you've ever tried to heat a bucket of water, one at a time, dumping it into a tub, but what you end up with is lukewarm water edging on cold and worn out arms and a lose of patience. So a gutter bath was just fine by me. Yes, I finally found those leeches. After painfully removing the disgusting things and patting myself dry with a clean cloth, I got dressed in a fresh pair of gray-dyed burlap suspender pants, tucking an apricot long-sleeved blouse with sewn little white baby's breath flowers along the neck. I tied my hair back, loose with a green ribbon. They were my going-to-watch-men-punch-each-other-in-the-guts clothes.

Keefie set out a very late breakfast of dried sausage, slightly-too-runny red berry jam and buttered hard toast on the table for us. A modest bit of food, but all we had at the moment. She sat opposite me at a small wooden table watching me gnaw on the toast. She sipped water from a little wooden ale mug.

"And, then I dove out the window," I finished my story.

"I never heard you come home," Keefie finally said.

"I couldn't tell you much about it after the bourbon

hit," I replied. "Tapper dragged me in. Remind me to get a nickel from him. Hey, do you remember Lady Tabitha?"

"Yeah, she still tossing you coin for a strump through the streets?"

"Well, yeah up until last night I'm guessing." I paused for dramatic effect. Keefie narrowed her brow at me, waiting. "So, there I was in the Cistern's high rooms making short introductions of myself to a nice pure lad called Samuel as I said before, when who would show up?"

Keefie tilted her head. "Lady Tabitha?"

"Burrow no, I wish. No. Lady Tabitha's masked friend."

"…Abby?"

"Very one. Also, my mask is gone. I checked already."

"Odd." Keefie reached across the table and snatched a dried sausage from my plate.

"How did you find your night?" I asked after we pondered the implication of a missing mask. Someone had been in our little place, that much was obvious. We kept it discreet, no one was allowed here and we always made damn sure no one ever followed us. Tapper was one of the exceptions; I did trust the boy, even if he was a dirty thief. He wouldn't steal from us, not that we had anything worth fingering.

"Not much different than the one before," Keefie said. "A new lad came in, paid up for the entire night to just talk. He kept asking if I knew Conley Mahren, had business with her. Too bad because if he were in my garden I would have opened my window curtains and showed em' while I'm called the Bearmaiden."

"Keefie…" I blushed, which was hard for me. She could do it though when what was left of her Irish Da came out of her. She'd been in the States long enough to lose most of her accent, but occasionally it slipped. Quite charming when it did, I'll say that.

"What? He was a good looking sort, not like the fat doughy tradesmen that usually drink themselves limp before coming in."

"Who was it?" I asked.

"Like I said, no idea. Never saw him before last night. He had a way about him though, he talked classy-like, not from Washmaid or Harklow. Maybe Breige or somewhere else just as fancy we don't have privy to. England maybe? I honored his coin by giving him a peak and sent him on his way, but not before he folded me three cash dollars to keep my mouth shut. Left out the window and never looked back, left his calvary helmet. That's a two-story jump down you know? I ordered a few pints of ale sent to my room and spent the rest of my night drinking alone since he'd already paid me for a full rut. Pondered the paint on the wall, drank until I got bored and came home sweet home."

"Three dollars? For that?" I was impressed. Even a full night of sheet-wrestling typically didn't cost that, unless you were doing something extra fancy.

"Yeah, minus the ale pints, I put one dollar into the can and called it good fortune." As Keefie spoke she held her arms out for me to tie the front and back pieces of a silver breast plate. She slipped her head through a chainmail coif, pulling her blonde hair up and letting it fall back. Soft, tight black wool leggings contrasted nicely with the silver of the armor. She finished off with a little bit of red powder across her lips. She would be the most noticeable person at this affair, other than Folks Emery himself. Advertising I reckoned, or maybe she was looking to try a new gig other than Bearmaiden for a change.

"You looking to get the eye of Folks Emery tonight?" I laughed as she shrugged her shoulders "maybe".

"Conley, there's something else you should know about that dandy man from last night." She looked at me, her red-lipped grin had faded into a more serious affair.

"He mentioned Pynes," Keefie finished, knowing what that meant. "Said he had a friend who knew how to find him."

I felt my heart drop heavy at the mention of that name.

CHAPTER SIX
Worry'd

If I can recall correctly, the first time I'd heard of Pynes Oak also happen to coincide with the first time Rye O'Keefe killed a man. First time *I'd* seen a man die in such a manner as well. It didn't seem to bother Keefie as much as I wanted it to bother me.

It was cold that winter. I remember that. This was years ago.

"You are a woman of unusual size ma'am," the man bleated, unable to contain his awe at my largeness casting a shadow above him as he sat on the bed.

He leaned his Sharps rifle against the wall were several emptied mugs of ale sat on a nightstand close to the bed, within reach. I *carefully* placed a full mug of ale next to the empty ones, as was tradition when entering the room of a impatiently waiting client. A gift. "Keep them from being thirsty, but also keep them thirsty." Biddy Larough taught me that. I didn't know what the hell it meant, but she allowed me to stay in her brothel (long as I kept it clean, which is a funny thing considering, you'll understand later). As payment of sorts for allowing me to stay at The Alley-In-The-Back, I allowed her to offer me wisdom in things such as men even if the *wisdom* was more confusing than actual men. The truth was, Biddy didn't have a daughter of her own, and she was dying to pass down the skills of the manual labor she'd learned working in the Farrowyard. She had Keefie and myself for that.

The man standing in awe was a Ranger of the Crossed-Iron, one of the elite shootest in service of the Deluge. Now, the Rangers typically followed the teachings of Low the Kind deeply and profoundly - even more so than most of their Deluge comrades. And, on account of how valuable they were in keeping the city of Charleston in line with their Sharps rifles they were considered the most venerable men in the entire Charleston Chapter, other than the High and Second Chancil of course. But, a Deluge is a Deluge and there was a certain amount of debauchery these lads were needing before being reined back in.

I couldn't help but laugh at the Ranger's surprise seeing my rolling girth squirming under the large bustle I'd chosen to wear under my dress for such a special occasion. I elbowed the squirming under the bustle and issued a harsh shush, echoing another shush back to me, followed by a little ouch.

I stuck to the shadows of the small room to keep things a mystery for the lad. Didn't want to ruin the surprise.

"Are you okay ma'am?" the Ranger asked, watching and squinting as I fidgeted with the tight strings holding the bosom of my dress.

I let out a groan.

I was just trimming seventeen years old and fully aware, though very inexperienced in the handy skills of debauchery that went down in the Farrowyard. Coin was on my mind even that early of an age and here I knew it was passed under the table to open hands easily and away from the eyes of Low the Kind. I couldn't help it, I saw early what coin could achieve you. I'd been to the Breige and back, between the Undergrowth and Washmaid Row and there wasn't a problem in the world that couldn't be solved with wealth. Literally, every problem I had could be solved with money. I wanted more than what I had. Which was nothing. So, I was willing to pull the strings loose on my morality and show this little bee the flowering blossom he was so eager to pay for.

Before I untied, the Ranger held his hand up and stopped my own from the untying and started to speak. My wriggling girth giggled again under my dress and the Ranger, mouth half-opened made a sound of pure confusion echoed out from the back of his throat.

"Should I come out now?" my dress asked.

"What did you say?" the Ranger bleated.

"Shh," I put my finger to the Rangers chapped mouth

and urged him lay back on the bed. I backed away into the darkness of the room, away from a lantern sitting bedside, where the Ranger was lying. I bumped into a hutch, toppling a small wooden vase over. He'd placed his hawk-beaked golden helmet on the hutch, next to a Beaumont-Adams revolver. I was quite fond of those guns and there were so few floating around the Parish, let alone Charleston, I'd learned to keep my eyes tight when I saw them lying around. They sold on the Grey Alley for more than most girls could make in a full year of working in Washmaid, so yeah it was hard to overlook. The Beaumont-Adams was a little more rare than the Colts you'd typically run around here in the Parish, which made me want it even more. This one in particular had the carved figure of a nude lady on the grip. One, disjointed arm ran down along one side of the barrel, pointing a finger as if to say "shoot that way." Even if you were a dullard you could see the anatomy of the woman didn't make a lick of sense in correlation with the layout of the revolver, but it was art, so I'm forgiving.

On the other side of the barrel was the word "Worry'd", carved as if a child had been practicing their letters. Little did I know the worth of this thing at the time, but it makes sense now on thinking back.

The Ranger started to undo his privy and I - not quite ready to see such a member unsheathed - kicked the hutch holding the hawk-beaked helmet and Beaumont-Adams sending it falling off the edge. It hit the ground with a hard series of clanks before it slid under the bed.

I gasped. He gasped. My dress gasped.

The Ranger reached for his revolver and snatched it from under the bed.

"Do you have any idea what this is worth?" his voice cracked.

Of course I did.

"No I don't, I'm so sorry!" I whined. "Is it ruined?"

"For your sake, it better not be," he said as he examined the weapon. "No way of knowing though unless I fire it, but that's not going to happen. I'll have to take it back to Knots for a look. That kid is a genius." His voice was surprisingly calm which I found reassuring and profoundly sad at what I knew was coming. I didn't know this lad any more than a dog on the street, other than this moment we were sharing. As I was pondering and watching him handle his revolver with intimate care, he tipped a mug of ale up, then took a swig, draining it of its remaining liquid.

My back was starting to ache from holding the weight and cause of my girth up. I dropped myself into a chair close by, let out another groan, then motioned for the Ranger to sit back on the bed.

"Not tired already are we?" he asked. He looked at me. "I'll be honest to Low the Kind, I wasn't expecting someone-" he started.

"I'm not to your liking?" I giggled, working on those damned dress strings again. Who the hell tied these so tight?

"No, not at all, it's just that-"

My stomach lurched, then kicked.

"What is that?" the Ranger stood up.

I stood up as well and out poured Keefie from under

the hem of my dress. She hit with a thud then stood up.

"It was getting too hot in there!" she cried.

The Ranger reeled back, gagged, then threw up all while hissing something about his heart. Keefie's entrance must have broke it. He was on the older side of forty I was guessing and probably spent half his earlier life eating greased sausages and taking very little steps, so a scare like this probably did him (or his heart) no good.

"What did you just birth?" he stumbled, looking for words.

Keefie snatched the Ranger's Beaumont-Adams from his hands and fell in behind me as I pulled the extra large dress over my head, revealing my true, not-girthy self wrapped in a twisted ensemble of buckles, belts and ropes. I was the starving girl of Charleston after all, just barely a twig and unable to hold Keefie up for that long without assistance from a cleverly bound contraption to support her weight under my bustle, which later came in handy involving a mermaid tail and one conch shell. I can see you may be confused as to how a girl not much smaller than myself could fit under a dress so well hidden. Imagine her head resting on my breast, arms around and under my ribs grasping to my shoulders and both of her legs wrapped around my waist, like a Devil's Hug. Got it now? It worked.

"Did I just birth what?" I began. "Come on man. Have you not seen a baby? Look at her." I pointed to Keefie, standing holding the Beaumont-Adams aiming it toward the Ranger. "You mean to think I just birthed someone of her size. That would have wrecked me. Surely-"

"Your coin or your life!" Keefie tossed in before I was done speaking, then, "Buckle up those breeches you *plonker* there's not enough room in here for that."

"No, Keefie we are not here for thieving. I already told you that."

The Ranger was dumbfounded looking at the pair of us.

He said, "I just thought, a woman of your size could-"

"A woman of great stature you mean! In business. Certainly not size."

"Yes, yes," he nodded. He started to stand. "What's this all about then? Why the rouse?"

"Why? Because I know what you fancy and it's a little more exciting this way. For all of us," I said, then changed the subject.

"Well, I didn't bring any coin. Low the Kind doesn't have wants, nor do I now. And, besides anyways, its all been drank away," he nodded toward the upturned table of ale. "You just said you were not robbing me. Now, give back my lady-iron."

"We are not robbing you." I took the revolver from Keefie, examining it as I held it to aim. "You came to a brothel with no money? Farrowyard isn't much for charity."

"Point it away," the Ranger demanded.

"If I don't?" I wiggled the end of the revolver, teasing him.

"I'll be forced to take it. We don't want that."

He took a slight step closer to me and tilted his head. "You're one of the Widows. L'fowl's girls. You're his little watcher. Always watching you are."

I only shrugged. "I'm no Widow."

"What do you mean to do then?" the Ranger asked.

I shrugged again.

"Well?" he repeated.

"Do you not see her shrugging?" Keefie said. "She's doing that because she ain't sure yet you dolt. Do you know what shrugging is?"

"I see. Then we have a problem," he said. His voice dropped its endless friendliness and went straight to stern. Here we go. Always the fatherly voices come out when some lad much older than I was about to offer me a choice of some manner. Only it wouldn't really be a choice I'd prefer, no matter.

"Seeing as how," I began, "that you are standing on the other side of this Beaumont-Adams now, *and* assuming she still works, I'll be the one suggesting we have a problem. I'm not here to watch. No one sent me. No one paid me. You're a man of Low, for God's sake lad. Do you not think about what you're doing to the reputation of the Deluge? Now, I myself, being of who I am couldn't give much of a chewed on horse tit what you do with your free time."

Listen, I recall the moments as they come back to me. I'm sure I wasn't this eloquent with my word choices back then as I'm telling, but just the same. I'm an admirer of embellishment. If there's any part of this that sounds too absurd, I wouldn't fault you for believing so. The reality of a seventeen year old girl with not but an ounce of muscle on her carrying a girl of sixteen under her dress to rob a man of his revolver is as far fetched as it goes. Truly, in looking back, we probably kicked the door down and robbed the poor bastard mid-trousers-down with some trollop from Farrowyard, then shot him on account of us not knowing better. Believe what you want, but the mermaid tail and one conch shell are certainly true.

I held up the Beaumont-Adams revolver. "Now this here. I could fetch some decent silver for this. Good coin. Not a lot, but it's honest-ish and it keeps me from spreading twig for men the likes of you in a place the likes of this." I looked at Keefie. "Can you imagine that?"

"Everyday," Keefie nodded.

"What?"

"What?" She repeated.

I turned my attention back to the Ranger.

"Point it away, I won't ask a second time," the Ranger said, glancing toward the Sharps rifle waiting for him in the corner of the room.

"You just did," Keefie said.

"Just did what?" he asked.

"That was the second time you asked. If you ask again, it'll be the third. You're not going to ask a third time is what you mean," she corrected. Keefie held her hand out for the revolver when I offered it to her. "I've never held one of these, let alone shot one."

She twirled the revolver around on her finger, caught the grip in her palm then brought it to her face for a look. "What's it say then? Worry'd? The hells does that mean then?"

"Means when it's pulled, you'd better be worried," the ranger smiled.

"Okay, I like it. Now, I'm no school girl but that's hardly how you spell it, is it?" Keefie laughed.

"Used to say something else, I fixed it. I made a mistake and couldn't go back is all."

Keefie squinted at the revolver. "S - something. What else?"

"Don't recall. And, I don't care. Now, hand it back over."

"The honest thing, Mr. Ranger, is that we actually came here for this very Beaumont-Adams. We knew you had it, because you took it from a girl not much older than… what? Nine? Ten?" I said.

"Girl shouldn't have the gun," was his reply. "Guns ain't allowed in the Parish, you know that."

"Girl said it belonged to her. Was important to her," I said. "Hardly up to you-"

"I don't give a sh-"

"And, sometimes we do things not because we are being paid, but because…well, we just want to. I want to get that gun back for that little girl you see. She left quite an impression on me."

The Ranger chose to make a mistake that night. That being, he lunged toward us to try and snatch his revolver back.

His hands twisted in frustration.

Keefie pulled the trigger.

I was instantly deafened by the force of the damned

thing. Keefie cried out as she stumbled back against the wall.

Looking up I saw the Ranger lying on the bed with a smoking hole in the center of his chest. I'd heard rifles fired before across the city, but never a revolver this close. I opened and closed my mouth. My ears rang. Seeing what it did to this old lad sent my stomach in a knot. Keefie was on the ground, holding her hands over her eyes.

"Guess it still works," I whispered.

I gathered her up and when the pounding started at the door, we took that as our cue to vanish. Where there was one Ranger of the Crossed-Iron, there were usually more to follow.

We didn't think much on being hanged or beaten so we fled.

After a few minutes of hand-holding and tugging an overly excited sixteen year old through the streets of the Harklow Down District, Keefie and I finally arrived at the front door of a building quietly hiding at the end of Washmaid Row.

I didn't look back as I pulled Keefie through. No one batted an eye at two young girls bounding into The Perky Daughter laughing to themselves as if sharing a secret joke.

I paused in the doorway.

A single fiddle whined a lone chord, standing out from the rest of the ensemble playing in The Perky Daughter.

"Conley Mahren, here to work? Say you are," the mustached man behind the bar said.

I looked at him and blinked. "Not yet, Sterling. Give

me a couple more years, then the Wash Guild will take me in. I promise, then I'll be golden with the things I've seen in Farrowyard," I yelled back across the busy bar.

I let go of Keefie's hand somewhere in the mix as I pushed my way through the crowd toward Sterling and his well shined bar.

I leaned on the finely polished bar top.

"Wishing for work in the Breige but settling just the same for Washmaid Row," I added.

"Bah, those Breige girls are all spoiled up their own asses-" Sterling looked out over the gathering crowd in his bar "-higher born, fancy girls that wouldn't know which door to use if the callers came banging late at night. Now, Farrowyard lads could bang on any back door they wanted, someone would answer their calls. For coin. Not much coin, but some."

"Not much to do around there unless you're willing to knock on those back doors. Which I'm not. Not yet. Girls there say I'm ready. I kindly disagree. So, in the mean time, I'm the *robbering* kind." I held the newly nicked Beaumont-Adams revolver up for him to see.

"That's because it's the Farrowyard, Conley, nothing can be done to help about the reputation." Sterling turned, grabbed a bottle of brown, poured a finger into a small glass of water and offered it to me. Without waiting for me to nod a no, he went back to wiping his counter clean of the dribble. "Nice iron by the way," he did add, nodding back at the revolver.

"Lad won't be needing it anymore." I pushed the

bourbon away without sipping. I didn't have a throat for it, let alone a stomach that could contain the burn. "I'm looking for a little girl. Real skinny thing, brown hair. She wore a crown of daisies, couldn't miss her. Called herself Burrow of all things. Don't think she was quite right in the head."

The fiddling stopped and was replaced by the low and constant hum of bar room chatter.

"Well, there's lot's of girls here, but none by that name. Or, that young. A few of these girls are not right in the head however-"

A stiff elbow shoved into me from the side, nudging me away from the bar.

I was just about ready to offer an elbow back when I-.

My world stopped.

I almost threw up. Hell it was hot. I felt beads of sweat run down the tip of my nose and the small of my back. I'd known countless lads, none ever so enthralling as the one that just walked away from the bar.

"Who. Who. Who?" I stumbled.

Sterling laughed as he twiddled his mustache.

"Who? Who."

Words were hard, but I did manage to at least nod toward the retreating lad.

"Pynes Oak. He's a local fiddler and tonight's entertainment, other than the girls of course." Sterling grinned, then grew it to a frown. "Don't look at 'em too long though. He's one of those educated types. A philosopher. Like Fair Nathaniel. Not by design or long study mind you.

His was a fortuitous journey into the dark education of…"

His voice faded away.

I listened to Pynes play *Low, In The Valley* on his fiddle, but he did not sing the words. It was the only time I did.

That night those many years ago still held a place in my mind that I never could rattle loose, no matter how vigorously I shook. And just when I thought I'd escaped those days, someone came along and put Pynes' name right back in my mouth.

CHAPTER SEVEN
Bare-Knuckle'd

Maybe I'll start again so you can understand better. This, after all, was Fair Nathaniel's fault. The whole thing. It's funny how directly my life had been guided by a man I'd never even met and know shit to little about other than a lad I had a one night encounter with was deeply obsessed with his philosophies. He wouldn't shut up about it. But, that was Pynes, obsession took him over. He was too smart for Charleston. He belonged somewhere smarter, like New York or Chicago.

Keefie snatched my hand, pulling me out of my day dream and back to her presence, she demanded it. We made our way from our home in Harklow Down. Knowing my mind was elsewhere, she fidgeted with the buckles of the silver breast plate she'd wedged herself inside, pulling them tighter into her bare skin as I watched with almost absent intrigue. Dressed and ready to watch the fight, I let the memory of Pynes slip to the back of my mind once again. I wanted to be present for Keefie, I wanted to enjoy myself.

"How do you breathe in that?" I laughed.

"I don't," she replied. "I hold my breath. Breathing is overrated anyway, don't you know?"

Transient kin from the Shake, girls from Washmaid Row *and* Farrowyard, government men from the State House, fancies from Breige, tradesmen from Hawker Square, even a few Deluge filed through the back alleys trying to wiggle their way closer to the roped off circle where Folks would make his glorious appearance. New coal miners mixed with the old salt briners for a moment, not worried about which industry held the best future. Everyone was content. Everyone turned out to watch a Folks Emery bare-knuckle fight.

Folks knew me, and knew me well, but even I wasn't allowed an invite to the rope line when time came for Folks to box, one had to box for that right. I tried my best to pull Keefie through the throngs of people crowding around so we could at least see the man, but his escorts held everyone back; they were all fighters themselves and you didn't want to cross their line. Orleans "Skinny" Oleerh was there; Sallow Salazar, the scalped man was Robert McGee, even Knots was there; all encircled around Folks Emery like sentient stones as he pushed his way toward the ropes.

Folks stepped over the ropes surrounding the

makeshift hay-matted boxing ring. The fights never took place in the same place twice, hence the quickly assembled fighting ring of rope and hay, as was tradition, even though L'fowl stopped caring about stopping the illegal bare-knuckle fights years ago or else face a riot. They drew in too large a crowd to stop, and the coin being passed around was too tempting to break it up. No one cared. It was fun, it was illegal and occasionally it became an effective way for the city to execute some of its unsavory and intolerable. This specific fight was a celebration, not an execution.

Folks would trade knuckle and teeth with a man half his size today (double the heart), didn't matter, anyone could fight if they were brave enough or stupid enough or a mix of the two. This poor lad standing across the corner from Folks tried to get the crowd on his side, waving his arms around and bouncing up and down like a little bug. No one gave a shit, we were all here for Folks Emery.

Keefie and I finally managed to push our way through the tight crowd. The streets were narrow here leading into Hawker Square, where this week's fight was taking place. Short, red brick buildings suddenly ended to a wide open square, where several permanent rows of merchant stalls stood, selling anything you could possibly want.

Folks was thick like a redwood and quick like a rattlesnake. He was a dock worker from Fell's Point, Baltimore that grew up too big and mean for them to handle there. He'd just missed out on the war on account of being too young to fight, but even to this day he still talks about the Buffalo Soldiers as if they were gods to him. And he, "certain as shit wasn't going to be a bugler or drummer boy for no damn company of white men," his words. When the war ended he came here to Charleston looking for work. But, Charleston doesn't have proper ship work, or a even much in the way of docks, except for a handful of steamboats putting in on occasion. If it hadn't been for the Serpent, steamboatin' could have been a decent living for those brave enough. Folks was left with not much else to do. He wasn't going to the coal mines, and he sure as shit wasn't going to be a briner. So, he beat men up.

Folks spent all his time getting drunk, fighting and spittin' his way through Charleston until he found something, or maybe Ale found him first. I'd seen Ale the Unhinged more than a few times skulking about, proud as she was, unlike my own Burrow - who I never see, as timid as she is. I supposed Ale hated Low the Kind just as much as any of us degenerates, but I couldn't speak for a Hallowfulk.

The skinny shit about to get his eyes rearranged by Folks stepped forward. I pulled Keefie closer giddy with excitement; close enough I had my hand on the ropes trying to hold tight soes not to get pulled away. Close enough I could smell the hay and sweat and desperation.

The fight was practically over before it began. Folks danced his dance as long as he could to keep the crowd from leaving and Ale entertained, but he couldn't hold back the wicked one-ending punch he bare-knuckl'd straight into the skinny lad's brown teeth. It may have killed the boy had Folks not caught him before his head hit the ground. Folks was something, but he wasn't a murderer. Like I mentioned earlier, this fight was a celebration, not an execution. Folks didn't fight in those.

I felt Burrow's fingers itching at my chin to look across the ring, so of course I did. You shouldn't ignore divine intervention when it arises. I narrowed my vision to one darkened corner across the street, right outside a barbershop called Chatty Gann's - called so on account of how damned chatty he was while he should have been cutting hair. Took hours for a simple trim job. Couldn't even trust the man for a shave. He didn't charge by the hour.

It was there, something in the shadow, watching me. It stepped forward and I saw the mask. My mask.

Black Abby. He started moving forward through the crowd, urging people aside and no one seemed bothered.

I went to squeeze Keefie's hand, but realized it was empty. She left the ring side. I quickly looked back where Abby had been pushing through, but he was no longer there. I panicked. I scanned the crowd.

Folks Emery was helping the lad he just whooped out of the ring as the people in the streets were growing oddly quiet.

I was too out in the open, too exposed for a knifing. I looked around the balconies and roofs. Mostly empty; no beasts stalking me. I turned to leave, to go find Keefie. My heartbeat was kicking my chest like I haven't felt in a long time. I was accustomed to panic, odd things, scary things, but usually all for coin. This was different. This was real and I had no idea why.

"I'll fight!" I yelped. The crowd looked my way and

Black Abby shrank down, disappearing into the mass of swaying lookers.

"What?" Someone's voice cracked.

"I'll fight. I'll fight Folks." What the fuck was I doing? Getting my ass out of the crowd and away from the stabbing knives is what.

"Conley Mahren," Folks said under his breath. The big man picked me up over the ropes and plopped me down in the center of the ring. I will say it's quite embarrassing to be handled in such a way, but he was too fast and very likely just saved me from being poked in the guts. He took a light jab at me, right in the nose. It hurt like shit, but I let my eyes water and cross, then shook it off.

"That felt personal," I moaned.

Folks took another low swing, but he let me side step it. I'm sure he didn't want to break any ribs. He would kick my ass, but keep me whole. We *do* know each other, I swear.

There was a reason I'd been such a shit to get closer to Folks. Fucker owed me money and it was time to gather some coin from the man, being pulled away from Black Abby was just luck I guess.

I squeezed tears from my eyes, dropped and kicked his leg out from under him. It was a low blow, a cheat move and the crowd made me pay for it in "boos". "We'll call it even," I huffed, then stretched my muscles out. I wanted to give the appearance I knew how to handle myself.

He laughed from the ground. When Folks stood, he swatted hay away from his hind and grinned. "Never got straw on me before." I tried to land a cheap slap across his face (I know) but he grabbed my wrist and picked me up to dangle me in front of his face. "Too slow little bird," he breathed right at me.

I'll take a moment to tell you what Folks looked like, because I can't imagine you are getting it right in your mind considering how I've built him up so far. The tattoos he had carved over the whole of his body were barely visible on his black skin, more so because they were inked in black as well. Still he wore them with pride of all the places he'd been and all the conquering he'd done (in boxing). He was slightly balding, with tufts of black hair circling the outer-banks of his head like a half crown of sea foam receding from a particularly shiny part of a beach. His jowls sagged a little too much, like his belly, which was held from jiggling by the high-waisted, brown linen knee breeches he wore pulled up entirely too high. They were the sort of breeches you'd see tucked into high boots, had he been wearing any. I liked to call them *pantaloons* because I knew it pissed him off.

"So, how does this end?" I asked. "I'm very new at this."

"New? No, you love this. And, I don't owe you anything." He knew why I was there. Folks dropped me to my bottom on the hay and circled me like a turkey vulture ready to nibble at my bits. "That transgression was seventeen years ago."

"All the same," I muttered, waiting for him to kick me or something.

"I didn't know you were *working* working, I

thought…you know."

"What?"

He *did* kick me. The big bastard kicked me. I thought he was a bare-knuckle boxing champion, but yeah, kicked me right in the ass. Then picked me up by the suspenders holding up my pants and *presented* me to the cheering crowd. I took this opportunity to look for Black Abby, didn't see him. Maybe he went away to find me in a dark alley to stab me alone while I was passing piss.

I've had a lot of men pick me up, none this strong. I didn't remember what being a baby felt like, but I would imagine it's this.

"I'm guessing I'm not going to get the coin you owe then? I gave you a pretty good tumble that night, sir." I tried to crane my neck back toward him.

I don't know how far I actually sailed through the air. It couldn't have been far right? A grown man can't just throw another person like that, even if I don't weigh all that much. But, there I sailed. Over the first couple rows of mouth-gaped onlookers. The door to a nearby tea house that broke my fall didn't hurt as much as the hateful look Folks gave me.

CHAPTER EIGHT

One Silver Owed To Me

"You should have known that. You should have known it was for coin."

"Can we just drop it? Please? We've been going at this for years. Folks just give her a damn dollar and be done with it. I know you have it, we all know you have it," Keefie raised her voice, interrupting Folks and I. We stopped to looked at her across the table. We sat at the far end of the table, closest to the fireplace, as many empty chairs between us as we could afford from the rest of the crowd in Bearmaiden. We did have the famous Folks Emery here and since Bearmaiden only had the one large dinning table in the middle of the place, it was hard to keep eyes and ears from wandering too close.

"You held me all night in your bosom," Folks was already three glasses beyond deep in beer. He held up another wooden mug, his eyes watered a little and he drank.

"That's what the coin paid for!" Again I said. How many times have I said this? Over the years, too many.

"Conley Mahren," a familiar hand placed his hand on my shoulder. I don't know why people insist on using my entire name, as if I'm in trouble. Nine out of ten times I was, but still. I cranked my neck to see Samuel standing behind me. The whole of the table quieted to hear the young lad. "I need to talk to you."

"You look so out of place here Samuel, why are you here?" I was trying to be civil. I already knew where this was going to go. I hadn't enough drink in me yet to ponder the murder of L'fowl, or the soiling of his cherished virgin soldier.

"May we speak?" He asked, then glanced around at my company. "Outside?"

"Pull up a chair boy, I'm going to tell you about your Conley here," Folks looked around the table at each of his lads, boys from his crew that earned their mighty place under his mighty shadow. Ale approved of them as well, likely in that they could tussle and toss as well as Folks. Or, damn near close.

"Can we just sit peacefully and enjoy our drinks?" I asked.

"Not at all, no trouble at all." Folks grinned his dumb grin. He then looked back up to Samuel as he kicked an empty chair out for him.

"Oh, here we go, fuckin' Jesus, Mary and Joseph," Keefie muttered.

Samuel wiped stray crumbs from the seat before sitting. He then scooted forward, leaving his hands at his sides. He dare not touch the table or the filth around. He stare straight ahead, glancing occasionally at me and the boys around the table, then finally at Folks.

"This couldn't have been, what? Seventeen years ago?" Folks started.

"You know Burrow-well it's seventeen and a half," I reminded him.

"I found her wandering through Farrowyard-"

"*You* didn't find shit, and certainly not in Farrowyard." I've never.

"How old were you back then *kiddo*?" Folks looked at me, I hated when he called me that. "May I even start this story or would you prefer to tell it?"

"Please, by all means entertain your lads." I took a shot from a bottle of whiskey left in front of us. I was the only one nursing from it, while everyone else drank beer, the service of choice at Bearmaiden. No, I didn't bring my own bottle of whiskey to the event. I said, "I was seventeen, give or take some days."

His crew leaned further in to the table. Robert, Sallow, Skinny Oleerh and Knots all kept their drunkard eyes fixed on Folks, occasionally stealing teasing glances my way. I only shook my head.

Folks continued. "I was out looking for some trouble back then, before I started boxing. Didn't matter what kind of trouble, I just wanted it."

"Before you became the belle of the ball you mean. Sweetheart of the ring." I couldn't help but give this man as much shit as he gave me.

"Yes, before then. Thank you. Must have been right outside Farrowyard if I'm remembering correctly. Came across Conley, all dressed and no where to go. Except to drown in a whiskey river of sorrow. See, she had her heart broken. Broken right in half. I approached her and asked the matter. Which she replied…" He looked at me.

"Sully off you limp-goose dick." Or, something like that I suppose.

Samuel cleared his throat.

"Yeah that was about it. Insulted my manhood, but I let that slide. Fellas you don't defend the size of your manhood in front of a weeping girl, there's just no point unless you're really ready to prove show, which, again, the situation didn't call for that. I left her alone there in the gutter covered in grief and filth. Not worth my time I figured.

I returned to the same spot the next day, again looking for some sort of trouble and there she was. Crying, like the night before. I was going to rob her."

"I wasn't *crying*." I reminded him.

Knots patted me on the shoulder. "It's okay to cry Miss Conley. Sometimes you need to let it out."

"Thank you for that. I was seventeen," I pushed Knots' hand away.

"What could I do for the saddest girl in Charleston? I couldn't rob her while she was crying. I'd have to wait. She was just too sad and I didn't want soiled coin. I did what any man wielding the kind of pride I had would have done. I sat down next to her and I'm not afraid to admit this boys, remember this. Remember what Ol' Folks Emery is about to admit because it will be the last. I wept with her. I don't know what brought it about at first. I found a reason. I wept for my home in Fell's Point. I wept for the father I lost and hardly had time to know. The mother I lost and her other children. I would never see them again.

I continued to meet Conley there over the next few weeks when I could find the time. Eventually we stopped crying together and started talking. We asked the kind of questions you ask when you don't know what else to ask. Where are you from? What do you do? What brings you here? To those such inquiries I found out Conley could fight, she told me so after I mentioned I was considering going a few bare-knuckle bouts to earn some coin. Then she put a coin where her mouth was and showed me so. Damn fine fight. Damn fine. I taught her a few things. Boxing lead to wrestling; it was one of the only ways she could win. Wrestling lead to…well. She told me of a place we could go. The Perky Daughter. Or, well at least behind it. I had of course heard of the place, but never really much wanted to go anywhere near Washmaid Row, on account how expensive such a hobby could be, but Conley's quick and warm hands changed my mind. On we went. We lay out in the open on a quilt we'd found in that alley. It was a cold night, I remember that. I also remember there being two dead cats not far from us."

"Three," I interrupted one final time. "It was three. Which I remember, because I was bored out of my mind lying there getting tossed, and looking around for anything to entertain my mind and thought, 'Oh, that's three dead cats right there. One you don't think much of and two there's a story there surely, but three cats? Unheard of. Unnatural even."

Folks shook his head, "The moon was glad for it. Glad for what it spied us doing. I was glad to be there in her arms that night."

Ugh.

"It was a deed worth doing only one night," Folks ended. "Can't top that again."

"Though you tried," I would have the last word.

"It had been a while. I told you that. You said it was fine."

"Still owe me a coin," I slammed my whiskey glass upside down on the table. "You'll owe me this debt forever before I let you cheat me out of it."

"Oh for..." Keefie sighed and stood. She excused herself, heading to the upstairs of Bearmaiden. She said she wouldn't work tonight, but coin is coin and Rye had a taste for it just as much as I.

I stood up and leaned forward, putting both of my hands flat against the polished wood surface of the table. Samuel stood as well and placed his hand on the table, sort of like I was, but his way wasn't nearly as...staunch.

Before I could say anything, Folks laughed. "Oh don't look so sour my young Deluge friend. It was a mutual arrangement. Conley would never cry over a lad, that's not her style if you know her at all."

Well that's not completely true, I *was* seventeen and figuring things out in my own.

"Where you from *friend*?" Sallow Salazar asked, chewing the last word like a coyote. He squinted from across the table through eyes that had seen far too much sun.

"Here," he simply said. As if where else could he possibly be from but here?

Sallow nodded. It was enough of an answer for him.

"You're not," Samuel returned.

It was a simple reply, but in typical Sallow fashion he took it to paranoia.

"And, how would you know that?" Sallow asked, putting his broad-brimmed hat back on like he was ready to leave. He was an old *vaquero*; hated being in the city more than a stray coyote. "Deluge got papers on all of us," he stood, sliding his chair back, then looked around at his lads, waiting. "All of us. They know who we are. I told you, Skinny." He looked at Skinny Oleerh. *"Todos estamos jodidos ahora…"*

"Your accent," Samuel started, cocked his head confused at the obvious as his eyes lit up, "You're not from here. Mexican?"

"What? Never seen a Mexican before?" Sallow Salazar stood a moment, considering, then finally sat. He nodded toward Orleans Oleerh, "Skinny's from around the outers of New Orleans, before you Deluge boys purged it and stopped letting people in. Took the hoodoo out of the damned place and replaced it with your own version of it. Just as worse. People of his skin weren't exactly welcome there after that, if you know what I mean. You ain't mention his accent."

"He hasn't spoken," said Samuel. I was invested in where this was going, just like the rest of the lads at the table.

"Fair enough." Sallow nodded toward Knots. "Okay, well, Knots, he's from here. Charleston. Breed here and born here. Don't look much like you does he? He's the only one of us that has any sort of out with the Deluge on account he fixes their bastard rifles."

"And, that mean looking cuss, with the half scalped head, that's Robert McGee. You probably have heard of him. No? Well, he's from Kansas far as we all know. He doesn't quite recall much before the Sioux got a hold of his head."

"I don't mean to offend." Samuel shifted in his seat, taking it all in. "And you?" he asked, looking back at Sallow.

"Mexico."

For a moment the table was silent.

"The world is a lot rounder than the Cistern my friend," I said, patting Samuel on the thigh. "And, don't let Sallow get to you, he's actually from Texas."

"Close enough to Mexico you could spit on it," Sallow corrected. "No one counts miles down there."

"I still swear to Ale I had no idea this girl could fight so well, someone taught her solid," Folks then said, barely paying attention to the rest of the table. He tried to soften his eyes for me. "I didn't see you again for five years. You just up and disappeared."

I needed to sort some things out. Had nothing to do with Folks Emery, even though he would probably brag otherwise.

"It'll be a cold, lonely trip into the dark of the Cairns before you get between these sticks of mine again. Or, you pay me what's owed and we can have an honest talk if you got more silver you're willing to knuckle up. But, until then, no sparring. Beers are on me, lads, have fun. Don't listen to this cunt, he's a liar and a horse thief and he takes advantage of young impressionable girls with his cock-headed charm. Put any leeway on this man, he'll take it for all it's worth and never pay you for it."

I offered them my ass side and started to walk away, then remembered the entire reason I came to the Bearmaiden with Folks and crew to begin with, other than story time for Samuel.

"By the way, someone asked about Pynes," I said with my back still turned. I spun and looked around the table then let my gaze fix on Folks. "Know anything of the such? Any word?"

He let out a sigh. "Why would you ask me about him?"

"Great man of your social standing ought to know what's being told or asked in your kingdom I figured. Where better to start asking than the king?"

Folks nodded his head a few times and pursed his lips, then clicked his tongue against his teeth. He didn't know anything. "No word I'm afraid," he confirmed.

I had no money to pay for their drinks and before they realized, I spirited myself away into the night. Folks wasn't a bad guy, but giving his crew that little speech kept their eyes away from the coin-less table.

I left Samuel there in good company, not wanting to look back at him knowing full well he would follow me.

"Here's to your next High Chancil, Samuel and hoping they'll leave us the hell alone to trade fists to face," I heard Folks say, followed by some mugs being tapped together. "More drinks around!"

I really needed to find some way to make some quick coin.

CHAPTER NINE
Silence And Ghosts

I poked Lady Tabitha with a stick I'd fetched from outside for poking after I discovered her in her estate. No movement. She'd suffocated. She was slumped in her chair, tied up with a silk bag over her head indicative to the way she preferred it with me, when she was paying. You could breath under a silk bag for a while, I've done it. The key is you have to control your breathing and not panic. Lady Tabitha did neither of those things. Her wrists bleed from the ropes tied around them, pinning her arms behind her back. Same with her ankles, all gone bloodless white.

Our nights running around the streets of Charleston, me playing as Black Abby always ended back here on her estate in the Breige, where I would tie her up, put a loose silk hood over her and "torture" her until she said the magic word. Which was "okay, that's enough". She was not that original in her olden age. A widow since little, married off to a self-made and wealthy olive oil producer from Apulia, Italy before she could even walk. Tommaso was his name I believe, Lady Tabitha didn't speak of him much, hell how could she, he died when she was two. Left her everything. The estate's gardener raised her until she was fourteen then the cook took her on. The cook died when Tabitha was fifteen, then she just kind of figured she could do the raising by herself.

She was lovely and then she was cold.

I took the silk hood off Tabitha and tried to close her terrified eyes. I pissed the wrong person off in Charleston somewhere and I hated it. I hated not knowing who I'd wronged. I mostly kept my head down and did as I'm asked, knowing damned well once the Deluge start looking my direction it's hard to skirt their gaze. And, besides I couldn't afford to lose more patrons. Two was enough. The only two I even had at the time. Poor, headless Pockets and now Lady Tabitha. I couldn't even fathom who would know how to do this to Lady Tabitha to get at me. Was someone watching me?

Lady Tabitha couldn't do anything for me now. I searched her house for any money she had tucked away, she owed me nothing, always paid up front, but if I knew her (and I did) she wouldn't want me to starve or make for Farrowyard. On her nightstand there was a Donegal Tweed and skirt, folded with a little bow on top. Likely a pricey

Breige gift from my patron. Her fashion sense was well wasted on the likes of me, but it was a nice gesture, so I slipped the tweed jacket on over my clothes as a sign of goodwill to her ghost. I didn't want to be haunted after all. I also found ten cash dollars tucked under pillows tossed to the floor in her bedroom and knuckled them.

"Consider this a tribute to *my* future and *our* past endeavors," I whispered as I tucked the cash into my blouse.

The rest of the house remained quiet and empty, even of ghosts. Wind blew through the open windows upstairs, creating the odd draft. Lady Tabitha didn't leave windows open and mostly left her home bright with lanterns.

I should have noticed the lanterns were all blown out when I first came through the door.

I bolted out the front door, leaving her house and Lady Tabitha as I found and undisturbed.

Once outside in the streets, I stopped immediately. Or, I should say I *was* stopped.

Two Pickney stood outside poking around Lady Tabitha's gardens; slick, greased down hair and Burrow-May-Care attitudes apparent on their toothy, shit-eating grins. One had a short hammer hanging in his sausage-fingers hand; he looked like a mean bastard. They wore their drab green collared shirts, buttoned to their throats and tucked into unsoiled, tan over-sized trousers which they pulled up way high above their bellies. It was a uniform meant to inform you of their tidiness or absolute order.

"What are you doing, girl?" Sausage-fingers of the

Pickney asked, his voice was gruff like boots on sand.

"I could ask the same of you." I said. I knew better. Burrow, help me I knew better.

The Pickney looked at me, then over my shoulder at the house. He didn't even need to ask me why I was there. He already made his assumptions. It wouldn't help me to say I knew her, or that I worked for her, or any other sort of reasonable excuse I could fathom. I looked the part of someone that didn't belong here simply in the way I carried myself and the fact my hair wasn't did up in a fancy bun like all the other Breige girls. I didn't matter what I was wearing, or not wearing. I was sold as a Washmaid girl the minute eyes were laid on me. The bruises on my face also likely gave me away. No Breige girl would have bruises, or if they did, they'd have the makeup powder to cover it.

The second Pickney was smaller, thinner, hunched over like an old spinster. Shuffling forward, he dropped one end of a thin rope he'd had wrapped around his wrist. Guess he was already planning on tying me up.

"You rob the place?" Spinster grumbled. Oh boy here we go. I shifted my eyes looking for options. "Look like you should be back in Farrowyard." The nerve of this guy.

"Listen-" I started.

Sausage-fingers slapped his hammer in his hand; the crack echoed across Lady Tabitha's estate. That was a wicked looking hammer. "Martin, stay here I'm going to have a look inside," he said, looking to his fellow Pickney.

Martin simply nodded, keeping his eyes on me.

"Don't thinking about running," Sausage-fingers said,

then disappeared inside Lady Tabitha's home.

He would find her, but not right off. The game we played when I was Black Abby took place in a small room toward the back of her house, and she hadn't been dead long enough to give off any rot scent.

"Keep your hands where I can see them," Martin growled, his voice and body language already pushing escalation. Pickney kept the streets of Breige clean and safe with the spilled blood of whoever dared them wrong.

Kor Eloise hired half the Pickney out from the gutters of Harklow Down, giving them just enough of a better life to keep them wanting it. The other half were children born in wealth with not much to do, bored and looking for violent solutions to problems that didn't even exist. They were also there to keep reminding the Harklow Down hired Pickney their place, keep them in line and following orders. It was a weird division within the ranks of the Pickney, but one thing kept them all like-minded and that was violence. No one broke laws in the Breige without fear of these boys breaking your bones, or killing you; or worse.

Martin eye-fucked me with his nasty little bulgy eyes and dry lips. He ran that thin rope through his fingers, cocking his head to the side, keeping his eyes on my legs and back to my lips. Burrow, what I wouldn't give to offer him the pointy end of Sparrow to his gut. Bleed him out while I ran back to the safety of lower Charleston. A dead Pickney on top of a murdered Lady Tabitha would do me no good however. Sausage-fingers had already seen my face, and would seek permission to tear about in Harklow Down looking for my ass to hang from a street lamp as an example to the rest.

"Want to see a trick, Marty?" I asked. His eyes somehow got slightly bulgier.

"No, turn around, be a good girl and make this easy," Martin said. He inched forward, meaning to tie me up until Sausage came back out with the news, and permission, for my beating. No judgment from me, had I been him and found someone like me leaving the place, I'd make the same fair assumptions as well. I didn't hate these lads, but I didn't take kindly to dying here in the Breige. If I was going to die it would be somewhere further and sunnier than here, and hopefully with a young lad (or two) in my arm, bourbon on my breath and wrinkles on my face.

"No trick then?" I asked again. "Suit yourself." I turned. I offered him my wrists behind my back, no fight, no resistance. "Come on Marty, you'll love it."

As I was facing Lady Tabitha's house, I saw Sausage-fingers through the front door making his way toward the back rooms. He would find her soon.

"Marty, come on, it'll be worth it."

"What? What is it? You have nothing I want."

"A simple trick, before you beat me. Something just for you before your boss gets here."

"He ain't my boss."

"Oh, don't be that way, I know a Harklow Down lad when I see one. Don't worry we are the same, born on the streets down low. I can tell. That big man about to come out here and order you to beat me doesn't know what it's like down there where we are from. How *hard* it can get. Just tie me up now, say I tried to hit you, whatever you want. There's an alley back where you can break me, or whatever you Pickney boys do." I winked. I would not be telling Keefie about any of this. "Just you and me, no coin. No Breige-born. I heard the way he talked to you, the venom in his voice."

"He ain't my boss," Martin said again.

"Yes he is and you know damn well he is." That earned me a fat slap. I turned back toward him and held my hands for him to tie. I pushed them forward into him. "Come on we are running out of time. Can't beat me twice for the same crime, your boss knows that. You know that. Get you licks in now before he does."

"Shut the fuck up," Martin pushed me back, I faked a stumble and landed on my stomach, offering my hands to grab and tie easy. They were tied within seconds and I was on my feet being dragged away to an alley between Lady Tabitha's estate and her neighbor. It was hot that day, folks of the Breige were all probably staying inside to avoid the sun on their pale, wealthy little bodies. No one would see, or if they did, they would look the other way anyway as Martin pulled me into the alley. He was already getting a little too aggressively handsy.

I had a plan.

Martin slid his leather belt from the loops around his waste.

"Come on now, I'm not your daughter," I teased, hating the moment. I could already tell this man's breath was going to smell like onions. "Take your clothes off, make it quick now."

He did.

"If you were my daughter, you'd never be here in the first place." He snap-cracked the belt. It echoed off the walls of the alley and startled us both. "You should know better. Now…what's that trick you want to show me?" He inched toward me with his little worm. His meager scrunched up body made me take a second glance. What an unfortunately shaped man. Like a skeleton wrapped in a thin canvas blanket, dipped in water.

Oh yes, my plan.

I screamed. As loud as I fucking could.

Yup, that was my plan. I screamed again.

I couldn't even describe the look Martin gave me. Shock? Joy? Pleasure?

A third Pickney entered the alley through the far end from where we stood. Pickney were everywhere in the Breige and I knew that. He was a medium sized bloke judging from his silhouette and already he had pulled some sort of weapon from his side. A baton. The Pickney loved their batons.

I kicked Martin's clothes away toward a stack of fruit crates. Then like any reasonable girl would do. I screamed again.

The Pickney newcomer ran down the alley toward us. I shriveled into a ball, pulling my knees to my chest. I even rocked back and forth a little.

"What's this about then?" The Pickney asked.

"Doesn't really need much explaining does it?" I hissed. "Just look!" I held my tied hands up to show the man and nodded my head toward the nude Martin. The Donegal tweed jacket and skirt gift from Lady Tabitha sold me as a beaten Breige girl, even if the fashion was a little late.

Martin stood naked, hands covering his shrinking Willis. He tried to speak but-

The Pickney struck Martin across the bridge of his nose with a wooden baton, crumbling him down to the ground. He went in for a second blow to secure swift justice. Before I heard Martin's skull crunching under the wood, I stood up and ran. It wasn't difficult with my hands still behind my back; that's one of the things I've done more times than I'd like to count.

I ran all the way down to Harklow Down, keeping my head down and cash tight to my chest. Humid wind blowing in from the river kept my hair stuck to my face. I gave up on trying to hold it back for the hour walk it took me to reach my home in Harklow Down, seeing as how my arms were still tied behind my back. No one paid no mind to me. Didn't look, kept their heads down. I stepped over a gathering puddle of water by the door, dripping from the gutter above our door. It was backed up again from the filth of Harklow Down and I didn't feel like cleaning it anytime soon. Maybe tomorrow.

It was mid afternoon; I had been awake all night with the boys at Bearmaiden, spent my morning in Hawker Square wishing I had coin to spend, then headed up to Breige to check on Lady Tabitha and by the time I walked back to Harklow Down I was exhausted.

Keefie was asleep in bed. No armor on this time. Pieces scattered in front of the bed and her black bear fur on top of her being used as a blanket. It was too hot for that, so I lay next to her on top of the fur and let myself fall asleep. Keefie could untie my hands in the morning. I hated to disturb her.

CHAPTER TEN
Lady Tabitha's Game

Let me set to you now a scenario, acted out by two of the finest players when the moon was high enough in the sky to guide us along those dark and empty streets of Charleston.

It was late summer somewhere around the year of 1870. If it got any hotter, I would have been obliged to take things off and flaunt the things I reckoned a young lady as myself shouldn't be flaunting off in public eyes. For free anyhow.

That dreadful summer was also the first time I'd fully stepped into the Cairns.

Up until that night, I managed to avoid the terrible place all together. Of course Lady Tabitha knew that and she also knew I would stop chasing her if she ducked inside.

Knowing my fear of the unknown, she used that to her advantage. And, since she had balls big enough to stuff inside a canon it was a strategy she engaged quite often.

She'd also managed to untie her hands.

I'd work on my knot-tying in the years to come.

Lady Tabitha didn't see me. I was on the roof of a small cottage about one block over from where the Cairns bled into Harklow Down. Some nights the Cairns would be a few blocks further in and other nights it would reach out past where I stood, flowing in and out like a tide. Most of the homes this close to the Cairns' border were abandoned. Wasn't worth the risk of being home when the dark Keening rolled over your home and you found yourself inside the Cairns dealing with all the horror that usually brought.

Even just looking inside the Cairns you could see the sad, shadowy forms of the men and women trapped inside. Those Cairnborn. Watching, just waiting for you to make a mistake and step into their realm of shadows and haunt.

Lady Tabitha froze in the street below me, stopping to listen. She looked up at the roofs towering over her. I ducked back and away just before her eyes found me.

Something caught her attention. She tilted her head and held her hand up to her ear. She was listening.

I removed the wooden mask of Black Abby and took a long, deep breath of the damp night air.

It was humid. A low, faint haze hung in the air.

I reached back to untie my hair and let it fall, wiping stuck strands away from my face.

Maybe Lady Tabitha was done. I didn't have the

energy to keep up the chase. It was hard enough to breathe in this damned mask and jumping around on the roof tops during, what I'm assuming, was the hottest night of the year didn't relieve me none. Normally she'd leave a small pile of coin before disappearing for the night, but this time nothing was there when I noticed she'd gone.

I heard it then. A low murmur coming from within the black of the Cairns. Now I understood why Lady Tabitha was gone. It was a creepy sound to hear murmuring in the dead of night coming from the haunted place.

I wasn't afraid though. Maybe I should have been. A comfortable warmth washed inside me.

Curiosity came over me as it would anyone in their seventeenth year, already burned out of life, looking for anything to spark their flame again.

I jumped down and walked toward the night-land border. It was like a breathing wall of black. Somehow darker than the night, but my eyes could still make out the shadows beyond.

The murmuring continued.

Now, I'd already said I'd never been this close to the Cairns before, let alone actually stepped inside. I knew the dangers, from tales and songs performed around Washmaid Row late nights around the table when everyone was bored and full of whiskey and ale. They'd tell you to stay away. Whispers that everyone knew. Stay away. Don't go inside, there's nothing inside but devils and twisted things. Dark things.

I stepped inside.

It wasn't instantly as terrible as the songs sing. I wasn't washed over with an impending dread of an endless, breathless night. The moon was absent, but it wasn't pitch black either. Something was giving off some sort of glow. The Keening itself seemed to flow in the air, in the sky and along the ground. I could still see. I could still breath.

It felt like swimming at night. You knew there were things lurking just below you, and peering down into the depths would only make it worse, so you kept your head up and just kept paddling.

Shapes did lurk in the shadowed streets and buildings, but they kept to themselves. Only curious for now. I was an invader in their world.

Not clouds, but something moved in the sky above me. I could barely see it in the absence of the moon and stars. A void shifting in the even darker dark.

I followed the murmur further in, one block maybe, passing houses with boarded up doors and windows. Figures would dart by me, ending their quick trek in safe, tucked away places. Behind piles of old and rotten wagons, alleyways, around corners. I felt their eyes follow me through the Cairns.

One such figure came close behind me. When I turned it was gone again. Starving wolves begging for handouts, but afraid. Were they afraid of me? I would find out later that no, in fact they were not afraid of me. They were testing my resolve. My fear. Wanting me to flee so they could hunt.

I pressed forward until I came to the sound and saw hooded figures forming a loose circle in the middle of a crossroads. The Keening twirled around them, reaching in from the nearby alleys. Rifle-armed Deluge lurked around the circle of the hooded figures, watching over them as the men chanted. I couldn't hear it all, but I heard some, "unsullied, undefiled." I saw now in the middle of the circle was a young man, not much older than I and he was on his knees looking up at the sky. His eyes were wide and black; his hands reached out as if grasping for something. Anything. He screamed in silence as a darkness vomited out of his mouth, mixing with the black of the Cairns, adding to the Keening swirling around him.

I was careful to creep forward. Both of my hands were on a building as if it were a damned safety blanket. I couldn't force myself to let go.

Another figure stepped out of the darkness. An old man. His eyes were kind, but with a volatile sea lurking just beneath the surface. He moved toward the boy vomiting up the black into the Cairns and knelt to embrace him. He wrapped his arms around him, whispered something for a moment in his ear and the boy collapsed in his arms.

"Cairnborn, coming from the alley," one of the hooded spat, interrupting the chanting. He pointed toward the opposite side of the crossroads from where I hid.

The hooded men all turned to see where their companion pointed. The Deluge took aim with rifles.

I would miss what was to come.

A cow of a Cairnborn crashed into me. My safe wall couldn't hold me as I tripped over myself, tumbling into the ground. I squealed like a child. Hell, I was a child.

Seventeen does not make you less a coward no matter how much you know. This was all fresh territory for me.

My squeal drew the attention of, well, everyone present. The hooded men and the Deluge turned to see me tumbled, ass up on the cobblestone with a massive mound of a Cairnborn woman on top of me. The Cairnborn woman used her meaty hands to smash into my stomach. Her girth was smothering me. My head lulled to the side. My eyes closed. I was out of breath.

Then freedom. I don't know why. She fell off me with one loud squelch, so I didn't wait to roll out. I rolled and rolled.

Until I hit a wall, then stood.

I wasn't going to look back.

Whatever was coming out of that boy with its reaching tentacles of darkness could fuck off for all I cared at the moment. The Deluge fighting off the Cairnborn could fuck off. I was getting out of there. I didn't belong. I belonged next to Keefie, in our tiny home in Harklow Down and Burrow-willing, eventually in Washmaid Row, belly up thinking about how I'd spend all my coin. The Cairns were no place for me. I should have listened to the songs. They sang of warning for a reason.

I heard the beefy steps of something heavy chasing me. I didn't turn. I wasn't going to turn. I was going to run straight to the Breige and maybe past Miner's Bridge into the Allegheny's, maybe even all the way to the Blue Ridge. Maybe beyond that. Where it was sunny. Not dark. Shadows didn't try to kill me and fat ladies were only fat ladies, not Cairnborn crazies looking to squash me.

If I knew back then what I know now about the Cairns maybe I would have stayed a kiss longer. Just to see. Maybe not.

I'm not much afraid of it as I was back then.

I was young, but I was no fool.

I ran that day.

Hell, I'm still running.

CHAPTER ELEVEN
A Dimming Light

I took a couple days to myself to lay low and let the glow-hot wrought iron of the Pickney cool down before striking out again.

Pickney hated the Deluge and had no love for Low the Kind, or well anyone other than themselves for that matter. Low, Burrow, Ale the Unhinged, Thread the Gadabout or any of the others. The Pickney didn't buy into it. Their minds were free and blank, left to roam and beat with no providential compasses guiding them.

It all felt insane. I'd been plucked from the streets by two of the highest ranking members of the Deluge, the High and Second Chancil, for the task of souring a lad (which I didn't hate, but I'll be the first to admit, did seem kind of degrading. Why not just take him to Farrowyard? Quality I suppose). Someone running around as my own Black Abby, murdering my only remaining client. My gutters needed to be cleaned, I ran out of money and I was growing bored out of my Burrow-damned mind. Two days stuck at home was two too many.

Keefie ran food for me and kept me up with any sort of goings-on, good or bad. In her own Keefie way, she found out the Pickney *were* asking about, but keeping it quick and quiet. Secret. For when they found me they could act out their justice and none-the-loss for my life. I'd be well to dead before anyone went looking for me

On the third day in solitude, Keefie came through the front door with a dried salami, white cheese and a loaf of hard bread. She dumped them on the table where I sat and smiled. "You need work," she smiled again.

I nodded, broke off a piece of the bread and chewed on it.

"Couple of Pickney were asking about a girl last night at Bearmaiden. I wasn't working, just heard. Been kind of dry lately, Jesus bless. Everyone seems a little on edge with the Breige business. You know, the murder. That doesn't happen in the high streets often." Keefie sat with me at the table. "Meh, who knows, that's about all I know about it." She wiggled the salami at me.

"What of the Pickney last night?"

"All they have is a bit of a description. Built like a young lad, lanky arms, frightened, messy hair. Nothing that could amount to anything." She laughed. "Flat as Nebraska in winter, and just as cold, one of the men did say. He was the one that saw you first, he said anyhow."

"I see. Awfully rude of him." I had it where it counted.

"The other Pickney, the one that I guess 'saved' you in the alley, only caught your arse-end as you ran away. Then the two men had a small disagreement discussing the shape of your figure for reasons of the law and drawing up a poster ad in your likeness. One said twelve year old lad, the other said fully grown lass. They really did catch your two sides I guess, coming and going I mean, depending on the angle."

"You're one to talk. I wasn't given the extra padded blessings from my mama. Like a Burrow-damned hour glass you are. No wonder Bearmaiden does so well compared to me. No one of moral standing wanted to see a…what did you say? Twelve year old lad. Burrow help me…"

"Meh, those blessings keeps me warm at night. And, buy you something to eat on occasion. Funny what men will focus on, even in life and death. Pretty hair or shapely arses, doesn't matter to them. It's all they see."

"Yeah funny. Now that you've gone and properly hurt my feelings, what's the point of telling me all this?"

"My point, wee Conley Mahren, is the Pickney have no idea who they are looking for and they are too nervous about the Deluge to come much closer to the Cairns. You're safe to roam, not coddin' ya."

I wanted to get out and earn some money. No more dry salami or cat naps in the sun. I snatched the salami from Keefie's fingers and tossed it aside. "Come on, let's go earn some coin then."

I got dressed. Simple black wool leggings, sleeveless cotton shirt, matching color. I tied my hair back with a yellow scarf today, hiding my messy honeyed hair. I reckoned it to be a hot one today. I then knuckled my two remaining cash dollars from Lady Tabitha and went out the door where Keefie stood waiting.

She wore a dome helmet with a nose guard and two gray bull horns on the sides. She'd also managed to strap herself into some sort of leather corset, with steel studs running up and down the length of it and a matching leather stripped dress that ended just above her knees.

"Working today?" I asked.

"Yeah, the man that came to Bearmaiden, the one that asked about you, British lad, called for me again. I can't go with you today, but we can meet up later if you want."

"This new client? What's his deal?"

"I'll find out."

"Tell me if he asks about Pynes."

"Will do. He seemed more interested in you though, he only mentioned Pynes the once. I'll try to poke more out of him."

"Keefie, the stuff you said about the Pickney looking for me. They way the described me."

"I was teasing you. But, not about having little to go by. They truly don't know who they are looking for. You're okay."

"Thanks." Brat.

The Perky Daughter was barren. I sat with my back at the

bar, looking at the lack of anyone of interest coming and going.

"Just going to sit at my bar and not have a drink, or you don't have anyone to con into buying?" Sterling said from behind me.

"Yes, much the latter, unless you're feeling generous bourbon man," I said, not wanting to drop my two dollars here on drink. Should have left them at home to stave away any temptation. I felt them warming and jostling under my shirt; wanting to be spent. "Not here dollars, not here," I said under my breath.

"I'm not."

"Any news about?"

"None concerning you I'm afraid," he said. That's good.

"Any *shavers* looking for something to ease their loneliness?"

"Going back to your roots, eh?"

"Not likely, just bored. Need some coin. Any gray hairs looking for a rough-about? Breige girls looking for a tea-buddy?"

"Not that I've heard." Well damn. I turned to face Sterling. His mustache twinkled. No I wouldn't ask him, best keeping him a friendly bar tender and not a quick handy just for a drink. Spend your dollars, it's fine. No.

Ugh.

I was bored.

"You've got two dollars on you, what's the problem?"

Tapper. Didn't even feel the lad.

"Still warm," he said. He hustled up next to me at the bar, like he does and handed one of my dollars back. "I was looking for you."

"A lot of people are looking for me," I returned. I put the dollar on the bar and winked two bourbons from Sterling. "Pynes' name is getting dropped again, know anything about that?"

"Maybe a little, just some rumors." His overly lippy mouth owned the shot of bourbon and it burned going down; his eyes told me. Too young to be properly drinking right, but no one would say anything. He wasn't too young to lift a dollar off an unsuspecting lass and hand it right back to her, earning him a drink paid for by her shirt money. "I have a job for you if you're interested. Big place by the Cairns, I'm only going for one thing, but you're welcome to the usual deal. Maybe grab some things you could use while you're inside."

"By the Cairns huh?" I asked. I raised my eyebrow at him. "What could I use from somewhere by the Cairns?"

"I dunno, like I said it's a big place. Owner never moved to the Breige, but he may as well have."

"I'm in. You have a way inside?"

"Window."

"That easy?"

"It is if you're me."

"What if you're me?" I asked.

"I'll hold your hand. Don't mess this one up." He took my bourbon and tossed it down his throat before I had a chance. Lucky bastard. We got up and left The Perky Daughter and this time I actually paid for my drinks.

"We are not going to wait until night?" I asked. We stood outside the house. Two-story wooden thing with a basement built into a stone wall. It's one of those buildings you pass all the time, assume it's haunted, probably is, but continue on thinking nothing of it.

"Really this close to the Cairns? I'm not that brave." Tapper ducked in an alley, peaking out every few seconds waiting for the streets to clear. When they were clear enough, he ran across the street toward the house, sliding behind a short stone wall standing guard at the front of the building. He motioned me over. I walked. He fumed.

"No one was looking. You're being way more suspicious than me," I scolded him. I watched him as he squeezed his much smaller body through a little square window same level with the street, leading into the basement of the house. "Are you planning on going up to open a door for me? No way in Burrow's buttocks I can fit through that."

Tapper didn't respond.

I took to watching the streets into the Cairns. We were too close. I could see Cairnborn lurking around the edges watching me back, but something else had their attention. Finally it caught my eye as well. A dim light a block down the street stood at the border.

Deluge.

Except something was off. The low glow from the lone figure felt off; despondent was the light that was fading out. It flickered like a lightning bug in the late summer off the tall stacks of rocks that earned the Cairns its namesake.

I'd decided then that Tapper would be fine.

I crept further down Virginia St toward the Deluge, keeping to the houses lining the street; the Kanawha River was only a block over from here and I could hear its waters gently rinsing off the low shores. As I got closer I saw Cairnborn massing toward the figure and moving with me, but leaving me out of their gaze. They were more interested in the Deluge and his fading light. He was slouching and losing faith. The Cairnborn could see that. Anyone could see that.

"Man, whatever you're planning, I wouldn't!" I cried from down the street. Burrow, I didn't want to get any closer. I was not going to sacrifice myself to pull this fool from the edges. Self preservation was one of the few things I had left and I rarely spent that on a fool.

The Deluge turned toward me.

Samuel.

He drew his Winchester from its sheath and stepped toward the Cairns. The Cairnborn were in the dozens, I could see them plainly, salivating and waiting for the lad to step inside their starving, savage boarders.

"I swear to Low, Samuel you ass, if I have to drag your body away from here I'm going to kill you," I said as I jogged toward him, trying not to rile up the Keening. Already I could see its dark clouds reaching out, searching for us.

Samuel didn't stop. I grabbed his arm and forced him to look at me.

"What the fuck are you doing?" Again I asked.

"Earning back the will of Low. The purity *you* took from me." He didn't raise his voice. He remained resolute, no animosity toward me.

"You offered it in kind. Twice," I said. "Stop. Walking."

"I was going to be the one to end all this." He motioned toward the Cairns and the Keening with his Winchester rifle. "I still can. I still can do as much for Low as I can."

"You will die. Have you tried dipping into the Basin yet? That'll do wonders. I haven't done that or anything like that naked for a dare. I'm only saying is all."

"I died that night with you."

Well, that was uncalled for. "It won't be a pleasant death. I've seen what the Cairnborn do. Hell I've just about been killed a knuckle of times myself by them. Not pleasant."

"I'm ready for that." He turned back away from me and went into the Cairns. Quick was the Keening that enveloped him. Samuel's light dimmed to almost nothing as the sorrow on his face became visible.

I'd could already feel the affects of the Keening wrapping around my mind as well. Aiming my thoughts toward my worst memories. Memories of things better left tucked away like the sister I lost to the river. She was there, in my mind.

I threw that afore mentioned self preservation in the gutter and went in after him, secretly hoping more Deluge would soon appear, but since the death of L'fowl it was lately hard to find a random Deluge patrolling the streets. Other than Anrose, the Deluge were currently without much leadership and he wasn't much around neither.

A few Cairnborn lay already dead at Samuel's feet, smoking holes peppering their bodies. Others stood back working on surrounding him. More came from the shadows deeper within. They came out broken windows and open doors from the long abandoned buildings.

It was the middle of the day but the sky was a deep pool of black from the Keening and no moon or stars offered any light above for us in the Cairns. Our only true light was from the faint aura Samuel held. Maybe he *could* do it. Maybe he could fight off the whole of the Cairns.

The lad was a brilliant warrior. He kept back at first, spending all the iron from his rifle where he could, moving away from the Cairnborn looking for opportunities to down another one. Bullet torn Cairnborn piled the slick cobblestone streets. Those he didn't shoot, the ones that got too close, he butted with his Winchester until they fell.

I tried my best to stay out of the way. Sparrow in my hand as I offered it to whichever Cairnborn tried to slip through the smoke of Samuel's spent rifle. I wasn't needed. I was only blocking him from destroying them all.

The air shimmered around us. I believed for a moment Samuel really was going to do it. He was determined to erase the sin I put on him (twice) and earn his place back in Low's graceful hands. He was going to become the sword the Deluge raised him from birth to be. How could I stand in his terrible way. I stepped back toward the edge of the Cairns, ready to abandon the lad to his fate. He looked back once at me and gave me a knowing nod. His eyes were death and a bright light. His love was for Low the Kind. His body began to give up the light that flowed from all Deluge when Low was giving his blessing.

Just as quickly as he cut down the Cairnborn, the remaining few retreated back with the Keening toward shadow. Samuel was standing alone in the middle of the empty streets, his shoulders rising and falling with his every breath.

A baying of hounds echoed from deeper within the Cairns. The air was too thick to see. With the scratching of claw on stone and wet growling drawing nearer, the rising of Samuel's light begin to dim once again back to nothing.

The Hounds of Agerhead were on Samuel before I took my next breath. Big bastards, all black fur and fury; they were once the hunting dogs of Lord Agerhead now consumed by the Keening's black temptations.

Samuel held his arms up to stop the snapping jaws of the first hound reaching him but the beast was too big. The hound's maw closed around Samuel's head like a bear trap. Other hounds closed in on the lad. He was on the ground trying to wrestle himself away from the awful beast. The hound shook its head and reared back pulling Samuel down to his stomach. I pounced on the hound at Samuel's head, slitting its throat with Sparrow, then pushed myself off the hound to hold the rest of the hounds at bay.

Both Samuel and hound lay still on the ground.

A long whistle from deep within the Cairns drew my sight away from Samuel.

A tall shadow calmly walked toward us. The Hounds

of Agerhead sat on their hinds, watching their Lord Agerhead casually take his time as he strolled toward the scene of horror, as if he were just out for a lovely jaunt on a spring day. The Keening reeled back as if watching the man from a safe distance, even it was wary of the lord. He whistled once again, quick this time and all but the dead hound lying by Samuel ran off, blood from its cut throat pooling under the lad. Samuel rolled to his back. One of his eyes was ruined, barely held into place by a loose thread of torn muscle and nerves. The other eye gazed up at the impossible midnight sky.

Lord Agerhead stopped above Samuel. He kicked Samuel's rifle away, then knelt to one knee. It didn't take much to remove Samuel's ruined eye with a small blade Lord Agerhead drew from a tall boot. The poor lad didn't make a sound as Lord Agerhead cut the eyes' nerves, severing it from the socket.

Lord Agerhead tossed the ruined eye to the largest of the hounds. All the hounds gave chase, looking for scraps, snapping and biting at the lucky hound with Samuel's eye in its jaw as it ran down a long street.

Lord Agerhead looked at me. I held still. Samuel's Deluge light was no longer burning. Agerhead looked at the boy then pointed toward me, then toward the edge of the Cairns. We had an understanding. Samuel's debt was paid in flesh and paid full enough to appease the hounds and Lord Agerhead, and for now the Cairns.

I knelt down by Samuel, now unconscious, then dragged him from this place of nightmares. Once in the warmth of the sun and far enough away from the reach of the Keening the abjection felt from the floating dark thing soon burned away from my mind. I left Samuel on the streets of Harklow Down.

The Cairns won and for its trophy claimed Samuel's eye. Samuel had gone too deep, his love and greed for Low the Kind suffered him.

I found the nearest Deluge and pointed him in Samuel's direction. I had done nothing wrong and didn't consider concealing my face. I pulled their once and future hope from the Cairns and saved his life. It was a rare thing for me to concern myself with ablutionary of the sinners seeking providential retribution in the Cairns. But it was my fault Samuel sought to find his forgiveness there and it was my hand that redeemed him his second life. An opportunity to be something other than a failed prophecy for the Deluge if he survived.

And, if he survived he would owe me and I *would* call in that favor.

CHAPTER TWELVE
The Mermaid

I'll tell you now when you're posing ass-over-elbows for some lad, the *last* thing you want is for his mother to walk in. I grabbed my clothes and bumped my ass on every single stair heading down after I slipped at the top, finally ending up standing outside in the street with nothing but sunshine on my bare ass and shadow over my bruised ego. I looked up at the window and caught a coin the lad tossed out, followed then by the angry old gray head of a mother spitting not very nice things my way, a silk mermaid tail and one tiny conch shell. The shell wasn't real of course, I carved it from wood. I'd lost my real one. It bounced on the brick road when I missed the toss.

"Keefie!" I yelled, angrily getting dressed.

When no call back from her came, I marched straight to Bearmaiden to seek her out. I walked through the saloon and upstairs to her room.

"You were suppose to warn me," I said, scolding her with a frown.

"You were taking a crow's age," she countered. "I was knackered."

"I can't just slide out of this thing at the sound of an angry mother's foot steps pounding up the stairs, now can I?" I asked, holding the tail up to show the intricate tangle of shoulder straps and belts to hold it to my rump. "You don't seem *knackered* now."

"I will never understand you." Keefie sighed.

"Bah I've grown past opening my legs up for coin, seems too boring now. No offense."

"None taken of course." She smiled.

"Unh, can you not bugger off?" the man under Keefie groaned. He lifted his head and glanced around Keefie's back to see me standing in the doorway with my hands on my hips. To be polite I kept my eyes on Keefie. She fell forward slightly, putting her hands on the man's knees to steady herself and looked up at me.

"Are you going to see this *client* again?" She huffed.

"Maybe? He came into the Perky Daughter looking for a muse, only wanted to paint me and what better opportunity to wear this beautiful thing? He only finished my bottom half before I had to bolt, and now he has a nice painting of a mermaid ass and I have one silver dollar for the posing."

I sat in a chair next to Keefie's bed and waited. The man shifted his gaze back at me, his eyes widened and he motioned his head in an inviting way toward the bed. I quietly shook my head no and nodded back toward Keefie. This was her show, not mine.

I shuffled through the pile of clothing at my feet. Keefie's mixed with her clients, hastily thrown. Under Keefie's blouse I felt something hard. Lacking anything but curiosity as to wonder what it could possibly be, I bent and tossed Keefie's blouse away.

"Want to go spend that coin?" She asked, not fully paying attention to me or my probing feet.

The twig mask of Black Abby stared back at me from the floor.

I hesitated to answer Keefie.

I looked at the mask and back at her, but her head was turned back, watching her client. He lay still, lost in the moment.

I tossed Keefie's blouse back on top of the mask and went to the window to look out over the streets of Washmaid Row.

"Naw, I'm gonna knuckle this one away with the Gypsies. Probably going to head over to the Shake later, to uhh…do something," I answered.

"Are you finished then, Mister?" Keefie asked. "Kinda stopped buckin' back there."

Her client sighed. "Yeah, I guess. Kind of distracting you know."

Keefie stood up on her bed, jumped off, then crossed

the room to get dressed in a fresh dress, abandoning the clothing on the floor. The man shuffled out with his head down, but not before tossing three folded cash dollars on the bed, then took one back on account of "not finishing".

"Are you feeling all right?" she asked.

"Pretty as a peach," I replied.

"Don't want to talk about the Cairns? Or Samuel? Anything?"

"What more is there to talk about? It was weeks ago. What's done is done and what's gone is gone. He isn't getting that eye back from Agerhead or his hounds. It's meat now is all it is. Nothing I can do about that." I kept it short to stop her from probing any further. Honestly, there was not much to talk about. I didn't know Samuel that well other than intimately and briefly. I'm sure he was a good lad, if given the chance to be someone other than a tool for the Deluge.

We crossed the street leaving Bearmaiden for the day.

The sun was directly above. Tradesmen worked the streets of Harklow Down, going about their heads-down businesses. Rivermen chopped and cleaned fish heads from the Kanawha River, they were odd little men; tough men completely capable of dealing with the awful things that lurked in the water, so I did my best to avoid them. A briner sat by himself at a table sipping from a metal canteen of water watching the rivermen as everyone in Charleston tended to do when they were around. He nodded toward me as I walked by, and I returned his pleasantries.

Keefie had gone ahead, eager to be where ever she

was going.

Dirty faced children huddled together searching for things to keep them from the eyes of the Deluge; tasks not considered sin, like stealing and the such. Some children filled their days cleaning and mending cloth, folding them into neat bolts to sell back to the tailors of Hawker Square. Since Washmaid Row is no longer a station for actual *washing*, then the task was taken up here.

Two wide-eyed children separate from the pack of others were staring at me as I walked by. Their eyes seemed far-seeing, almost as if they could see through me. And then, together, as if one, they opened their mouths.

> *Tis'ill luck to follow a lost child*
> *Don't follow me, don't follow him*
> *T'will you cover your eyes with your hand*
> *Don't follow him, don't follow me*
> *T'won't get you there faster'n dead*
> *Don't follow me, don't follow me*
> *He's comin', He's comin'*
> *Fair days a comin', Fair's comin'*

It was only a nursery rhyme, the type you'd sing to your little one at bed. Really it was a warning about following lost children in the woods, but that last part, the last line wasn't in the rhyme as far as I could recall. I continued to look at the two children as they repeated the last line, *Fair's comin'*, over and over until I was far enough away.

> *Fair's comin', Fair's comin'*

Keefie was stopped at the edge of Hawker Square, chatting with a merchant who was just sitting out his wares.

She grabbed two cakes; the kind with the sweet frosting and handed me one.

"Listen, I have a nice job for us. Could set us up for a while, if you're willing."

"Willing to what? I'm almost willing for anything you know. Mostly. Almost anything. Within reason."

"Got us set up *Tristing* for some Breige boys later. Just have to be there, handing out drinks to the fancies or something like that. Didn't get much into it. Shouldn't be hard."

"Seems easy enough," I said.

She gave a wicked grin.

"Listen, the mask - " Keefie started, but hesitated. "I couldn't find *Klagemuhme*, so I borrowed Black Abby. That's all it was. The client wanted something less…creepy he said. More exciting. Was best I could do up with at the time. T'wasn't nothing of it. I promise."

"And nothing nefarious? That you'd fail to mention to me?"

I had no reason to even *question* Keefie's motives, if she said a thing, then I believed her. So I put it out of my mind that she'd be masquerading around as Black Abby trying to murder me and ruin my day.

"No wicked deeds done," she confirmed.

CHAPTER THIRTEEN
Here's To Low The Kind

"Love me," the girl whispered, finishing the song. I recognized her as Anrose's wine girl, sitting alone at a table in Pleasant Bottom with her back mostly to the rest of the saloon, ignoring the debauchery as best she could. She had her nose buried deep in a small leather book.

"Fuck me," I whispered over her shoulder as the young Scottish lad performing tonight - whom I only knew in passing as Dublin MacCrory - finished belting out the rest of the song with the rest of the saloon. I'd like to buy a whiskey for the Irishman that convinced a Scottish mum to name her freshly born son Dublin, but he died during the child's birth. Had a weak heart and fainted of fright due to all the screaming, never woke up to hold his little Dublin. Sad story.

I circled the table to slide a chair across the boarded floor to sit across from her. I held a knowing smile, matching her own toward me. Her hair was black and her eyes were blue. She was not holding wine today. "Those are the words."

When she made no effort to entertain my knowledge of lyrics so I asked, "What're you drinking then?"

"Tea," she replied, tipping the mug toward me. "You should try it."

"It's a little late for tea to my taste. Keeps me up all night." I held two fingers up to the server walking by, then looked back at Anrose's girl.

"Two whiskey's to start?" she asked.

"Oh, one's for you my dear *belly-dweller*," I smirked. "I'm not going to be drinking alone tonight I'm afraid. Got a big job later, I want to unburden myself. So, congratulations, I've chosen you for that."

The server returned to our table and placed one whiskey before each of us.

"The lyrics are 'Fuck me,'" I said again after taking a sip of the whiskey as to not be too impolite in front of my new friend. "Not 'Love me'. It's a play on words from one of your…never mind. You get it, I'm sure. What's your name? I can't bare to think of you as just Anrose's wine girl a moment longer."

"I know what the lyrics are," she replied, finally making eye contact with me across the table. "Rhone."

"Rhone?" I looked, puzzled.

"My name," she nodded.

"You've got to be kidding me."

"Well, as you say, I only pour his wine."

"Odd coincidence for your Ma to name you that and then find such a station in life, but who am I to question the great Rhone the wine pourer her name?"

Rhone took a small sip of whiskey to match my own and said, "And who am I to answer to the *memorable* Conley Mahren? Good thing you're name is not labeled as someone in your profession." She smiled. It was faint, but still there.

"Aye, Belly-Down-On-A-Table Mahren is a bit of a tongue twister, but I suppose that is what I'm known for. Twisting tongues. And, speaking of that, how's Anrose fairing since L'fowl was brutally murdered in his room? Is he sad? I bet he's real sad."

"Fairing as well as anyone. The Deluge are never short in the line of succession to replace the High Chancil, which is Anrose's top concern at the moment. Though…I wouldn't know much about it."

I finished off my whiskey letting the burn warm my belly.

"Nasty hanging today," Rhone said. "A man and his two sisters."

"Guess I missed it," I replied. "What did they do?"

"Smuggled guns into the Parish," Rhone frowned.

"Well, that's a hanging I guess…" I frowned back.

Dublin MacCrory was just starting a new song, one he'd written himself and was rightly proud of it. It was about a girl he'd met in San Antonio last Christmas Eve.

She lover'd me thrict 'n bed that night
Aye ow'd er three copper
Aye ow'd er three copper
She lover'd me twict 'n the dewy light
Aye ow'd er two copper
Aye ow'd er two copper
She lover'd me onct 'n quiet requite
Aye ow'd er one copper
Aye ow'd er one copper
And now she's my wife'r
And there's no more lover'n

I turned my attention back to my table guest. "What'cha reading?" I asked, poking the little book Rhone had pushed off to the side of the table.

"Nothing." She clearly didn't want to talk about it, the way she placed her arm over the book. "It's called *The Damning of Yor'lfallen*."

"The hell is it about?" I asked.

"I'm not quite sure. I don't speak the language it's written in."

"You're not reading it then."

"What?"

"If you can't read the words, you're just looking at it."

"Well, I-"

"So then…" I waited for her to correct me.

"No, I'm not reading it, I'm just *looking* at it. I think I'm close to figuring it out."

"Figuring what out? How to read it?"

"Something like that." She could see I wasn't going to just drop it. "Figuring out where it is. Where Yor'lfallen is. It's…an old place. I think. I like to study old places." Her cheeks blushed slightly at the allowance of letting me know something about herself.

I noticed Rhone looking up over my shoulder and before I could turn to see what drew her undivided attention away from me, a gentle hand rested on my shoulder.

"Samuel!" I stood to embrace the lad, reeling back when I saw the wound where his eye was, then motioned toward the table. It had been two weeks since that night in the Cairns, I'd kept busy with myself trying not to think on the lad, but here he was to remind me. I offered him a gentle smile. "Always coming behind me when I least expect it. Have a seat with us. This is Rhone of the valley, High Chancil of the Deluge and also the ever diligent and finest disperser of the wine. She was there when you and I first met, you may remember her - "

"We need to talk," he said as he as he dragged the chair across the floor all the while watching Rhone with a look of familiar trepidation. Annoyed eyes looked up from their drinks all around Pleasant Bottom as the sound of the chair being dragged disrupted the so far quiet evening.

Before any more was said, the server leaned over my shoulder and plopped a single, wooden mug of ale in the middle of the table. And, as was tradition in Pleasant Bottom, I picked up the ale and took a drink, "To the Deluge, with whose mighty company I share tonight, although *both* would probably be elsewhere than here-where," I said before passing it to Samuel after.

"No," he replied. "We really must speak."

"It's just something we do in Pleasant Bottom, take a drink," I pushed the ale closer to the lad. "We'll speak later, when our guts are full of courage and our hearts are full of honesty. And our loins, well we'll just have to see how the night goes. Probably full of lies if I'm reading this table correctly," I shot Rhone a wink. "I'm getting some wicked tension between you two already."

"There's an old story," Rhone said, taking the ale from Samuel before he could fully take a sip. "Sharing a drink with someone forever intertwines their lives together."

Rhone lowered the mug from her mouth after taking a drink. White ale-foam lined the top of her grin. "To Low the Kind, in his *mighty company*…I will always share."

"I think my life is already too intertwined with hers," Samuel said, nodding my way. "Not sure it could be anymore intertwined than it is." He took a long drink, finishing it off. "To L'fowl," he added.

"To L'fowl," I parroted, followed by Rhone doing the same.

We all three looked down at the table a moment, then after the pause, looked back at one another as Pleasant Bottom whirled around us in revel.

Rhone was the first to speak.

"It was a messy death. Messier clean up," she whispered. Would she have known I was there when L'fowl was murdered? She poured the wine and wished me well that night next to Samuel, but the lad and I went into the wee early hours, thieving sleep from the night in those soft satin sheets when I should have been home next to Keefie. "Samuel told me you were still there, when L'fowl died. It took some convincing for him to come from the closet, but when he did, you were the first thing he asked about."

"I…the chair fell in front of the door," Samuel stammered. "I couldn't get out."

"Yes, indeed. The room was in quite shambles. Chairs everywhere."

This mood, which I knew where it was heading, was interrupted when food was delivered to our table. It was late morning, and I wasn't terribly hungry, but I felt it rude to ignore food paid for by others and this was Rhone's treat, so I thanked her by eating. Sometimes, doing a mundane, everyday task such as eating a small plate of buttered, scrambled eggs can show your appreciation. My two table companions picked apart their plates waiting to continue the conversation where it had left off. I was hoping they'd move on, talk about more pleasant things like the booming coal economy, or the might of the storm clouds brewing east from the Blue Ridge but I could tell we were not done talking about L'fowl yet, so I continued for them as much as it pained me.

"The Rock of San'ctu," I started. "It was the last thing L'fowl mentioned as he lay dying."

"The Rock of San'ctu," Samuel chewed on eggs. "I heard him as well, he also said something was under the Cistern, whispering, reaching. I don't know what he meant."

"The Stone of San'ctu. Not rock," Rhone corrected.

I glanced at her, puzzling what difference it would be.

"Yes, well, rocks can be as big as mountains but the Stone…is just a tale. A small one. Something that gives the Deluge…hope," she continued. "Not much was known about it other than one of the founding apostles of the Deluge, San'ctu, had with him a stone when he first came to this land, long before the Cistern was built here. It was through his will alone that the Deluge found a foothold here in the old settlement bringing the teachings of Low the Kind before it was even called Charleston. The stone was lost, or hidden, or…didn't even exist to begin with, no one actually knows for sure. But, what's been told about it, is that it would bring forth such a catastrophic change in the very foundation of the Deluge's beliefs, that such a thing should remain hidden. The story is told that his teachings were carved on the underbelly of the stone, out of sight while the pillars of our faith were recorded on the other side. It was San'ctu's way of maintaining a balance in the Deluge. He was unique in that way. He understood that while he truly loved Low the Kind, other's did not share that love equally. It was those others that continued to pass the story of the Stone down. To continue its existence, continues the doubt."

"How could a stone hold on it the pillar of our beliefs? Such a simple, small thing. The very thought that it holds the key to our salvation and destruction is a silly one even for the

Deluge. It's almost silly for me to even say." Rhone watched me, then closed her eyes. "The Chancil's say, 'The Cairns are and always will be our only answer'. Not some Stone of San'ctu. And, I tend to believe them, for I'm only a servant of Low. But, I also concede that the Cairns can only do so much to hold the Keening back and all the wicked things that live within it."

"So the Deluge have given up on ever finding the Stone then?" I asked. "You said the Stone was another way. A way to-"

"It could destroy. Why would any one of us choose to destroy this holy foundation? The Deluge keep this town - " Rhone shrugged as if searching for the right word. "Pure. When the Keening leaks from Hell, it's us who fight it back when the blessed rocks of the Cairns fail."

I let the word fall on me. *Pure* was hardly what I'd call the underbelly of Harklow Down or the alleys of Farrowyard. The Deluge have always turned their eyes away while preaching of how pure they kept the order. I stood up, looked at both Rhone and Samuel. "Come on," I said, walking away. "I'll show you the *pure*."

After leaving Pleasant Bottom we stopped a few blocks away from Washmaid Row and found a spot in Harklow Down where the pleasantries of Rhone's Deluge were not so pleasant. In a window high above the street, on the third floor of an old wooden building a man leaned out. He was old, sunken cheeked, severely under weight and lost in a daze as his eyes struggled to follow the passersby on the street below.

"Do you see that man up there, in the window?" I asked, pointing, though it was terribly obvious whom I was speaking about. Both Samuel and Rhone nodded *yes*.

"Every night he cries out for his two daughters to come home to help him, because he's crippled in the legs, can barely walk, certainly can't come down those stairs. The only problem is, his two daughters are long dead, murdered in the back alleys of Farrowyard not but maybe four years ago? He's been up there since, crying out. I know this because I knew his daughters. Not well, but I knew them. They were good and honest for taking care of their father and now he sits up there alone, starving slowly as the world fades out from below him. Occasionally I'll toss a loaf of bread or some dried meat through his window and he'll eat for a day, but it's hardly enough is it? The Deluge won't help him, so I do what I can."

"Why is it up to you to help him?" Rhone frowned. It felt like she was scolding me, but it was genuine curiosity.

"Harklow Down is a bond, we huddle together like family because the Deluge leave us no choice. The Deluge could improve the lives of everyone here if they just chose to."

"The Deluge *are* improving the lives of - ugh, you don't have to point out all the wickedness of our Charleston to prove your point. You fight us, you fight us because you love the devils you are."

I pointed to a skinny boy vomiting behind a barrel of dried out river fish. Rhone shook her head. She'd seen enough.

"Seems most of you are happy to just watch, or just ignore us. We've surrendered ourselves to the Deluge. Some of us have given everything and maybe more." I looked toward Samuel when I said that, his absent eye was a harsh reminder of what sacrifice could look like. His hand went up, conscious of my stare. "I could see the appeal of thinking Low is an answer to your problems. I'll surrender that to you."

"Yes, well, just because you love one doesn't mean you can't acknowledge others." She looked at Samuel when she said that and wrinkled her brow at him.

"You're smart for someone that pours wine for the lords of the Deluge," I said. It was hurtful, I know. "Don't let them hear you speaking of Low the Kind as if he's not the one and only solution."

"Low knows my feelings."

Samuel's hand was still on his eye when he said, "Low left me in the Cairns."

"What happened to you is…unfortunate," Rhone said, taking Samuel's hand down from his face. She traced her fingers along his palm. "I'm sure the Deluge will always have a place for you. We drank from the same cup together." She laughed, but it was of weakness.

After that we went our separate ways with out much more to say to one another. I made my way toward Breige by way of Harklow Down and stopped by the edge of Elk River and watched its glassy-topped waters drift under Miner's Bridge. Something bulged the surface of the water and continued down the stream. A Deluge preached his gospel about Low the Kind to a group of Salt Briners huddled together in the middle of the bridge. He spoke of Low's truth and love. He had them enthralled with his sweet words.

I walked away, not wanting to listen to his lies anymore.

I needed the comfort of Keefie to clear my mind, so I crawled my way through Washmaid Row to find her.

CHAPTER FOURTEEN
Bastard Of Low

"Have you seen this then, Conley?" Keefie ran her finger along the dome of a steel helmet, down the nose guard and flicked it. "Solid work. Functional. Bit rusted, but functional." She looked up, then added, "You remember the lad Jorey? He's drinking his sorrow away for hanging a lad this morning."

"Shouldn't have smuggled those rifles in the Parish. That's a hanging," the Deluge slurred. He was wicked with drink, barely keeping his head from being too intimate with the table. He was wearing the Deluge black surcoat with a white unbuttoned shirt underneath. Missing was the chainmail gorget the Deluge were rarely without. He was off-duty then from the lower rooms of the Cistern where he would have been attempting to convince the girls of Washmaid Row that Low the Kind was their only salvation away from whore work.

"How could I forget," I said. "Still stretching girls below the Cistern? I've heard about you Mister."

He held up two mugs of red ale, one in each hand. "Cheers to that! Let them stretch until they break. Low, I've always said that."

The Perky Daughter was busy tonight. The crowd was the usual from Harklow Down just looking to drink or looking to ease their loneliness while tossing some hard-earned pennies to the *pettiwaist* working tonight upstairs. Tubwater was picking *Blue Juniata* on his catgut as he sang the lyrics with a quick tremolo.

I joined Keefie and Jorey at the table tucked back against the far wall listening to Tubwater. When he'd finished, two sweet young sisters out of Savannah stepped up on the corner stage. One began thumbing away at a mandolin while the other sang high and fast like a couple of whispering gossip-women going back and forth. They'd called themselves Shuck's Sisters, but I didn't know who Shuck was. The song went:

> *To sing the song of Black Abby, as is,*
> *surely one I shan't repeat, she was.*
> *Fury and calamity and storm and tide,*
> *sunken and drowned, the sea's sullied bride.*

The song wasn't that great - they were just getting their feet and the rhyming felt desperate - but I'm mentioning it here because I'd never even been down Savannah way, let alone as Black Abby, which caused me to ponder if the legend of Abby was spreading in a way I wasn't too keen on. Could explain the fake Black Abby that was trying to off me like a bug. What if there were more?

I couldn't help but laugh at the ridiculousness of the whole thing. The song. The company. Keefie was at least enjoying herself, looking around the room, glaring at anyone who wandered too close to our table. Her senses were up, highly aware of what it must have looked like. Two known Washmaid girls sitting at a table with a rowdy Deluge known to not particularly be terribly fond of girls like us. We must have been up to something, they'd think. Keefie kept them all at bay with the meanness glowering on her freckled face. She'd gained a reputation and everyone knew behind those freckles and sweet little smile was a devil waiting for someone to mouth the wrong thing, or throw too long a side glare at her. So they didn't.

She wasn't drinking tonight, so she sipped away at some heavily watered down honey-wine (mostly water) and fingered away at a small plate of sugared blackberries. A loaf of dry bread sat uncut in the middle of the table.

I took a sip from a mug of red ale (only a little water added), caught Keefie's gaze as I nodded toward Jorey.

He plucked at the loaf of bread absently smiling across The Perky Daughter as he watched the room.

"I had a girlfriend once," Jorey admitted.

"Beg pardon?" I asked.

"The song, it's about a girl," Jorey said.

"I guess…" I had to admit.

"Sure you know lots of girls," Keefie said.

"There's one in particular though, sweetest thing." Jorey looked out over the Perky Daughter again at no one in particular. Was he waiting for someone? "Can't know her anymore, on account of, well you know…"

"Conley don't do that kind of work anymore if that's where you're going," said Keefie.

"Why? Is it because of your haircut?" He was looking at me.

"What?" I asked.

"Nothing, nothing. It's fine. It's a fine haircut. I wouldn't say it's modern by any means," he said. "I'm sure some men like it. You'll get back in there."

I twiddled the tip of my hair.

"I know your type. We all know your type. *Goddamn* braggart," Keefie crossed herself when she said that. "Wouldn't shut the *feck* up about it while you were stretching me on that nasty rack of yours," she said to Jorey as if she were not even present in our conversation.

"You didn't tell me you got stretched," I said, following her lead in the change.

"Yeah, not long ago," Keefie sighed. "Wasn't even doing anything worth nothing. Jorey here didn't care. Said it was a preemptive stretching to keep me honest. Threw a hood over my head, took me down to the Cistern's under belly and strapped me into one of those machines of his. Stretched me until my bones popped and I cried. But, I withheld. I withheld."

"A man is allowed to like things," he laughed. "She's

too skinny and you-" looking at Keefie, "too…I don't know. Too mouthy I guess."

"That's ashame, and I was just starting to grow fond of you Jorey. Our time under the Cistern meant… so much to me," Keefie said. "What's this girl's name? The one you're so fond of, yet can't do anything about?" Keefie thumped a blackberry across the table and watched it roll along the ground, then smiled when it was stepped on. "He told me all about it, had a girl that's willing to meet him in dark places, but-"

"Taffy," I said.

He perked up.

"You know her?" He asked.

"Know her? In a word. We've shared a few moments. She used to beat me up all the time when we were girls."

"You two wouldn't know what it's like to court someone. Impossible these days. The things you have to do, not that I don't mind them. But Low the Kind…"

"Bully Low the Kind," Keefie said. "You just have to take the girl and-" she made a fist motion, then punched out, "You know?"

Jorey's eyes grew darker. "Now, listen. I can't have you speak ill of Low. Won't allow it."

"She's only trying to say sometimes you just have to make an exception," I said. This was taking a turn.

"Just get this Taffy and…listen I know her too. She speaks of you all the time Jorey." That was a lie. "Between girls you know. She talks about you. How good of a rifleman you are, that kind of thing. She likes you lad. Take her. In the light and for good."

"But Low doesn't like…relations to be had within the Deluge. And she's a Widow. Her body is committed to Low."

"Bah, sounds like you've already worshiped at that temple. What's stopping you from paying more penance?" Keefie asked. She was pushing him. She wanted to push him. She wanted him angry. "I've heard her speak your name when she's alone. If I could tell you what girls like her-"

"Enough!" Jorey said. He slammed his hand down hard on the table. The crowd in The Perky Daughter paused a moment, like a breath being held until Dublin MacCrory stepped back in and started thumbing away at a banjo. The sisters from Savannah soon joined him.

"Speak ill of her again and I'll take you back below the Cistern and stretch you further than your body can take, both of you," he growled quietly.

"Me? What in Burrow's name did I do?" I sipped my red ale. "Besides, I'm pretty stretchy."

"Bah, you're all the same. Whores. You push men into thinking too much about your cunny then you close up shop right before we've decided to pay. What's the bloody point then? Tease, whores. Dirty daughters and ashamed, both of your folks should be. Ashamed. Low is ashamed. Low is always ashamed of the likes of you."

"I could just about count on all my limbs on how little I care about the shame of Low the Kind, tell you that," I said.

"You're sitting here, in your own mind, thinking of bending our Taffy over in a back alley just for a chance to shop at her window and you have the nerve to preach on us about shame. I know you're type too well Jorey. Deluge. Man of Low. You've no standards. Only when someone is watching you, or you're preaching to others about how we should behave. I see you looking around to see who's watching us. I am a dirty daughter and I never had the privilege to know much else, Keefie either, but I know who I am. Unlike you. Bastard of Low. And don't think I don't feel your leg shifting under this table as you think about pulling iron on us. Bad place for it though. Look around man, you're the only Deluge here. No one would bat an eye at another Deluge shit gone missing. Think about it. Think about it before you pull that iron out of its sheath."

Keefie slid her chair back slowly to the sound of wood on wood, no one turned this time. "If you'll excuse me, I have to go pass some of this honey-wine."

Jorey was red-faced staring at me. Both of his hands had returned to the table where he shifted a mug of red ale back and forth across the table. Ale sloshed out a little each time.

"All you have to do is ask her. Ask Taffy. She'll beg you for it before she says no, is all I'm saying. I know her. She's wound up tight like a kitten trapped in a box." I wouldn't think a man's face could grow more red, but he proved me wrong. The Deluge light started to rise out of him, faint, but it was there casting a faint aura over our corner of the room.

"Girls like-" he started.

Keefie returned. She was standing behind Jorey, leaning down to whisper into his ear.

"Girls like Taffy, are the reason girls like us exist," Keefie hissed in his ear.

He didn't turn toward her. His eyes only narrowed before they widened.

A thin trickle of blood ran down the side of his neck forming a small red pool under his collarbone. The front of his shirt began to blossom red, yet he stayed erect, his hands on the table propping him up.

Keefie wiped her blade on Jorey's surcoat, then sat back down.

Jorey struggled to take one final breath, then his head lulled down.

"You ready to go to work?" Keefie asked.

CHAPTER FIFTEEN
Terrible The Donkey

I lay with my back to the hay and belly toward the sky, pondering. It wasn't much of a ponder, but it was enough to start a revolution in my mind. A revolution to stop pondering.

What could I have done to offend Keefie as much to end up at the ass end of a donkey named Terrible, getting tugged through the Burrow-damned Cairns in a wooden cart full of itchy straw and biting fleas - almost entirely from the afore mentioned beast leading this shit parade?

"What's that new scent Keefie?" I asked.

She lay next to me, keeping her eyes up at the clouds, traveling in their silent journey across the sky, slowly disappearing the further into the Cairns we'd traveled, so far, mostly undisturbed.

We came in on the opposite side of the Cairns - the side not often visited or spoke of - for reasons other than there was shit to do and only fools made homes here. Fools and the destitute. People that had nothing left to give, nothing left to take were mitigated to this side. The forgotten side. No, we didn't go through the Cairns, we kept to the border of that dark place, skirting around the outskirts of Charleston and finally here, in the Deadlords. The Deadlords was a place kept from the eyes of the Deluge, it was a long abandoned old part of the city. Like I said, nothing worth doing here.

That is, unless you're a fancy from the Beige looking to test the weight of your stones in the Cairns. *Tristing*, they called it. It was a hunt of sorts and the kind not many knew about, or if they did they didn't talk about it, or if they did talk about it, likely you were there, in their inner fancy circle and one of the few privileged enough to be in the know.

Or, you were in a donkey cart.

Keefie and I were to be their darlings, "darlings of the *Tristing*," they said. We would dress in the finest silk clothes and drink from rested red wines that we couldn't recall the names of while listening to the tales of our brave lads from the Breige as they prepared for their hunt. It was a way for them to kill untethered and recklessly without worry or guilt, not that they had that to begin with.

Darlings.

Bait. We were to be bait.

In truth, this is exactly where I *probably* belong, here in the eyes of the Breige boys' sullied intentions, a vision of their expectations, and I knew they intended for me no good.

And, if you're wondering why I would return to the Cairns after such a night as the one shared with Samuel and his eye departing his head; maybe, just maybe you haven't been paying attention up until now.

Did you feel like you knew me? Know me *really* well? Or, is it still too soon to really get it? Money was my one true motivator as to place myself in precarious situations as this, knowing that once I'm done and the money was warming away under my blouse and bed I could stop; I could buy myself a nice place somewhere not here, maybe down Galveston way and say, "Conley, you've once and truly deserve this."

"Deserve what?" Keefie asked.

"Nothing," I said. This flea cart was my stage, where I belonged. A bed of hay under the open sky, free of stars and full of terror, being pulled by a *lovely* donkey named Terrible.

"Cinnamon," Keefie nodded, snapping me back to my reality. I felt hay poking me in the back.

"I'm sorry?"

"The scent. It's cinnamon from the Shake. Or, well right outside the Shake I should say. Young girl was selling it."

"Oh, well it's nice. Suits you."

"Thanks, you look pretty in those silks," Keefie smiled, looking at me. "Kind of big on you, but all the same."

Already the streets of the Cairns began to shift as the

Keening rolled through the streets toward us, leaving a trail of Cairnborn in its black wake.

"Well that's horrifying," Keefie whispered.

"I really hope those Breige lads know what they're doing." I sat up next to her and looked where she looked.

"Just think of the pay," Keefie half-laughed.

"I'm trying, but I'm also thinking about that Cairn-shit that's getting a little to close to our cart. Are we allowed to run? Or, do we just sit here and stew in our own pissed in under-clothes? Not that I'm wearing any, you should have told me to pack accordingly. Do we get some sort of signal? You know I really think we should have discussed the terms of this job a little fuller in detail." I held my arm out to stop the Cairnborn from getting much closer. My hand was on his head keeping him at bay as you would a small child throwing a tantrum toward you. Luckily, this Cairnborn wasn't much bigger than a child, so it didn't take much.

Suddenly an arrow bloomed out of the side of the Cairnborn's temple, dropping him to the streets. I looked over my shoulder and saw one of the Breige men standing on the roof of a low building, holding a bow. He gave me a thumbs up. What could I do, but smile and give him one back. Different finger. He smiled.

He was Henrold Nanibold Merigold. It's near impossible to say the man's name without rambling off all three. He did go by Henry if you'd like, but I didn't. I'd found out later that Henrold was the man paying the British lad that kept paying Keefie a visit at Bearmaiden, the one asking about me. I met him briefly before this all began, shook his hand, gave him a wink, that kind of thing. Henrold explained the job - not in much detail, I accepted, that's about all I can do. As the leader of this little endeavor, he promised us we could live a healthy few months with the coin they would knuckle us, *if* and only *if*, we kept our "pretty mouths" shut as to what we were witness. Easy choice for me as I usually keep my mouth closed to the perversions of what I was being paid to perform. But, this was also a test of trust between Henrold and I.

I trusted Keefie not to get me killed, but when our cart shook and Terrible the donkey ran off taking us with him, I began to second guess myself, which I try not to do, because if I can't trust myself, who the hell am I going to trust? This donkey? He seemed at least smart enough to run when fondled by the Keening's choking sadness.

I heard the boys from the Breige yelling for Terrible to come back and noticed an arrow sticking out of the poor donkey's ass. I looked toward Keefie, but she was holding on to the cart's railing, eyes closed trying not to get bucked out by the rattling cart and startled Terrible as the donkey did his best to avoid the large stacked rocks of the Cairns.

A Cairnborn crashed into in the cart with us, grabbing on to me with clawed and awful fingers just as Terrible turned a sharp corner. I was pinned to the side of the cart, with my hand behind my back and leg twisted and bent under my ass from the Cairnborn's thrashing body. My free arm held his bitter, dead breath away from my face.

Terrible and the cart lurched on a rock, sending Keefie out the rear and into the streets. All I could do was watch from under the Cairnborn as she bounced on the streets, rolled, then quickly vanished from sight as Terrible pulled me further into the Cairns. Keefie was on her own and I asked a favor of Burrow to see her free from any horrors. She would be of no mind to survive this nightmare. As far as I knew, Keefie had never been into the Cairns, not even on a dare or job.

"Headbutt!" I hissed as I threw my head into the Cairnborn pinning me down and felt his teeth cut into my forehead. A small trickle of blood seeped down, blinding me in one eye. I coughed when the blood went into my mouth as I wasn't prepared for the irony taste.

The Cairnborn reeled back just enough for me to untwist my leg from under myself. Enough for me to get into a squat and push my weight forward, placing me above the foul man. I was already bleeding from my head, so I figured it wouldn't hurt to offer a few more headbutts to the Cairnborn's face ending his flailing tantrum. When he stopped I rolled his body over the side and turned toward Terrible.

He was too far pissed to settle into a trot so I did the next best thing I could and waited for an opportunity to jump out of the cart; I didn't want to end up being taken deeper into the Cairns. Before I could jump the cart flipped, I was tossed and Terrible broke free. The poor donkey lad with an arrow in his ass would not survive on his own in the Cairns. Soon the Keening would consume him in some nightmarish way. He panic-ran away from the flipped cart and disappeared out of my sight.

The Keening rose like murky water around my thighs. High ground. I needed to climb and get out of the streets. I glanced around for anything. I was too deep into the Cairns now for more Cairnborn to show up and didn't want to wait around to find whatever surprise came for me so I ran toward a decayed inn, with a chipped painting of a bed and moon on a rotten wooden sign. Next to the inn, nestled down an alley was a small house. I heard a murmur down the alley, a voice whispering to me. I soon felt the Keening rising higher on my thighs, pulling me like a slowly flooding river from seasonal rain toward the house, toward the whispering. Above me something gathered in a black mass of shape. Shaking, I turned from the odd little house, then kicked the inn's splintered door and ducked inside.

I wiped the blood from my face and took a breath to gather myself. Nothing was inside the inn with me except the memories of a forgotten and stolen time before.

Burrow's hand grazed my own, urging me to move toward the stairs. I wasn't one to not do what she suggested when I felt it, so I went and ran up the stairs. The Keening filled the bottom floor of the inn as soon as my foot hit the upper most step of the stairs. I turned and looked back. Something tall and long-limbed rose up from behind the old bar, beginning its slump toward me slowly.

It felt as if Burrow's hand kept urging me up, so I kept going. Onto the roof.

I looked out over the whole of the Cairns from the roof of the inn. Once inside the Cairns, this deep, you can't see the rest of Charleston, or even much further than a few city blocks. The Cairns were massive, spreading out over a large portion of Charleston's once forgotten old city; reaching and wanting more, the dark tentacles of the Keening undulated at the borders of day and night. I looked down into the streets below me and watched the Keening receding. And, I was safe for now.

Something shimmied quietly at the opposite end of the roof. I turned to see a figure stand up, drop something, then dart off, jumping to the next closest building - a warehouse next to the inn. When I went after him I stopped when I saw what was dropped.

It was a hat knit out of yarn and it belonged to Pynes.

CHAPTER SIXTEEN
Lovely Knit Hat

Pynes Oak.

No, impossible.

I called out his name and he looked back up at me, but now he was far enough away I couldn't be sure, it could be anyone at this distance, but the knit hat did belong to him. I would know that ocher wool thing a mile away, could I see that far. I was the one who knit it for him. That's not right, I knit it for me, then he stole it at the corpse rock down by the Kanawha River banks.

He turned and kept running.

I looked for a way to follow, but other than jumping the way he did and risk landing in the streets below there was not much else. So I jumped to the next house over. I landed like a Burrow-damned tossed sack of potatoes and felt my ankle twist under me. I tucked and rolled as gracefully as I could, stood then fell back over. Soon as I could, I hobbled over to the edge of the roof and watched for Pynes.

Pynes continued away. I wasn't going to let him go. I readied myself at the edge of the roof.

Hands snatched my hair and pulled me back. Hard. I fell, landing on my back and looked up at whoever had the damned nerve to interrupt my desperate chasing of Pynes.

Burrow bury me alive and call me dead-

Black Abby stood above me, already twin daggers hanging in hand. I didn't wait; I pulled Sparrow from my back and rolled away.

Pynes stood two house roofs away, watching. Mocking me to draw chase. The Keening gathering around him.

Abby lunged forward.

Let me tell you a joke.

What was currently trying to kill me, had twin daggers, my Black Abby mask and tits?

I know, it's not very funny. Not funny at all you even might say. I need to work on the delivery, but what the hell?

Abby was a woman.

I don't know why I would assume otherwise, she was wearing my clothing, my mask and had my body, or at least close to it. I'd only known a few men in my life that could match the same and they had entirely different professions than roof stalking.

I could feel her deceitfully concealed body deliver up, pressing into me from under the tattered cloak she wore as we wrestled for our blades on an abandoned roof in the middle of the damned Cairns.

I'm was just as surprised as you. Really I was.

The Cairns had a way of bringing forth whatever ailed your spirits and mind at the time, a true place of nightmares and undesirables. This was real enough. Those twin daggers were real enough. They already sliced my forearm, making it impossible to hold my own Sparrow with the slick blood flowing into my palm.

When my dagger dropped I tackled Abby to the roof, grabbed her wrist and pounded until she lost her grip on her weapons. They skittered across the roof away from us, leaving us in a desperate battle of slapping hands and shit-bad attitudes.

"Who are you?" I hissed at the mask of Abby. I tried to push the mask away but she was too quick.

She reared her leg back and smashed her knee into my notch. I hate fighting girls. We don't fight fair. I've kicked my fair share of men in the prick before when they had a height and weight advantage; I'm not going to fight out of my league and not cheat you know. All's fair and all that. Abby stood a little over my eyes by not much but kicking my sweet cake was totally uncalled for. I felt my belly cramp as I tried to roll away. She jumped on me again, squeezing with her thighs and grabbing for my wrists.

It was dark up there on the roof. For a moment I

thought I saw a star through all the midnight above me looking down at the madness below, but it was actually the middle of the afternoon; the darkness was just brought about by the wickedness of the place and the Keening. What a lovely thought to be safe on the moon watching this nonsense and keeping uninvolved. Unfelt things flew and dove in the sky above, massive shadows that were not clouds.

I felt strands of her hair tickling across my face. I hated it. She held both of my wrists stretched up above my head with only one of her hands (Burrow she was strong) and dug her knees into my side, pinning me to the roof. She used her free hand to reach for my bloodied dagger, just a few feet from us. I tried to kick out from under her, but she was too good of a wrestler.

Abby's fingers were at the dagger, she leaned to the side just enough for me to roll her off, but she was able to grab the blade in her dismount. She stood, retrieved her own dagger and held it before her, then tossed mine to me.

I stood. We circled around one another for three quick beats of a heart, then I jabbed forward with my dagger hand. Abby swiped down, just catching blade on blade, sending my arm away to the side. I spun and slashed a wide arc to keep her back. It worked, but she came forward fast, her free hand grabbing at me; dagger hand slashing. I leaned back enough to only receive a small slash across my waist, but tripped backward on a loose tile from the roof.

I was quick to my knees and quicker to look for Pynes. Still he stood spying us from the safety his roof. I truly was concerned at his lack of concern for me.

Looking back just in time, I saw Black Abby fling herself right toward me; one final attempt to end me here. I still don't know why and I didn't think I was going to have the time to ask at the rate things were proceeding. Hey, why are you trying to kill me everywhere? Yeah, see no. Hard to talk with a mouth of head blood pooling around your tongue.

A shadow, quick and heavy caught her mid-jump; slamming her away from me to the side of the roof, where she flipped over and fell into the darkness.

Henrold Nanibold Merigold stood there, with several of his Breige men along side him, all dressed for the *Tristing* and looking terribly darling in their little outfits. I was never so thrilled to see a lad from the Breige in all my life.

"You looked troubled," Henrold grinned.

"How did you find me?" I asked.

"When in the Cairns, we stick to the roofs. Seems safer somehow," he said.

"Keefie?" I asked, looking around for her.

"Not yet I'm afraid," he returned.

I scanned the jagged horizon of dark houses. "Did you see a man run off? He dropped his hat."

"I did." At that moment Henrold whistled and the man I thought was Pynes approached.

"Where did you get this hat?" I asked under my breath.

Henrold dismissed the man, leaving me no chance to ask further about the hat.

"I'm sorry for the cunning ruse," Henrold said. "I just

had to be sure of your intentions."

"My intentions?" I believe I must have looked quite a mess, judging from the looks Henrold and his lads were offering me. I felt my hair, dry and sticky-sweet from blood and filth from the Cairns. Hay stood from my hair like switchgrass by the lake. My legs itched from fleas. And my clothes, shambles.

"That you would do anything for Pynes. Come on, first we will find your Keefie, then there is someone that I would like you to meet. Come on, don't sulk." Henrold jumped houses to the next roof, then looked back. "I'm sorry! Yes, figure it out. This was all for you. He needed to know."

Who needed to know? Know what?

As I stood on the roof I noticed the faint scent of cinnamon crossing my nose with the mix of blood. I smelled my arm and clothes. The scent lingered on me.

CHAPTER SEVENTEEN
Henrold Nanibold Merigold

Hours passed as we waited in a room too fancy for my own taste, not to mention the sight and smell of me stinking up the niceness of the place all while not belonging here.

Keefie was with me. I watched her from the corner of my eye, stealing glances back and forth as she kept shrugging, wondering as I was to what we were doing in a place like this. We sat in silence in the middle of that room, on a couch just close enough to one another to graze our nervous bouncing knees.

It took hours of searching until we finally found Keefie in the Cairns, huddled under an overturned donkey cart, passed out.

"Are you mad at me for any reason?" I asked,

breaking the silence of the room.

Keefie startled. She looked at me and asked, "Mad? Why would I be mad?"

"I don't know. Forget it."

"Are you okay?"

"Not really. You?"

"No, not really." She laughed a little. "I could go for a bath."

"What happened to you after the cart flipped?"

"I…" She looked down at her hands as if looking to them for answers. "I can't quite recall. I remember flying out of the back of the cart. Landing. Darkness rose around me. Shadows and buildings moving. Crooked things watching me. It was like the Cairns were alive. Like it was a cat and I was a mouse, frozen. Conley, I've never felt anything of the sort before."

"That was your first time in the Cairns wasn't it? With the Keening?" I asked. I felt bad for Keefie, it's a thing no one should like to experience, to be so vulnerable and alone there.

"Yes."

I didn't have words to give her.

She looked back up at me and asked, "Tell me what happens when this all catches up to you?"

"What do you mean?"

"The burden of what's inside that terrible place. The Keening made me feel…I don't know. Like the world was burning. Like I missed my Da dreadfully and my Ma. I never even knew her, yet, I felt her sadness. Does it stay with you?"

I nodded my head. The smell of her cinnamon filled me again as she shimmied closer to me for comfort. I placed my hand on her thigh and patted.

"We can talk you know," I said.

Keefie made a "huh" sound.

"I've known you far too long and far too well for any sort of difficulties to arise between us, if you ever want to say something to me, just say. Anything of mine you ever want to borrow, just ask. Coin, comfort, bed, ear, anything. Mask." I watched her looking down. Her eyebrows furrowed as she pondered the oddness of what I was saying. Light from a nearby lantern haloed around her blonde hair. She was too lovely for this life, a life of the burden carried from being inside the Cairns and being inside what I've just offered her.

"I don't understand," Keefie's voice felt odd, away from me.

"It must be strange," a new voice from the room's only door caused Keefie and I to both quickly look up.

Henrold stood, with a small entourage of Breige men standing behind him in the adjacent room. They did not enter when he did, and he closed the door behind him after he sneaked inside.

"It must be strange, no frustrating maybe," Henrold started again like it was the beginning of a speech he had rehearsed, "to have Pynes' name resurrected to you after all these years. I know what he was to you."

"And what was that?" I asked as I watched Henrold

cross the room and pick over a plate of cheeses left sitting out for Keefie and I. I liked the sharp Irish white the best.

"I'll be blunt. I am sorry again, for the ruse of taking you into the Cairns, but it seemed necessary. The truth is we did indeed find Pynes."

He waited for me to respond, but I didn't.

"A report came back from a logging camp up north of a man acting in ways the people there are not accustomed to."

"How could you be so sure it's Pynes?" I asked. "He's been missing for years and never told me where he went."

"Yes, and that's why you are here. Because you, of all people, he would have told. But, since he apparently didn't, the truth of what he and Kor saw in the Cairns must be absolute. Kor Eloise would like you to go north, find what you can find. And if it's Pynes, convince him to come home."

"You speak for Kor Eloise then?" I asked.

"Kor Eloise speaks for Kor Eloise, but come with me, I would like to show you something. Rye you may come too, I have a feeling your part in this will run parallel with Conley's." Henrold finally popped a cheese in his mouth and left the room. We followed through a long hallway filled with paintings of dark things and dark places. Rotten buildings with black beasts standing above them blocking out sun and stars. Ruin and death with spears and lances crossing fields of war, ravens flying over, shadowy fogs crossing endless abysses. A black shape in the middle of all the paintings, void of any light or shade. A shape like a man in some. Clouds of black in others. Evenly placed sconces illuminated as well they could considering the war they waged on the perpetual midnight through the hallway. After the black hallway, Henrold slowly opened a door and squeezed inside. We waited, then he peeked his head out and invited us inside.

Kor Eloise sat in a chair with his back to a wide, open window. The city of Charleston splayed out forever behind him. Beyond that were the Cairns.

Kor's office was brighter than the rest of the house. There were ancient looking things hanging from the walls and on displays; artifacts under glass domes, things I've never seen, things from another history, much older than us. Stone tablets, tiny carvings of busty women, horns with ruins carved all around them, curved swords; all on display next to busts adorned with various sets of armor. Keeping an eye out for any small exotic armor pieces I could lift for Keefie (because I knew she wouldn't), I crossed the room to stand in front of Henrold's desk, where Kor Eloise was sitting, a plate of barely touched food behind him.

His face spoke of a void as he tapped his finger absentmindedly at a map laid out on the desk.

Henrold said something to the man and returned to us. "Kor is not who you once knew him as, I'm afraid. The Keening…broke him. But, before he lost his mind he whispered one thing to me."

"So you're making decisions for him?" I asked. "You do speak for him?"

"Me…and a business partner. We do, yes. Before Kor completely retreated into his own mind, he asked us to never reveal this truth and to continue as he would have."

"Ensuring the Breige is untainted by people like me…" I whispered.

"No, lord, we need people of your morality offering shelter against the Deluge, or else we'd all go insane," he laughed.

"Okay, let's not go that far, I don't have those." I looked at Keefie who was holding back a scoff.

"Don't have what?" Henrold asked, still smiling.

"Morals," my reply.

"You obviously don't know our Conley," Keefie said. She was staring at something sitting on one of the bookshelves under a box of glass. "What's this then?" she asked, looking at Henrold.

"Beautiful isn't it?" he replied.

"May I?" Keefie asked. "I'm an admirer of things like this. Mostly armor, some swords. But this…I've seen this before. Conley?"

Henrold appeared to think for a moment, then nodded. "Just, be very careful and do not finger that trigger."

Keefie reached into the glass box and pulled out a revolver, rolling the cylinder after pulling the hammer back. She studied it, held it up arm-length out and looked down the barrel. "Worry'd," she traced her finger along the writing on the side of the revolver. She held it for me to see, "S'what I thought. Remember this?"

Keefie was right, never had much of a chance to return it to its owner after we swiped it from that Deluge, so I dropped it where I could. Fetched me a few good coins back then. I'd always wondered who Sterling had sold it to. Funny how things like that come back into your life.

"Does it work?" Keefie asked, looking at Henrold.

"It does," Henrold said, moving over to stand much closer to Keefie. "Do you know much about them?"

"I know they can put a hole through just about the biggest Ranger you ever saw and sit them down right quick."

Henrold laughed. "That about sums it up I guess."

At that, Keefie moved it around the room while aiming at different things, sure to keep her finger away from the trigger.

Henrold held his hand up, taking Keefie's hand in his own, then slowly peeled the revolver from her grip.

She finally relinquished the revolver and let Henrold take it, lingering her hands in his a little longer. "You're right, it's a right beautiful piece."

"I'd be more than happy to show you other things, had we the time. But, everything else would pale compared to this. It's such a rare piece. The art on it is exquisite. Almost ruined by the word carved in the barrel. Worry'd. Don't know why anyone would do that." Henrold put the Beaumont-Adams back in the glass case and carefully closed the lid.

"Use to say something else," Keefie said. "Before it got all scratched up with Worry'd."

Henrold Nanibold Marigold frowned.

"Just saying, have a professional look at it closer sometime if you haven't. The man that carved Worry'd there, carved over something else. Though can't really see what was there before anymore. Depending how you look at it, and if you squint just right, what ever it read started with an S, and looks like the d used to be a b."

"You can carve your dick on it for all I care, can we just get to the point where you tell me what you want, what Kor wants, and where Pynes is," I changed the subject.

Henrold sighed, clearly he was enjoying showing off his collection. "As I said, go to the north and bring back Pynes. If you can. He might have information that could greatly benefit this city."

"How?"

"He saw, just as Kor did, the truth of the Cairns. He went in far enough to see what they hold, just as Nathaniel Faire did before them. Unfortunately for us, Kor returned as he is now, unable to properly communicate. The Keening stayed with him, over him like a shadow, ruining him."

"Fair Nathaniel, he was like a god to those lads," I said. "Pynes held his ideas in high regard. They were obsessed with his philosophies."

Henrold nodded, thinking.

"Anyway, Pynes left. Walked across Miner's Bridge and never looked back. Not even for me," I reminded Henrold.

Not even for me.

"There was a third man, Everett Thayne. He went into the Cairns with them," Henrold said.

"I met Everett once as well, but we barely spoke," I mentioned. "None of them really spoke much, Kor or Everett. Pynes only spoke to me when I pushed him. They had plans I couldn't be part of. It was like…it was like I was sitting outside a window, barely allowed to glance inside. But Pynes opened it for me one time. It was enough."

"We don't really known much about Everett or how he ended up. There was a story he was left inside the Cairns, becoming part of it. There's another rumor he's out in the wilds somewhere plotting a return to end all of this," Henrold gestured vaguely around him. "It was the city that wronged these boys."

"Everett was quiet, but smart. He's the one that tracked down Fair Nathaniel's notes about the Cairns, got the idea in their heads about going in," I said. "Don't know if I forgive him for that."

"The Cairns swallowing people up," Henrold scoffed. "Silly children's tales to keep curious little feet from going inside. Probably conjured up by the Deluge to 'keep us safe'. Who knows what's inside. I'd like to know."

"I still don't understand what any of this has to do with Pynes. He wouldn't have left without a good reason. He wasn't a fool," I said. "I just…I just don't know what his reason was is all."

"Now's your chance to find out. For me it's simple, Pynes has information that my fellows and I could find useful to getting Charleston away from the growing hand of the Deluge. We can't allow the Deluge to grow any further and we think the Cairns may hold the answers. There is a lot being played here and we do not wish Charleston to become another one of their holy outposts for Low anymore than it already is. Come, let's enjoy the night for what it is before you depart. A new partnership of sorts."

I cocked my eyebrow at Henrold.

"Trust me a little, like you once trusted Pynes." Before Henrold, Keefie and I left Kor, I leaned in close to the map he was tapping on. It was map of New Hampshire, around the White Mountains and scribbled on it in red chalk were locations of several logging camps. He sat quietly as he watched us leave. His eyes followed us; tap tapping his finger steadily at the map. He was still in there, somewhere, his body had simple given up.

We went into a small waiting area with a few chairs sitting back to back in the middle of the room and hooks even spaced along the walls. Henrold shut the door behind us, then went to stand by a door on the opposite side of the room.

"Remove your clothes. All of them." His tone changed. However it was softer now, not proud or forceful or wealthy. He was not demanding we do this. He sounded like a regular man.

"I can't imagine a situation beyond that door where we would need to be naked," I said.

"Your clothes are filthy and should not be a presentation of who you are. Please. There are fresh clothes for you in that closet. Only more silks I'm afraid, nothing of what you're accustomed." Henrold turned his back to allow us our dignity. "You as well Rye, if you plan on accompanying your friend into the north."

"I never said I would do this for you," I reminded him.

"You agreed the very moment I mentioned the rumors

of Pynes still being alive. You just haven't said it out loud yet," Henrold said. He opened the door. "Do this all for me and you'll never have to worry about collecting coin on your backs again."

"It's rarely on my back Mister," Keefie said.

CHAPTER EIGHTEEN
We Would Be Statues, Still

I was keeping my mind busy counting how long I'd stood in a decorously genteel dining space, watching Henrold Nanibold Merigold from across the room. Four hours sounds about right. I knew everything I needed to know about him by watching how he interacted with the rest of the Breige, all pomp and no circumstance.

When I heard the heavy breathing of a fancy from the Breige in my face, I switched my attention back at hand. A woman, maybe slightly younger than myself, early thirties if I were to guess and all the niceties of life dripping off her that I'd been missing. She wore jewels around the crown of her head weaved into her long black hair and like all the other women floating around the room a long evening dress with a deep cut down the center of her breast. It was a dress designed purely for presentation. More strings of jewels and shiny things were tied in loops around her arms going wrist to shoulder.

This wasn't hard work by any standards. I was holding a drink. I was holding four at one point, but now just one sat on my tray. The woman ran two fingers along the long stem of the wine glass watching me before she picked it up.

Keefie was absolutely enjoying herself. She loved the attention. She loved the way she looked. This was her scene. I hated her for it, but I loved her for knowing me well-better than myself and knowing I'd rather be doing this than lifting my twigs and rubbing bellies in an alley somewhere desperate for coin with some dusty coal miner. I had to pull what little weight I could. For her.

People used us. We knew the drill, it wasn't anything new for us and we were perfectly fine playing our part and earning some decent dollars to the coin for it.

My boredom must have clearly been on display.

I didn't care how the jewel-armed lady was trying to see into the mask I was wearing. She didn't give a good crooked shit about me and the smug look on her lips told me she barely even saw me. I stood like a statue when she ran her finger along my collarbone. Seeking what? An arousal of some sort? A wicked grin seeking some sort of secret between us? Not fucking likely. I coughed loudly, drawing the attention of the room toward us, which had her pull her hand from my chin quicker than a turnabout hand-trick in the

Farrowyard. A rattlesnake we called em'.

The room moved about with other Breige owners of lecherous hands, grabbing the drink holding girls standing like still statues around the borders of the room. In the middle was one big table, another girl lay in the middle with various morsels of food splayed out around her, and even on her. Vanilla mousse tipped with strawberries stood perky hiding her breasts, which really stood out to me at the moment as a brilliant design of custard usage. I won't go much further into the detail of the other sweet treats and honey's she wore, but I will say she would require a long bath after.

I'd taken to sipping the drinks (mostly wine) when I didn't think anyone was looking, only so I could experience the finer sides of Charleston. All around were foods too fancy to do anything with other than admire, so I gazed at them as I walked by too afraid to eat. I wasn't much for eating slimy little things that looked like they would slide down my throat without chewing, so my belly was left an empty cavern for the aforementioned sneaked wine. The electric lights of the room began to spin, the floor even more. Strangers clung onto and groped one another around the shadowed corners of the room.

Henrold stood at a bar which was serving mulled spice wines and chilled apricot champagnes in tall crystals. Nothing cheap like mead or whiskey here. Only the best for these people.

I shimmied my way over toward Henrold, inch by inch trying to remain a drink holding statue for anyone interested.

Keefie eyed me, shook her head and scowled. She didn't want to lose this job and knew me well enough to know I could mess this up for her with my fuckery. I'd try to keep my fuckery to a minimum to appease her. Plus, starting trouble in the Breige usually led to disappearing if you're someone like me, not worth a silver nickel to them.

Fuckery aside, Keefie was pulled into dancing, as she usually was. Wine gets her legs and lips loosened and unwise while it seemed the man doing the pulling maybe didn't recognize her as hired help. She, like me, was suppose to stand like a statue and hand out drinks and absolutely not be on a table kicking cups of wine over, twirling the hem of her silk skirt like a sail in a storm showing the Breige her newly acquired fashion-forward trimmed mound. Something she said would soon be picked up by the fell ladies with higher fashion standards.

"I wonder if he'll ever ask her to dance?" I whisper-laughed as I did a little wiggly-dance in front of Henrold. I was far past recognizing that any decision my body made at this point was the fault of the wine. As usual.

Henrold looked up from his glass of water; he was not drinking anything fancy. "I don't have any money," he said.

"Oh, it's like that then," I laughed once again. I removed my statue mask to let him see me better. I like to imagine his breath caught in his throat at my beauty, but, I think back on it now, he was simply reminded that I was even here.

"You're still here then?" he laughed back.

"Where else would I be, but the most interesting

place? Which is currently where I am, currently." If these lips could close.

"Interesting? Hardly. Look around."

"I've been looking around."

"Everyone is watching," he said. "They all want to see what Henrold's next move will be. I have an eye for people eyeing me. Call it intuition."

He took my tray of empty glasses and set it on the bar and looped his arm into mine.

"What are you doing?" I asked.

"I'm asking if you're dancing."

"I'm hardly here for dancing. I'm working."

"What are you here for then? You approached me asking if I was asking if you were dancing. Lighten up."

"You'll be paying me for something else besides if those hands keep getting handsy."

"All the same, I just thought, before you leave." He looked over my shoulder around the room.

I perked at that and squinted my eyes. I sucked my bottom lip in and popped it back out, then said, "I doubt any of them know who I am."

He laughed, then said, "They all know who you are."

"Ha, maybe some," I replied, then nodded to an older man holding the hand of his wife. "That guy for sure knows me. Or, well did. On the weekly. Before his money dried up. Think his wife caught wind of his transgressions. He had a saddle that just barely fit him."

I pointed to a young woman sitting alone in the corner. "Her, she knows me. Look how she watches me when she thinks I'm not looking. She always came to me for lessons. I won't speak on those, what ever you're imagining is probably accurate."

"Well, they'll all be whispering your name soon enough," he said.

"How's that then?"

"When you're old and bored, on some cold night thinking fondly back on the day you got to dance with Henrold and you get that itch needs itchin', you're going to remember this night," he said. "And, so will they."

"I'm hardly ever bored," he said. "And, I certainly don't want you to give me an itch."

"No, I don't imagine you-."

Henrold paused for a moment looking me up and down. I felt pretty that night, wearing a pure white-as-bone sleeveless shift with a little slit cut from the side for just enough hip to poke out for a tease. Keefie was dressed the same, as were all the other drink holding girls. We were to be quiet girls for the rich, unheard but seen. Alluring, but untouched. Henrold's design.

"Looking is free Henrold Nanibold Merigold," I whispered in his ear. "You asked me earlier to trust you as I trusted Pynes. I barely knew the lad remember? But, that night did leave quite the impression."

"I'm going to change the subject now, for my sake, of course," Henrold said, then asked, "Are all of your affairs in order?"

"My affairs?" my reply.

"To leave for the wilds. In about fifteen minutes or less

it will be dawn and you have a long way to go."

"But-"

"These Breige folks do love a show," he sighed. "If you survive, I would leave the city immediately. Are you ready?"

"No, I'm not. If I survive?"

"Are you quick?"

"At what?"

Henrold kissed my cheek and whispered into my ear, "Consider this motivation. I wouldn't come back for a while."

He cut the shoulder strap of my shift with a quick knife, put his hand to the dimple of my back and gave me a shove to the middle of the room. He had my Sparrow in his hand for only a moment before he threw it, flipping it end over end right between the shoulders of a man wearing a green leather vest and pulled back, slick-black hair.

The room filled with the whispers of those watching.

"Was that necessary?" I seethed.

He only smiled. "Someone paid me extra to do it this way," he said.

Then, "What did you do?" Henrold cried out to the crowd of Breige.

I stood in the middle of that room, holding my shift up best I could and every single, fancy eye turned toward me. I let my shift fall around my waist and I shrugged. I plucked Sparrow from the back of the slick-black hair, green leather vest wearing man and dove out the window like a Burrow-damned naked goblin into the night.

It wasn't until I was fully awake the next morning and I saw Keefie, did I realize we both were covered in bloody hand prints, both our own and much larger ones.

"Let's never talk about what ever the bullocks that was…" Keefie moaned from under cover.

"I think you killed a man," she added.

I lay back down next to her, kicked the covers from the bed and slept the rest of the morning covered in the bloodied hands and I realized I did it all without getting a single silver coin.

Not a single one.

I was losing my touch.

CHAPTER NINETEEN
Horses

"Will you bloody drop it. I already agreed to your ridiculous terms big man," I looked at Folks Emery through squinted lids. He was already wearing on my tail about unimportant details.

"Say it once more then, Conley, loud enough for all," Folks looked around at the group, his big dumb mouth smiling ear to ear. He brought his lads along with him; the scalped man Robert McGee, Sallow, Skinny Oleerh and even Knots - who will only answer to just Knots by the way. Not even fully sure on the big lad's real name, just the nickname, which had nothing to do with an awkward, physical hump on the lad as one might expect like that Quasimodo fella. No, his name comes from something quite more embarrassing, maybe he will tell the story one day over a camp when we are all looking for amusement.

I looked at Keefie for support, she only shrugged.

"It wasn't just for coin," I finally admitted reluctantly, as if my tail were being pulled from a warm bed and I wasn't ready.

"And, you'll never ask for the coin again?" Folks cocked his brow at me.

"We shall call it even," I said.

"And, you'll admit that what we did that night was more than just for coin?"

"I just said we'll call it even didn't I? I'm not one for charity."

"Fine."

"Fine."

It was an easy payment to make, although a difficult one to form my lips to say. All Folks wanted, for my asking of him to accompany me across the great and far hills was to call it even, never ask of coin again and even, if I'm willing, admit that night was mostly for pleasure. I succumbed to his terms, only because I knew I would need him because Keefie would feel safer, and he would drag his lads along with us. And, he wasn't terrible company on the long road.

Now, there we were, an hour walk from the edges of Charleston, past what little scatterings of small wooden and stone homes, where, Burrow willing, we would cross the Allegheny unhindered by what ever tried to hinder us. So far it was only this conversation with Folks which had me considerin' turning back around and calling the whole damn thing off.

The smell of horses littered the wind. We stopped at the horse stables at the edge of civilized lands.

"Horses are a good idea Miss Conley," Knots said as we walked toward the stables. He let his bricklayer's hammer fall to the ground as he adjusted the rope belt tied around his waste holding his breeches up. Once done he picked the hammer up and kissed the rusting iron head. "Sorry, Mamaw," he said, then tucking the hammer back into a loop at his side. He loved that damn bricklayer; carried it everywhere with him and given the opportunity, I'm sure he wouldn't hesitate to insert into the side of someone's head if they crossed him, or questioned him as to why he called it "Mamaw". I'd known Knots for a while now, and I'd still no idea. Just assumed the love he had for it equaled the love he'd had for a special lady.

Small patchwork fields separated by low, stone-walled fences and trees lay across the hills like an uninspired quilt.

"I have no damn intention of traveling on foot, Knots," I responded. "Even *with* horses, it'll take weeks of riding to get where we're going and we don't even know for sure where that is. I have an idea, but it's a loose one."

"Horses travel much faster than people, I've always said that," Knots reminded me.

"Yes, they do," I said.

"And, they will not mind if we ride their backs," Knots nodded. I didn't know if he was seeking my permission. I didn't care. Knots always spoke the truth of the matter in all aspects, I could count on him for that. He wasn't addle-headed, just saw things different as the rest of us. More honest.

I went inside a small stone hut to the south of the horse stables, but not before I counted all the members of my group. Seven of us there were.

"*Cuatro* horses please, horse man," I called to a stringy Mexican fella sitting in a chair next to a stove in the middle of the mostly empty room. The man stood up and whistled four times out the window toward the remuda.

"Four?" Sallow asked.

"We double up, you want more horses you'll have to pony up for them. I ride alone, unless you want to toss a dime to ride with me, but I ride in front. You hold the hips, nothing else. And, I don't go slow."

"I'm too big to ride with another," Folks muttered.

"We'll get big horses then. Geldings, like yourself," I said, knowing it was uncalled for. Folks only smiled. "Four of your *biggest* horses please, if you will. Appaloosas or Morgans if you have em, none of that Tennessee shit. We travel north and east, make sure they're steady and don't mind the trails." I looked at Folks Emery. "See the big man about pay," I finished as I started to walk out. My transactions here were concluded as far as I was concerned.

"No one said anything about me paying," Folks said to my back as I walked away.

"Seventy-five a head ain't bad and I know you can afford it Folks, let's just go," I said. "I'll pay you in kindness once we're over and done and returned to Charleston. We'll sell them when we get back."

"That's not the point. In kind you say?" His brow rose slightly.

"We can't the seven of us ride to New Hampshire on four horses," Sallow spoke up. "It'll kill the horses. I would guess in less that one day of riding. We would be better off just walking the whole way."

"Horses are faster than people," Knots said.

"Not if they are carrying you *and* me at the same time, poor beasts," Sallow said.

"Okay, Sallow you and Knots won't ride together," I nodded.

"What about me?" Keefie asked.

"Keefie's with me," Folks said.

"I'd rather ride with Conley if you don't mind," Keefie said.

"I'm alone, no offense." As the four horses were brought out, I chose mine - a tan Kentucky Saddler with a white-spotted ass. I patted his neck and he nibbled at my hair. "Kind of reminds me of Sarah Roy with that rear-end, you remember her?" I asked, mostly looking at Keefie who only nodded once. I looked back at the Kentuckian, "Think I'll call you Sarah Roy."

"It makes more sense if you two ride together, you're both way lighter than us," Folks said. "That horse could easily handle you both. I'll ride alone, I'm the heaviest."

That earned a scoff from Robert McGee.

"What? I am. Just look at me."

"Belly doesn't count," Sallow said. "You'd need

another horse just to cart that barrel around."

"That's the point I'm making ain't it? Of why I should ride alone," Folks laughed.

"What if we go north by Elk River?" Keefie suggested. "At least for a bit."

"Ferry's don't operate on the Elk," Sallow answered. "It would only go as far as Sutton before turning south again if they did. Plus, I ain't riding no ferry. Not again. Those waters…the ocean, I…no, never again. And before anyone does, no one even think about suggesting a train. I ain't never stepping on a train with those devils on them."

"There are other rivers that go northerly," Folks said. "Safer ones. We could head toward the coast and catch a boat there. A ship even. A decent one that can handle what the sea gives. It's not that bad if you don't show fear. The devils would hardly know you're there. In and out."

"We would lose weeks of travel. We'll do horses. We are getting horses. No boats. No ships." I could do this journey alone right? Just me. It couldn't possibly be harder than this.

"Okay, horses. What do we do with all our gear if we are doubling up on horses and don't have a mule then?" Sallow then asked.

"You brought gear?" Keefie looked surprised. "I was told I couldn't bring anything. I left all my clothes at home. All I have is what I'm wearing and a couple hard loafs of bread I snatched up last minute from a bakery real cheap."

"Keefie, I said you couldn't bring *all* your stuff, not that you couldn't bring *anything*," I looked at her. "We are going to be gone for likely weeks."

"No extras? What if we run into *ladrones* or Kelpie or something even worse than Kelpie? *Esqueletos…* skeletons," Sallow shrugged at the mention of every dangerous thing, quite comically. "You didn't bring extras?"

"Are my hands empty? Are they, Sallow Salazar? Does it look like I'm wearing extra clothes right now?" Keefie glared at him. "Skeletons?"

"I don't know what you're wearing truly, I don't know. Is it fur? Bear fur?" Sallow reached out and pawed at Keefie's cloak. "It's the middle of summer."

"We are going North, have you ever been North? Into the mountains? Da taught me to be prepared for the mountains, always."

"I have. And it ain't winter yet, so yes, to me at least, furs seem slightly out of the question."

"Well, when we get more north, your *bollocks* are gonna tuck themselves right up at night I can tell you that," Keefie said motioning toward Sallow's pants. "For now I'll suffer. Though it's starting to get quite stuffy in here. And, just so we are all clear, I was planning on washing my underclothes every night at camp. Until I could find a shop that sells more I suppose."

"I'll shall be on for walking then." Skinny Oleerh stepped from the shadowed corner of the small hut, reminding me he was even here.

"You're going to walk? All the way?" I looked at the tracker from New Orleans.

"Yes, by the time you get this all sallied out, I'll shall

be there." And with that he walked out the door and started walking north.

"Okay, great, one less horse," I said to the horse keeper. "Can you *un-whistle* one back."

"You can't just take a man away and then take away an entire horse!" Sallow hollered.

"I don't even know how many horses we have now," Keefie sighed. "Who am I riding with?"

"Me," Folks smiled.

"What if we run into those skeletons? They'll take your clothes, right from you," said Sallow, still looking at Keefie. "Have you thought of that? I don't even know why they need the clothes but they do."

"Sallow what are you on about skeletons for?" I asked. "You're causing Keefie anxiety about it all."

"Conley rides with me," Folks said. "Keefie you're with Robert, Knots you can double up with Sallow or one of you can run with Skinny, I don't give a shit, now let's just go."

Robert smiled at Keefie, then tried to slick his long hair over the pale scalped part of his head.

"What if we just got two horses and had those pull a wagon for us, we take turns riding?" Sallow asked.

"Wagon would only slow us down in Vermont," I reminded him. "I ride alone."

"We can't go through Vermont," Sallow said. I sighed.

"Now why the hell not? It's the direct way?"

"*Esqueletos?*" Keefie asked.

Sallow shook his head, "No, no, Kelpie, not

skeletons."

"Jesus Christ, would you stop?" I glared at Sallow. "Sallow, you're a top notch tracker, but I'm starting to regret my invitation to you for this trip?"

The hour was growing late and the sun was well on its way toward the horizon, putting us behind where I would like us to have been by now.

"Give us a fifth gelding sir," a voice came from the door way. I looked.

"Samuel! What are you doing here?" I was astonished to see the lad. His eye was wrapped neatly in clean bandages and he wore travel clothes, not those of the Deluge. His rifle was rattling on his hip and he had a small travel sack strapped to his back.

"It's Samyel now. I've left the Deluge for a new life."

"What? Why?" I asked. Two questions for the price of one.

"I was no longer useful for them. Or, anyone. As a gesture of kindness, a man told me where you were going. He seemed to know that you and I had a history of misdeeds, and thought I would like to see you through this."

"History of misdeeds," Folks laughed.

"He means they had relations," Knots said. "Of the kind-"

"Thank you," I whisper-hissed to Knots. Samyel looked at the floor, then back up at me, he kept his eyes locked on mine, his face turned the familiar shade of red I was accustomed to drawing out of him.

"Twice-times Miss Conley said," Knots added.

"Burrow help me, we get it," I shook my head. "Yes, just so everyone is clear and to relieve any sort of doubt being cast on the validity of this lad's honor *and* shame, he and I went for a round. Twice as long the second go, first was practice. For his sake." I offered a wink to the once Deluge.

"And he paid you for this?" Folks was looking at Samyel when he spoke.

"Yes, dear Folks. I was paid. Unlike with you… though the coin felt dirty so I drank it off. Everyone, this is Samyel. Once Samuel."

"I don't hear the difference," Sallow shrugged.

"She rolled her tongue different the second time," Keefie said. "Like this," she made an odd gesture with his tongue flicking the top of his mouth. "Samuel. Samuel. Samuel. Samyel. Much less tongue now."

"Samyel rides with me," I said.

"Horse man, whistle it up to eight," Folks hollered to the man at the stove, who had already reclaimed his proper seat, but whistled three more times to bring the total to eight fine horses.

Sallow looked back over at Keefie as our horses came trotting up. "Won't be no underclothes merchants in those woods I'm afraid *chevrette*," he said. "Or, well any merchants selling anything worth your coin for that matter."

Keefie pouted, mostly looking at me.

We rode off, everyone on their own damn horse.

We even brought one for Skinny Oleerh, who was well on his way walking north when we finally caught up to him. To hell with all of us.

CHAPTER TWENTY
A Brief Reprieve

The farmhouse was built from the same stones as the walls which surrounded the farm and had a two story wooden barn across a dirt field, plowed and ready for seeding. It had only one bedroom and a small kitchen off to the side of a cozy sitting area with a couple of chairs next to a fireplace. A pile of sheep wool rugs littered the floor in the sitting room in front of the fire place. That was what I needed. What we all needed after being in saddle for nearly two weeks sleeping with the bugs and rocks. Travel was slow through the hills. Slower than we initially expected.

"Let's get the fire going," Sallow urged. He opened the flume and a puff of black ash filled the room. "We'll give it time to clear out, in the mean time let's get some firewood and figure out what to eat." He pulled his longbow from over his shoulders, followed by a quiver of red hawk feathered arrows and tossed them all in the corner of the room, where he lay claim to his territory for the night. He then pulled a pair of worn Schofields from holsters at his side and set them down as well, with a nicety he didn't spare for the bow and quiver. The Schofields were old and no longer functioned, but he'd fashioned them with leather around their long barrels and rounded off the butt of the grips into a smooth end, meant for bashing. An effective weapon in a time we weren't allowed to brandish firearms. And, even though they didn't work, Sallow did tend to keep them hidden from Deluge eyes, just in case.

Everyone else took their cue from Sallow and began settling in for the night. Robert McGee chopped his tomahawk into a wooden bench within reach of where he sat on the ground. Samyel leaned his Winchester against the far wall closer to the door than anyone else and Skinny sat on the ground next to Sallow, a broken calvary sword across his lap. Sallow told it that Skinny broke the sword on the ass end of a sassy steer during a cattle drive to Nebraska. Skinny only smiled when Sallow told the story, never bothering to correct his old friend.

We each ate a handful of blackberries we'd found growing along one of the stone walls. Since there was not much room to spread out and everyone was gathered in the sitting room by the flickering fire, the house had grown stuffy.

I stood up and excused myself from the room. We'd just crossed over into Pennsylvania last night and the fresh air chasing us from the Allegheny Mountains filled my lungs with the feeling of freedom I hadn't felt in a long while, since my first time away from Charleston, I guess. It was a feeling I sometimes wanted back, away from the city and the eye of the Deluge. Those righteous Deluge were getting worse by the day, mucking things up for the city and people like me, just trying to earn an honest coin. Honest enough I mean.

A barrel of clean rain water sat next to the farmhouse. The moon was bright enough I could see my reflection on the surface of the dark water.

My lips had grown even more pouty since last time I looked at myself. Small creases were starting to form around the corners of my eyes; I was getting old. New freckles sprouted around the bridge of my tanned nose and forehead. I was sunbaked and exhausted from the trails. I tried to smile, but it was hard.

I dipped my hand in the water barrel and splashed my face, holding it for a second in the water.

"You still look as young as the day I met you," Samyel said from behind me.

"Well that was barely a while ago, so I hope this short time on the trail hasn't aged me that much you horse's ass," I said. He smiled back. Samyel was loosening up a bit from the strangle of Low and the Deluge.

"May I join you?" he asked.

"Splash away," I said, moving away from the barrel. "If you take your clothes off and try to clean your under bits in that little barrel, I'm leaving."

"No, I'd like to join you on a walk."

"Oh, yeah."

"Good, I could use a stretch. Room was feeling small." Samyel started walking toward the edge of a short cliff overlooking a tree-lined valley and waited for me to catch up.

"I don't really know what I'm doing anymore, Samyel," I admitted. We started walking, with the cliff to our right. The moon was almost directly above us, it was late. "I feel like I can admit that to you."

"You got us this far," he said.

I couldn't help but laugh. "And where exactly have I gotten us?"

"I don't know. Here, into Pennsylvania. Look how beautiful this valley is. Never thought I would see something like it."

"It's hardly anything to gawk at." I looked out over the dense woods below us. "I guess beautiful in its own empty way, but I want more."

"Since I've known you, you always seem to want more."

"Always will. And, I'll stop when I have it all."

"You can't have it all."

"Then I won't stop," I smiled. The wind kissed the wet hair across the front of my head and ran a chill through my body. Samyel was looking mighty fine in the moon's light. It could have been the fresh air getting to me, I don't know.

"No, I don't imagine you ever would," Samyel laughed. "You know you have a way of naturally drawing people to you. Folks and Keefie adore you. They would do anything for the great Conley Mahren."

I grinned, "I know people love me, it's how I make a living ain't it? All the love you want for a knuckle of coin." I stopped and looked out over the valley, listening to the wind rolling through the red maple. "Keefie spied you in a river once washin' your bits, still talks about it."

"Oh I know, she's always asking me where I'm going. I haven't bathed in a long time. Not alone at least, that I know of."

"Just drop your guard and accidentally join her. Fall into her honey trap. She may forget she ain't working and actually enjoy it for a change. You too."

"What exactly is your plan?" Samyel quickly changed the subject.

"Keep going until we reach New Hampshire. Then the logging camp. Then Pynes."

"And if none of that works?"

"Guess we join the loggers and live the rest of our lives in woods doing logger things."

"Sounds peaceful. But, then what?"

"What else are we going to do? Turn around?" I asked. "Either way we go, it's a long trail."

"No. No, can't fathom going back at this point. We've come too far to just turn around. It's been a nice ride, I've enjoyed it. Not the parts with the chiggers or the Low Stack goats, but other than that. It's…refreshing to get away from the Cistern. Into the world and under open sky. When was the last time you remember seeing this much sky?"

"Oh, but you were a sheltered baby child weren't you,

Samyel. The things I could show you."

"You've shown me enough already."

"You're a young lad, lot's more to learn. But, I'm not the one to show you. I hope you know that," I looked at him.

"The Cistern was always my home." Samyel looked up at the sky. "I don't think they had plans for me beyond sending me into the Cairns. Die in the Cairns or live dying for it, that was always how I saw things, but now we've gone past familiar, but I'm not ready to turn back. I want to see this through with you."

"We all really are just living the same lives, I guess," Samyel said. "Conley, remember the journey itself is really the greatest reward." He smiled and nodded. "Folks said that."

"That's the dumbest damned thing you've said Samyel," I said. I had turned back around putting the cliff on my left side. "Folks was fooling with you."

"I liked it," Samyel said, joining me as I walked back toward the farmhouse.

I looked back at him. "Oh, bugger off, you're not being serious. Samyel, the reward at the end of the journey is the reward. That's the whole bloody point isn't it? I was told to bring back Pynes, so Pynes I shall bring back. Earn more dollars than I could count for doing it. And maybe get some answers from the boy that left me wet by the river and more desperate for attention than I've ever been. I won't say much more on the matter, not to you anyway."

I took his hand.

"Now come on, I didn't ride all this way to stand here and have meaningful conversations. No lad. We get to New Hampshire, find this logging camp to steal Pynes away from whatever it is he's doing and get back to Charleston to pick up where we left off. Drinkin' and earnin' coin. Probably at the same time."

"Sometimes you sound a little too much like Folks," Samyel said. "And, you still want to continue toward these White Mountains? I couldn't change your mind about that? About going into New Hampshire?" He got quiet at the end, as if something were bothering him he didn't want to admit.

"What are you afraid of, Samyel? Something got you spooked? Better speak up if you know something I don't."

"I'm afraid of what's in the woods there."

"Now you got me all riled up. What's in it that's got you so scared?"

"A devil. Best you ask Sallow. He told me about it. Something he said he heard about back in Sutton when we stopped for the night."

But, I never did bother asking.

With sore asses and nodding heads we rode until it became night. The eight Kentuckians we bought from the stable were lean and fast and Folks was right, we needed all eight of them. I'd become quick friends with Sarah Roy as he took his sweet and thankful time over the rocks and slick trails making sure he didn't dump me in the mud. He was a fine horse and I trusted him.

We followed a small, but quick creek north as much

as we could, taking advantage of its fish and clean water before we broke off slightly more east. So far we were harassed only by a handful of coyote snapping at the trotting feet of our ponies as we navigated along trails going in and out of the woods. Sarah Roy even kicked one coyote right in the snout when it got too close to him trying to get a bite at his unders.

When we found a clearing we stopped, just before full night and hobbled our horses. The low, rising moon was our guide, allowing us to set up camp amongst a scattering of large white rocks. The nights out there were cold, as Keefie warned, but not yet unforgiving.

Keefie climbed to the top of the tallest rock over looking camp, looking north as if she were being called by something I couldn't understand. Maybe a call to the mountain home she never really knew in Germany. The bear fur she wore lifted in the wind and even from here I could see her flesh turn goose from the cold. She shivered once and looked back at me smiling, pulling her bear cloak tighter. This Bearmaiden looked more at home out here in the wild than she ever did in the summer city streets of Charleston.

I had a hard time smiling back.

Later, I decided to stretch my legs, knowing I would not be falling back to sleep anytime soon and to enjoy my solitude under the deep-water sky full of floating stars.

The moon was midnight high, illuminating the far distance and I watched the wind sway the tops of the tall trees on the horizon.

"What do you see girl," Folks said from shadows

between rocks.

"Nothing. Peace." I said. He moved over to me and sat. He smelled of horse and dried meats.

"Tell me why we are doing this. It's been years since Pynes left," Folks said.

"Closure I suppose. Even if he is still alive and rejects me, I will be happy."

"And you can move on? Hell, you only knew him for one night. Surely there's someone else."

"Move on?" I repeated and I thought about how he was right. I cocked my eye at him.

"Oh, that's not what I meant. I know. My stomach is too flabby and my hair runs further away from my eyebrows every passing year. I'm getting old. Besides, I've only eyes for Ale now, she's my only mistress. You're different than when we first met."

"I'm older, too."

"Not that way, before you were less… I don't know."

"Corruptible?"

"No," he laughed. "I think Pynes took something of yours when he left and you went to find it, but came back empty. Like part of you was missing and this is your second chance to go lookin' again."

"I came back didn't I?" What was this fool getting to?

A scream from camp startled us both. It was Keefie.

Folks grabbed my outstretched hand and tugged me up quicker than I could stand myself. We ran back to camp to find Keefie sitting up, not where she fell asleep, but a few feet further away from the fire and the trail dusted up where she had been dragged out. She looked like a bear in silhouette; her shoulders heaving up and down as she struggled to catch her breath.

The sleeping lads now all woke from their own dreams and sat staring at Keefie, unsure of what was happening. Keefie looked around back toward the camp.

"Something was pulling me, something was dragging me by the legs toward the woods," she said, catching her breath.

"I heard nothing, Conley and I were awake." Folks looked to me. "There's nothing out here."

"Well I didn't bloody drag myself out here did I?" Keefie swore.

"The Moon-eyed people," Sallow whispered. He quickly stood and glanced out toward the woods.

"Quiet, they ain't real," I hissed.

"The wind isn't real either, yet it's all around us," Sallow said, waving his arms around as if feeling the air. "Oh, the Moon-eyed people are real."

"Wind isn't real?" Knots asked.

"Can't see it can you? Don't see the Moon-eyed either, they stay low. Wanted our horses I'd reckon. Must have thought she was a horse." Sallow glanced toward Keefie. "They take them back to their caves and mate with them. Viciously, use them up until there's nothing left. Scary little things. *Cosas espeluznantes...*"

"Mate with horses? What are you getting on about then?" Keefie puffed her chest up toward Sallow, to feign courage. Her eyes and brow said otherwise.

"Moon-eyed are real, consider yourselves all warned now. Sleep in shifts or be taken away."

"Thought she was a horse?" I laughed, to ease Keefie's mind. The whole thing was silly.

"She's furry as all hell ain't she, like a horse!" He paused. "Fine, I'll keep first watch." Sallow sat back on a rock and within seconds fell back to sleep, head slumped under his tilted hat, chin touching chest and snoring. What an asshole thing to say before falling asleep.

The rest of the night Keefie snuggled into my back as I lay close to the fire, watching out over the thick line of trees not far from camp. They shifted and moved, lulling me and tempting me until I finally closed my eyes.

We woke the next day covered in morning dew and a silent, warm breeze.

Samyel stood over me, pointing west. His face was as solemn as his spirit.

All the horses were gone.

Along with the scalped man Robert McGee.

CHAPTER TWENTY-ONE
Those Are The Options

"Okay, so what's the game," Sallow asked. "Are we still making our way through Vermont? I suggest we cut slightly south and east through Boston, then back north. We could stop in Manchester before heading up toward the White Mountains. I know someone there that would take us in for a spell."

"Our plan was always going through Vermont, Sallow. You knew that from the beginning," I said. "It's the quickest trail."

There was a slowness; a weariness to our journey since leaving the cave of Gone. We were out in the middle of the wild hoping to come across any sort of trail other than bent grasses and broken limbs to reluctantly follow. We'd found a small gaming trail that eventually led to crossroads where we were crouched behind a small stone wall on a hill overlooking a three story inn on the corner of a crossroads. Looking back, we should have started this journey better prepared. Also looking back, we should have followed the coast. Probably my fault for rushing everyone out of Charleston to go after Pynes, but I was eager, you understand.

Our days in New York were mostly uneventful ducking in and out of taverns along the way to get resupplied or realigned with directions. It offered us a chance to regroup and since we'd left the Parish, a chance to breathe. I shared in frustrations with the lads over their loss of Robert McGee and our horses. I'd barely the time to truly get to know Sarah Roy.

"I said what's the plan?" Sallow asked again, nudging me out of my planning and reminiscing.

"Keefie and I go down there and umm, get those horses," I shrugged. The truth was I was tired.

We needed fresh ponies to keep going and we were looking at more horses than we could possibly need stabled behind a place called Crossroads Inn.

The rest of the lads lay back behind the wall, catching up on their peace under the open stars.

"Seems as good as place as any to get horses I suppose and proper food. And maybe a bath," Keefie sighed. "Not too keen on stealin' them. But, what do I know about horse transactions. *Bollocks* is what."

"If we want horses," Sallow submitted, "this is where

we get them, unless you want to continue on foot. Would take an awfully long time. What's your plan, Conley?"

"Okay, right. Keefie, go down there and use your blessings that your Ma gave you," I suggested. "See if some lads will just…give you some horses on a whim."

"I don't feel…*blessed*, at the moment. In fact I feel downright filthy. Plus I lost my cloak in Gone. Some renegade, hillbilly *gobshte* is probably wearing it. Stinking it all up."

I went with her of course. I wasn't going to send Keefie down there by herself and risk losing our chance for these horses. I kept my eyes on her backside as we trotted down the hill toward Crossroads. The horses in the stables shifted, nervous as we walked by, inspecting them. Fine horses, a good assortment. And, plenty to go around, unless the inn was full of passers-by, but out here that didn't seem likely, so maybe the owner would sell us a few.

We went into Crossroads, one after the other.

The entire room turned toward us as we stepped inside the fire-lit room. The piano player hesitated his entertainment. Every single eye looked at us in the doorway. Every single eye belonged to a damned Deluge.

An entire patrol of Deluge as a matter of fact.

"Seems the wilds have sent us in a pair," one of the Deluge said as he stood from his chair. He was a big bastard. His Winchester rifle leaned on the table by his side, he put his hand on the barrel and offered me a big, mean grin. "Come on in girls and hear the word of Low the Kind. Seems you could use it."

We stepped into the Crossroads, confidence shot.

"You'll have to excuse my friend for her lack of wanting to hear the telling of Low, we've been on the road a very long while and are looking for some horses. Ours were stolen," Keefie said. I kept my head down on the table and played my part of the weary as she played her part of the plump Irish-German girl looking for some men to help her back home. A part she played very well, and this far out into the wild, where saucy Irish-German girls are lacking in number, it wasn't hard to get the attention of some starving Deluge men who had only seen the ass side of the horse in front of them as they rode single file on these narrow, wooded trails looking for lost travelers just like us to speak the telling of Low the Kind.

"And, perhaps a place to wash up," Keefie added flavor to the stew of our thrilling conversation. These Deluge lads were not sipping.

The Deluge that stood and offered his telling of Low the Kind was named Connor.

"And you said you needed how many horses? Now, before you answer me, know that all ours are spoken for. We have no extra," Connor said. His voice easily carried across the inn's dining hall. "There was an ox out back, working a small onion patch when we arrived. Maybe you could ride him if you asked the locals." This drew out a politely forced laugh from his fellow Deluge.

In the middle of the Crossroads inn was a single, long fire pit with various pots of boiling things. Things that all smelled delicious. Long wooden tables bordered the room with benches tucked under the unused ones to free space up for floor activities like dancing or hatchet throwing.

However, the dancing wasn't to be had with our current company, else Low frown on them. I had my head down on the table as I pondered what Keefie was planning to say. Connor was no idiot, asking for more than one horse would draw out questioning, two horses would be a stretch at that but reasonable. Seven horses would be unthinkable. There were at least a dozen Deluge around the table, sitting on all sides of us. A few scattered patrons sat around the other tables in the room, listening as well for lack of anything better to do. Mostly local dairy workers. A single middle-aged woman stood behind the bar with her arms crossed across her port, thin eyebrow cocked, watching and waiting to see what Keefie said.

"Seven-" Keefie started as I lifted my head.

"You already said you couldn't spare a single horse," I interrupted. "Why ask how many we need now?"

"Oh your friend does have a tongue," Connor said. "Boys, she can speak. I'm glad you could join us from borrowing our table as a pillow. Maybe you'd like to sleep on it and in the morning we can have this conversation at your leisure."

I had to watch my mouth. It would be difficult. Deluge in the wild outside the Parish would be traveling there for a reason. That reason being to spread the telling of Low and extend the territory of the Parish. Or, they were looking for more places rising up to move against them like the Springer

Rebellion and put them down. They weren't out there to rile up locals but to let them know by show of presence they could squeeze their knuckles tighter if they had to, so best not to mess with Connor and his lads. I wasn't looking for trouble and Connor was probably looking for a reason to honor his Low with purity through punishment.

"Well, I could say we needed one horse, and Keefie and I could ride together, squeezing our hands around each others hips as you do when you ride tandem - I'm sure you boys know, but say that one horse twists an ankle on a rock. Then we are left horseless, again, and in the same position we are in now, except further away from horse-getting opportunities. The smart thing, would be for us to ask for two horses right? One each. Or, one to carry our supplies, except you already saw we didn't bring supplies in with us. Unless we left it all outside with our lads. Oh, our lads. So maybe the third option would be for us to ask for a dozen horses, maybe even all of them. Leave you with none? Maybe we are horse thieves and we have this place surrounded and we are the charming, incredibly fine-looking distraction sent inside to…well, distract you." I looked over at the cross-armed middle age lady behind the bar and subtlety shook my head *no* as to only she could see. She smiled back.

"But, we are not that either. Why steal from our holy Low the Kind and damn all ourselves and souls…do you boys believe in souls? Sure you do. Why would we damn ourselves to all that nonsense going after the very thing we are trying to preserve in our young Keefie. Her very soul.

The mountains have it. We go to get it back. Don't think too much on that. We are not horse thieves. We are just two traveling girls looking for a handful of horses to get our sweet little bottoms to the next inn over, which I'm told is never over, until we can beg for the kindness of strangers there as well. Maybe it'll be a logging camp and we can chop-" I chopped my hand down and hit the table a little too hard. "-our way into their hearts and hope just hope, that they, like yourselves will be kind in their charities, but that also seems impossible since I haven't seen a Burrow-damned tree that wasn't full of rot in days, maybe weeks. You lads know of any logging camps just far enough north and east of here to be in New Hampshire? What about any in the White Mountains? Ever been there? Naw, you probably stay pretty local. I bet the girls around here feel pretty lucky to be around educated Deluge - and handsome Deluge - such as yourselves."

"I have no desire to test my tally with the devil in those mountains, let alone anything else that might be up there. Aye, I've been, and I won't be going back," Connor said. He looked across the table at Keefie. "I see why you do the talking. Now in all that rambling, she did say a 'handful' of horses."

"I'm not going to lie to you anymore, Connor, I can tell you're all smart Deluge lads, just looking to enjoy your evening and I really must apologize for our wandering into here, we clearly interrupted something special. But, we have a problem." I looked at Connor until he asked me what.

"What?" He asked. Good lad.

"We have no money. And you being the *pious* Deluge you are, will not be tempted into giving us…well anything, no matter how sweet the offer." I stood and leaned over the table. I flicked my finger on the barrel of Connor's Winchester, then ran it down along its length to get a rise out of these lads. "So that really only leaves one option."

"Which is what?" Connor asked. He was really good at this game. "Keep your hand away from that rifle with those deft little digits of yours or you'll be counting to only nine from now on."

"Seven horses," I replied.

He laughed. Then rest of the Deluge joined him, filling the inn with a buzz of confused chuckling. The locals didn't join in the merriment. The lady behind the bar didn't do much other than tighten her crossed arms and probably her buttocks. I really should have asked her name before this ruckus.

"You're going to have to do better than that girl," Connor said. He went back to sipping on a thin chicken broth. "You have nothing we want. Seven horses. Get out of here you cocked-mouth whore."

"The forth and last option," I raised, "And, in my opinion it is the best. Hard to pass up."

Connor looked at me and raised an eyebrow, waiting.

"You talk to him about it." I nodded toward Folks Emery standing in the doorway of the Crossroads inn.

"Box ya for em," Folks smiled.

CHAPTER TWENTY-TWO
The Legend Of Folks Emery

"Do you boys know who just walked through our door?" Connor stood. "Fuckin' Folks Emery. The nastiest bare-knuckle fighter this side of the Mason-Dixon."

"Other side too," Sallow said as he stepped in behind Folks. Knots followed. Samyel last, keeping his head down as best he could.

"And his outfit of Ale worshipers," Connor finished saying. "Men, sit down there will be no fight. I have no desire to gather my own teeth off our host's floor. Come on Folks, join us. Other side of the table boys, make room for Folks Emery." All the Deluge moved to the opposite side of the table, with their backs to the wall, making room for Folks and the others in a terribly uneven seating arrangement.

I couldn't help but shake my head, of course they would know who Folks was and wouldn't even consider fighting for their horses; even a friendly padded-knuckle fight would be out. You don't throw cookies at a bear and not expect to be chased up a tree for a whooping.

Connor studied Folks, then each one of us. His Low-judging eyes stopped on Samyel. "I don't know you," Connor said. "Should I know you? Your face seems like I should. Doesn't seem bloodied and whored out like the rest of your pals."

"He doesn't speak," I interrupted, not that Samyel was going to speak anyway, but just to make sure. "Got into a fight. Cut his tongue out."

"I'd like to see that," the Deluge next to Connor said. "Never saw a tongue stub before. Seems like something I'd like to see. Must have been a hell of a serious fight. What got you riled up so?"

"Someone asked to see his tongue stub," I said.

"That doesn't-"

"Listen, are we getting horses or not. Whatever it takes. We need to get into New Hampshire before summer's end and I know damn well we can't do the rest on foot," I said.

"Horses are not on the table for discussion anymore," Connor said. "You all hungry? Least the Deluge can do is feed the poor and weary travelers."

Eggs were brought to the table. Hard boiled, cut in half with a sprinkling of black pepper across the top and a little shivering of green.

"So, what really takes you north and east through Vermont?" Connor asked. "Kelpie ran all the good Low loving people out. Nothing there but haunts and ruins. And empty forest. Long walk through there to get to New Hampshire. Even if you don't get turned all around on your own, those woods will do it for you."

"Just out seeing the world," I said. "Our Keefie here keeps family there. Thought maybe we would take in the mountains and the high air for a while there. Get away from it all. You know?"

Connor laughed. "Well, good luck with that. You'll have to be damned sneaky or have an awful lot of luck to even get through that cursed place. Those Kelpie have it locked down, guarding the only paths in or out. Deluge sent a patrol there not long ago. They never returned."

The Deluge ate as we sat and watched. With a mouth of hard boiled egg, Connor looked at our side of the table again, stopping at Keefie and myself. "Surely you two don't take your licks with Ale the Unhinged like your boys here. You both look half a stepped on pile of dog shit right now, but not fighters."

Aware of how absolutely filthy Keefie and I must look after what we went though in the caves of Gone, which I can't even begin to get into and never will, then walking here, I let the Deluge's assessment of our filth stand, it was only fair. "Burrow," I said, "not that it really matters on account of getting us horses."

"Burrow. Never heard of that one," Connor nodded.

"What do you have against Low the Kind. He keeps you all safe you know. You owe him a lot of safe, sleep-filled nights, keeping the beasts at bay."

"I'm sure we do," I said. "Four horses."

"Oh, now that I think about it. You do look familiar," he suddenly looked at Keefie. "The whore of Bearmaiden."

"Okay, whore is a bit of a stretch, though I won't deny she is me," Keefie said. Her face grew red. "Fancy to see why I'm the Bearmaiden?" Keefie looked down at herself then said, "Oh, shoot, I just remembered I lost my namesake, sorry lads. Got a spare fox fur or even a weasel? Might be a bit *tight*, but worth seeing me wiggle in to. We could make change for those horses."

Connor shrugged. "Think I whooped you a few times like your daddy should have, for stepping over your *tolerated* duties. Tolerance is one of the things that L'fowl had an abundance of, unfortunately for your ilk, the new First Chancil does not."

At that, Samyel slammed his hand onto the table, causing everyone to startle and look up.

"The mute has something to add? I offer penance if I've offended your bear, my friend," Connor said.

"He has a tongue, I seen it," the neighboring Deluge said. "Look at it in there looking to flap out at us. Say something. Come on now, don't be shy. Our Low isn't shy about telling his holy word of truth for you, why should you be?"

"I'm wholly aware of just how *shy* Low the Kind is *not*," Samyel said. Aw, he remembered our first night together. Here I thought I was a footnote in the lad's sexual awakening.

"I don't know what that means, but I feel it's an insult to something you know little about," Connor said. I heard the dragging of his boots along the wooden floor as he shifted his body just enough for a better angle at his Winchester. An insult toward Low is an insult toward all Deluge.

Folks stood up, "I'll tell you what. Back to my original offer. All your horses for one fight. All of us to all of you." He smiled.

"You've got to be mad, man," Connor said. He remained seated, looking up at Folks. "You're outnumbered a dozen to six. And we have iron. Wait, you boys aren't armed are you? Guns are not allow in the Parish."

"We're a long way from the Parish, *necio*," Sallow sighed.

"That we are, *huevos*," Connor replied.

The Deluge sitting next to Connor set his Winchester across the table in front of him. A simple gesture that it was time for us to leave.

"You say you've heard of Folks Emery, but I'm starting to think you've never *really* heard of Folks Emery," Folks said. He looked down at the Winchester on the table and slammed his knuckled fist right behind the rear sight, fracturing the rifle just enough to render it useless. "These are harder than your damned Low iron you rotten twat," he snarled. Burrow help me, I'd never seen such a thing in my life.

All the iron came from under the table, as the rest of the Deluge drew their Winchesters and pointed them all toward us. We stood faced with a dozen rifles.

Connor held his hand up. "I noticed you are missing two of your gang of Ale drinkers. Tell me where is that scalped man, Robert McGee and the skinny black one. I'd be more comfortable knowing you're all in front of me."

"Robert left the outfit," Sallow said, looking from Winchester to Winchester. "Went back to trackin' wolves."

"As for the *skinny* one. Orleans "Skinny" Oleerh. Remember his name now? You'll like this," Folks said. "He ain't dead. No, he's very much alive. And, he's here. Do you remember what he did before he took in with Ale? Do you remember that, Deluge?"

Connor narrowed his eyes and looked toward a window.

"He was a horse thief. And a Ale-damned good one." Folks flipped the long wooden table toward the side of the Deluge, sending them all flailing backwards, rifles and all.

I grabbed Keefie's hand and pulled her out the front door, following Folks into the night outside the Crossroads inn where Skinny Oleerh waited, with nine horses ready to ride. We each jumped a pony and took off down the road away from the Crossroads inn, dragging the two extra horses behind us to keep a greater number of Deluge from giving chase. They wouldn't dare send such few numbers after us as cocky as they were and they knew we knew that.

We rode half way hard, pushing our horses through the night away from Crossroads. Without saying much of a word to the lads I led us north and east to the edges of Vermont and broke its border with the low sun rising before us.

CHAPTER TWENTY-THREE
Long, Black Trails

"The key is fat," Sallow said. "Sizzle the bacon up real nice and use some of the grease frying your eggs. Yeah, bacon fat. Makes them better." He flipped a half-cooked, unseasoned potato over on a small skillet.

"All you've been doing is talking about bacon the past two nights, Sallow, drop it already," Folks said. "It gets my belly sad for the stuff."

"I'm just saying I wish we had some for these damned potatoes."

"We all do," Folks said.

"Make em taste like something other than dirt," Sallow grumbled. "I'm sick of tasting dirt, Folks. We've been riding these *caballos* though Vermont on these Conley-thin trails for five long days, tripping over rocks, sleeping in puddles. I'm right sick of it. I don't even know where we are anymore. Seems like we've been going in circles for days. I told you we should skirt this place, go more east to Boston."

"You knew what you were signing up for," I said. "Conley-thin trails, huh. Okay. Bit hurtful, but still funny. Good for you."

"Thanks." He couldn't help but laugh.

"Burrow help me, Folks I didn't mention it until now, but that wasn't a good idea, riling up those farmers as you did," I said over some dry-frying potatoes. "Were you planning on fighting the entire town? With your fists? You had no weapon other than your wit. Which is pretty slow, I'll say it. Did you even think about poor Keefie in there before you did that? She was working her charm over on that farmer lad, trying her way to get us fed and a roof. And, now that we are speaking on it, where was that courage with the Low Stack goats? Where were those iron fists of yours then? Next time Stack goats are nipping at us, I want, no I demand that same reckless behavior. It's why I brought you out in the wild after all, you dick. And, I'm sorry if my attitude is bare, I'm hungry."

Folks widened his eyes, caught a bit off guard, "I'm not going to mess around and get horned by those asshole goats. Then dragged off to Ale-knows-where. Have unspeakable goat things done to me in their weird little goat-people villages." He shivered, then looked me up and down. "Besides, I gambled that I could just outrun you. You need to work on your running away. Bah, you're mostly just stick, of course they'd want to eat me first. You're nothing but an appetizer if anything."

"Appetizers get eaten first you asshole."

"Hmm, maybe they wouldn't be as hungry after that."

"Have you ever had the thing they do with potatoes at The Eager Wife? Probably the only thing she gets right there. Deadly that," Keefie mentioned.

"I don't go there. Doesn't feel…morally right." Sallow squinted at his potato, going along with Keefie's change of topic, as I'm sure everyone here was tired of Folk's and mine shit. Sallow tossed the potato over his shoulder into the bush.

"Well, you should try it. The potato not the wife. She's really not all that eager by the way, as the name of the establishment would imply," Keefie said. "You know they really should change the name of it. Potato something. I dunno, I'm not that savvy with names. Maybe Conley could help them out on that front."

"Bah, she's doing just fine there on her own eagerness to sell those spuds, better than we are out here. Burrow but it's getting ball-shriveling cold out here, right lads? These nights are the worst. Does Vermont just seem…colder?" I asked. "Could just about slice this potato up with how hard my nipples constantly are out here. Chapped too. Burrow help me, I'd kill for some proper underclothes, I have two bloodied spots on my blouse where my nipples use to be," I was in a mood. *Hungry* was the mood and also angry and cold. Something had to give quick and soon before the chilliness of the moon sent me on a misguided errand to warm my bottom up against one of my companions. I looked across the fire at the lot of my lads. Ugh.

"I shouldn't have brought up the goats," Folks laughed. "Conley, I'm sorry."

"Apologize to my fucking nipples." I shoved Folks' arm.

Knots glanced a peep at me as I held my hands across my chest. Across the pan of roasting potatoes he said, "I'm sorry nipples." Then looked away flush with red.

Folks and the lads couldn't help but laugh.

I glared at Keefie. "How are you even dealing with this shit?" I asked.

"Oh." She thought. "Oh, I'm just used to being miserable I reckon."

"What day is it?" Keefie asked.

A pair of squirrels spit-roasted above a low burning fire.

"Not sure. Tuesday maybe?" I said.

"Sunday," Samyel nodded. "Holiest of the days."

"Don't matter out here though," Sallow admitted. He took a cut from one of the squirrels testing it, then cut the rest and passed a bit around to each of us. "All that matters out here, right now, is if this will get us through to the next squirrel. Easy."

"What's the wildest thing you've seen out there?" Keefie asked.

"What do you mean, Rye?" asked Samyel. He sat

next to her on a moss grown log.

"I don't know, just something that stuck with you. Something you'll never forget," Keefie answered. "I'm bored. Entertain me."

"When Folks first 'discovered' the milk from silfrnymphs…" I offered as I twirled Sparrow around my fingers. I shuddered to emphasize my horror.

"Second that," Sallow laughed.

"Okay, okay not counting that one. That was weird for all of us," Keefie said. "Poor little thing."

"I was dyin' of thirst is all," Folks blushed. "Those little nymphs were everywhere that night. They lured me in." He paused chewing on squirrel and looked around at all of us. "It's not my fault!"

"You disappeared for two days!" I said.

"Probably Wolf Mother," Knots was quick with a second suggestion.

"She was just a wolf. A skinned one at that now that I recall, but just a wolf," Sallow said.

"Big wolf. No fur. Wild."

"I saw a black stag," Sallow said. "Moss hung from its antlers. Must have been as tall as a cottage, maybe taller."

"You were drunk," Folks nudged him.

"I most certainly was not."

"Sallow doesn't get inebriated," Skinny shook his head.

"He was in the tree line, and I was alone, standing by the river having a leak. Looked up and there he was. Didn't even see me."

"What about you big man?" I turned to Folks. "Surely nothing in this forest would surprise Folks Emery."

"I saw a young girl." Folks nodded. He closed his eyes trying to remember. "I was afraid."

Keefie laughed and nudged Folks. "Of a girl?" Keefie snorted.

"If Folks was afraid of a girl, what chance do we have?" Sallow said.

Folks shook his head and smiled. "She was by the river, just alone, no one around. She seemed happy. I barely caught a glimpse of her."

"You were spying on a young girl by the river?" I asked.

"*Spying* is a strong word," Folks responded.

"I mean that's what it sounds like you're saying," I said. "Spying on a girl taking a bath in the river. And that's the wildest thing you've seen. Did you know her? No. Then, that's spying. Even if you did know her. Spying."

"Never saw her before or again. Anyway. Like I said. I barely saw her. I didn't want to get too close."

"You should always be weary of river girls," Knots said. "My Mamaw always said that."

"You just had to be there I guess. Damnedest thing," Folks added. "She weren't no serpent or river devil like that."

"And be a third wagon wheel? No thanks," I said.

"Was she pretty?" Keefie asked.

"I wasn't that close." Folks replied.

"Must have been," Keefie said.

"Maybe we can go back to the river and look for her," I suggested. Folks shot me a look. I couldn't help but grin.

"Yeah," Folks moaned. "She was beautiful."

I looked over at Keefie. "What about you? I'm assuming you asked us, so you could tell us yours."

A hollow breeze blew through the woods, rustling the limbs and leaves in a gentle, wooded song. Everyone sat in their own silence for a few moments.

"I saw a turkey," Keefie said, breaking the quiet.

"A real one?" Sallow asked.

"Yeah, couldn't believe it," Keefie said.

"You're lying," I cocked my brows at her.

"No really. He was just out there. Pecking at bugs and just doing his turkey stuff."

"A real turkey." Sallow didn't seem to believe her. "How do you know it was a turkey?"

"Sterling has a few old paintings of them, up in his room at the Perky Daughter. He loved the creatures. Used to paint them." Keefie responded.

"Did it do the sound?" Sallow asked. He was shaking his head in disbelief.

"No, just pecked bugs," Keefie laughed.

"Well, we are all but doomed then…" Sallow moaned.

Another breeze pulled through. This one colder.

"How deep into these damned woods are we going?" Folk asked.

"Until we find them," I replied.

"Or, they find us?" Keefie asked next.

"I don't know where they live, yes," I said. "Or, they find us."

"So we are just out here walking around, no real destination, bumbling through these woods, hoping these loggers find us? Am I to understand that?" Folks slapped a low branch out of his face. He looked back at the trail, shifting his eyes up and down. "I want to go home Conley. I went along with this for as long as any reasonable person would, maybe further. The lads are ready to go home."

The trail was narrow and muddy. Slick leaves slid under our boots as we sloshed through an early, wet snow.

"What would be the point in turning back now, Folks," I said. "I'm not going back emptied knuckle and no Pynes. Came too far for that. Are we going to have this conversation again?"

"I'm getting older out here in all this. We've already been fighting these trails for I don't know how many damn days. I'll give it another day then we turn around." Folks sat on a fallen log and kicked mud and stones from the bottom of his boot.

"We rest," Sallow said.

I looked at him. "Yeah, we can rest."

CHAPTER TWENTY-FOUR
Grey Sir Greggorty

"I can't really imagine what was in it." No one was really paying attention to me, eyes on the trail, leading their horses on foot, looking for any sort of evidence of loggers. Felled trees, oxen trail marks, filers tools, anything.

Sallow stopped, then squinted at a tuft of brown bear fur between his fingers he'd plucked from a nearby thorn bush. His bow was in one hand and he dragged it along the dirt leaving a little line behind him, the reins of his horse in the other.

"Peaches, I know that much…and well I'm not actually sure what else goes into it on account I'm no baker," I continued. "Crust of some sort. The peaches go under the crust, but I don't know what goes into that."

"What are you going on about? All morning with this." Folks looked back at me as he ducked under some low branches, then through some bushes and crept forward best he could through the heavily grown trail.

"The cobbler. The peach cobbler."

Keefie stopped walking and looked back at me. "Wait, what do you mean? The cobbler from Gone?"

"You mean the cobbler from that cave," Folks laughed. "Gone weren't no town. Just a cave we found with a vagabond living in it. Took us in for a couple of days and fed us. I don't want to talk about it."

The frown on Keefie's face spoke for her.

"Haven't really thought about it, huh? Been on my mind since we left Gone," I frowned back at her. "And those eggs. There were no chickens in that cave."

A standing of stones eventually rose from the trail before us as we approached. Cries and yelps from forest creatures nearby rang around the trees creating a rising tide of sound that eventually died out as we approached the stones. Neat piles of them, hundreds, all standing alongside the worn dirt road as some sort of trail marker. It all reminded me of the Cairns back home in Charleston.

There was a rotting, overturned wooden cart, overgrown with weeds and taken by the vines and plants of the forest. A stone bridge crossing over a small trickle of a crick greeted us a few yards past the standing stones. Lichen-stained skeletons of some small things poked up from the shallow, watery-mud under the bridge like garden flowers that had given up.

These woods belonged to ghosts and beasts and the filthy things.

My companions and I marched across the bridge, slow and ready. I stopped when I saw a man standing on the far opposite side of the bridge under a cyclopean stone archway where the trail picked back up. He held a bayoneted musket planted firmly on the bridge, his hand ran up and down along the long barrel. He was wearing tattered Confederate grays and tipped his wool kepi up slightly as we approached. We traveled too far to be stopped now. No. I would go through this fool if necessary if he chose to not step aside.

"I don't suppose you're this…*devil* of the forest I've been hearing so many things about?" I called out to him. It seemed a reasonable question at the time as he was the only other living thing we've seen since entering haunted Vermont.

"S'I am," his answer.

"Great," I returned. "Now what?"

"All hinges on what you want," his reply, his accent deeply Southern.

Sallow stepped forward and squinted at the man as if looking at him closer. I could see the disappointment.

"I kind of expected more," Sallow said.

"Is he witched or something? A beast? A Hallowfulk, maybe?" Samyel asked. "Is this a woodbugger?"

The man of the bridge called out. "Come on up a piece, girl."

Everyone, including me, turned to look at Keefie. Her face sank to milk white.

"Not her, ya shunters, you. The head of your posse," the man called back.

"Oh, she's not the leader," Folks yelled back to the man. I looked at him and smirked.

"You're the man in charge then?" the man asked.

"No, he's not," I said.

Folks looked at me and frowned. "You get us into too much trouble." He looked back at the man on the bridge. "I wouldn't follow her anymore than a mule follows a horse."

"I've seent mules after horses," the gray bridge man said. "They are pack animals I reckon, it's what they do. They follow the things what are ahead of them. If they're not too stubborn."

"She's a stubborn one, going to get us killed, one by one likely," Folks said.

"Hey," I looked at Folks and frowned. I pushed a finger into Folks' chest. "You have something to say? Say it."

"You brought us out here, Conley," Folks said. "Still trying to figure out what for."

"You came on your own accord, Folks," I said. "You're welcome to go back any time you want."

"Bah, who would watch your ass then? Samyel and Keefie?" Folks glared at the two of them. "Can't have that can we?" He started walking across the bridge toward the man. The water barely trickled below.

I handed Keefie the reins to Good Horse, my new pony. She neighed once and went to nibbling at the moss on the trail.

I had no intention of settling for fools, so without much

thought, I reached for Samyel's Winchester before he could protest, cocked the lever then trotted toward the man on the bridge.

I stayed focused on the man in front of me, aiming the Winchester as I slowly approached him. He had, perhaps, the biggest musket I'd ever seen. And, I've seen plenty of big-musketed men.

"Quite a musket you have there," I nodded at the weapon.

"Thank you ma'am, quite nice of you to mention," the man's reply. "It do tend to draw lots of stares."

"I can only imagine." The man made no effort to lift his musket. "What's it called? The musket I mean. You seem the type to name his weapon, pardon if I'm wrong. It's an Enfield, single-shot I should note. 1853? Early design, but clean."

"Ain't got no name," he said as he spat some brown liquid on the ground. "After my Pa, whose life was lost in a knife fight before I had a full account of what to call 'em other than Pa." The man now picked up the Enfield musket, letting it rest it at his shoulder. "Go home. Ain't nothing here for you."

"And your name, sir?"

"Greggorty. Two *g's*. Three if you do count the first."

"Well, Greggorty with three *g's*. We traveled a very, *very* long way to get here and I grow tired of sleeping in the dirt and long so badly for a real bed. Now, are there any loggers in this forest here? Maybe a camp of some kind?

Answer that question and you may pass this bridge."

Greggorty cocked his head to the side, "No loggers in these woods. And they ain't receiving visitors at present." He shook his head.

"They're not? Isn't that part of the deal being attendants of these woods? We are after all in their woods seeking refuge. Wouldn't it only be polite to take us in? Where are the manners? The hospitality? Of these loggers, I mean."

"No. They're very busy. They ain't loggers here. No logging camp a piece north and a piece east or nothing of the sort."

"I'm very confused. As you can imagine."

Greggorty now held the Enfield out in front of him, with both hands spaced evenly on the barrel as if inspecting it, still, not aiming in my direction. "Does your weapon have a name? I shall like to know it to get an idear naming mine. Never thought of that a'for now."

"Oh this? I'm only borrowing it," I said and looked back at Samyel. "Does your rifle have a name? Greggorty would like to know it."

"Beth." Samyel called back.

"Beth? Who's Beth?" I yelled back across the bridge.

"Baker girl. Doesn't matter," Samyel said, looking down at his boots. "Doesn't matter."

I knew enough about getting shot at to know speed wouldn't be enough here. With that musket, Greggorty had exactly one shot before needing a reload - if it even still worked - which offered me the upper hand with Samyel's

Winchester.

Greggorty's eyes focused on mine.

"So, you're not the devil of woods we keep hearing about are you?" I asked.

"I have to apologize. I am not." Greggorty stood still. He glanced over his shoulder at the stone archway behind him and took a few steps back toward it.

I looked back at my companions waiting by the bridge, then back at Greggorty. "I was so looking forward to telling everyone how I was the one to slay the devil. I have to say I am rather disappointed. This whole damn trip has been disappointing."

"Again, I apologize, ma'am," Greggorty said, bowing his head.

"You are very polite for a devil. Tell me, how near New Hampshire are we?"

"I ain't no devil, I'm just watchin' after this place is all," He looked over my shoulder. "I'll tell you what, tell the young lad to come forward. I'll fight him instead."

"What?" I was shocked. "That seems awfully rude. I'm already here and ready."

"No, no, you seem too grumpy to account for this. It ain't often I get visitors to duel me to cross my bridge."

"But, I'm…we could just walk under it. Look there's barely any water in the crick. Just a tinkle of piss in it in fact."

"You there boy! Step forward, we are dueling."

Samyel put his finger on his chest, "Me? No by all means, go ahead with her. She likes that sort of thing. It's the attention. She loves it."

"I refuse." Greggorty pointed his Enfield back to the dirt. "Please, for honor's sake."

"I have to say, I'm really quite offended," I said again. "I'm the best fighter among my group."

"Hardly true!" Folks yelled across the bridge.

Keefie shook her head when I looked at her.

Samyel stepped forward and I handed him his Winchester back. I frowned at Greggorty.

"Forest's tits boy, keep your hands up!" Folks shouted out over the rocky bridge. "It's like the boy can only use one arm at a time," he added, to whom he spoke I wasn't really sure, but we all nodded in agreement. "Hold the thing with both hands like your mother taught you!"

Samyel forced a harsh glance toward him, but Folks only smiled a toothy grin back.

"Samyel come here," I called out. I waited calmly as he approached.

"Take the ass end of your rifle, this part here and bash his face in." Folks intercepted Samyel before he reached where I stood at the edge of the bridge.

Roughly placing my hand under Samyel's jaw, I forced his head to turn toward me. "Samyel, do you remember the night we met? What we did?"

"Yes, of course," he sighed.

"Good."

"How does that help?"

"It doesn't. Now go back across the bridge and

smash his face in like Folks said so we can get about our business." I let go of Samyel's chin and offered him a sly wink. He rolled his eyes.

"Are you listening?" Folks yelled. He held a stick and with it, mimicked striking Greggorty in the face with one end.

"Couldn't he just shoot him?" Keefie asked.

"Who? Samyel or Greggorty?" I asked.

"Either one?"

"Yeah, probably."

Samyel returned to the center of the bridge and waited for Greggorty to stand in front of him.

"You ready to give up and skedaddle?" Greggorty asked.

"Unfortunately, no. We could easily just outnumber you and take the bridge you know?" Samyel nodded his head back toward where we are all standing as a group watching. "Are you a woodbugger?"

Samyel and Greggorty walked circles around one another. Samyel patiently waited for the Confederate man to make his first move. Samyel teased Greggorty with a few quick swings of his Winchester in hopes of knocking him back off the bridge, but the last swing was blocked, sending Samyel's rifle clanking to the stone. Seeing an opening, Greggorty lunged hard using the bayonet but overextended himself, stepping past Samyel. Samyel drove his foot into Greggorty's backside, sending him sprawling to the ground. He recovered quickly and kicked Samyel's rifle away, sending it far off the bridge to splash in the crick. Then he turned back toward Samyel and punched him hard in the nose. Not hard enough to break anything, thank Burrow, but hard enough to water his eyes.

"You done lost your weapon for a lowdown hit," Greggorty cheered. He wiped a patch of dirt away from his shirt. "You ought be dead. But, I'm a man of hon-"

Samyel reached out, grabbed the Enfield musket from Greggorty's hands and stuck the bayonet through his heart. Greggorty lurched forward, placing his hand on the back of Samyel's head and pulled it toward his mouth. He whispered something into the lad's ear.

Samyel then turned toward us with an anger in his eyes I'd yet to see from the lad. "He said don't walk through that arch there. Go around it." Without another word he continued across the bridge into New Hampshire.

"It was a solid move," I whispered as I walked by Greggorty, who was dropped down to his knees, bleeding like a stuck doe with the musket still in his chest. I plucked the Enfield from the Confederate man and tossed it to Samyel. He'd earned it.

Greggorty fell to the shallow crick below the bridge and there remained with the small things in the mud.

CHAPTER TWENTY-FIVE
The Shepard

We rode as fast as our stolen ponies would let us, carefully for half a day following a small game trail through the southern forest of the White Mountains. It was a cloudy night and we'd set camp up in the midst of a tight circle of felled trees. It felt like we were closing in on our destination, through none of us knew exactly where that was to be. We knew it was a logging camp, and when we left Charleston the assumption was there wouldn't be too many of those in New Hampshire, but all of us were foreigners to this state and now after seeing the great amount of fallen trees on our half-day ride we were beginning to second guess our initial thoughts. Luck came our way that night as the moon peaked out from behind a thick bank of clouds.

The ponies shifted in the tree line where we had them hobbled. Good Horse went about her business with no concern toward me, she was no Sarah Roy, but I didn't fault her that since I stole her.

A grunt came from the dark beyond the ponies. They settled as a figure stepped out, hushing at the animals.

He was tall and dark bearded; had a felling ax hanging from his hairy-knuckled fist and a pair of foxes in the other. The man pushed a low branch out of his way with his ax and stepped into the light of the fire. He stood, taking us all in as his eyes scanned the fire lit trees around the camp. From the side of his mouth he said, "I'd offer you something to eat, other than your potatoes, but I suggest I take you straight to camp instead. Before the rest of your tits freeze off, can't have that now can we boys?" He laughed at that, quietly. The woodsman looked around the fire at my lads and let out a hearty laugh worthy of this broad forest. "Come on now, let's pack up and head in. The hour's late and the moon's offering to guide us home."

"Who the hell is this?" Folks asked. "We're not just going to follow some bastard that stepped out of the woods further into the woods."

The woodsman looked up at the moon and sighed. "Forest tits, this one has a tongue doesn't he. It's fine to speak this way where you're from I'm sure, kept secret by the muffling of the branches and pines and the hills, but in these woods, I'd watch that fleshy flapper else the *devil* remove its impurities. He's always listening, as the first white snow and the very bottom of the sea. My name is Yasper and the woods and trees you've been borrowing for shelter belong to him." Yasper nodded toward the woods. "And, I'm here to help you."

"The devil?" Keefie asked.

"Camp is this way. Keep behind me, eyes on the trails. When we move, do not look out into the woods. Ever." He looked back at our ponies. "Your ponies will stay here. They will be safe. I promise."

We all got up from our spots and started after him.

"Wait, we are going to just follow this man, who just wandered up out of the woods on us by the way, further into the woods even after he told us not to look into the woods?" Folks said from the end of the line.

The moon grew dim as another low cloud passed before it.

"Language," Yasper said, continuing forward.

"Sorry," Folks said.

"I like your beard," Keefie said. She was directly behind the woodsman.

Not even an hour following Yasper further north and I forgot I was not suppose to look into the woods from the trail. I didn't really forget, but when something is looking at me, I tend to look back. "What's that watching me right now?" I asked.

Yasper froze and held his hand for us to stop our march.

"I told you not to veer your eyes from the trail," Yasper said.

"Something said my name, I looked, anyone would have looked," I said, looking immediately toward my feet.

"I didn't look," Sallow said.

"Me either," Keefie followed.

"The man said don't look," Samyel said.

"I watch my feet and walk forward," Knots added.

Skinny only shook his head.

"Thanks guys," I said. "Okay, but what's it? Something is out there. I can see it in my peripherals, skulking about. It's dark, but just look! There is goes. See it? Did you see it, Folks?"

"I'm not looking, I was told not to look," Folks said.

"There are a lot of *'somethings'* out there, but this is the reason I asked you not to look. Did you hear me say not to look? I clearly said, 'Keep behind me, eyes on the trails. When we move, do not look out into the woods. Ever.' Right? Did everyone else hear me say that?" Yasper was fully stopped now and looking back at me, I think. I was told to look at my feet so I was, I more sensed his eyes on me. I wasn't looking. I was told not to look. I wasn't looking.

"Listen, is something awful about to happen?" I asked. "I am *completely* sorry. I really am. Tell…this devil of yours I really fucked this one up."

"Language," Yasper whispered. "The camp is not but a mile from here, still north. Don't stray from this trail, no matter what. And do not look into the woods. On my count, be ready to run there. Eyes down. One."

"Wait! Is something going to chase us? I can't run a

mile," I said. "Keefie can't run a mile!"

"Yes I can, I can run a mile," Keefie said.

"Well I can't! I get winded and my side hurts." I kicked mud off my boots. "And it's bloody night time!"

"Two," Yasper continued.

I felt myself beginning to panic. "Yasper, is a man named Pynes in your camp? Pynes Oak? I need to know before I go."

He winked and then offered a small nod.

"Three." Whatever was in the darkness lunged out of the tree line toward me, but not before Yasper tackled it, taking them both down. A guttural howl rang through the woods around us. I ran.

I didn't have time to look back.

I ran.

I was the last to pick my heels from the mud and run, following quick behind Knots as we crashed through the trail a mile north into the further north.

I never looked back. We ran for what seemed a full life time of burning breaths. We ran into the dark toward the low burning fires of a camp ahead of us. We didn't stop. We just kept going.

Somewhere far behind us was the sound of a man fighting for his life. The cries of a bearded woodsman we only just met, fighting off whatever crooked devil I called from the woods by looking into them, like he asked me to not. If this man died it would be because of my dumb curiosity and fear of the unseen.

I thought of Pynes Oak, fiddler, lover, bastard.

Crook's father. And, even though he left me in Charleston with a swollen belly and not a knuckle of coin worth a piss, I was going to retrieve him.

Or, at least just ask him why.

So, for that, my feet carried me.

CHAPTER TWENTY-SIX
Flea Hovel

We fell through the open gate of the logging camp one by one into a heap of fired lungs and bloodied heels. A mile doesn't seem that long, I know, but running on the muddy, rock strewn trails in the middle of the night with only a faint moon to guide you is no easy task.

"I couldn't see what was back there," Keefie breathed out. She lay on her back, not caring about the muddy puddle she pillowed as it soaked into her hair.

"Be glad for that," Sallow said. He was standing at the gate we'd just barreled through looking back out over the trail. "Sounded awful what ever it was. Hope he had it handled."

The gate was open to the woods with no sort of

barrier or door to seal shut behind us, but it felt warm here, even if it was just the fires burning in the camp providing the illusion. Warm felt safe. I let my anxiety burn away from the top of my belly. I sat up, raking mud and leaves from my hair.

I looked around the camp. A few buildings sat tightly hugged together inside a circle of high, erect logs reaching up along side their still growing cousins. A filer shack, hitching posts for oxen, a large hovel for the men and a blacksmith shop were scattered around the camp, though all seemed abandoned. The camp sat butt against a short cliff, protecting it on its northern border. A vein of clear streams ran through the center of the camp, down from the cliffs trickling to a vast lake on the easterly side where a tight group of cabins sat, facing the calm water. The pines around the lake still stood tall, with very few cut down. No where was there a clear-cut where the loggers would have been working, unless their logging operation was further away. Hay and straw were strewn everywhere to keep the cold mud underneath at bay.

A tall silhouette appeared at the gate.

Yasper.

"The hovel is empty. The water there trickles down from the mountains, so it's clean. If you don't mind the cold of it, you can wash yourselves. I recommend you do that, and sleep. I'll have some food for you in the morning. I hope you like elk," Yasper said, then returned to the wide-opened gate and squinted his deep set eyes toward the woods. He watched the trails, then waved his lantern back and forth.

Like he was signaling something. Or, someone.

"He's right, let's get cleaned up before anything else," Keefie suggested.

"What about Pynes? We are so close," I said, eager to look around, but I was tired. My legs and lungs burned and I felt some sort of critter crawling around the bottom of my cheek, trying to burrow into the mud caked there. I swatted it away. "Pynes can wait," I concluded.

We plodded through the hay covered mud toward the empty hovel. It looked much smaller on the outside, but was in fact pretty roomy. It was one large room, with bunks along ever side except one which stood a simple kitchen setup. Cabinets above a iron-belly stove and skillets hanged on hooks above it. The iron-belly stove was lit, already warming the room for us. Summer was drawing to conclusion and the small fit of fall was only just beginning to blow in, but with these long nights out in the woods, we'd grown into longing for any sort of warmth.

Keefie and I went first outside to the water falling out back behind the hovel. Yasper was right, the water was freezing, but clean. It felt good on my muscles as I stood letting the water tease my body to get fully in. Keefie didn't wait, she stepped in without a full thought of how cold it was. Call it a German blessing of stubborn skin. I watched the goose flesh rise on her skin and admired the bruises around her hips, up to her belly and below her chest. Some men liked to get rough with us, came with the work unfortunately, made them feel better about what they were doing when their wives weren't looking. Keefie bore those bruises like a jeweled belly dancers belt; she would never believe it brought something fierce to her.

She stood in the falling water, staring at me through wet hair. "What is going on?"

"What?" I ask. Lately, there was a lot going on; I needed the specifics narrowed down if I were to follow her.

"Why are you not talking to me much lately? Don't seem yourself of late." She shivered in the water. "You've been acting damned strange," she said, squeezing icy water from her hair.

"Something's got me rightly rattled is all," I said. I rubbed my shoulder poke. "Been thinking about a lot of things, can't help my mind."

"Why didn't you mention it earlier?" Keefie whispered. Her voice was small.

"I-" I began. I could only return her gaze as I found words hard to admit. "I don't think anyone can help me with this one is all."

I watched her, waiting for anything she may offer. I couldn't live like this. With the fear of her following me further into the unknown. Not my cup.

I narrowed the space between us, letting the cold water fully have me and flicked a muddy leaf from her hair. "Keefie. I'm scared," I said. "I'm scared I won't be able to find him. I need to admit to myself that it's a possibility we are wasting our time. Before anyone gets hurt. Or, killed."

"We're all still here aren't we. Out here in these wilds with you," Keefie said. "We won't stop either."

We said no more words as we finished washing, then

returned to the warm hovel. The lads went next and went quicker than us. They all returned complaining of the cold water and mostly did a good job cleaning themselves. Knots was really the only one that smelled fresher than when he went. The rest were good enough.

Fleas bit our feet as we tried to sleep that night. The wind blew throughout the camp in long breaths and somewhere, deep in the mountains something howled.

Thump.

We rose the next morning to sunlight peering through one of the windows. I looked out; smoke rose from a burning fire in the middle of camp. A shank of elk leg turned on a spit above the fire, sizzling fat drips hissed at every drop.

I slid into a pair of doe-skin trousers and a simple button up boy's shirt - likely from a lad that came here and outgrew it - before heading out into the camp. I'd blend in mighty well with a group of loggers if I wasn't such a scrawn and I tucked my hair up.

Keefie came running up behind wearing a fox pelt fur shoulder mantle, held in place by two leather straps criss-crossing above her breast. Under that she wore a simple, low cut blouse with a string of sewn flowers across the neck. One of the fox heads could pull up over her head like a hood with its little arms hanging down the sides of each of her red-flushed, snowy cheeks. Another fox head hanged down her left arm, about half way. Whoever did this for her knew how to work the skin, stretching it to get the most out of each of the portly foxes. She looked lovely as usual wearing it. Of course she did. We would have to change the name of her place to Foxmaiden by the looks of her smile, and the lads'.

Someone went to effort to provide Keefie with something other than logging clothes, and I was a little jealous. Just a little.

"You look chipper," I said to her.

Thump.

She smiled and ran her hand through her hair.

"Thanks," her reply. "You going logging this morning?" She laughed.

"No, I'm not going logging." I moved over to the elk leg basking over the blaze. "Someone took an eye to you it seems."

Keefie looked around. "Notice that we are the only ones here? I looked around a little right after the sun rose, before you did."

"Yeah. Bit odd isn't it. Quiet here. Kind of nice," I said.

Thump.

"So, what's the game?" Sallow asked. He took a bite of the elk shank I tossed him. "Mmm, good."

We sat around for the rest of the day, lying in the sun, eating elk and poking around the camp looking for any trace of Pynes.

We found nothing.

CHAPTER TWENTY-SEVEN
Another Night, Another Elk Flank

The merriment of Yasper coming home for the night rose our spirits from doing scratch for most of the day. Time was spent looking for Pynes in the nearby woods, but the old hunting trails usually ended overgrown with bush and thistle, making it difficult to go forward. The lake that shored the camp was too wide to attempt to hike around before nightfall. With a warning from Yasper, we were to always return to the logging camp well before the sun first teased the top of the trees. Every night we greeted Yasper like bored little children would with their father returning home from working the woods.

Folks and the lads returned to the hovel earlier than Keefie and I, taking their food and water with them. Folks said he didn't like the cold. "Felt off," he said.

Keefie stood next to me at the entrance to the camp, waiting and watching, wishfully expecting more logging men to march in any minute from the night trail, carrying lamps and humming songs of the woods as you'd expect them to do, but none came. Only Yasper. Keefie ran her fingers through the fox pelt mantle on her shoulders and smiled at Yasper as he passed. He nodded.

Around a campfire, sipping boiled wine, I looked up from my mug and asked Yasper, "Pynes Oak? Is he here then?"

"*Here* is a general term," Yasper said.

"Okay, what does that mean?" I pressed. I didn't want to sit around another day in this camp waiting. "Don't sass me, Yasper."

"It means. There is a *man*, but not 'here'," Yasper held his hand open toward the rest of the logging camp.

"Just tell me woodsman. Where is he?" I asked again. I could feel a rash forming on my neck from all this nonsense. "We looked all over. And, where are the other loggers? Surely you are not it?"

Yasper looked at Keefie, "Is she always this way?" he asked her.

"Honestly, yes mostly," Keefie smiled. "She has a hard time not getting her way."

"Thanks, Keefie," I glared at her over the rim of my mug.

"Don't get mad at your companion for pointing out the very obvious," Yasper said.

"Oh, I'm sorry, no one made *me* a beautiful fox mantle though, so yeah I'm a little upset. I'm dressed like a dolt of a logger boy and want to find Pynes and go back home. These barely even fit." I pulled the waste of my trousers away from my hips and kicked my heels up to show bare ankle. "And damned fleas bite up my legs all damn night."

Yasper nodded. "Language."

"Where is Pynes? Please?"

Yasper sat for a long time staring at the fire, then grunted as he stood.

"You're just going to leave without saying anything? Surely the logs can wait?" I asked, again.

"I'm no logger, only a shepherd," he replied and stared right at me for a long while.

He disappeared into the dark without a word, leaving lamp and ax behind.

After Yasper left, we retired to the hovel and slept with the biting fleas at our ankles. The wind pulled outside our window.

Thump.

We woke again the following morning just as we did the last, with a rump of elk roasting on a fire outside waiting for us. For days, we'd been gnawing mostly elk meat and I was surprisingly not tired of it yet.

"What do you think's out there? In the woods?" Knots asked. His half-terrified eyes were looking through the only entrance into the logging camp. He tilted his head to try looking further down the trail. "Sallow, what do you think is out there? More Moon-eyed to steal our horses?"

"No *gran hombre*, Moon-eyed don't come this far north. I wouldn't think at least," Sallow replied. He patted Knots' arm. "Probably skeletons. Although they do prefer quieter things. Quiet roads and such. Valleys where the sun barely visits. Not crypts or the like, those are for worse."

Thump.

"What about *el chupacabra?* Keefie sat up, teasing Sallow with a word she'd heard him mention only once before he grew stone white. Meat dropped from her mouth as she laughed and she tried to catch it only to send it flying over the campfire. "Does anyone else hear that damned sound? Like a distant pounding?"

"Don't talk about the *chupacabra*! These woods ain't right. Nothing about this is right," Sallow said, looking around at all of us. "There's no one here but us and Yasper! Who comes and goes so often by the way, I don't even know if he's real anymore! Last night I was looking at him, really looking-"

Keefie laughed again.

"No girl, not peeping, just looking. And, I ain't afraid to admit I saw through him. I don't mean in a way he's trying to trick us and I saw through his traps, no. I saw *through* him. *Through* him."

"Did you see through him then?" I asked.

"Yes."

Skinny Oleerh sat away from the group on an overturned log, whittling away at a small piece of wood.

Samyel sharpened the edge of the bayonet on his new Enfield, a trait I soon realized he did feverishly and nightly since retrieving the musket.

Thump.

High above us, at the tip of the pines, early snowflakes whirled around the low hanging clouds as they moved in and out of the valley. The edge of the lake was starting to see a kiss of frost on these early mornings, but by afternoon the young ice would melt away again leaving the yellow and orange fallen leaves of Autumn to float about their way with the waves lapping at the shore. Signs of animals burrowing in and burying away hidden stocks of berries and nuts were starting to appear all around us as they prepared for winter coming. Fall was barely arriving, but winter seemed ready to push in.

"You're an odd fellow Sallow, but I'm happy to have you around," I said. He looked around the camp. "Just where is Yasper anyway? Have you seen him today?"

"Saw through him last night," Sallow said. "Just sayin'."

Thump.

CHAPTER TWENTY-EIGHT
To The Scalped Man

The cabin was lit by the warmth of a small fire place. Drying herbs hung from a rack attached to the ceiling above a pot of stew simmering on a little iron belly stove in the kitchen. A large window above the iron belly stove overlooked the lake. On the opposite side was one single window allowing the sun to brighten a large bedroom. In the room off the kitchen was a row of eight beds with quilts and piled up pillows as if made for us. I would have liked to sleep forever in that little room.

"Good, you found her," Sallow said to Keefie as he walked over and stirred the stew. It smelled briny like the ocean, simmering in a rich white peppered gravy. My mouth watered.

"What is this?" I asked. I felt a sigh escape my lips.

Thump.

"Peppered crab," Sallow replied. "Keefie found this place. Feels safe here right? Don't know why, can't much explain it. Lake breeze I reckon."

Folks fetched two bowls of stew and paused to look out the window. "Big winter coming in. The hovel was full of holes and fleas, good riddance."

Keefie and I both took our bowls and sat at the table. I blew across the top. The warming, peppery scent wailed through my body.

I took a bite of stew, then said, "Why do you still stay with me?"

The stew felt warm in my belly. I took a sip of white wine Skinny Oleerh handed me from a nearby cupboard and I continued.

"I could never have made it here without you. Keefie. Folks. Skinny. Knots. Samyel, even Sallow." Why was I admitting this all?

"I believe you would have, girl. I know people. It's my gift. And your gift is you are stubborn. Sometimes that all it takes." Folks took a long draw of the wine, sharing my cup.

"Stubborn, huh." I said, not asking. "Oh, Burrow help me, what are we even doing here?"

Sallow took my bowl and filled it again at the iron belly stove. His gazed stayed out over the lake for some time, he pointed out a small black bear poking around a dead fish while it stormed in the distance. "I don't know about you, but right now I'm having white pepper crab soup and being at peace. Robert would have liked to have seen this lake. He missed Kansas something fierce and loved it during a good storm. Said he thought it had to be like the ocean with how open it was. Wrote a handful of poems about it, likely never read them though." His voiced cracked a bit, then he coughed. "I know it's only a lake, but still. He's a fine cowboy and trapper."

"That man was a poet?" Keefie asked. "Robert?"

"And, a damned good fine one," Folks Emery said.

Thump.

"I want him back." I didn't bother with names, it was more for myself to admit what I was doing. Out loud. Everyone knew I wasn't speaking of Robert McGee.

"To what end?" Folks asked.

"To the very end."

Sallow nodded his head, still looking out the window.

"Then to the end we follow," Folks said.

Thump.

Somewhere out over the lake a loon call carried through the open window, chilling my skin.

I looked up from my soup at the window.

"That seemed ominous," Keefie moaned.

We all sat at the table and ate the rest of the soup in silence, enjoying the moment while we could. A breeze blew through the kitchen, carrying with it the gentle sound of the waves lapping lakeside.

Thump.

Folks brought a bottle of spirits - covered in dust and red like coral - that he'd found tucked away in the back of one of the cabinets.

"It's too somber in here," Folks roared. "Let's drink and eat and toast to Robert McGee until we are too drunk to stand and too full to sit and then we can pass out in those nice looking beds in the other room."

"It's barely mid lunch yet. We have things to do," I said. "Why are we talking like Robert is dead? Man stole our horses and now he gets a toast?"

"Pah! What better reason for this fine liquor and good company than a toast?" Folks asked, taking a long draw from the bottle of coral red. "To Robert McGee. The Scalped Man. The only man I ever saw swim down a mermaid and part tails with her!"

Keefie shot me a curious glance. I shrugged.

Folks passed the bottle to me and I held it up for Robert. "That man wore a lot of hats," I said and took a drink, then passed it to Skinny.

Skinny Oleerh took the bottle. "Finest cowboy I knew. Better trapper. Decent horse thief. The bastard…"

"I went with him to track a mountain lion once that killed some of the remuda. When the traps didn't work he tracked it down one night and choked it with his own hands. And, the babies too. He was a tough *caballero*, too tough for the Sioux when they tried to skin his head." Sallow held the bottle for a moment as if thinking, then took his swig.

"He was afraid of moths," Knots said.

"Absolutely terrified of them," Folks added. "T'was the fluttery sound they made."

"I don't think I said a single word to him," she said,

taking her drink.

She almost spat it out, but kept her lips together then swallowed. "It tastes bloody awful!" she coughed. "Like a fish that's sat in the sun too long!"

Samyel passed on the drink, but nodded in agreement with the words spoken for Robert.

I pushed my empty glass back across the table toward Folks. He quickly stood and bounced toward the small kitchen to retrieve a different bottle. This one containing a greenish-black liquid that sloshed slowly as he returned. He stumbled and slid the bottle to Sallow.

Sallow poured the green-black liquid into my glass and pushed it back. "Squid." He said, smelling the spirit.

We'd been at this for hours. Testing the reserves tucked away in the cabinets that reached further back than any of us were born. Old whiskey, old wine, old brandy. Some of it was tossed when the cork popped, due to a noxious odor that sniffed out having gone to ammonia, but most seemed fine to drink. And the more we had the more our inhibitions were gone, which in turn allowed us to go back and try the nasty smelling stuff. Wasn't going to kill us after all. Not me at least, I had a throat for it.

"The hell do you mean squid? Like the fish?"

"Mollusk. From the sea. Must have traveled a long way to make it here. Like us."

"Hopefully it taste better than the last," I said as I tossed this one down. And no, it did not. It was thick like mucous as it slid down my throat. I gagged. Then when the liquid hit me I felt a tingle in my spine running down to my southernly bits.

"That one hits where it counts does it not?" Folks laughed as he took a longer swig of the stuff. "Gives you a healthy dose of the squid dick!" He burst into a deep laugh before tumbling out of the chair, landing on the ground. We could see, clearly, the squid spirits were affecting him as well.

"I haven't felt this way in years," he whispered from the ground, then picked the bottle up and spoke to it. "Where were you a long time ago? Bah, with this company what would have been the point." He looked at me, then his face glazed over.

"Oh no you don't you degenerate, besides I need a good wash," I took another drink for some reason. "So do you big man. Might go step out in the cold rain for a bit. Let the night and the moon wash you off. Just sayin' is all."

"Someone say degenerate?" Keefie asked. She stood at the door between the kitchen and the bedroom, looking at us sitting at the table, then yawned.

"What did I miss?" she asked. "I was just lying down for a spell. Those beds are nice."

"This cabin is really nice. Was it here the entire time?" I asked. I thought for a moment and couldn't recall seeing it before.

"Think so," Skinny added. "Stuck to the hovel Yasper told us to use."

"I found this one when I was snooping. Better than fleas biting our asses," Keefie grinned.

"Better than fleas biting our asses!" I held my squid spirit up and took another drink.

"I'm going to lay down for a while," I said, suddenly standing up and instantly regretting it. I took Keefie's hand and dragged her into the bedroom with me, where we got undressed, then crawled under those soft quilt covers.

Samyel and Knots were already in the bedroom, snoring in a peace I haven't seen since we left Charleston. I wanted to join them. For that night, I had everyone I needed right where I needed them to be. I wanted to sleep with a belly full of warm soup, mollusk spirits and nice thoughts, tucked into Keefie.

So, I did.

CHAPTER TWENTY-NINE
Bounty Hunter

"A man is coming," Knots said. He pointed out the window toward the logging camp's only entrance. We all stood and hurried toward the door.

Thump.

In walked a man, slightly older, wearing a patchwork fur cloak over the black surcoat of a Deluge. He had long, stringy white hair clinging to his scalp and chainmail coif around his throat. A Winchester rifle hanged from his back. If not for his hair I would have told you he were Deluge, but out of the Parish, it was just as likely he could have stole his attire. Or found it.

"Can we help you old man?" I asked, calling across the small amount of ground between our cabin and the entrance to the camp. The patchwork man walked in without looking up. Behind him he pulled a small wheeled-wagon with a bolt of burlap cloth strewn across the top, concealing whatever the wagon held.

The old Deluge paused in the middle of camp, not a few yards from us and looked back at the gate. We moved out of the cabin to greet him halfway, where another chunk of elk was roasting nicely above the fire. "You wouldn't know of a handful of horse thieves what came this way would you? You lot don't look much like loggers," he called back.

"We don't?" I asked, wondering just how my logging outfit wouldn't sell the fact that I was a logger. Lack of muscles on my part I presume. Chopping wood all day would give you bigger sticks than I carried under these clothes. I looked toward Keefie in her Foxmaiden arrangement and laughed. She was obviously the one giving us away I convinced myself. No self respecting logger woman would dress as she did. It just wasn't practical out here.

"She's uhh…" I couldn't think of a thing to say here. "She's getting ready for a ritual. A sacrifice. One involving foxes. And trees. And probably some dark foresty things. Which, by the way have you seen a logger on your way in? Ah bugger, no we haven't seen any horse thieving to answer your original question, old man."

The Deluge looked at me and grinned wide, his two front teeth were missing and his tongue clicked in the black hole. "Well. Fair enough then."

Thump.

He spun toward the wheeled-wagon and threw the burlap cloth to the ground.

A rifle came out.

Skinny Oleerh found himself with blood blossoming from his gut before I even registered the snap of the rifle let go. He fell backward, tripping and landing behind a log we would have sat on to eat elk and discuss the fleas. Every one of us scattered before the old Deluge could grab another iron.

I put my hand on Skinny's bullet wound and pressed, worried he would bleed out soon enough. Skinny grimaced as I shoved a piece of cloth ripped from my sleeve into the hole in his gut.

"I have been shot," he said.

"Yeah you have," I replied.

"Then tell me, where is Sallow?"

"He's just over there."

"Apologize to him for me."

Another bullet bite into our fallen log cover as the shot echoed out into the forest.

"A few horses were stolen not long ago from a place called the Crossroads," the old man said. "Know the place?"

"You walked right past them on the trail you asshole!" I called out from behind the log. "You could have had them."

"Forgive me. But, stealing from the Deluge is stealing from Low the Kind and well, that just ain't allowed. Horses returned or not, you're still a bunch of dirty horse thieves."

The cloth in Skinny Oleerh's wound was darkening with blood. Too much.

Thump.

"Come on out, we can talk. Just the mouthy one, the rest of you stay in your cover," the man said. I assumed he meant me, they always do, so I peeked my head over.

Samyel was beside me, his own Winchester across his lap. "I can't cover you," he said. I spotted Sallow in the shadows next to a cabin, unaware that Skinny was bleeding out to Harvest. He watched us.

I stood up, then walked toward the Deluge with my arms held out to my side. "Are we going to talk then?"

"You've got nothing I want, just wanted to get one of you out in the open is all. Damned fool."

Without thinking - and taking the gamble I could reach him before he put a bullet between my eyes - I dove forward and rolled. I stood up, then ran at him. Out came Sparrow from my back. I tossed her as the old Deluge stepped to the side, pulling his patchwork cloak off his shoulders, throwing it over my head. He smashed me in the face, spilling me backward on the ground. I heard scuffling beside me. Groaning.

Thump.

I ripped the cloak from my face and spat blood.

Samyel was kneeling by the Deluge, holding Sparrow firmly in the old man's jaw. The Deluge pawed at the blade, but Samyel held on to it, then placed his hand over the dying man's mouth as we all listened to his final moments.

"It had to be that way!" I hissed at the Deluge.

When it was over, Samyel stood and picked up the old man's Winchester.

We buried Skinny Oleerh right outside the logging camp under a giant black oak tree that was as quiet as him. Wind blew through its branches, but it held firm and silent against the breeze.

CHAPTER THIRTY
Whiskey Business

A whiskey-soaked tabletop came up quickly to meet my face. Or, was it that my face came down to the table? I was well into having one too many whiskeys to remember and the table and I were quickly becoming intimate.

We didn't question where that whiskey was from, Sallow pulled it from the same cabinet he'd earlier found the wines. Yasper, I assumed, was supplying us for our stay here with whiskey, wine and elk. Lovely ghost that, if I haven't mentioned before. Yes, we decided the man was a ghost. Did we have proof? Other than he was occasionally see-through and Keefie swore he walked through a wall to spy her one night. No. We really didn't.

Skinny Oleerh died quietly behind a fallen log out in

the middle of New Hampshire in some flea infested logging camp. In the middle of no where, with no one by his side when he breathed his final. All the lads, and Keefie ran to me when that old Deluge tried to saddle me with a shotgun. That was how Skinny died. Lack of pressure on his wound saw him bleed out quickly, while everyone was up my ass about playing it safe. To Hell with safe. And, to Hell with that old man for killing Skinny.

We didn't give the old Deluge bastard the luxury of any sort of proper burial. I could see Samyel's rising questions and concern for the fellow follower of Low; maybe even wondering if when he died himself, that was how he would be treated. Dragged out and left alone in the woods for the wolves. Dead for the foxes so Low would never know him.

Samyel's claim of love for Low was wanning. I could tell, it wasn't hard. He was becoming bitter, questioning things, becoming a killer like us. But something like *love*, something you were raised into your entire life to believe was an absolute truth, the absolute truth, didn't just leave your blood and your heart after a quick tumble with an incredibly attractive woman and a long trip across the wilds. It didn't even leave after you witnessed two good men die for no reason. It would take some time for the lad. He would need time and until that time and his mind came to fruition, let him question himself and his Low I say. Let him wonder just how *kind* Low the Kind was to send an iron from a rifle into the flesh of a man for stealing a horse. Or, at least in act, through his Deluge. Low the Kind was no good.

I would continue to guide Samyel as best I could, equaling the determination he was showing me. My own determination. He would follow, I knew. I just hoped I could lead him home before he was truly well and lost.

Questioning everything you've ever known tends to change a man.

I looked around the table. Folks, Sallow, Knots, Samyel. Keefie. Afraid to lose another. I couldn't lose another.

Another round of whiskey went around and the hour was getting late. I took two more shots of the honeyed amber and pounded the empty glass down.

"Slow down girl, you'll wake up next week and miss the winter," Folks laughed. He was trying at least to lift my spirits. The others sipped patiently on their drinks as they watched me drown myself.

Sallow slammed his empty whiskey glass down, bouncing it toward Folks. "Keep drinking, you'll need that courage won't you," he growled. "Useless death. All for some Pynes I don't know goat balls about. Just so you can split your twigs with…what? One more time from what I'm told. Surely there's other lads out there who'd mend your basket? You're young still, get after them. Stop wasting your time on this man. He left you and here we are."

"It's more than that, Sallow," Keefie took no notice of Sallow's bite.

"How old are you Keefie?" Sallow asked, looking at Keefie. There was a snap in his voice as if slapped sober.

"Thirty-three somewhere around, I suppose, last

count," replied Keefie. She pouted out her bottom lip, thinking. "Why? You already know this…"

"Let's call it that then," Sallow said. "Thirty-three. Ale, when I was thirty-three I was caught up with the Kelpie, doing who knows what to who knows who. You're both just babes wasting out here in the wilds. The city is where you belong. Charleston. New Orleans. Boston, hell even San Francisco. Anywhere but here. There's no count for it being out here, girls your age. Bah, what do I know. I'm just an old man. Let's say that when you're no longer a child, because you still are for now. Let's say you look back at all this and wonder just what you were doing out in these woods, in this camp, looking for a man that may or may not even still be alive-"

"-Pynes is alive," I broke.

"Maybe, maybe not, how could we possible know…" Sallow sighed. His shoulders slouched and he leaned back in his chair. "The curse of the young is watching the old get older. Fade away. Die off. And, knowing that it's coming for you too. One day it'll be here. It came for Skinny. We were just kids once, Skinny and I. So full of ourselves and each other, just like the two of you. Age comes for us all. Look at your girl here. Just a baby compared to us. What am I saying? She is a baby. That face. That's a curse too I tell you. Everything's a curse. She could have just about anything with a face like that and she doesn't even realize it. Never have to work. Instead she's out here wasting her time for you! Find someone worth giving it all to, someone that cares about you is all I'm saying. It couldn't be hard with a face like that. Stop looking at me. Skinny looked at me like that when I was rambling."

Keefie put her hand on Sallow's shoulder. "Meh, call it what you will, Sallow. I wouldn't say it's a curse. I know what it's worth. Earned me some good ol' cash money with the lads back home," Keefie laughed, but Sallow was right. She knew it. We all knew it. Live or die out here in the woods, or go back to Charleston and be safe. Live a safe life.

Folks looked up at her and frowned. The thing about Folks was as he let the spirits take over he became too fatherly. Call it fault, call it from being such a big man, maybe he couldn't help the nurturing. Keefie frowned back.

"I'm trying to straighten up," Keefie said, avoiding his gaze.

She then added, "I ain't looking to settle just yet. In the wilds is where I'm at right now, with you all. Having a drink. Having a drink for Skinny."

I thought I caught Sallow's shameful glance toward me, but I could have been mistaken. I was feeling paranoid. Drunk and paranoid. I didn't even want to speak.

"He shouldn't be dead," Sallow puled.

Instead Folks surprised me, "Where were you with that bow of yours Sallow? You could have ended that Deluge before he even spoke with one arrow." He reached across the table and placed one straight finger on Sallow's forehead, tilting his friend's head back just enough to look at him. "Right between the eyes. You're that good. I know you are." Folks exaggerated of course, I don't even recall if the bow was within reach at that moment. But, it set Sallow to look back down at the spilled whiskey in front of him. He frowned.

"Doubt that," Sallow finally muttered. "This journey has become a waste of our time. I'm just drunk enough to say it out loud."

"That's enough-" Folks grumbled.

"You didn't do a thing when Skinny died either, Folks Emery. Legendary Folks Emery. Left him there to just bleed," Sallow growled. "We all just left him."

A sad anger rose in my chest. The whiskey was hitting him harder than the table hit me.

"I told you… what happened," I slurred. A spot on my head began to throb where I'd banged it into the table. The room was moving an awful lot tonight. Wind pulled smoke from the cabin's fireplace outside.

"I would have jumped in front of Skinny and taken that iron and you know that is what." Sallow was now pointing a finger at me. "She stood there. And watched." He looked back and forth between Folks and myself and decided it was best to leave it at that. "Bah!"

Folks leaned back in his chair. "Conley went forward to stop the Deluge from putting iron into any more of us. What she *did* was stop him. Samyel, too. I don't know what you would have done different Sallow, Ale knows you're brave. We all know you don't fear much in this world. Conley did what she could. End of it."

Sallow dropped his head. "I really miss him. Already, it's this hard. I'm not going to be able to do this," was the last thing he said.

"Skeletons," Knots said.

I looked at him. We all looked at him.

"Sallow is scared of skeletons."

Silence from Sallow, then a slight shake of his head. "Fucking right I am…" Sallow sighed. That was the only time I believe I'd heard Sallow curse.

We sat in silence for the rest of the evening finishing our drinks and elk eventually deciding to call it a night.

When Folks and the lads left, taking Keefie with them, I sat at the table, starring at Sallow until he sobered up. It took all night, but I wanted to make sure he was fine.

CHAPTER THIRTY-ONE
Tend To Kill Back

"Whole mess of Deluge coming through the gates," Sallow said. He was at the door of our cabin looking out and after he announced what he saw, he shut the door and bolted it.

Thump.

"Deluge? More of them?" Keefie sighed, mostly annoyed. She started looking around the room. "They already murdered Skinny. Those Deluge have never done me any favors other than trying to scrub off the sin of Washmaid Row and we just killed one of their own. This won't end well."

"It's the ones from Crossroads Inn," Samyel said. "Connor's out there."

"How did he find us all the way out here?" Keefie

asked.

Sallow looked at Samyel as he crossed the cabin to retrieve his Schofields sitting on the table. He spun them in his hands, then tucked each one away in their side holsters. "Why don't you tell them how the Deluge are like a hornet's nest. One of you goes down and all of you feel it."

"He's right. We shouldn't have killed him. Should have tied him up, anything other than death. Sent a pain through even I could still feel." Samyel moved next to Sallow, he wiggled the bayonet on his Enfield musket checking its sturdiness, then reached back and tapped his Winchester, making sure it was there.

Thump.

"I tend to kill back when someone tries to off me," I said. I pulled Sparrow from my back. "Besides he murdered Skinny, remember? Don't ask forgiveness for that, you offer death right back when it's time."

"You can't be serious?" Folks looked at me.

"Serious as death to that Deluge," I replied.

"There's just too many, Conley," Folks said. "*We* do this. You leave out the back. Take Keefie, get out of here."

"I'd prefer to die along side all of you if it's all the same," I said.

"Well, glorious as that sounds. I don't plan on dying just yet," Folks laughed. "Just scare them a little. Connor doesn't seem like the shoot first kind of Deluge. I intend to buy you the time to get out of here. Samyel take them out the back way. Climb over those damned mountains if you have to then cut back south and follow what ever trails you can until you're out of the woods. Do not wait for us."

"Folks, I don't need you to do this," I whispered. "We stay together."

"No, what was it you asked me earlier? Where was that damned reckless behavior? Well, this is it."

Folks shoved me out of the way.

CHAPTER THIRTY-TWO
The Gentlest Man

I crossed the cabin and took the Winchester rifle that Samyel plucked from the dead Deluge. He handed it over with no objection. "Got one shot for it," he added as I then handed it over to Sallow.

"Hey Connor," I called out the door. "You got a man named Denne out there? Should be old as sin by now."

A long pause.

Thump.

"Yeah, he is me," the man Denne answered. "You got my interest peaked."

"How's that danglingly dick of yours Denne? Still sticking it in round jolly Haina?" I laughed. "Wasn't that her name?"

"Conley Mahren," he said. "You knew damned well what would happen to that girl after you found us and didn't take your proper hands. Now, come out and we can finish what we started back those days."

"I can't believe you're even still alive," I said.

"From what I know about you I could say the same," he said. "Come on, let's get this over with. Now come on out."

I spotted him over the field. "The problem with you Deluge is that you're all hypocrites, do what ever the hell you assholes want," I said.

"I reckon as long as I bring more meat to the table than I eat, he's willing to turn cheek," Denne said. He fingered at the trigger of his Winchester, aiming it toward my voice from the cabin. "I've got something here for you. Let's have that meat."

Thump.

"This is getting a little awkward Denne. You're saying all these sweet things to me in front of your friends, and here I don't have anything nice to say back."

"They sent me outside the Parish after you, into these damned wilds," Denne said. "Cunt."

Uncalled for.

He took a step behind Connor who was pacing in the center of camp. The other Deluge were spreading out, forming a loose circle around the two, nervously aiming their own Winchesters at shifting shadows around the camp.

"I changed my mind Folks Emery. I do want to fight you for those horses," Connor said, interrupting my words with Denne. "What do you say?"

"How many Deluge do you have with you there?" Folks cried across the field between them.

"Oh, numbers hardly matter with you right? You're Folks Emery. *The* Folks Emery. Fists so hard they break steel. Balls so big he can satisfy the whole damned States. That right?"

"Sounds about right," Folks said, peaking his head out the front door just to be seen.

"Sallow Salazar and the Knot," Connor said, looking behind Folks. "They in there too? Where's the rest?"

"That's it I'm afraid," Folks said.

Thump.

"Knots," Knots reminded the Deluge, calling out.

"Yeah…just Knots," Connor said. "Apologies. Are you to suffer the same fate as your Folks? You too Sallow? You're all horse thieves in my eye and in the eye of Low the Kind, but I would forgive your insults if you just walk away and let us sort it out with Folks. No offense, but his reputation far precedes your own."

"No offense taken," Sallow said.

Now, that is where it got tricky.

Denne saw me in the window from across the yard.

This suddenly wasn't a matter of dick swinging with the boys anymore.

We were outnumbered as far as bodies went, but each of my lads could hold their own, as they would prove.

I could tell by the hateful lust snarling on Denne's lips that this was about revenge and worse. Never in his old twisted, long-lived mind did he think he would be here, out in the wild with the one girl that sent him here to live with the filthy forest vermin in the first place.

Like the shit bird I was and still not waiting around on the advice of less capable men, I hustled through the front door. Past Samyel, past Folks.

"Everyone just wait!" I called out, staying just outside the threshold of the cabin. "I got something here you'll want to see!"

Thump.

Before they could reply, I nodded back toward the cabin. Sallow aimed the Winchester at Denne through a window and spent the iron.

The camp ruptured into pure chaos. Dirt burst around us, shattered wood from the cabin splintered, loud cracks broke the silence of the woods as the Deluge opened fire with their Winchesters.

I ran out the cabin at Denne. I wasn't willing to wait for him to put a bullet in me. I had my Sparrow ready to knife him.

He was on his knees now, eyes locked forward.

I lunged at him, but he was already quite remarkably dead what for the bullet lodged between his twitching eyebrows. I gave him a final kick to send him to the dirt.

Samyel was next out, he stopped when a bullet split the frame of the cabin door, the Enfield musket was resting on his shoulder waiting for permission to follow me across the yard under a hail of bullets. With a quick nod, I gave it.

Knots charged three Deluge alone, taking a bullet in

his left shoulder as he ran toward the man that shot him. His bricklayer's hammer, Mamaw, dragged a line in the dirt behind him as the other two Deluge each missed their shots before the mad lad tore into them. One Deluge lunged, Winchester first. Knots side stepped it quick enough to grab the Deluge's arm and pull him down to the ground, then swung his hammer down, smashing it into the back of the man's head. Knots was already turning to face his other two Deluge as they tried desperately to back away and steady their rifles for one more chance to get a shot off. They never did.

Sallow was working his twin Schofield's over on a Deluge at the edge of the logging camp. After the Deluge tripped as he retreated backward, Sallow was on him, and it was over within a breath. Sallow moved to the next nearest Deluge that was aiming his rifle at Folks.

A blade slashed behind me, stopping a Deluge from braining me with the butt of his Winchester. I jumped back, seeing Samyel recover from his wide swing and follow back through with another twirl of the musket above his head. This time he stabbed the bayonet in the Deluge's shoulder. The Deluge dropped his rifle and slumped as he held his bloodied shoulder, snarling at Samyel, saying quite nasty things about the boy. Samyel didn't take it kindly and ran bayonet through the Deluge's stomach.

I heard shuffling behind me.

Thump.

I turned and saw Folks and Connor squaring up in the yard of the camp. Connor was dumb. Dumb enough to try to squeeze his arms around Folks to contain him.

Now, it goes without saying that even someone like Connor couldn't hold onto a man like Folks Emery for very long. A fraction of a second in fact, before he was flipped over the bare-knuckler's shoulder and slammed into the ground. But, what came next astonished even a seasoned viewer of complete bullshit as myself.

Connor stood up and held his fists before him, ready to bare-knuckle box the bare-knuckle boxing champion of Charleston and maybe beyond. He had to. He had no weapons other than his fists and unfortunately the fear of seeing his Deluge patrol broken before him left his mind in a state of unreasonable thinking. Connor was about to box a killer.

He actually held his own longer than I thought he would, trading punches with Folks, who actually seemed to ease up on the smaller fellow. Connor laughed, almost like he was enjoying it. Who knows, maybe he was. I know that not having an outlet for your depravity can cause you to unleash in a wicked way when offered the chance. I've seen it a thousand times with these Deluge assholes. Given the chance, they'd fight you or kill you as long as they thought it would put them in a better eye of Low the Kind. Convenient their morality was only as strong as what fit into their own individual narratives. And narratives told outside the Parish were a little more loose than within the city. There was a reason Deluge lads like Connor and Denne were out patrolling the wilds and it wasn't to spread the kind word of Low. It was to enforce it. Spread chaos. Violently.

Connor connected a left hook into Folks jowls, stunning him backward a moment. Connor forced the attack, pushing Folks back, but Folks wagged his finger at the Deluge to scold him.

Connor threw a right cross, but missed and was gifted a succession of quick low jabs to his side. He doubled over and went to his knees, then looked back up at Folks moments before the boxer hammered him right in the middle of the eyes. Connor fell backward in the hay and mud, but for what it's worth, he gave a good fight.

Folks grabbed Connor by the collar of his surcoat and lifted him back to his knees. He punched him again, sending him back down. Then Folks was on the Deluge, hammering blow after blow into Connor's ruined face. His jawbone popped out of its socket. The sound from him made me gag. You don't forget a man gurgling for his life under the relentless assault of bloodied fists.

Connor turned his head to the side, no longer able to watch the assault coming to him. His head jerked with each blow, oblivious. He was becoming a bystander in his own death. I turned my eyes down. But nothing else came. It stopped.

Folks held his fist up, ready to keep striking, but something held him. He slouched.

Thump.

"Go back home," Folks whispered.

Connor could barely roll after Folks moved away from him. He reached for a Winchester close to him. His hand was shaking.

I walked over to the scene, Keefie was behind me, emerging from the safety of the cabin. Knots and Samyel were already there, looking down at Connor. I didn't have to say anything. Nor did they. I think all of our thoughts were on Skinny Oleerh and his silent grave under the silent tree.

"'uck 'ou," Connor moaned from his broken jaw. "'ow 'or'ive 'e…" Connor asked Low for forgiveness, as if *he* failed *him*. My heart felt broken. Even with a ruined jaw, broken and teasing death, this depleted soul still had grit. A dedication to Low even when he was failed. I would never understand that. I couldn't. I've never loved anything like that.

"Go home," Folks repeated. He bent to pick Connor up by his chainmail coif and held the Deluge before him. "Go home."

The skirmish in the logging camp was over as quick as it began, everyone that needed dying was lying on the earth dead, soaking up mud and giving back its blood.

Connor tried to kick at Folks.

"Look around you. It's over," Folks begged. "It's over."

Lost in the middle of a logging camp far north in a forest in New Hampshire, where he swore to spread the love of Low, Connor wept alone. The sound would haunt us for the rest of our lives.

Everything that Connor was had been taken by the gentlest man I knew.

I sat alone watching the fire fade into glowing embers.

"The stars are different out here," Samyel said from behind me.

I moved a bit over on my log to allow Samyel to sit next to me. His closeness felt off. Unnatural. Awkward. It wasn't him. Place anyone next to me and I'd say the same this night.

He looked back over the log at a small travel pack I'd tried to push hidden.

"You're leaving?" he asked.

"You don't need me anymore."

"That's hardly for you to decide, what I need." Samyel wasn't smiling. Only watching the fire.

"You've killed, Samyel. You don't go home from that the same as you were."

"No, I don't reckon you do. But that's my walk, not yours. I've killed before."

"Cairnborn. It's different when it's a man. How many now? Three?"

"Reckon. That old gray Confederate at the bridge, Greggorty if I recall, probably didn't deserve what he got. The others did."

"If it makes you feel better, I'm not sure that Confederate was…well, doesn't matter now I guess. Still feels the same don't it?" I tried to smile.

I looked up at the sky. "Folks won't understand me going."

"He'll be okay." he said, then asked, "Will you be okay?"

I shook my head. "Get them home."

I left the logging camp.

CHAPTER THIRTY-THREE

Thump

Thump.

"-owe me a coin!" I felt myself bark. My own gravelly voice snapped me awake.

Thump.

That bloody, Burrow-damned sound. I'd hardly noticed it missing until it recently started again, sounding more often than when I'd first arrived in these woods with the lads. I was ill-prepared for its tenacity with nothing to distract me from it.

I rose from my hay bed, kicking my feet out from my pile of furs and straw. I didn't worry about getting dressed, or putting boots on, those things were long gone. Taken by the forest. I would tell people later it was a Dunnie that stole them.

It was early morning. The sun was rising over the trees casting a haze through the mist that covered the valley where my cabin nested. This was a nice valley. The way a valley should be, with birds chirping, deer peaking in on me as I rose, squirrels chasing one another around trees, chipmunks running under bush. Water trickled around the camp from last nights rain running down from the mountains in veiny streams. Peaceful.

Thump.

Except that.

Again, the sound. I stood up and glanced out across the valley, trying to pinpoint the sound echoing out over the trees.

It would be a while before breakfast, not because I was feeling lazy, but because I had lost my only way to catch fish in the streams around the woods and the thought of eating a knuckle of random forest berries didn't seem all to appealing at the moment, so I chose to finally follow that damned sound instead.

Thump.

I wrapped a raccoon fur around my waist and tied it paw to paw, concealing Sparrow at my dimples and about half of my rump and called it clothing. It was all I had. Didn't know a damned thing about turning dead critters into clothing, other than gut them and use their skin and fur as it was. I didn't even kill the poor bastard, just found him in a stream drowned. Plus he was a big boy and thinking back on him bouncing at my ass, paws tied together around my waist as I trod through the woods, my hair all in braided tangles and covered in dirt had to be a sight. No one out here but me and the moon.

I walked for several hours following a muddy path through the woods before the trail began to transform into rocky moss-covered terrain. The tree canopy above was thick here, blocking most of the sun from the forest floor. The air felt old to breathe, dank and the trees leaned crooked over, bending into one another in a gnarled embrace. I found a trail overgrown enough with crossing branches and snapping weeds I struggled to break through. Once through, I crawled for the last few yards until I came to an archway of large, olden stones, which the trail lead under. Ahead of me was a clearing of felled tree stumps.

Thump.

The sound was louder.

I looked across the clearing past a stack of felled logs, where there stood a man swinging an ax into the nearest tree.

Thump.

I slowly approached, feeling my heartbeat thumping heavy under my breast. I tried to slow my breathing.

I whispered. Not a name or anything like that. Just a whimper of sound. What could you actually say with any meaning at a time like this?

The man made no attempt to turn toward me. He swung his ax, sticking it into the tree one more time. *Thump.* And stopped.

I put my hand on his shoulder. "Pynes?"

I turned him gently with my hand.

"Oh-" the only sound I could make.

"I…" I started. "Everett…"

Everett's eyes were far-staring, long with the distance of lonely night. His face held no weight to it. His cheeks sunken in, but not in a starving kind, but the way that happens when tragedy works its ugly hand over on you. Long, wavy hair stood straight up like a tree fighting for sun and his beard fell down his chest like turning, searching roots.

His face let up no emotion of any recollection on my part or even the sight that I was standing before him, nude save for a raccoon embracing me. A stick tumbled its way from my hair and fell to the ground.

"No, no, no."

He was unresponsive and turned to continued to chop ax into the tree.

My knees gave out and I dropped to the ground, feeling my fingers slip back behind me searching for Sparrow. Why wasn't it Pynes? All this. For nothing. Lost. Alone. For Everett Thayne. I let my hand drop down to my side, then slammed my fist into the ground. A small rock bit into my knuckle.

Thump.

I stood and held my hand out toward him, afraid it may pass through, then stopped. Grabbing the back of his hair I tugged back hard, then put Sparrow under Everett's chin. I buried my face into the man's back and kept it there. I wanted my hand to glide the blade across this impostor's neck, to spill out the blood that walked me across the long hills and black woods and through the dead lands of Vermont, that caused me the death of Skinny and the lose of my friends.

I felt a portending heat rising up from Everett's body, pressing into mine. Warning me. Let go.

"What is wrong with you? Do you not care?" I whispered into his ear. He only stood, letting me hold the blade to his neck. "Fuck!" I yelled, dropping Sparrow and releasing Everett's hair. "Fuck…"

I reached back out and took the ax as gently as I could, like a mother taking a dangerous knife from her babe. Careful not to cut them, or more importantly get myself cut.

I rested my hand on his cheek and guided his eyes to mine. I could see in his eyes this man had been to the edge and seen things worth forgetting. Seen things a man had to travel far and forget everything he knows about himself to move on. I hardly knew Everett, not like I knew Pynes, but then I didn't know anyone like that. This man was not much more to me than an associate, someone you meet in passing one night and never really think on again. He'd been there that night I was with Pynes, before they all disappeared, but no words were passed between us, if any. I didn't really owe him, but I'd come all this way, I didn't want it to be for nothing. All this way for a man that wasn't Pynes, for a man that was Everett Thayne.

I took his hand in mine. Gnarled hands and roughed with calluses, not the hands I wanted though. Definitely not the hands that glided smooth across my body on a night so fierce I could hardly breath. Not the hands I begged to hold me after. Not the hands I held onto constantly in the back of my mind.

Unfamiliar hands on an unfamiliar man.

I pulled Everett away from the tree, lightly at first, until he took a few small steps backward with me.

"You're not who I was expecting, but I will take you home," I said. "I'm glad I arrived. It's an end of sorts."

I led him out of the felled woods. I never let go of his hand.

I'd had enough of this forest.

That night I'd found out the devil in these woods was holding my hand as I guide him through.

I didn't know truly how dangerous Everett was, but I'd known how scared of him Yasper was and I trusted that fear. I tied his hands to keep him safe. And me. I was soon to find out that the pull of whatever awful thing held Everett's mind came out at night. Sometimes he would remain calm, but anything could upset him, and then hell came.

We traveled this way through the woods for days, finally arriving at the Crossroads Inn and instead of going inside to politely ask for a couple of ponies like last time, I outright stole a pair, convinced Everett they wouldn't bite him, then rode off into the night. I didn't name the pair of them.

We continued traveling west toward home, eventually coming across a farm that had clothes hanging outside drying on a line that seemed about my size, so I took em', finally abandoning my raccoon fur attire. Felt good to have normal clothes again and I was glad for it, glad that I wouldn't have to wander into Charleston looking like a feral wood child.

We made quick haste across the last dying sunlit hills of the Virginia's, past the scattered mining villages and farms and arrived at the gates of Charleston late the following day.

I'd been away for over a year.

CHAPTER THIRTY-FOUR
Familiar With Low

"Why is there a queue to enter the city?" I asked, glancing at Everett knowing damned well he wouldn't answer, other than a blank stare. I dressed him in a cloak with a hood, which was pulled up over his head to keep his profile low. I feared any moment someone might recognize him and soon find out what he'd become, mucking up my plan.

"What are they checking?" I pointed to a pair of Deluge, fully armed, speaking to people as they took turns approaching the Miner's Bridge into Charleston. Another patrol of Deluge lingered a knuckle of yards away with a group of Rinmnir, searching their wheeled caravans, tossing things out into piles along the dirt road further from the city.

Approaching Charleston felt wrong. Something was changed. The mood floating around the air was sour. Held breath and scowling faces greeted us as we approached the Deluge guarding the bridge into Charleston.

Horses roamed without owners, nibbling on the overgrown weeds poking from the unkempt brick streets all while dropping shit where ever they pleased. Green and rotting breads, mushy vegetables and spoiled barrels of briny water were pushed off to the side of the roads, while people stick-thin picked over them looking for anything to eat. There was a foul smell in the air, like over-worked, pressed in bodies standing in line for a bathhouse. The bridge into Charleston was a damned mess, much more so than before I left.

"Conley," a nervous voice cracked from behind me. I turned to see Samyel sitting on an overturned wooden crate of horseshoes not far from the Rinmnir commotion. His hair had grown ragged, longer and he was unshaven. There was a wildness in his eyes and he no longer had the Deluge demeanor about him. The overalls he wore were stained soot and black with coal dust. In his hand hanged the Enfield Musket he'd taken from Sir Greggorty outside New Hampshire. The bayonet was replaced by a longer spearhead and was permanently fixed to the end, secured by leather wrappings and bolts. On the butt of the Enfield Samyel had whittled figures from the forest: bears, wolves, even some sort of beasts I'd not recognized. His old Deluge Winchester was sheathed at his side, the only reminder of who he once had been.

I tugged Everett with me and approached Samyel. Things felt shaky, like seeing a jilted lover in the streets when you least expected it years after you broke their heart. What was I to say to him that I hadn't already gone over in my mind thousands of time on my journey back to Charleston. I would have a conversation with all my companions, I was sure of it. Awkward ones. Ones that would explain why I'd left them in the forest after having gone through so much. Ones that would get us all on equal standing again, they would forgive me and they would embrace me back home.

The broken look on Samyel's face told me enough. He began to cough which then turned into a full fit and spat out a thick wad of phlegm on the street.

"Samyel, I…" My rehearsed speech tore apart as I watched thick, soot-black drool slide down Samyel's lip and he wiped it away with the back of his hand.

"Me and the lads were waiting out here for you a while back. They didn't want to keep waiting, said you were not coming back, said we shouldn't go inside," Samyel explained. "They talked about leaving for the coast for a while to dodge the Deluge. I didn't want to leave just yet," he grinned, almost child like. "I think it's because I knew you'd come back. Eventually."

"Yeah…about that," I started, but he shook his head. I tossed a glare toward the Deluge at the gate. "You should have gone in. You shouldn't have waited out here."

"I can't," he whispered.

"Why Samyel?" I asked.

"I'm a murderer." Samyel walked behind me, looking

over my shoulder at the Deluge we were slowly approaching. "We left Connor alive, I shouldn't have allowed that as much as I regret. Sure as a holy shit he would have come running back with exacting revenge on my likes, and the lads. You too, if you're asking." He was sounding less and less like Samyel and more like Folks and his crew. Those lads had a way of rubbing off on you right quick. Can't say that's a bad thing, especially for someone like Samyel. Open up a lads views to the world a little, open his eyes and he'll stop sounding so damned contained and proper all the time.

"Well I ain't asking, never am, no count for it. Besides, the amount of Deluge looking to set me right you could just about fill the Kanawha to the top. Nothing new for me."

Samyel scratched his beard growth, "It is for me. I don't right know what to do. I don't know who I even am. The coal miners took me in for now, been staying in a camp with them. Decent living."

"Well, come on, you can stay with me until we sort you out. I owe you that for waiting at least." I put my hand on Samyel's shoulder and patted it. "Sounds like a start then…in figuring who you are."

He nodded then said, "I need a bath."

"I couldn't agree more." I wiped my hand on the leg of my breeches.

"Familiar with Low?"

"In what way?" I asked.

The toothy looking Deluge only stared at me, as if I'd had a tit on my forehead and he'd never had the privy of seeing one.

"Familiar with Low?" He repeated, this time slightly more annoyed.

"Probably more so than you, if I'm telling the truth, which I am."

"I doubt it," Toothy said.

"No, really. Went belly to belly with a lad while your Low watched up in that high tower there. Now, tell me what this all is then? Let us in." I looked around, then caught Samyel's eye and winked. He was slightly shaking his head while holding Everett's hand so as he wouldn't wander off. They lingered back, but still close enough to obviously belong to me.

"What's wrong with that man," Toothy asked. "I didn't like your answer about Low, and if you soil his name with that slippy tongue of yours, not only will I drag you through the city, I'll have it tied at the Cistern. Now what I say goes at this gate, and what I say is, you don't get to come in this holy place of ours with filth spewing from your holes. Got it? Keep it clean. Now, what's wrong with that man?"

I looked back at Samyel.

"No, the other one," Toothy said. "Is he sick? Has a pale look on him."

"Sick in his head only, brother of mine. Got into way too many fights as a kid and never won a single one," I said. "Promise. Can we come in now? I'll toss a coin your way when Low isn't looking. Or, you know, something else." I nudged my head a couple nods toward a Rinmnir girl quietly waiting behind us in line. She smiled wide at the Deluge and tried not to laugh.

"No."

"This is our home, it's where we live. And if we can't come into where we live, then where do we live?" I asked.

"Not my problem. Are you daft girl?"

"A little bit," I replied. "Like my brother. We had a rough childhood. Too many bumps to our heads, not enough hugs."

I peaked at the sun setting soon on the horizon. This was about to get three crooked shits to sideways if we didn't get Everett inside the gates before the sun set and someone went to upsetting him.

"Listen, buddy," I said. I stepped probably a little too close to the Deluge as he quickly stepped back. My hands held up, offering him palms to apologize. I ran my fingers through my hair to settle down any stray fizzles. I looked back at the second Deluge on the opposite side of the gate, letting people in. "Why are they getting in so easy?"

"They are familiar with Low, as I asked you earlier."

"I already said I'm familiar with him. He grabbed cheek, isn't that right Samyel?" I looked for him for any help.

"Samuel?" The Deluge from across the gate asked. He approached and both Deluge now stood before us, blocking our way inside.

"Wilyam," the second Deluge started. "If this is who I

think it is, which is to say, if this is the same Samuel that-" He stopped, looked at me, then Samyel, then back at me, held his hand to his mouth and nodded. "I suggest you let him in or at the very least take him straight to the Cistern. Truet would, I'm sure, love to meet him."

"She called him Samyel, not Samuel," Wilyam said. "This isn't the same lad, Jerme. Couldn't be. Samuel died fighting in the Cairns. We are looking for a Samyel though, got some papers here says he's wanted for…murder, horse theft, and public lewdness. Among other…unnatural things."

"Samyel not Samuel, what's the difference, she already said she's dumber than a mule so maybe her tongue can't roll the name right is all. This is Samuel if I'm not blind. I saw him raised from a babe in the Cistern myself. Even changed his nappy a few times," the Deluge named Jerme said.

"Oh, this is Samuel the great. Err, chosen one. Pure one. Whatever, this is he, I simply misspoke earlier, rolled my tongue in the wrong place as you said. Mama always said tongues were for other things than rolling proper words out," I said. "We are escorting him on the holiest of missions for Low the Kind to get this sick, sick man, my brother, help at the Cistern. Right away. Now, let us in. He's not dead. He's in front of you know looking to go in to see…uh, Trudy. Samuel." I probably over exaggerated pursing my lips a little too long to speak my point.

"Truet," Wilyam correct.

"How do we know it's him?" Wilyam, the toothiest of the Deluge asked.

"How do you-" I started. "Samuel, tell them of yourself. Show them your rifle."

Samyel pulled the Enfield musket from his back, presenting it as if that's what I was talking about.

"Your other rifle Samyel. Samuel," I sighed. "Your Deluge rifle. Show them Beth."

Samyel shrugged, then pulled Beth the Winchester from the sheath at his side. A faint light cast shadows on the immediate area, just enough with the setting sun to barely see.

"What does this prove then?" Wilyam asked. He pulled his own Winchester out, and there it glowed a light cloud around it too, only slightly brighter than Samyel's own Beth. "I have one too. As does Jerme. Show them your rifle Jerme."

"Keep your swords sheathed lads, we believe you. Listen what's it going to take to get into the city?" I asked. Soon the sun would be under the horizon and Everett's rage wouldn't wait for niceties to be sorted out.

"Take me to Anrose. And this Truet," Samyel spoke with fuller authority than moments ago. "And, let them know I've earned back my purity. They would know me."

I guess Samyel wasn't above lying anymore then.

Maybe he was learning something from the lads.

CHAPTER THIRTY-FIVE
The High Chancil

Everyone within the walls of Charleston kept their eyes down away from the Deluge escorting us through the city toward the Cistern. The people were afraid.

We'd only been inside the city for a heartbeat, but already I could read that the mood had changed in the time I was gone. The Deluge's numbers had grown. Patrols of them walked the streets, looking through windows, standing at intersections, staring down anyone brave enough to walk too close. They'd had the city by the balls.

I aimed to change that. Samyel got us across Miner's Bridge, but I would have to be careful and I would have to mind my manners with the new High Chancil, who I knew shit all about.

Jerme and Wilyam stayed behind at the bridge, manning their post and hollering out another Deluge to take us straight to the Cistern. Right away, no delay. I never caught this Deluge's name, didn't matter, all that matter was ducking Everett away before we crossed into the Cistern's walls and hope this Deluge didn't realize he'd lost one person on the walk here. He wasn't much paying attention to us, spending his time glancing down alleys, shoving anyone that got too close and generally cursing everyone around.

We stopped for a moment in the streets as a large, pock-faced Deluge set about work on a young girl trying to buy bread outside a bakery. The Deluge went about asking her where she earned the money, was it honest work? Did she steal it? Did she fuck someone for it? I felt my mouth wanting to open to defend the young girl, tell that Deluge it wasn't any of his god damned business, but that's when I noticed Tapper standing off to the side trying to get my attention.

Oh, young, sweet, Burrow-blessed Tapper. What a sight to be seeing, and I shouldn't have been too surprised to see the lad so soon into entering the city.

I doubled winked at Tapper and threw a few "bugger off" hand gestures his way, one's we'd practiced one boring night when the rain was keeping us at bay and no one in the Breige wanted to knuckle up coin our way.

Our escorting Deluge shoved us quickly through the last street of the Breige where it rolled into that weird part of town between here and Washmaid Row - you know, the taint part of town where it's a little bit whores and a little bit fancies. We as a town collectively decided to call the place the Undergrowth. You didn't really want to linger much in the Undergrowth. The place gave Harklow Down a run for its coin, but at least in Harklow if you were going to get stabbed it would be to your belly and not your back. Too many people looking for their opportunity to escape meant lots of backstabbing and back-table trading which led to folks disappearing only to wake belly-up, covered in straw on a table with your guts hanging out. We didn't dally and let our Deluge push us through toward the Cistern, following the Undergrowth's streets all the way there, which I thought was weird for a Deluge to take this path.

In the chaos of the streets of the Undergrowth we lost Everett to Tapper's quick snatch without our Deluge even noticing and by the time he did it was too late, they were gone. Tapper would know where to take him to hid him away until I met up with them later.

Once through the Undergrowth we made our way past the outer walls of the Cistern, through a small grove of fruit trees until we were within the building proper. We crossed a narrow bridge over the Basin to stairs going up to the upper floors. The Deluge guarding the Basin eyed us feverishly to make sure we didn't do anything to foul their holy waters.

Working our way up to the chambers of the Chancil we were then sat in an all too familiar room. The Second Chancil Anrose's room. Our Deluge left Samyel and I alone in the chambers.

"Remember this room?" I asked, smiling at Samyel.

"I see you two are still cozy with one another," Anrose said from the door. He stepped inside, followed closely by his wine girl. "Lovers now I assume? That was quiet a night you two had here last time." He laughed. "Unforgettable, I'm sure."

"I'm glad you both were brought here first." He held his hand toward the young lady behind him, and she stepped forward. "This is Truet. *High Chancil* Truet."

My shock must have been obvious.

"I didn't know they would allow women in this role," I mused, looking at Anrose. "And, so young."

Then, looking at the girl, "Thought your name was Rhone…"

Truet moved toward me. Her confidence, even in just the way she walked countered any doubts she gave off with her youth. "One of my names. To earn a position such as this so quickly, I've learned to be known as many things. And, I'm seventeen if you're counting, soon to be eighteen. Yes, young. And, like your Samyel here, I was raised pure."

"I don't know how you kept that way, looking as you do in this fortress of men," I said. "You're tall for soon to be eighteen. I know some clients that like tall girls. Does Anrose know you go to Washmaid?"

"Lust is discouraged," Truet laughed. "In all forms. But, I do get bored. Not lonely though."

"I remember you," Samyel added.

"Well, you should. We did share a cup. I *am* the High Chancil now, Anrose is my Second and my guardian. He willingly offers me guidance on things I'm so far unfamiliar with. Raised as I was, purity and holiness are really all I know in a sense. Dealing with things opposite of that are well…a challenge. I know right from wrong, black from white. But it's the gray areas that confound me."

"Are we a gray area then?" I asked. "What do you care what we do?"

"You two are the grayest of them all," she laughed. It was more of a giggle. Watching her, I couldn't imagine someone as her running the dailies of the Deluge other than as a puppet. I surmised in our short time sharing ale in Pleasant Bottom that Rhone, now Truet it seemed, was intelligent, well read and humorous, but those things could only get you so far, and with what I knew about the Deluge, those things were usually frowned upon, especially in young girls. She settled herself, then looked back up at me, changed, "I can't allow you to undo now what we've accomplished. It's your fervor and reputation that bewilders and frightens me. Someone as tempting as you can't be tethered to boredom for long."

"Surely you understand-" I started, then said, "I know I can't appeal to you, but you can't hate me for trying."

"I could never hate you, but you won't be able to appeal to my youth. I'm simply not the same as you," Truet said.

"I think it would be fair warning you that the city is different now," Anrose said. "Under Truet's guidance, we've cleaned up the streets. Starting with the Undergrowth as you saw on your way in."

"Yeah, well that place needed a good rinsing," I said.

"Glad to have done it," Anrose nodded. "It's not hard to wash dirt off a dog, but keeping him clean is another task. One that requires diligence and a firm hand."

"And you are that firm hand," I said.

"And Truet is the diligence. Through her we have a fresh start. A clean start." Anrose crossed his chambers and looked out the window. Streams of the sun's light illuminated the flaws on his Deluge surcoat, highlighting frays and grim I don't recall ever seeing on a Deluge. His surcoat was used and tainted, dirty, and no longer just for show.

"Cleaning out your gutters only keeps the water fresh for so long before it starts to muck up again," I reminded him.

He started to continue, but Truet held up her hand.

"You know someone else use to challenge the love Low the Kind has for us, like you do," Truet said, then paused. "I find it so funny how quickly things are forgotten. How quickly they slip from our collective memories. Do you know anything about Nathaniel Faire or his *teachings*?" The way Truet said *teachings* bleed with enough sarcasm even Samyel picked up on it.

"Of course, a little, odd that you'd bring him up," I said, sensing a turn in the conversation. Why did my life revolve so much around a man I never met?

"You two are alike. You fight against everything, everyone," Truet frowned. "All the time."

"Yeah, because everyone is mostly wrong. Just look around you, look at what you two are doing. You know Burrow-damned-well this isn't right, yet you now try to appeal to my senses. It doesn't work the reverse on me either. If you know anything about me, you'd know that."

"How could people forget about something that happened so few years ago?" She looked at Anrose and frowned, then to Samyel. "Samuel, do you recall the stories?"

He shrugged. "Some, I was a child when Nathaniel's writings were read to me. We had a lesson, L'fowl read the scripts one time and never mentioned them again."

"Yes, well L'fowl seemed to have a soft spot for the man before he disappeared," Truet said.

"He was taken," I whispered.

"Taken?" Truet looked at me.

"The Keening *took* him. It takes people."

"Hmm, then *our* books must have it wrong," Truet said. Her black surcoat matched Anrose's, fraying and worn, with hints of stained blood on it. She kept her hand on the hilt of her Winchester, and I only just realized she had yet to remove it, like a baby holding its favorite blanket. "A single man, rising to challenge Low the Kind, *taken* by the Keening, interesting." She laughed, then said, "How would you know something about this that I don't? Wonderful."

"In between all the debauchery I found time to read a book," I said.

"I don't know if that means you read a book about Nathaniel, or you've only read one book, once," Truet smiled.

Then she asked, "Why did you come here, Conley?"

"We didn't really plan on stopping here first, but those

Deluge of yours at the gate were so inviting. Plus, thought I could use a hot meal and maybe a bath seeing as how I just got back."

"I'm glad you came."

"Do I get a bath?"

"No."

"Fair enough."

"Listen, it was nice meeting you and all again, Rhone…Truet, but I have some rather important business to get about and this history lesson you're about to get into, while informative and quiet lovely to hear, especially the part were I knew something about Fair you didn't - which I would like to circle back around too next time we meet - it is in fact keeping me from that important business."

She only laughed.

"Fine," Truet sighed, looking over at Anrose. "I'll hasten the story. One of the things, well the *only* thing I was allowed to study was history. Specifically the history of the Cairns, Low and Nathaniel Faire."

"Okay, go on," I said.

"These things are all tied together. We know for a fact that Low does have some sway over us. Can interact with us. I've seen it, you say you've seen it as well." Truet asked. "Low tries very hard to keep everyone happy and safe-"

"You mean standing at the edge of a chair with a rope around their neck," I said.

"See…see there, this is why I bring you here, Conley. You'd put that rope around Low's neck just as Nathaniel tried! To end his love for his children!"

"Since you were raised in a prison with mostly men, I'll forgive you for your loose understanding of love. Love is not being a slave to someone else's beliefs," I said.

"Can you imagine what this town would be like without Low and the Deluge?" Truet tried.

"I imagine it everyday. Warm, I imagine. Free. Lots of whiskey, a lot more nudity I'd reckon."

"You have all these things already!" Truet spurt.

"Chair's edge." Thought that said enough. "Listen, I really need to go. Nudity, whiskey, before it's all gone."

"I can't have another situation like we had with Nathaniel." Truet rolled her eyes, then clicked her tongue. "There are too many here already drawn to Charleston and its filth."

"Oh, they've been here a while, I can say that much. Just leave it alone, Truet. Love your Low, but let everyone else be." It wasn't a threat, but I couldn't help but think she heard it as one. "I wasn't much on giving a shit about anything before that didn't involve me. And, if you know me much at all, you'd know that I still don't. But, you've brought me into this. Tell me why." I looked toward Anrose, hoping to appeal to his sense of calm.

"Because you brought Pynes back to Charleston," Anrose answered after a moment. "Yes, we know. We have little birds chirping everywhere for us."

"This was Pynes' city," I went along. "It's where he belongs."

"This is my point," Truet held her hand up to Anrose who was about to speak. "We can't allow Pynes..." she stopped, then said, "because he went into the Cairns he is too much of an uncertainty…an uncertainty like Nathaniel was. He saw behind the world, like Nathaniel did except *he* returned."

I stopped her. "He's in no condition to do much. Something is inside him. He's a prisoner. I don't know what. You don't have to worry about him. He's not like Nathaniel was."

"How deep into the Cairns did Pynes go? Did he ever tell you?" Truet asked.

"No, I never saw him again after he went in. I assumed he was taken as well, or dead, but I didn't want to give to that."

"How deep?" Anrose asked.

"I don't know."

"And he never talked about stopping Low? Harming him?"

"I already said I never saw him again. You really are afraid of the lad, huh?"

"If you bring him here, we can give him a full life. A safe life. We may not be able to fill the empty vessel he's become, but we can try to offer him comfort," Truet said. She was standing in front of me now. She smelled of cinnamon and lavender, like you'd expect someone like her to smell. I was twice her age and she stood only slightly taller than I, but in her thick surcoat, with a Winchester at her side, she was imposing. So I looked like a child next to this young woman. It was all I could do to not want to be cradled in her charm and arms.

"Kor Eloise went in with him," I said. "Get him to scribble out what he saw for you, if that's what you're after."

"Unfortunately Kor is untouchable," Anrose said, "but, he also makes no play at going back into the Cairns. The Breige keeps him safe from us and from himself. He's of no concern."

"Pynes, Kor and their third; a man named Everett, were the only ones to go that deep into the Cairns and come back out," Truet said. "We don't know what they saw, and now it seems our hope of finding out is trapped away in the minds of two broken men." She held her hand for me to take. I didn't and she dropped it back to her side. "I'm sorry Pynes is this way. I don't know much about what he was for you, but I assure you, I know what loss is. I know what it means to have things taken from you beyond your control."

"I doubt it," I said.

"Maybe you're right," she sighed.

"Where does this leave us then?" I asked, looking at both Truet and Anrose.

"I will say this. Keep Pynes with you for now and if anything changes, you'll let us know. We can't leave such a risk unguarded," Truet said. She started pacing slightly in front of Samyel, all the while looking at him.

"And, me?" he asked.

"You've chosen your path," Truet said. "I can't say that I'm not a little jealous of the trail you walk. But I have a duty, as you now do. If you still have any love for Low and your brothers of the Deluge, you'll *watch* over Pynes and

Conley. Can you do that for me? As a favor of course."

"I've felt empty without Low. Without a guided purpose, without my fellow brothers of the Deluge. Without my new sister and High Chancil. Being free also means feeling untethered and weightless. Like I'm drifting away on a ship, watching the shore grow further and further away until I'm surrounded by nothing but a great and quiet sea all around me." He stopped to nod his head as he looked down at the floor, then finally said, "This sea I'm in is peaceful."

"I could be your tether from drifting too far into this lonely sea," Truet winked.

Samyel did not reply.

"Anrose will show you out," she said. She moved toward the door as if in a hurry. I watched her go, saying nothing.

Anrose gave Truet a moment as she stood looking at me, then herded us toward the door. "She's very busy, as you can imagine."

"That went better than I expected," I said.

"And what did you expect?" Anrose asked.

"Torture, I don't know. Not pleasant things. I don't have fond memories of being dragged beyond these walls," I admitted. "Last time I was here, I witnessed a murder and jumped out that very window."

"Yes, L'fowl's murder was an unpleasant thing for us, but it also gained us Truet and the means to bless the city with Low's teachings."

"I'm surprised you didn't pin his death on me, considering," I said. I walked past Anrose into the hall with

Samyel dutifully in tow.

"We knew it wasn't you. We are honest people," Anrose said. "Truet means it when she says keep Pynes to yourself and safe from Henrold. She wouldn't mention it, but we know of your dealings with the Breige and while they are a thorn under our skin, they stay on their side of the city. Henrold is not a man to be trusted."

"And Truet is?"

"Sometimes Truet's eyes are looking beyond the ones right in front of her."

"I'll see what I can do," I said.

CHAPTER THIRTY-SIX
Everett Thayne

"Tell him Conley's here with his man and I want the damned money what's owed," I yelled up the stairs to a man standing at the top guarding the door. He was a big burly type and I wasn't going to forcibly handle my way through him with Everett in tow. Besides, I wasn't aiming to cause trouble, just collect. Had to start somewhere, after all we just got back and had no prospects of knuckling any promising coin. Tapper made it a point to tell me this was a good idea, so I was going with his advice and taking responsibility solely out of my hands if it went bad, I just didn't tell him that.

Yeah I was breaking my word with Truet, but I don't recall owing her a damned thing.

"He's expecting us," finally I said to the guard above.

We were lead through the lavishly dark halls of Henrold Nanibold Marigold's estate.

Kor sat at his desk as usual, gazing out over Charleston through a stained-glass window of an exotic bird with long, bright tail feathers flying over a setting sun. Kor didn't turn toward me, but continued to stare outside toward the setting sun.

I was lost looking at the stained glass window when a voice from the edge of the room said, "We just had it made for him."

Henrold Nanibold Merigold stood in front of me and all his gloriously self-pampered, handsome self. "Gives him something to look at while also keeping his eyes away from the Cairns," Henrold said.

Three very rough-handed looking lads circled the room. I recognized them from the *Tristing*. Plus, the guard that escorted Everett and myself through the halls stood close enough behind me I could feel the heat from his breath on my neck upping that number to four. His awful hands slid too casually over my hips.

I didn't hesitate to kick him in the groin, his hands withdrew from my hips immediately and he went down. He rolled around on the rug, holding his busted dick, saying something under his high-pitched wheezing directly at me. Not polite things. He growled a few times. I didn't take it too personal; I did just kick the prick right in his manhood. I made to go kick him again. I'm not above kicking a man when he's down if it can all but guarantee he stay down and out of the fight.

Before I could reach him I was grabbed from behind. One of the big lads managed to grab hold of my arm, twisting it behind my back and forcing me chest first into Kor's desk. The man's free hand pushed down on the back of my head until I turned it to the side where I could see Henrold standing, shaking his head as if saying *"chht chht chht."* That sound your dad might make if he were wagging his finger at you for touching something you shouldn't have. Like a rabid cat or hot coals or a young man's rifle. Henrold added to the insult by wagging his Burrow-damned finger at me.

I saw that old Beaumont-Adams revolver sitting under some glass on the book shelf and it reminded of Keefie. I should have gone to Keefie first. I should have gone home and checked on her.

A rough hand probed the back of my leggings lingering a little long toward the insides, then withdrew Sparrow from my back, tossing it aside. I felt his hand ease and he allowed me to stand up, turning me to face Henrold.

"Sorry about your man's plums. I'm sure he had it coming," I said, nodding to the grounded man.

Henrold only shook his head and expelled air from his nose in a sort of half laugh. I liked this fancy guy, just couldn't help it.

"What brings you here? To your home?" I asked. Keep em' guessing, this game was going to be easier if everyone just kept their wits about them.

I was looking for a way out that didn't involve me diving through that expensive stained glass window. I quite liked it.

"Relax, these Breige boys have a long memory of the trouble you've caused them, but what's done is done. No harm," Henrold said. "I told them they could get a little handsy, but not kill you." He smiled.

"No harm, right? Well, that one owes me some coin for where those thick fingers of his went while he was searching me," I looked back at the lad. "Don't think I won't come collect."

I turned back to Henrold, "Not quite the greeting I expected, seeing as how I-"

"You brought Pynes," Henrold interrupted.

I smiled, "I'm here for what's owed."

"I can see he is as catatonic as Kor," Henrold sighed. "Maybe even more so. Disappointing."

"I believe you said I'd never have to 'worry about collecting coin from my back again', well here I am. Standing in front of you with Pynes wanting to never have to collect coin again after this."

"He can't speak. Can't even look at me," Henrold wasn't paying attention.

"Not my problem now is it?"

"What would you have me do?" Henrold asked.

"You hired me to bring him back and bring him back I did. I went through goddamn Vermont. Vermont. Lost more than you know. Pay me now, and I'll be on my way."

"What a useless thing this man has become," Henrold sighed.

"Better here with you than the Deluge," I admitted, a

little more for my own than to him. "I see the way you're taking care of Kor over there, why not this man as well?"

I found myself pacing Henrold's office. I felt nervous. Cornered like a stray dog. I stopped by the bookshelf with the Beaumont-Adams revolver, tapping on the glass. "May I?" I asked.

"I think it's best left in the case," Henrold replied.

A small manner of a man crept into the room like a child. "They are here," was all the man said. He waited patiently for Henrold's reply.

The sun was just about to dip below the horizon.

"I'm afraid our affairs may have to wait awhile," Henrold then said after taking a long breath. "Allow them in."

I watched as the little man step from the room as silently as he entered then turned my attention back at Henrold.

The sun was only a thin sliver on the horizon, just barely visible above the city.

I could already feel the temper in the room shifting.

A patrol of Deluge entered Henrold's office, weaving through his men like sand through fingers. Small, glowing light swarm around them like moths. Low the Kind lurked in the far corner; I was barely able to focus my eyes on him, but he was there. I could feel it if anything. No one seemed to react to him being there other than the Deluge, who made quick glances his way, almost uncomfortable themselves. Knowing they were being watched by their beloved, they made room for him, stepping out of his way as his shape weaved into the heavy shadows of the room.

"Oh, yeah, I did just come from the Cistern and they definitely told me not to come here. Which was the first thing I did obviously. I'm sorry, Henrold Nanibold Merigold," I admitted, wanting to break the tension in the room. But the tension lie only within me and Everett.

"They got here first didn't they?" I asked, didn't take long to figure it out.

"I'm sorry they did," Henrold said. "They arrived well before you, hours in fact. The Deluge are everywhere now I'm afraid. The Breige isn't what it used to be. My hands are tied."

Henrold changed his attention toward the Deluge. "We had an agreement that the Deluge would limit their reach from the Breige, if only momentarily. There are things happening more important than even you, Conley."

"I'm sure I can explain," I started, speaking to the Deluge nearest me. He was very young and I don't know why I spoke to him. Maybe I wasn't paying attention to the room. Maybe at this point I was hoping for mercy from anyone worth a listen. Hoping youth would spar me an ear.

"'The world isn't ready for what we saw in the Cairns,'" Henrold said.

"Pardon me?" I asked, looking at him. "What's that now?"

"It was the last thing Kor said before he lost his ability to communicate," Henrold frowned.

"Where does this leave us?" I asked.

"I though Pynes would know what Kor meant, I really

did," Henrold said.

The room stood silent. Waiting.

Everyone's breath held.

Waiting.

Kor Eloise coughed, then shuffled in his chair.

Everyone in the room turned to him as he raised a dinner knife and scratched something across the face of the desk. Henrold went to him, his face went white. Numb, he looked up at me, then to the man standing next to me.

I let go of Everett's hand and took a step away from him.

"What does it say?" I asked.

"It says, 'Not Pynes,'" Henrold said.

I looked at Everett, faking hurt. "You're not Pynes?" I yelled. I looked back at Henrold, then around the room and shrugged. My eyebrows twitched.

The Deluge were watching Kor, but Kor was working his way back to his catatonic self after using all he had left to scratch "Not Pynes" on the table.

"You promised us Pynes," one of the Deluge stepped forward saying.

"That. Is Everett Thayne," Henrold muttered, then looked up at me. "The third man." Had he known it wasn't Pynes?

Everett watched my eyes as if he were waiting for the sky to finally fade into night. It felt like ages.

"Hello, Everett," I muttered.

Everett burst with a furious scream. I dove behind the desk with Kor Eloise, pulling him over with me.

Kor's eyes grew wide as the room turned to absolute murder.

A voice cried out through the violence. Henrold's voice.

I threw Kor's chair through the stained glass window, shielding my eyes from shards of glass, then rolled out.

When I hit the ground I turned to look back up at the window.

The silence of darkness lingered around me, shifting the corners of my visions.

Up above, the awful sound of Winchesters extinguished Everett's fury as quickly as it began.

CHAPTER THIRTY-SEVEN
The Torture Of Conley Mahren

I'd barely time to start plucking broken glass from my ass before my hair was yanked back.

"Didn't take you long," I hissed, jerking my head and hair forward from her grip.

I turned, reaching back for Sparrow but stopping midway remembering my blade lay on the floor of Henrold's office.

Black Abby slapped me hard across my cheek. She slapped me again the other way.

I blinked back tears and focused on my attempt to keep Abby at bay. Knuckles and elbows, whatever it took.

Her twin daggers spun forward, toward me.

"Can't you see I'm occupied right now you twat! I

don't have time for this," I yelled, keeping in mind the nonsense happening above me. Which was rather quiet now, but my mood and my mind were still soured.

Abby slashed again and I stepped back, not wanting this. Not now.

She came at me fast like a spark from steel and flint. It was all I could do to duck and dodge her attacks before finding myself up against the wall of Henrold's estate, glancing up toward the smoking window where Everett's rage was extinguished one story up. Soon the heads of Deluge men started poking their heads out to see the commotion Abby and myself were causing below.

One of them shouted. "She's here," he said before jumping out and over me. His landing wasn't graceful, but enough to cause Black Abby to stop her assault on me and turn toward him. Abby hesitated and shook her head at the Deluge man, her mask wobbled back and forth.

I reached out and grabbed her cloak, snatching hair and pulled down as hard as she'd done me. "Hurts doesn't it," I hissed.

A Deluge crashed down into us, leaping from the window above. I fell forward, then quickly rolled myself to my side and stood. More Deluge were now coming out of the window.

I didn't have time to think, only react. I grabbed the closest Deluge by his surcoat and pushed forward into him. His eyes grew wide and he tried to keep up, running backward as I put what I had left of my strength into pushing him. We took a few steps together, him backward and me pushing forward, until we stumbled. I was on top of him and his comrades were quickly coming to his side. I slammed my head into his nose, once and twice until his nose shattered. He let out a gurgled yelp and tried to push me off, but I tightened my thighs around his side.

Something struck my back from behind. I pitched forward, leaving the broken nose Deluge on the ground and got to my knees, pivoting on one leg to face my new attacker. This Deluge wasn't large, so I lunged forward driving my shoulders into his stomach. For a smaller fellow it was like hitting a brick wall.

I crouched low to the ground to make myself a smaller target. The Deluge inched forward, all working in unison and none stepping closer than the man next to them. I couldn't single any of them out as they came forward.

"Stop!" cried a voice.

Henrold, whom had just sold me out, stepped out of a door from his estate, followed by a score of his *Tristing* men all armed with wooden batons.

"The deal was for Pynes, not Conley," Henrold said. He walked toward the circle of Deluge, putting himself right in the middle next to me.

I looked at him with a cocked eyebrow and shrugged "now what?"

Henrold's men entered the circle with him, outnumbering the Deluge by twice.

I looked around for Black Abby. Didn't see her.

So, I ran.

I ran back through the Breige, heading down toward

the new Washmaid Row, the boring one, not stopping until I was at the edge of Harklow Down. A few Deluge gave chase, but I lost them in the small and winding streets I'd gave chase through so many times in my life. I felt Burrow's tug pulling me different directions. Last minute turns or ducks-under, a jump here or spin from someone standing around a blind corner. And, though I hadn't seen Burrow in years, I let her pull guide me through the streets like I'd always done before. I felt what presence still remained of her and how I missed her fully with me.

I lost the pursuing Deluge long before I circled back around to my home.

Or, where my home *had* been.

A smoldering pile of ash and burnt wood remained where my home once stood. Keefie's and my home. Everything was still hot. Nothing remained but char. This was a very tightly controlled burn. None of the neighboring buildings suffered any damage from what I could tell, other than from the smoke.

"They will be here within a breath." A quickly whispered voice from an alley nearby.

"Tapper!" I cried.

"Deluge will return here soon, they did this," Tapper said. He stepped out of the shadows, looking ragged and beat. "Not long ago, I watched. I couldn't do anything about it. Besides it's just a building and wasn't much. Better to preserve my life I thought."

"I don't blame you," I said, looking at the charred remains. He was right, nothing of much value was lost, just a place to put my head for the night.

"Keefie was taken," he added, looking down at his feet as he spoke. "I'm sorry I couldn't do anything about that either, as much as I wanted. I'm a thief, not a brave man."

"Deluge took her? Why?" I asked, panicked bile rose in my throat. "I knew it. Didn't feel right. I should have gone running to her right when I walked through those gates and no where else. Fuck."

"I think you know why they took her, Conley," he said. "She'll be at the bottom of the Cistern by now. Not much you can do but wait it out. It's you they want, not her."

I thought about it only for a moment then turned away from Tapper.

"Where are you going?" he asked.

I slunk off toward the Cistern to plead for Keefie and trade her life for mine.

CHAPTER THIRTY-EIGHT
A Conversation Of Violence

"Where is she?" I whispered harsh, spit from my lips flicked on Truet's face.

I pressed my hand harder down onto her mouth. Her head sank into the pillow. She tried to shimmy out from under me, but it was too late, I was already pinning her down. Sweat ran down her face and her hair was disheveled like she'd been fighting the Devil in her sleep.

My other hand held locked both of her hands stretched up above her head as I leaned down and toward her ear. My legs were all I really needed to hold Truet down and if you're one for remembering, I have strong legs. "Where is she?" I asked again.

Truet mumbled something under my hand. I pushed

down harder.

"If you yell or raise your voice I will gut you cunt to neck do you hear me? I'll do it." I dug my knee into her side and put my forehead to hers and bumped it one final time to emphasize my advantage and answering her unasked question about messing with me.

It was the middle of the night with the moon full and high above the Cistern; Truet's room was already well lit with lanterns when I'd arrived through the window. She must sleep with the lanterns on to stave away the dark, the Cistern was a terribly creepy place after all. Maybe she was a night owl stuck awake reading her books.

"Do you hear me?" I asked again, I wasn't giving her much of a choice but to nod a response, which with my tight grip all around her she could barely do.

I let my hand slip from her mouth and she hissed, "Yes, I hear you!" She took one deep breath.

I climbed from her, still squeezing both of her hands by the fingers above her head. A move I learned in Farrowyard actually, one of the the few thing I took from there worth a good damn. I slowly moved backward on my knees to the foot of her bed as she crawled forward as best she could without the use of her hands. Or, it could have been she just wasn't trying. I stepped off the bed holding her hands above her head, helped her sit on her ass, then stand before me.

I twisted her fingers around with my hand and spun her around, putting her back to me. Shoving my now free arm into her back, I pushed her against the bed and patted her down for any sort of thing that could poke me. Not that I planned on dropping my guard, but a girl like Truet, as young as she is doesn't get to be High Chancil without some tricks up her sleeping gown.

Which she wasn't wearing by the way. No, she was clothed. Trousers tucked into tall boots and a long-sleeved, button up blouse half way unfastened.

"Do you always sleep in your boots?" I asked. My hand finished my search, she had a dagger tucked in a sheath just at her waist, which I casually tossed to the side, thinking nothing of it. I slept with Sparrow, why couldn't she sleep with her own blade?

I released my grip on her and let her turn toward me as I stepped backward.

Burrow, seeing her as this I couldn't help think she wasn't much out from being a child. Without the surcoat of the Deluge she appeared frail. She stared at me as she unbuttoned her blouse the rest of the way and took it off, tossing it to the side of the bed. She was bruised, but the bruises seemed old and settled into her skin. A purple and white wound on her neck glistened in the lanterns faint light.

"I was just getting ready for bed, when you arrived. Besides, girls like us need to always be ready as it seems, for anything," Truet said as she slipped a nightgown over her head, then pulled her straight black hair up and through, letting it cascade back behind her. She sat on the bed and removed her boots, then her trousers. "Is your intention to kidnap me or may I take these off? I'm awfully tired."

"I find it a little odd you're wearing them in bed, but I'm not here for those types of judgments, I'm here for

Keefie and I know you have her."

She laughed. "I've had quiet a night." She tossed her boots aside.

"I guess most of us sleep armed in some way."

"I do trust my Deluge, but I do sleep with my window open. I get hot at night, and you never know who may slip in and well, here we are," she said. "I have a busy day tomorrow, if you'd like to make your complaints quick. Or, you can always make an appointment."

"I'm sorry, is this an inconvenience for you? I left here thinking that we had some sort of eye-to-eye on where we stood, then you up-"

She stopped me. "You went straight to the one place I strictly forbade you to go," she said.

"Forbade? I guess I'm not much on staying away from places I'm told to stay away from." I had a problem with being told what I could and could not do. Matters of coin and self preservation often were at odds in my heart, but I wasn't going to be a pauper begging, or a potato peeler at the Eager Wife, no. Truet be damned. If she truly thought me to be a sinner then I wouldn't disappoint.

"You betrayed my confidence," Truet said. She started moving about the room, shifting books around on her shelf, standing the boots back up proper where she'd tossed them, folding her clothes. Menial things. Unimportant things. Her room was a mess.

I couldn't bare myself to look at Truet, because I knew she would be looking at me with shame in those eyes. Shame for the very small amount of trust she loaned to me before I left the Cistern the last time knowing damned well that I would be a causer of trouble. That I wouldn't fall in line, like everyone else in the city and do what's told.

I did finally look at her. And, she was disappointed.

"Your man Samuel came back and warned us you'd crossed into the Breige as soon as you left the Cistern. He wishes to seek the bright grace of Low the Kind again. Already, I've grown quite fond of him and am considering a high place of council next to me. He will never regain his purity, but I'm sure I can figure something out. Low is forgiving to his children."

"Well that makes me sad," I said.

"Why? He is home," Truet said.

"I was growing fond of him as well," I said. "I guess everything he said was a lie."

"No, I wouldn't say that. Men are allowed to change themselves, as you know. Men have the uncanny ability to flow with the waters around them, fit into any vessel they so choose." Truet took ponder of the room. "Women however, we must remain the rocks in which men flow around, always steady where we stand. Some of us don't have the luxury of simply being free I'm afraid."

"That's where you're wrong Truet," I said.

"How so?" she returned. "Without me being steadfast in my resolve, not bending to the will of the men around me, I have shaped this town in a matter of months. Something L'fowl couldn't do in a life time. I have become a rock for Low in a world of men." She spun and looked back at her collection of books.

I cocked my head at her, then approached her from behind. I wasn't going to simply be ignored, so I put my hands on her arm. "Where is Keefie?"

She spun fast and slapped my hand away. "Get your hands away from me! You've touched me far too many times tonight," she growled. Her faced was changed, no longer did it hold youth and beauty, but anger. Sadness.

"I should have silenced your voice when I had the chance," she added right before slapping me across the cheek.

I slapped her right back.

Then, she slapped me again.

Then she was on me like a pissed off old house cat that'd been stepped on one too many times.

I quickly stepped back, but tripped over her boots and she went down with me. Landing on top gave her a short advantage, but I bucked my hips and tossed her to the side.

"I didn't think a sheltered girl like you would have any fight in her," I said. "Bravo, bravo."

"Don't chastise me," Truet said as we both watched one another from our knees, waiting for the other to make a move. Truet stared at me with her mouth half wide. "Why can't you just leave this all alone, Conley? What is it about you that just won't stop?"

"I don't know how," I replied.

"This town was full of girls like you, a plague moving throughout the city, sickening everyone it touches. I tried to be civil. I tried to *offer* you a chance to be someone different. I tried to send you out away from the city, hoping you'd find something, someone out there and not come back. But, you came back, you always come back. And, now we are at a crossroads. A problem."

"You're wearing me awfully thin," I said. "I'm not here to solve our differences, I only came for Keefie."

Truet rocked back and forth on her knees, then got to her toes. She bound forward at me, but this time I couldn't roll back or move out of the way. I bore the full brunt of her body slamming into mine, bending me backward. We rolled around on the rug for a moment, trying to gain traction over one another.

I was tired.

Truet ended up behind me, her arms tight around my neck squeezing my throat. I couldn't breath.

Banging at her door jolted her grip, letting loose just enough for me to squeeze my hand under her choking arm. With enough leverage I pushed her arm away and then threw myself backward into her. We both lay on the ground looking up at her ceiling.

More banging at the door.

"I can't do this anymore, Truet," I admitted, more to myself. "I'm tired. I'm tired of fighting everyone."

"My Deluge are at the door," she breathed.

"I'll turn an eye that you burned my house. Just tell me where she is," I huffed out. I rolled to my side and held myself up on one elbow.

Truet still looking at the ceiling finally admitted, "she was brought in for acting in an indecent manner."

"If she flashed her tits for a coin, that's hardly a reason to be taken to the Cistern," I said. "I've seen yours only just then and you're still standing, innocent enough. Your Low didn't strike you down or condemn you."

Truet smiled, "It's different when dishonesty is exchanged. I try to be understanding. I know there is lust in the city and I don't condemn that. But there is no room for someone like Keefie in my city and she will come to admit that. Besides, you messed this all up, not me."

"Surely you must-"

"You've tried to appeal to my loins before. It won't work Conley, we are very different." Truet started toward her door and cracked it open. "I don't even bother sleeping with my door latched. It's not within me to worry about such things. All I have to do is give them the word and they will come in."

I bound toward the window that I'd climbed up to get into Truet's room and stopped before going out. "You're going to hand Keefie back over to me, personally. You will."

"Keefie *will* concede to Low the Kind and finally turn away from you."

Deluge entered the room, but I had already flown.

I was to be a conquering plague then and with it here, I would bring war and death.

CHAPTER THIRTY-NINE
The Cairns

The world was crashing down on me.

But, I had a plan.

Reach the center of the Cairns.

See what Pynes saw.

I had nothing to lose at this point, and I was just pissed and petty enough to take it all out with me.

I didn't know what was there, but Truet feared the Cairns for what was inside, so I was to use that.

Besides, I really wanted to know what the fuss was all about.

Burrow-willing I could find a way that is. If the Cairnborn or the Keening and other nasties didn't kill me in the getting there.

I was moving too fast to give the Cairnborn lurking in the streets time to notice me. Shapes didn't undulate in the sky above me, they were not searching for me yet. It was dark, but the Keening's darkness seemed slow to gather.

I took this as a sign to keep moving and ran as quick as my feet could go toward the center, not wanting to allow the Cairns time to gather its evil around me.

I reached the spot where Lord Agerhead stole Samyel's eye, but there were no baying of hounds to pursue me. Just emptiness and a gut feeling of being absolutely alone.

It didn't last long.

"Take the blade from your back. Keep your back to me," Anrose's voice broke the silence behind me.

I turned to see him and a knuckle of Deluge behind him, already beginning to circle around me. They already had their rifles drawn and aimed. I held my hand out in peace.

The Cairn's sky and streets were returning sticky and stale black. The Keening was returning, pulling back in on itself.

Again, Anrose said, "Drop. Your. Blade."

"I have no blade," I said. "I was already robbed of her by your Deluge." The houses around us began to stir with Cairnborn, watching us. Black, empty windows somehow became more black with a presence standing in them. Eyes were on us now. The eyes of the Cairns watching.

He approached. I could hear his boots shuffling on the ground toward me growing closer.

"I'll make a deal with you-" I started, numb to his hands as he placed them on my shoulders.

"Quiet," his reply. "Keep your rifles on her," he said to his Deluge. Odd, I thought I could hear the leather on their gloves itching to pull the triggers. And at this range? The bullets would punch right through me.

One of the Deluge was in front of me now, tip of his rifle was almost kissing my nose like a sweet little baby. I smiled at the lad and couldn't help but laugh.

"You've done enough. You've spoiled enough," Anrose said. "You must think we are fools to not know you'd come here. Do you really not understand what's going on here? You've almost undone what Truet has worked so hard to accomplish. What Low has done for us."

"My heart bleeds for her, truly it does," I said. My mouth curled in a snarl, but it quickly faded. I felt Anrose's hands sneak around to my front, then up my chest, cupping under my breasts, under my arms, then down my sides and hips.

"Frisky," I whispered, my voice broke. Before I said more, my mind went back to Keefie. It's hard for me in situations like this not to use words as a way to lessen the direness of it all. It's a pathetic attempt I make. The truth was I was always losing. It was hard to even fathom a reason to keep moving forward, when everything I held dear was left so far behind. I know she would want me to continue, to not give up on her, but to where I didn't know yet. To find her.

He slapped the back of my head. I held my gaze at

the ground until my eyes stopped shifting focus. It hurt. His hand finished their searching work around my bits and thighs. "She's unarmed," he said. "Nothing smart to say?" he added. I had nothing else to say to that man.

As his Deluge lowered their rifles, the one directly in front of me kept his drawn.

"Tie her," Anrose said as he took steps backward, away from me.

I looked down the barrel of the rifle, then into the eyes of the Deluge standing before me as one of his companions pulled my hands behind me and started to wrap a rope around them.

"I'm to assume Anrose has no idea?" I asked the Deluge lad in front of me. "Thank you," I added.

The Deluge in front of me winked, then slowly, deliberately placed his finger on the rifle's trigger. He tensed, just for a moment.

The shot grazed my ear, deafening and within a blink the Deluge behind me was on the ground. His nose was caved in from the force of the shot between his eyes.

The Deluge in front of me pulled the lever of his rifle and aimed at another Deluge. Then pulled the trigger, sending another man to the ground.

"None," said Samyel.

Samyel's Winchester sang as it pierced the thick air of the Keening surrounding us looking for a victim. Another blink and Samyel shot into the next closest Deluge adding a smoking hole in the surprised man's chest. The three remaining, plus Anrose scattered behind nearby buildings.

Samyel put his back to mine as he aimed out into the Cairns, waiting.

"They were so fixed on you, didn't even notice me walk up," Samyel said. "Also, you should know, I decided I don't want Low the Kind to speak for me," he continued, looking over his shoulder at me. "Get us out of this and I'll follow you."

That's when the hounds of Lord Agerhead cried their awful howls.

Samyel's face went white.

"I'll-" he started.

"Come with me," I said, pulling at his hand.

"No, what ever it is you're up to, see it through," Samyel said. He was looking down the street toward the approaching shadows. The hounds of Lord Agerhead were coming and behind them the lord himself. "Go," Samyel hollered. "Go!"

Lord Agerhead wasn't a minion born from the darkness of the Keening, but one that had been consumed by it long ago. He and his hounds held no allegiance to the Deluge. This would be a bloody show if I were to stick around, but bugger all that. If Samyel thought this through for half a decent second, he'd let the hounds go at the Deluge and come along with me, but his face was full of rage. Or, confusion, it was hard to tell. Maybe it was fear.

I took Samyel shoving me as his final word that I needed to leave and leave now, so I ran.

I ran far enough until I was confident nothing was after me and I stopped to look back. The Deluge followed, with

Anrose in the lead. Turns out they didn't want to stick around to fight the hounds either, so instead opted to place their lives in their pursuit of me. Flattered, sure, but I wasn't half as deadly as those damned hounds and I had no real plan of attack other than keep going toward the center of the Cairns and if they wanted to follow me there, folly on them. Soon, Deluge reinforcements would start to file into the Cairns, emptying out the Cistern before I doubled back. Or, at least that was my hope.

I heard the cry of a hound behind me and hoped to Burrow it was Samyel succeeding in the revenge of his stolen eye.

I vaulted myself through the window of a house I prayed was abandoned and put my back against the wall. My hand stung. I looked down and realized I'd cut it coming through the window, but I could still wiggle my fingers. If I didn't get it bandaged soon, I'd likely lose it.

Not much of a happy deal.

When I no longer heard the pursuing foot falls of the Deluge I left this house of momentary refuge. I couldn't be far from the center of the Cairns. Things were darker here, the Keening more present. The air felt heavier and there were no longer Cairnborn glancing out from nearby houses. I didn't know what devils would await me the further in I went, but in I went.

I thought I saw for a moment daylight breaking through the blackness above me. A pinch of pain ran from my torn hand up to my shoulder and I grimaced.

I moved down the street slowly, careful to watch from

the corner of my vision for anything wanting to sneak up on me.

In front of me in the shadows there was a figure, head hanging half-cocked in defeat.

It was Black Abby, only this time she wore no mask and everything suddenly made sense.

"I won't try to fight you. Not anymore," Truet said.

"Move," I hissed. "I'm going."

"You don't understand the weight you are about to bear on this world," Truet said. Her twin daggers were sheathed and she held the twig mask of Abby in her hand. "You can't do this."

I didn't stop my march toward the center of the Cairns. I could feel it. I could feel the center and I knew I was close. I'd wondered if this is what Pynes must have felt. I felt the Keening trying to enter me, pull me further in.

Truet held her hand up and placed it in the middle of my chest to stop me from walking past her. She looked at me and I could see the anguish and pleading in her eyes.

We held it that way for a breath, then I kept forward. She dropped her hand away from me.

"What's in there you don't want me to see?" I asked.

"Exactly what you *want* to see," was all she said.

I left her behind standing in the darkness, then asked without turning around to face her. "It was you the whole time then..."

"Yes," Truet said, and then as if sensing I wanted more she said. "We knew you would be the ender of all this. Since you came to us that night in the Cistern to be with Samuel.

We had lost L'fowl to dangerous ideals. Ideas Low the Kind didn't approve of, but by then it was too late to stop you from spreading your…*corruption* on young Samuel. He was lost anyway, so it didn't matter. Too tell the truth he wasn't even Deluge, just a kid we found on the streets. I guess that accounts for most of them though…"

"Corruption is a funny way to say *life*. Which is what this all is. It's just living. No harm in that right?"

"Oh, so much harm. You have no idea," Truet said. "Why do you do this?"

"Because you don't want me to," I said. Mostly not true. Well, some truth, because at this point fuck her.

"I don't believe you," she said.

I looked at Truet, wearing the soft leathers and holding the mask of Abby. My creation.

"I'll tell you the reason," I started. "Because all I want is to exist and you can't even let me do that. So you don't get to exist either. None of you do. The Deluge are too powerful. Their little holy fingers are in every pocket, taking everything from us. I aim to knock you down a peg." I looked at her, felt my lip twitch. "And you have Keefie. That's unforgivable."

Truet sighed. "We just don't see things the same way. Come back with me and you can have her. She's yours."

I shook my head. "Kind of too late for that I reckon."

"I live for Low the Kind, true. The things we do for *him* are to keep this world safe, to keep it held together, because if you can't see that it's falling apart then you're an obstacle, like the rest of them. If we have to remove everyone that doesn't see that. We will. Pynes, Keefie, even our own."

"So you killed L'fowl because he was an obstacle?"

"Well, I was talking about Samyel, but yes also L'fowl. He had to be removed and it was assumed you'd take the blame, but because no one gave a damn about the old man's death we had to find another way to get rid of you. Your journey north."

"You knew it wasn't Pynes."

"Of course, but I also didn't anticipate your rouse. Truth is, I obviously didn't know who Pynes was, but I knew the man you brought back wasn't him. Henrold confirmed it was the third man on Pynes' expedition into the Cairns, so you did us another favor. Your lack of surrendering or giving up only helped us exterminate another potential problem. But that's easy for you isn't it? Blindly throwing yourself into everything. Low help you, you barely know yourself." Truet stepped toward me. Why tell me this all now? Was I really worth convincing at this point? I could hear her feet shuffling closer to me and I'd yet to turn to face her.

"All you've ever done is walk away. See it or not."

It was the last thing she said before I walked away toward the greater darkness. Truet didn't try to stop me and I never looked back.

CHAPTER FORTY
The Middle House

There was a small house at the end of a tight alley, tucked between two taller, ramshackle buildings. You wouldn't even notice it walking by, but it was there. Faint voices began to call out to me until they became a constant angelic hum in my ear.

I was standing before the house and reached my hand out to turn the doorknob. When I did a *pop* of dust cracked out of the door's rusted hinges, likely from not having been opened for years. I pushed the door open and stepped inside. At first it seemed normal enough. There was a kitchen with pots and pans hanging from a rack in the ceiling above an iron stove, long abandoned plates and dinnerware sat hosting dust on a small wooden table and across from that was another door, slightly propped open leading to what I assumed was a cellar. Off the kitchen was a living space with one single bedroom behind that. Fallen timbers from the roof caved in at the back of the living room barring the entrance to the bedroom, so I didn't even bother making my way toward it. I didn't have time to clear them out, plus my glass-pierced hand was now fully numb and feeling useless.

I cursed out loud to no one except the empty ghost-house. I could hear the voices of the Deluge echoing throughout the Cairns. They couldn't be far behind.

I had to be in the deep center of the Cairns. I felt it. Something about this house, but a quick glance around offered no clues until the cellar door creaked open a smidgen wider.

"All right, why the hell not." I said. "Cellar it is."

I sneaked down the stairs, careful not to trip and end up ass over elbows at the bottom. I could cry out for the Deluge, but at this point they'd likely just kill and leave me here. Out of sight, out of mind.

Once I reached the bottom I noticed the walls of the cellar were wet, moist, dripping with some sort of briny smelling foul liquid. Running my finger along one of the walls caused it to shimmer, so I quickly pulled back and decided not to touch anything.

There was a door across the cellar. Narrow and tall, unusually tall. It was carved out of a red wood and had worn down carvings from over its entire face. Time had worn the carvings down to small ridges and hills in the red wood, making it almost impossible to tell what it once was. A forest perhaps with something in the middle? A man with a crown? Black tentacles or maybe smoke rising from the earth? Hell if I knew.

Going against what my body wanted, I opened the door, after all it was only a cellar. Darkness stood before me like a great wall. I'd never seen anything like it before. It was as if it wasn't there, but something was there. I know, it didn't make sense to me either.

I stepped through the door and felt my way through with no light to guide me. All I had was my hand on one of the walls, my fingers guiding me along broken brick, then rough-cut stone until it smoothed all the way out and I felt no more crevices or cracks in the wall. The walls opened up as I went deeper, the ceiling rose above me. At first I was able to reach up and touch the ceiling, which I'll not lie, it gave me a small sense of relief to be in such a confined darker space, but now as it opened further up I had the sense of dread tugging me to turn around.

I took one final step and stopped. The world before me opened up into a great and flat plains. It was day here, with no clouds and nothing but a dull gray sky stretching out in every direction. Tall brown grass blew in a slight breeze like waves lapping on a shore. A sweet, rotten smell filled the air.

A man stood several paces from me, facing away, looking at a ruined city on the far horizon. He slowly turned toward me, then started walking.

His features shifted. I was barely able to focus. Try to open your eyes underwater and look at someone. It was like that. He was everything all at once until finally he was standing in front of me as just a man.

I looked up at the man, but he looked past me at the door I'd just came through and kept walking.

"They took everything from me," I whispered. I don't think I spoke to the man, but more to myself. A confession as to why I was here.

The man walked beyond me.

When I had a chance to turn and look back the direction I came from, I could see a cyclopean stone archway over a narrow crack in the flat side of a cliff. Had I looked up when stepping out I would have noticed the archway, but my eyes were on the plains before me stretching far into the staggering nothing. The cliff bleed up into a gray and brutal mountain range. Endless hills rolled out from the mountains in both directions, but behind me empty flatness. The vast prairies. It was hot, hotter than it should be for this time of year, but then again I had the feeling I wasn't even in Charleston anymore or anywhere near the Blue Ridge. I thought this must be Hell.

I turned my eyes back toward the horizon. Past the distant prairies, where the tall grasses faded into desert and there stretched the ruined city. Heat rose from the sands and there was another figure. Uniquely tall against the black silhouette of the city.

Not a figure, a statue. Unmoving. It rose from the sands and all around the base of the statue were people. And, a little girl. She turned toward me. I felt myself moving forward.

The little girl smiled at me, bent and she waved.

She was unfamiliar. I smiled back.

Then the little girl frowned and pointed behind me. Beyond me.

CHAPTER FORTY-ONE
Hallowed Was Thy Name

A voice.

A voice brought me back.

It was the voice of the man trapped in the gray Hell with me. Trapped? No. Too late I realized the door I'd come through in the Cairns had once been sealed on the Charleston side, and I'd left it wide open. I'd broken the seal.

The voice spoke again.

"Tell me, the door. Is it open?" the man's voice wasn't harsh, it wasn't awful, or powerful. It was gentle. Soothing.

I nodded.

I could see him better now, focused and no longer shifting. He was only a man, thin, but standing a shoulder and head above me. Unkempt, and an unruly wave of dark brown hair hanged down low over his kind, raised eyebrows, waiting for me to answer. His dark eyes held such a sadness, I found forgiving. He looked exhausted. A beaten man.

He wore a stained white undershirt with black wool breeches held up high above his belly by suspenders. One hand held a thick black jacket and in his other hand a black short brim hat, which was smashed mostly flat. He patted it, fluffing it back up before slicking his hair back and placing the hat on his head. The man looked like he'd been dressed for a funeral.

"Nathaniel Faire, but known as Fair to my friends," he said, taking my hand. "I am having quite a rough time." His smile was gently depressing. "I wonder, are you a friend?" His smile finally faded away as he waited.

Fair dropped my hand and shoved me aside, not hard, but enough to move me entirely. He then turned away from me and narrowed his eyes toward the horizon, no longer concerned with the likes of me. I was no more a threat to this man than a gnat was to me, and he knew that.

"You…" whispered Fair.

Under the archway to the Cairns I could see another figure standing. I thought it to be a salvation to guide me and pull me from the wrong I was intending in this Hell. The dark outline of his body was faint against the dull gray sky behind him, but he was there. Low the Kind was coming. The Keening itself appeared to pull through the stone archway toward Low, surrounding him. He was doddering, frail and thin, wearing an old Deluge Chancil cassock. He had a stark white beard that ended just below his chin and long white hair, slicked back over his livery spotted head. The darkness from the reaching long arm of the Keening flowed around Low as if he were guiding it.

I stood next to Fair Nathaniel and waited for Low the Kind to reach us.

I took a moment to just breathe. I decided to see how this would play out. I exhaled.

Fair cocked his head and looked at Low as if he were a parent trying to understand an upset child. The smallest hint of a smile cracked his lips. "You didn't create this place, did you? No more than you sealed up the gates with your towers."

Low the Kind lunged forward, hands held before him reaching for Fair, but he was slow, he was too slow. I didn't know what Low's plan was, but it was a disaster. He tripped before he reached Fair and fell to his knees.

Fair approached him and knelt, holding his hand out for Low, "You're just a tool for them." Low reached for it, but Fair dropped his hand before Low could take it. Then, he stood and walked behind Low placing his hands on the old Hallowfulk's shoulders. "I know what it's like for your kind here," he added, before reaching around Low's neck with one arm. "Worse than senseless things."

Fair's face grew grim as he squeezed. The Hallowfulk made no effort to fight back at first, then I began to see how insubstantial old Low was. He tried to move his legs out, he tried to pull Fair's arm away from his neck, but he was weak.

Low's body went limp in Fair's arms. And he dropped him.

It was over within a breath.

Fair Nathaniel turned his attention toward the stone archway and walked across the plains toward his freedom. A shadow of a thing passed behind the clouds over the mountains, though I could not comprehend it at the time.

"Does the tower still stand over the gate?" he asked. I don't know if he was talking to me, I didn't give him a response.

I heard a loud crack, like stone splitting, thundering across the plains.

I looked passed Fair at the stone archway. The whole damn thing was falling in on itself, threatening to seal me on this side of the Cairns.

But, I didn't feel like moving.

I wanted to just stand there and be at peace with the horror I was allowing into the city that wronged me so many times. There was nothing left. Nothing left.

My knees wanted to buckle. I wanted to be on the ground, just looking up at the sky. So calm. And the desert with the nice little girl smiling at me.

One half of the stone archway had collapsed and the other side was soon threatening. I didn't know what it would mean if it fell, but the massive stones would block the narrow crack in the cliffs, making it impossible to get through. The Keening lingered around the archway, then reeled back in on itself as if injured, fleeing back through. There were no more shadows here in the plains, no more darkness for it to hide in.

It took but a strained moment to reach the archway. Looking up, I ask a small word of favor from Burrow that the stones wouldn't fall on me as I trotted by. I'll be damned if that archway didn't collapse as soon as I was through and on my way through the narrow crack, working my way back through the dark tunnel.

My clothes were in shambles, but I felt no shame. My skin was bleeding from multiple gashes, but I felt no pain. I climbed up the cellar stairs back into the abandoned house.

Fair wouldn't be that far ahead.

CHAPTER FORTY-TWO

At The Hanging Of Rye O'Keefe

"Devils!" yelled a voice over the slow murmuring hum of a crowd. My head was cradled in my knees, but I picked it up when I recognized the voice as Anrose.

I'd been sitting on the roof of the Perky Daughter watching the city below, waiting for any sign of what was to come, if anything. But, so far nothing.

There was a sky above me. A familiar sky. Slightly cloudy with errant beams of sun light striking through like spears through a shield. An otherwise lovely day.

I could hear a low rumbling of a gathering crowd not far from Washmaid, but I didn't want to be a part of it. All I wanted was to be alone.

The Deluge had won. They'd emptied the

Undergrowth, Washmaid Row and Harklow Down as Low the Kind had wanted. Truet was his blade and she'd cut Charleston deep before it knew it was bleeding out. But what was it Fair Nathaniel said there at the end? Low was just a tool for them?

"Depravity!" Anrose cried.

I climbed from the Perky Daughter and began to walk toward his voice.

There was a wrongness in the city. I could smell it. Even in Harklow Down houses seemed like empty lots, abandoned. Lanterns glowed a dim bluish light and swayed to no wind.

I stopped where Harklow Down bled awfully close to Hawker Square.

The crowd was gathered in Hawker Square around large, wooden gallows. It was mostly a quiet crowd, listening to the words from the Second Chancil of the Deluge. They were there to mourn in their own solemn way the last threads being cut to the world they once had known as normal. This was to be the new normal. Public humiliation, excepting defeat and execution. Admitting wrong before the throws of half closed eyes and silent voices. They weren't there to protest. They were there to give up.

Anrose stood in the center of the gallows wearing a full suit of wicked armor as blinding plumes of light flowed from him like smoke. The armor he wore was styled medieval, a dark steel breastplate with even darker etched imagery of a beast I still struggle to envision, an awful thing, a flying thing consuming the dead with longed tentacled legs and bulbous, wide and looking eyes. Below the beast across Anrose's chest, was the gilded gold image of Low the Kind, palms together in prayer. Faces in anguish lined the bottom of the armor, as if Low were the only thing that stood between them and the awful sky beast.

"Wickedness."

The next word Anrose spoke. His voiced echoed across the square. I got the sense he knew I was there in the crowd and he was speaking for me alone.

Keefie was brought up the gallows and knelt in the middle, her hands were bound behind her back and she had her head down. Her hair no longer held the youth and springiness it usually did, but looked frail, torn in places from her scalp. She was wearing some sort of sack, covering her entire body from neck to ankle so as to show no skin. I didn't want to think about what her flesh would look like under that sack. Raw and purple, red with bloody slashes going across her once snow skin.

A lonely noose swayed at the back of the wooden podium. There was to be a hanging.

"We have tried to offer a chance for this one to *reclaim* the innocence she once had before giving herself away to sin," Anrose continued. "And I will offer it one final time. A plea to her, here before all of you." Did he look my way?

Anrose walked one circle around Keefie before stopping directly behind her. He looked toward the crowd where several people shook their heads 'no'.

I moved through the crowd watching, keeping my eye

on Keefie, hoping beyond Burrow that she would glance up just enough for me to see her. I wanted to offer her any sort of comfort, but she never looked up.

Anrose was at the front of the podium when he said, "We've tried and tried, O' Low how we've tried to reason with this one. Her name is Rye O'Keefe and she is sin. She is depravity. She is a wickedness *this* city can't afford to have any longer." Anrose waved his arms open toward the city as if presenting it. "Look, in these past few months what I - what *we* have accomplished. No more filth runs along the city streets. Murders, theft, lust, immorality, jealousy, all words for the same thing. Hate."

"You have noticed that the Keening has grown. That is a good thing. Do not be afraid of the reaching darkness. It searches for the beacon of sin and extinguishes it." Anrose started pacing around, looking down and out at the crowd. "What comes from the Cairns only wants to protect us. Do not be afraid of it. Look upon me? Do I look afraid?"

I pushed my way through the tight throng of people toward the podium. Toward Anrose. Toward Keefie.

Pausing, I glanced down toward my feet. Swirls of darkness gathered in a low cloud just above the ground. I felt it inside my mind asking, *where is he?* The Keening was searching for him, all the way from the Cairns it was trying to find Fair Nathaniel.

Anrose looked down at the crowd. Then, directly at me.

His eyes grew wide. With fear? Good. Fuck em'.

"This is the only way I can get you to listen!" He

yelled after seeing my face.

Rangers of the Crossed Iron moved from the crowd and stepped up to the podium, surrounding Anrose and Keefie.

With the Keening swirling around me, I'd appeared the devil Anrose always knew I was.

The crowd around the podium grew hush at the realization there were clouds of darkness gathering around their feet as the Keening reached further out and filled its way into Hawker Square.

No one moved.

No one took a breath.

A woman standing next to me covered her eyes with her hand, then with her other she pulled her child closer to her body in a hug.

The darkness was on everyone.

The Keening was on the podium, around Keefie and around Anrose. Around his Rangers of the Crossed Iron.

People around me were pulled to the ground by dark tentacles, pressed into the cobblestone by unseen hands. Black, shifting clouds of things moved in the sky above us, blocking out the sun. Shadowy Cairnborn people appeared, then disappeared in the undulating clouds of pure, pitch black terror that moved through Hawker Square. Were the Cairnborn moving inside the darkness? Was the Keening allowing them to move freely, far from the Cairns? Which I assumed was a prison for them? It was working *with* them.

Either way, the two moved, the Keening and Cairnborn as if one, pulling people into the black spaces, leaving nothing behind but death.

And all around me Hawker Square was consumed by the Keening.

All because of me.

I'd been to the depths of the Cairns and survived without going mad.

I saw into that Hell and released what it had sealed inside.

I bound toward Anrose, who was busy kicking a young girl in the face as she tried to climb onto the gallows to escape the Keening from snatching her away.

It was useless though. The Keening wrapped around the girl's leg with a dozen reaching hands and pulled her back down into its writhing, flowing black. When the darkness moved away, the girl was dead, poked full of open and bloody holes. Anrose's eyes must have been as wide as mine, but his were delight whereas mine were probably something you'd see and call *absolute terror*.

The Keening snaked up toward me as I ran across the gallows toward Keefie, who had managed to squirm her way toward the edge in an attempt to back away. Anrose ran to meet me and in the middle of the gallows we were bound to collide.

A flowing stream of oily darkness wrapped itself around his leg. It was just enough to cause him pause. I bound myself sideways away from the armored Anrose and let my weight instead crash fully into Keefie. She looked up at the last second and met my eyes before I slammed into her and we both went off the side of the gallows, crashing hard into the brick streets of Hawker Square.

It took a moment of a breath before I was on my feet again standing above Keefie untying her arms. She stood up and threw her arms around me, but I pushed her back and said, "Later."

I saw a small chance, an opening in the parting crowd behind where the Keening had already torn its way through and I took it.

I pulled Keefie behind me by her hand. She was weak and could barely keep my stride, but yet on I pulled. I wasn't going to let her go again.

The Keening stopped its bloody massacre in front of us and reared up like a snake about to strike. Watching me. Waiting.

I held Keefie's hand, pulling her as we ran past people trying desperately to flee Hawker Square. I tried not to think about what terror I just brought on these poor people.

I didn't glance back to see. I kept running.

I kept holding Keefie's hand and running.

That's when I heard him.

Anrose, from the gallows.

"Shoot her!" he yelled.

One thing I had yet to notice because my eyes had been focused on Keefie, were the Deluge soldiers littered throughout the reeling crowd.

Three of them looked toward us as we ran and their wicked Deluge Winchesters came out.

Since Keefie was in the rear she took the brunt of the

shot and she fell limp immediately.

My hand couldn't hold hers anymore.

I looked down at a gaping tear fresh in my forearm like a black flower bleeding red roots.

"Again!" I heard Anrose call. I glanced up in time to see he was off the gallows now, pushing his way toward Keefie and I, yelling for the three Deluge to let their rifles loose once again. The Deluge hesitated for a moment.

Keefie was on her knees, crawling forward on the blood-slicked bricks. Her head was hanging down. Three bullet holes bleed from the back of her legs, two in her calf and one under her ass. The first three shots had all stuck their target. Keefie wasn't going to walk out of here.

I reached back out to Keefie, but she couldn't take it. Another bullet punched her in her shoulder and she went down. Face cracking into the bricks. From this volley, it was the only shot that struck her, but it was the one that ended her flight from Hawker Square.

I looked up. Again, Deluge levered their rifles and aimed them toward us. Five of them now, as two more Deluge joined.

They motioned for me to stop running. Give up and get on the ground. One of the Deluge was taken by a strand of the Keening pulling him away from his comrades. They'd had no more luck not getting murdered by the Keening than everyone else. Merely pawns they were and as far as I could tell with my dealings in the Keening, it gave fuck all to what it consumed regardless of how loyal the Deluge were to Low. Maybe the Keening was just a tool of the Deluge, but if you starve and poke an animal with a stick long enough, soon it will start thinking it might not like it.

I shook my head "no" at the Deluge aiming at me.

The sound of a bullet whizzed by my head. Son of a bitch shot at me. Cowards, all of them.

A shot hit Keefie's body lying on the ground, in her arm, sending up a small splash of blood.

I dropped to my knees and started pulling Keefie's body away from Hawker Square.

I couldn't get far.

More bullets punched at the brick close to my feet.

With gun shots, the already panicked crowd of people now made it much harder for the Deluge to aim their rifles at us. One man next to me took a bullet to the chest when he stopped to help pull Keefie. He was dead before he hit the ground. His old man eyes looked up at me as if to say sorry, but why was he sorry? He'd only tried to help. Maybe he was sorry for dying.

I kept pulling Keefie's arm.

I stopped moving forward and looked back at her. She wasn't moving.

I let out a rage and hate filled scream.

The sound of a horn broke in sky.

CHAPTER FORTY-THREE
The Conqueror

And there was a silence that followed.

Everything in Charleston was silent. It seemed the whole world must have been silent. For a moment the Keening retreated back to the Cairns and Hawker Square wasn't fouled with the stuff.

A rider approached Hawker Square, mounted on an imposing white horse. Behind him was the setting sun, framing him a golden crown atop his head; neither of his hands held the reigns as they both dangled down by his side, one holding the horn he'd blown as his horse slowly trotted forward through the crowd.

Nathaniel Faire had arrived. His eyes slowly surveyed Hawker Square and then he grinned.

"Hell is empty," he started, speaking to the calming crowd, "and all the devils are here."

As he trotted his horse through the crowd one of the closer women to him reached up for his hands, to touch him. "Though I am no Caliban," Fair said. "Yet, I am here. I am here."

"Do not speak to him!" Anrose cried out. "Step back to us. Step back to my Deluge!"

"Stop him!" Anrose called out again as he and the Deluge ran forward toward the man. One Deluge fired his Winchester, but the shot went wide, and for such an attack on Fair, the brave man paid with his life as the crowd surged over him, crushing him, tearing and beating him. Anrose watched in horror as the turning crowd formed a circle around him and his men. I tried to flee, but the crowd was too dense.

Fair dismounted and walked toward Anrose. None of the Deluge stepped between the two men. No one attempted to halt Fair Nathaniel. He reached out and put both his hands on Anrose's shoulder. The two of them stood this way for only a moment. Fair leaned in and whispered something in Anrose's ear. Anrose's legs wobbled and he dropped to his knees. He tossed his Winchester aside as if it burned his hands. I never found out what Fair told the Second Chancil, I don't know if I would have liked to known, but it looked like Anrose just learned a terrible truth. His eyes grew wide.

Anrose began to weep.

Fair's hand was at the crown of Anrose's head.

Anrose rocked back and forth on his knees. I was going to throw up if his head exploded. I couldn't take that right now. I buried my head in my hands and didn't watch.

I could still hear Anrose whispering, "no, no." He screamed. He howled my name as he hobbled toward me.

I screamed.

Anrose stood before me, except Anrose didn't seem to be home anymore. Anrose was gone and in his place was pure hate and rage manifesting throughout the man's body.

He fell on top of me. It took every bit I had just to hold his face away from my throat. Even my bleeding arm knew the desperation and lent a hand. But it was all for naught. The enraged Anrose was too strong. His armor bit into every inch of my skin and crushed me. He was crushing me.

He leaned down, his face close to mine. He pushed his mouth down finding mine. His horrid tongue reached into my mouth as if he were just awakened to the needs of men. Searching, penetrating. I wanted to vomup. Gloved hands like claws, tore at my skin, shredding me.

He pulled back and threw his head into my face, splitting my nose. Blood filled the back of my throat. Again, his tongue went into my mouth. Whatever Fair Nathaniel said to Anrose sent him into a rage. Was he trying to suffocate me with the bloody, wriggling thing? Was it trapped up passion from years being with the Deluge, flooding out as violence all at once toward the woman who ruined it all for him? He was an uncontrollable beast, his instincts had fallen back to becoming a feral animal, bent on nothing but lashing out from fear. I tried to tell my mouth to bite down, tear the offending tongue from his mouth but I was too panicked. Breathing was all I wanted. All I needed. Just one breath.

My eyes wanted to close. Sink into the ground. I was giving up.

I was giving up.

It's what I do.

Or, don't do I should guess. I don't give up. I'm unpredictable. That's the thing with me. I'm wild and I'm untamed I'm told. All the things the Deluge had tried to torture from me over the years.

And, I just don't give a shit.

But, there. At the end, when all things were lost. What was the point of fighting? It would be so easy to just let Anrose close my eyes forever for me. I didn't even have to do anything. Just lay here and take it.

Let the peace finally take me.

I had a plan. And this time it was to surrender.

I let my head loll to the side as Anrose continued to rage on me with his pent up hate.

My body jerked.

I could feel Anrose ripping away at my flesh, but I didn't care. His furious hands were all over me.

Fair Nathaniel, a man I'd met only moments ago, put an aggression in Anrose that he aimed toward me. And, I was to feel every bit of it.

His eyes bulged.

A dagger - one of two daggers - pierced out of

Anrose's mouth. The other dagger reached around the front of his neck, spilling his life blood down on me as it was dragged across his throat.

He was still twitching when he was pulled off and pushed to the side. Anrose's body lay on the ground, looking up at the sky, pulsing his last life's breathes. Only it wasn't Anrose anymore. Fair's words had brought something from the man, turned him into pure and violent rage.

"Get up," a voice spat.

Truet was standing over Anrose pulling her dagger from the back of his neck.

"As much as I hate you, I'm not going to leave you here," Truet said, only slightly kinder this time. "You're going to help me fix this."

"I knew it wasn't because you loved me," I said, spitting on the ground. It hurt to talk. I didn't want to fix this.

I leaned on Truet.

Someone grabbed me by the arm where I'd been shot and I winced, almost passing out.

I looked up at Samyel. He held both of my arms tight and shook me. He was not wearing anything to distinguish himself as a Deluge, which I was thankful for. I'd grown fond of the lad and will, to this day, maintain that I held no ill will for anything he'd done or had yet to do toward me.

"Conley, what are you doing?" asked Samyel, catching his breath. "You're shot."

"Saving the day from the Deluge, what does it look like?" I hissed, trying to grin. "It's just grazed, bullet's not in my arm, it's fine. I'm fine."

Samyel finally let his hands drop from mine. "A man fled from here riding a horse. I've never - I've never seen a horse like that. And people were following along after him." Samyel said, his voice broke away in panic, unusual for him. Usually he was as stoic as a brave young man could be, especially one that had faced as many terrors as he had, but seeing Fair Nathaniel, trembled the lad's steady resolve. Something about the way Fair moved through the crowd, calming them, yet inciting them into dissent. It was okay, I'd twice pissed my pants by then.

"That was Nathaniel Fair," Truet said, looking at me. "Thank your friend for that. I tried to stop her. We all did. Anrose is dead."

"People are losing their minds. Deluge are fighting as best they can, but there are too many Cairnborn and they no idea who to even fight. The people following Nathaniel… they're fighting for him. Protecting him like the possessed." Samyel put his arm under me to help Truet support my weight.

I pulled away. "I'm fine," I said.

"Where is Fair? Where has he gone?" Truet asked. She let Samyel take over holding me erect, but the truth was I didn't really need it.

"Washmaid. Some Deluge there set up a blockade to try to slow him, but he rode that horse right through it," Samyel said.

I hesitated before saying, "He's going to the Cistern."

"The Cistern? Why?" Truet asked.

"He mentioned a tower and a gate. Asked if was still

standing. There's only one tower that I know of."

I was standing on my own now. I stopped to glance back at Hawker Square, it was in ruins. The amount of dead there was staggering and I faltered, stepping away from the place, thinking about what I'd done. About the horror I'd brought Keefie. I wouldn't be able to find her, even after all this was over.

Truet was still looking at me.

CHAPTER FORTY-FOUR
The Battle Of Charleston, West Virginia

Rain fell from high and heavy clouds.

As we crossed Harklow Dow into Washmaid Row it became clear the city was lost. Cairnborn tore through buildings, breaking windows, dragging people out of their hiding places. It was over.

An older Deluge lad was pinned to the ground by three Cairnborn. All women and much smaller than the Deluge, but their hate-filled rage overwhelmed him. They tore at him, ripping his surcoat and finally skin. One bite his nose off and swallowed it. She swallowed the whole damned thing.

He probably deserved it as most Deluge did.

Truet stopped and noticed me watching the Deluge man's suffering.

"Is this what you wanted?" she growled. "You selfish bitch."

"Selfish?" I said, my voice rose at her.

"I fought to end all this. To end what the Deluge has done to this city, my city for decades. I fought to stop this," I said. "Everything I've ever had was taken from me and you are going to call me selfish. Fuck you. Fuck the whole Deluge. They brought this one. You did, you brought this one. If you'd just left well enough alone-"

"We fought to keep Nathaniel sealed away!" Truet returned. "We've always fought for that! Low was the one holding this all back with the Cairns! Why can't you see that?"

"Because I don't want to. I don't want to think that this world was protected by something so corrupt that whatever it was sealing away could somehow be worse."

"To trap something *evil*, we had to be something *worse*," Truet said. Her voice cracked. Then, she looked up at me. "We are *not* bad."

"It doesn't matter now," Samyel interrupted. He stood with his Enfield ready in his hand, barely scrapping the brick at his feet. For the first time since seeing him, I noticed that he was covered in blood. How many Cairnborn had he already killed? "But, we can still go after Fair," he added.

"Why would Fair be interested in the Cistern?" I asked, mentally judging how much I actually wanted to be involved in this foolishness anymore. There wasn't much left for me, but to run away at this point. "What gate was he talking about?"

"Low only knows, I don't even want to consider it." Truet threw both of her twin daggers into the chest of a Cairnborn rushing toward us, a small boy with long hair covering most of his face. The daggers put him down instantly, like he ran face first into a tree as his hair flipped forward further than his little body. She bent to retrieve her weapons.

Truet faltered. "Low trapped Nathaniel in the Cairns for a reason and taught us that if he were ever released…" She looked at me when she said that last part. "I've studied all this, I've read all the books, but I've no idea. I got so close to finding answers, then just came up with dead ends. I know that Cisterns are unique, old, all of them were built for a reason. I just don't know why. And, now I probably won't. You killed us all."

Okay, it stung a little to hear that. The terror of that truth was starting to pull at my heart a little, but that pull wasn't going to bring Keefie back. It wasn't going to bring anything back. I knew this. I looked at Samyel, the last honest and decent thing I had left in my life at that very moment. The last person to truly stand beside me.

"L'fowl knew," Samyel said.

"And, you murdered L'fowl," I glared at Truet. "He could have helped us."

"It doesn't matter anymore," Truet said under her breath.

"It does. He knew what was under the Cistern. He

knew," I said.

Truet loosened her belt buckle, then tightened it, tucked her twin daggers into their sheaths and pulled her hair back. She put the mask of Black Abby to rest on the top of her head, then looked at me.

"*You* killed L'fowl..." whispered Samyel.

"We're wasting time," I said, pointing at Fair as he rode his horse past a street in front of the Cistern crowded with Cairnborn and Deluge. More people followed Fair as he reached out from his horse with his gangling arms and brought them into his flock. I say that because they'd become sheep following their good shepherd, willing to throw themselves between Cairnborn and the Deluge holding the Cistern. Anything to keep Fair safe with his sweet words, and a promise of breaking free from the Deluge. They'd seen Fair standing against the Deluge and offer protection against the Cairnborn, and through him they found sanctuary.

"No, no more," Samyel growled. He held his Enfield musket before him and checked the bayonet's edge. Then he ran toward the Cistern.

"Go after him!" Truet yelled, looking at me.

"What?" I asked, barely aware as I watched the lad running away from us.

"Fix what you've done," she said. "Go help the last person worth helping. You love him don't you?"

I don't love anyone.

Never have. We'll talk about Pynes again later, but even I've come to realize that what happened by the river Kanawha that night with Pynes was hardly considered love.

Dirty lust maybe, enough to rustle my *jimmies*, but hardly love. I did *love* what he did to me, yes. But, what young lady wouldn't love being ravaged by the river as such. No, not love.

"What? Of course not," I said.

Truet paused and looked at me, cocking her head. "You don't?"

"No. He's brave and stupid and I admire the lad's tenacity, but love? Absolutely not. He was only half decent in bed in fact. He has a lot to learn." I was rambling. I was slightly afraid, okay?

"You're impossible," Truet growled. She ran after Samyel, twin daggers back in her hands as the mask of Black Abby bounced up and down on the back of her head.

We were completely abandoned here in Charleston to the quickness in which this horror was happening in our streets.

Crossing the street, we stopped when we saw a red head sitting alone outside a vacated saloon, The Briny Pickle. What was visible of her body was criss-crossed in scars and she had two black eyes. Dangling from her swollen lip was a rolled cigarette, dried blood soaked into the paper. One finger on her left hand swung loose like a door on a broken hinge. She was leaning back in a chair with her long, thick legs perched on a broken, low brick wall beside her as a pair of chickens pecked away at grains beneath her.

A Deluge, wounded and bleeding from a deep cut above his eye wandered too close to the red woman, feeling his way along the walls outside the saloon. Ale the Unhinged stood when she saw the wounded man, grabbed his collar and slammed him against the wall. Over and over she slammed her fist into the Deluge's nose until he slid down the wall, dead. She took one long puff from her rolled cigarette, smiled at us and sat back down, continuing to toss grain to the chickens pecking away.

Truet and I continued on, dodging Cairnborn as best we could as we looked for Samyel.

A knuckle of Deluge held the door to the Cistern like a dam as more and more of Fair's flock crashed into them from the steps below. The Deluge didn't know who to fight anymore, Cairnborn or the Flock, none mattered, keeping them all out of the Cistern seemed their safest bet, but the Flock was more guided. They had purpose. Fair gave them that.

We found Samyel ahead of us fighting his way through a group of Cairnborn, stabbing several in the back with his musket. When the Deluge at the entrance of the Cistern saw him, they found some reserve from Samyel's tenacity and rushed out, fighting back the closest of the Flock.

Samyel saw Fair before Truet and I did, then yelled for us. Fair Nathaniel stayed back on his horse, lingering and waiting not a full block away from the Cistern for the Deluge dam to break, allowing him to enter. Fair kicked his horse into a full gallop toward the Cistern.

I couldn't hear Samyel's words over the chaos and waters of the Kanawha River not far from us, but he waved his arms toward the direction of the Cistern's steps where two Deluge had stepped in front of Fair, occluding the entrance.

Jerme and Wilyam. The two Deluge whose regular duty was the guard the gate into Charleston stood against Fair and his Flock alone. Jerme was badly injured and holding his right arm, which was dripping blood. Wilyam stood before him, tempting Fair back with his Winchester - long out of ammo. Fair Nathaniel flicked his fingers toward the pair and his Flock rushed in at the pair of Deluge. Wilyam yelled, his scream breaking Samyel from his own fight across the street not far from the bottom of the Cistern's steps.

These lads had no hope and normally I would let the murderous deed happen. I didn't owe these two Deluge anything other than a silent prayer to Burrow hoping they die quickly rather than a long suffer.

What's two less Deluge in the world?

Samyel, however didn't share my feelings of neutrality when it came to their death. I grabbed his arm as he rushed toward the steps.

"I don't love you," I said.

"What?" He pulled away from me. He was bleeding from a gash in his head and blood pooled under his left eye.

"I barely even like you," I added.

"I barely like you either," Samyel said.

Truet circled around us, watching out for any rogue Cairnborn brave enough to approach from the shadows. Luckily for the moment, none did.

I looked back up the steps of the Cistern. The Deluge

fighting at the door were dead, strewn across the stairs in their final act attempting to stop Fair from entering.

I would pay for this the rest of my days.

"Do you both trust me?" I said, looking between Samyel and Truet toward the Cistern's entrance. It was hard to focus. Charleston was falling to ruin behind me. People I had grown to know over the years were being slaughtered.

"Absolutely not," Truet said between heavy breaths.

"Fair enough," I said.

I took Samyel's hand in mine and placed it to my chest. The rain pattered ceaselessly around us as thunder rolled over the hills of the Alleghenies. Soon, the storm would arrive.

"You don't owe me anything. And, you can hate me when this is all done," I whispered. "You're a brave lad. Braver than me, I know. I need your bravery now. You've already walked this far with me and I can't understand why."

"What would you have me do?" he asked. His voice was flat, emotionless. He'd already buried himself.

"Let's see this finished."

CHAPTER FORTY-FIVE
The Tunnel

We passed the grand entrance of the Cistern, where we found no resistance and continued across the Basin's bridge. We found three Deluge guarding over the Basin's holy water, one of them was lying unconscious on the bridge. Rain water flowed through aqueducts in the Cistern's walls pouring like hundreds of independent waterfalls into the Basin, but it was designed to never overflow. Crossing iron rods were later installed at the bottom of the Basin after a girl from Washmaid fell in during a wildly inappropriate night and never came back up. She was found on the banks of the Kanawha River about five miles south of Charleston all chewed up.

"A man went that way, down. To the basement. I…

he…he wasn't, I don't know, like the man knew where he was going. We just let him by. I'm sorry," one of the Deluge said. His companion ignored us as he wrapped a wet cloth around the fallen Deluge's head.

"There's some old rooms for storage passed the correction rooms, not much else," Truet said, holding a lantern to see down the stairs into the darkness. Not much could be heard except the rain water continuing through the aqueducts.

"The torture rooms," I corrected.

Truet didn't even bother looking back at me as she descended the stairs. Samyel and I watched as her lantern faded the further she went. We followed through the Deluge torture chambers into the storage area. Wasn't much down there except a few old waterlogged wooden crates holding Burrow knows what, but it was all rotten by then. There were a few rolls of old rugs piled in a corner, and some broken parts of a cannon sitting on a table covered with a thick layer of mucus-looking rot. No one had been down here for years.

Water was dripping from the aqueducts running along the top of the room then flowing along the floor in little streams toward an opening in the far wall.

"We have a problem with flooding down here," Truet said. "This room will completely fill with water if the Basin's drain can't handle all the water. It used to be for - " She stopped. "It used to be something else."

The idea that so much water was directly above us paused me for a moment.

"Are those stairs?" I asked as I walked closer to the hole in the wall and peered down. After four steps down the stairs abruptly ended and dropped down into nothingness. It was awfully dark and I couldn't see a bottom, but I could hear the water not too far down. I would have guess if I tied my lantern to a rope and lowered it down, it wouldn't have taken long to see the bottom, but as it stood I couldn't see it from where I was.

Truet stood next to me looking down. "I wouldn't-"

"Don't you get bored sitting in your castle all day?" I asked, smiling.

"No, not lately," Truet replied.

Once I was lowered down below where the stairs broke off I gathered myself a moment. This was foolish. Samyel knelt at the stairs and peered down.

A narrow tunnel leading further into the darkness greeted me. I started into it.

I made a mental note of how many steps I took into the tunnel, reaching my hands out until I felt the slick rock walls. The walls felt smooth and natural, likely from water running through the tunnels for hundreds of years. My fingers traced odd lines and shapes in the walls, but it was too dark to make out what they were. As I walked deeper into the tunnel, I noticed some of the lines felt not quite as deep in the rock as others. The further I went the more shallow the cuts in the rock were, like some ancient creature was clawing its way through the tunnels until it reached a small, wooden door. It creaked open when I pushed, and I had to kneel to pass through. My lantern wasn't doing anything to illuminate much further than a few yards into the room. The flame flickered until it finally went out. I rattled the lantern, hoping the kerosene would reignite the flame, but I didn't have anything to light it with, so my hope faded. Have you ever been in something so dark it hurt your eyes to keep them open? That closing them was somehow not as dark as leaving them open? It was that way. I grew instantly paranoid, disconcerted. Was something follow me?

Faint noises ahead, voices maybe, continued to guide me into the darkness. I was surrounded by pitch black but could still feel the solid ground, which was something, so I kept pushing myself to continue hoping I'd eventually reach Fair and he'd have light. What a conversation that would be, "Sir, may I borrow your only light to find my way out of here? Go about your business please."

I closed my eyes, they were useless here.

"What ever you're planning, make it quick."

I jolted, then turned to see Truet crawling up behind me pushing a lantern in front of her. Samyel was following her, along with two more Deluge. I didn't scold them for following me, I didn't care. I was overwhelmed to just see the light again.

When I looked back forward, my eyes guided by the light of Truet's lantern I was able to see a massive cavern opened up before us. I stepped through the door.

Truet was through next. She used her oil lantern to light a row of primitive torches along the wall where the modernity of the Cistern faded into old stone walls.

The two Deluge joined Truet in lighting the wall

lanterns.

We were deep under the Cistern in a room very few could have known about. Room hardly described it. It was a cavern expanding well past the walls of the Cistern above us and even further still. How far it went I didn't know, but if I were to venture a guess it was at least to Harklow Down. Large columns reached up to the ceiling throughout the entire cavern.

Truet approached slow until she was standing next to me looking at what I was looking at. A shrine in the dark, hard to see even in the faint glow of both of the lanterns.

Truet turned to look at me. She had no words at first, until the look I gave her finally gave her permission to ask. "What?" Truet asked. "What is this?"

The shrine was set back in a hole a few feet deep into one of the columns. Using a torch I pulled from one of the columns when I first climbed in, I lit a few half melted candles around the shrine. In the shrine, sitting on a small throne built of ancient stone and clay was the body of a young girl, eyes shut with her head cocked to one side wearing a crown of daisies.

"Burrow…" I whispered.

CHAPTER FORTY-SIX

My Own Princess Of Moss And Mushrooms

From behind me Truet said, "Conley? I don't understand. Who is she?"

I sighed.

I dropped my head to the forlorn body of the little girl known as Burrow. The crown of daisies she wore upon her head that night we met all those years ago hadn't rotted a day. She looked like a princess of her own small kingdom of moss and mushrooms and bones surrounded by an unforgiving darkness, watching over whatever fresh Hell she'd found. Burrow had disappeared on me the same night Keefie killed that Ranger and the night I was with Pynes. I never saw her again to give her Beaumont-Adams revolver back.

Burrow had found a place to rest away from the awful horror of everything above. I'd falsely named her as Hallowfulk so many times because the truth was I had no one else. She filled a substantial gap I alone couldn't fill myself and I needed something more permanent than what she gave me in the few moments I'd known her. Someone I could speak to. I'd said before, the night I met her to get her Beaumont-Adams back that she'd left quite an impression on me in the small amount of time we'd spent together and that still held true. She was like no one I'd met before.

Burrow must have liked how quiet it was in the tunnels. But, I knew that peace was soon to be broken.

I set my lantern on the stone table, then looked at Truet, who was starring at my rotten princess. Flickering lantern light illuminated her confused and sad expression.

"Thank you," I whispered. I didn't know why, but it felt like a finality.

"What is she doing down here?" Truet asked.

"I barely knew her any longer than I'd known Pynes," I said. "She went missing around the same time he did…"

"I…I thought she was Hallowfulk? The way you speak of her," Truet said.

"I don't know what she is, but…I named her as such," I said.

"You can't just-"

"I can't what?"

"Stop," Samyel came between us.

I was ready to change the subject and back to the

matter at hand, the horror happening above us.

Holding my torch to see further into the cave, I noticed there were other notches carved into the other stone columns. Notches carved big enough to hold a person. There were several in fact, all of them sitting in their own little column thrones of stone and clay, looking out into the center area of the cavern. They all wore some unusual form of outfits; a panoply of ceremonial clothing. The man next to Burrow on the right wore a crown of gold and jade, with a mixture of teal and turquoise feathers fanning out of the back. His face was sunken in and hollow. On the left side of Burrow was a woman wearing a black waistcoat and a pair of black, men's trousers. She wore a black, wide brimmed hat with bleached-white bird's bones hanging from the rim, covering most of her face.

Every notch in a column held someone like that, watching, looking out over the vast room. All of them had their eyes shut, but they were watching.

I turned to see what would have their attention. What they were guardians over.

We stepped away from Burrow's shrine and I followed Truet to a massive black stone. Above the stone was an arch, carved from the same type of old rock as the arch in the Cairns; the same type of rocks that the watcher's thrones were constructed. A series of interlocking chains wrapped around the black stone, up through the arch above before finally disappearing in holes in the caverns ceiling. I held my torch up and pointed to a rough-cut, wedge stone at the top of the arch. And there, carved in the middle of the stone was the profile of an open hand facing downward.

Truet stood in amazement, she couldn't comprehend what it even meant. "Real…" was all she managed to choke out until she regained herself and added, "L'fowl knew about it. The Stone of San'ctu was under us. It was under us. But, that symbol. The hand facing down. That's not a symbol of Low. Not one I recognize."

"No, it's not. That symbol is something far, far older," I said.

"I see now why L'fowl called it the pillar of our faith. It's massive. Conley, what do you think those chains are?"

Screech.

A sound, like metal grinding on stone.

"This earthly saint, adored by this devil…little suspecteth the false worshiper," Fair Nathaniel cried from the safe darkness far into the cavern interrupting us. "The king is watching! The king is watching!"

"Stop quoting Shakespeare you asshole!" I cried back. My call echoed over the walls.

Truet smiled, "You do read."

"I hate to spoil this moment," Samyel said from behind us, startling. How long had he been standing there? "But we have a whole heap of trouble coming our way. Cairnborn found us. Coming through the tunnel."

Screech.

The sound was deafening in the cavern.

"Is this all part of your plan?" Truet guessed, looking at me. "Those chains are moving."

I grabbed Truet by the arm and faced her toward me, "Listen, we don't have a lot of time."

She pulled back some, but then let me hold her.

I pointed vaguely east and north passed the light of our lanterns, toward where I thought the Breige would be. "Take a lantern, if you're lucky, there will be a tunnel that way that leads up to the surface-"

"Stop," she started, but I shook her.

"No, listen. Go. Hurry," I looked back toward the Stone of San'ctu as its enormous mass slowly rose with each screeching of metal. The chains around the Stone tightened as they pulled it higher.

"Why would they leave chains on something they didn't want raised?" Samyel asked. Damn that was a good question I'd have to circle back around on.

Screech.

"As much as I would love to see you get what's coming, dying down here next to you wasn't part of my plan, so go," I shook her one final time before I pushed her away. She stopped and scowled at me. "Fair's going to have that thing raised real quick."

Screech.

Screech.

Screech.

The screeching of metal stopped suddenly.

"Maybe he gave up," Samyel whispered.

"No, look," I said, pointing toward the Stone of San'ctu. It was raised now, and a gaping hole was below it. "It's done."

Little whispers.

Screams from the hole.

Something wailed.

And then, in the brief moment of silence with only the slight breathing of Samyel and Truet, the thing came. Like the silence and a flash before thunder, a beast came.

It rose from the hole in the ground like ancient death, savage, blindly crashing into rock and wall.

The beast's hulking head jolted quickly, looking around the cavern as it climbed from its deep prison. Sacks of skin on its long underbelly filled and shriveled with each great breath it took. Four thin and useless legs dangled behind from its body, raking against the cavern floor as it dragged itself forward and up a wall to the ceiling with its two front legs, larger than the four unused ones. Its face was almost flat, lacking any sort of features except two abyssal-black, miserable eyes sitting in flaps of loose flesh, shifting around as they searched below. The whole thing's body, size and all (minus the weird dangling legs), reminded me of a rotting sperm whale carcass that I stumbled across once, only more wicked and more swollen with bulbous air sacks on its undercarriage. And this thing had a head. Which, whales really don't, or maybe they do, I'm no whale expert. Are they all body and tails? It smelled awful though I remember that. This thing climbing up from Hell faired no better.

I've seen the silent fear in sailor's eyes as they leave our rivers for the wide sea. I've seen what the ocean can do to man and ship. I've seen the giant beasts that lurk in the shallow waters and gulfs. And, I know what lies deeper. But, the *thing* that came from the earth's belly…I've never seen the likes of that.

It roared from the top of the cavern where it was now perched. The great beast inhaled and shimmied its bulbous body along the top of the cavern's high ceiling knocking chunks of nearby column loose. It was facing away from us, searching, but soon it would turn its head toward us. I shivered at what would come when it did. We shrank as well as we could back against the cavern's wall, not far from where we entered.

"That unsettling," I whispered.

"Yor'lfallen…"

I looked at her, then snatched her arm and pulled her into a small door in the cavern wall. It opened into a chamber large enough for us to sit. The chamber itself was a perfect cube, as perfect as I could tell, with stone benches aligned in rows facing a tall podium. Behind the podium was the same opened hand, facing down carved in the stone wall. This was a place of worship.

Samyel followed us in. For a moment things were quiet except for the scratching of the beast as it moved amongst the ceiling and the columns. its breath was heavy and steady.

"Yor'lfallen?" I asked.

"It…it translates to 'fallen worm'. I thought it was a place at first. I'm such a fool."

"You figured out your book?" I asked. "That's wonderful. It really is. What was the language? This is all very interesting by the way."

She smirked. "Hallowfulk."

"Hmm, I've never heard one speak - "

"Let alone have a written language, right," Truet finished. "It's very hard to translate without a reference."

I peaked out of our momentary haven, Cairnborn were crawling into the main cavern from the same hole we'd came in. The beast watched them from above.

"Truet you have to tell that thing to stop," I urged.

"I can't do that," she said.

"Technically, you're in charge," I reminded her. "It'll surely listen to you."

"Entire civilizations have fallen because of these… things. What can I do?"

Truet was lost, watching as the worm moved along the walls of the cavern. "The Serpent. Ammit, Gvelesphapi, Bahamut, Knucker, Apollyon…Yor'lfallen." Truet would have kept going, but I nudged her.

"Stop," I said. "I get it. You read your little book."

"Every single corner of mankind has these things in their stories," Truet was looking back at me. "The Deluge refer to this one as Reach. It's a - "

"Like the children's rhyme?"

She nodded her head. "Yeah, we tell those rhymes to scare children from doing shit like you do. *The Damning Of Yor'lfallen* was about how the Hallowfulk trapped these things…it's actually a very good book if you give it a chance. Starts off slow, but it picks up toward the end."

I knew then Truet was right, this was beyond us and

the city would be lost. Reach would rampage through the streets destroying everything once it found its way out. No one had time to flee, everything all happened so fast. I didn't know what I brought. I didn't know.

I turned back to Truet. I can't imagine how desperate my eyes must have looked, but I'm sure they matched her own.

"I know you've lived a safe life, but there's more than just what Low the Kind teaches. Just looked around you. The world can't exist under the palm of a Hallowfulk like that. What you did with Charleston in the name of Low truly scares me. But, people will follow you. Make better choices."

We sat for a moment in a quiet stillness as Reach skittered around on the ceiling.

"I would have liked to have heard Pynes play that fiddle of his one more time," I whispered. "Just one more time." It's a hard thing longing for the safety of your past. "My dad was a fiddler, though, not nearly as good as Pynes. Maybe that's what drew me to him."

"I never met my father," Truet replied. "It's funny how your life can still be guided by someone that's absent from it."

"No father, huh?" I asked. "Could explain a few things. You would have liked Pynes. Everyone did."

She frowned "Explain a few things like what?"

"Why you're so damned uptight. My dad was the wild one. The one who taught me you can't take life too serious. Mama was the worker, she cared deeply for us. So deep it hurt sometimes. I don't know if I could ever care for someone like she did for us."

"I don't know if my mother cared," Truet said. "She was-"

"We can't stay in here, the Cairnborn are getting too many," Samyel reminded us. "We have to do something soon." He was the first to crawl out of the smaller cave into the the main one to face the Cairnborn.

I looked hard at Truet for a moment, then shook my head knowing that our moment was over. I followed Samyel out. Truet after me.

I shoved her hard, away from a piece of column jolted loose. "If you run into Fair Nathaniel stick one of your blades in him for me."

Truet stood. Then, I watched as her lantern disappeared in the further black of the cavern without another word from her. There was no point. She understood my intentions better than me at the time I believe.

I crawled to where Samyel was kneeling by Burrow's shrine watching everything transpire.

"You intend to stay down here with me? To see it through?"

He only nodded.

I was overran by clawing hands and biting things. Hands and tooth tore at me. Cairnborn smothered me. Rank flesh filling my nose, filling my lungs. I was being crushed.

I couldn't breathe.

I couldn't breathe.

I couldn't breathe.

"Fight!" I heard. A faint scream, muffled by the mass of Cairnborn on top of me.

"Fight Conley! Fight!"

Samyel was out there, he too fighting for his life. Yet his concern was for me. He's too good.

"Fight damn you!" Samyel yelled again.

He's too good to die down here with me. Like this. Like a footnote in what was happening here glazed over by historians on a bored afternoon.

Facing Samyel, I could see Cairnborn were getting the better of the young lad. Samyel was outmatched by pure ferocity and primordial rage. He didn't have what Cairnborn naturally had. Instinct to murder. Fair won. His duty done. He released this Hell on us then fled.

The sheer number of Cairnborn drove Samyel further down as the lad tried everything he had to push back up with his Enfield musket.

Reach was above us, watching and waiting.

Samyel looked at me one final time. He tossed his musket my direction before disappearing into a dark chasm further into the cave. The old musket clanged to a stop just a foot away from my hand. I reached out and found its stock.

I let out a piercing sound. A scream mixed with dread. It was awful, as if my throat tore open. I coughed up a spit of blood.

Samyel was gone.

Cairnborn were at me again, this time I had the mind to pull myself up. Taking the Enfield in my hand, I stabbed everything within reach with the bayonet; I bashed where I could with the stock. It was a moment of freedom. I didn't worry about precision, grace, parrying, or any of the things that goes with fighting to preserve yourself. I was bleeding anything I could bleed. I laughed and the echo of the cave laughed back, drowning out the slaughter the Cairnborn were handing me.

But, my savagery just wasn't enough. Cairnborn swarmed me like hornets. There were just too many.

I saw Reach turning his ugly, wide open face toward me.

I backed myself toward young Burrow's grave. I thought that in my death I may as lean toward familiarity and comfort.

A small Cairnborn child wrapped his arms around my legs and tripped me. I fell back hard into Burrow's recessed tomb, toppling her frail body over. The crown of daisies on her head fell to my feet.

I yelled again, punching the Cairnborn child in the face, breaking her teeth and bleeding my knuckles. She was in her early teens I reckoned and likely would have been on the verge of woman hood, deciding if working in Washmaid Row was her destiny, but the Deluge would have stopped that I guess. Anyway, there she was with broken teeth about to die in this cave with me.

Reach inhaled.

I was on my stomach. The Enfield was on the ground next to me, out of reach. Cairnborn tore at my skin, biting my legs and clawing anything they could. My face was pressed into the stone.

I managed one arm free and reached behind my back to the weapon holstered there, pulling that Beaumont-Adams revolver with the word Worry'd carved in its barrel.

Yeah, those Breige boys searched and found Sparrow - a loss I still needed to redeem, and that gave me room to knuckle Worry'd moments before Everett exploded. Oh, well their mistake. This Beaumont-Adams was the only one in existence, so I was told and I wasn't about to just let it go. I'd tucked it away outside the Cairns before going in and meeting Anrose there planning to sell it again before all this nonsense with Fair Nathaniel happened.

As I was lying there, pondering my inevitable death I recalled Henrold saying it still worked. I asked a prayer of Burrow that it still worked.

Give me one last thing.

I put the barrel against my head.

It was my plan after all.

I would go out on my own terms.

What's the difference really?

I managed to sit up while the Cairnborn were once again distracted by Reach bellowing through the cavern. They sat calmly by, looking for him around the columns with wide and terrified eyes. They were as frightened as I.

I sat, locked in a moment of shared peace with these creatures from the Cairns, then I placed my finger on the trigger.

I wasn't waiting for the perfect moment when everything would align as I planned. I wasn't hesitating on the ending of it all. I was ready.

But.

I whispered one final and desperate word to Burrow as I looked toward her shrine. She was gone.

Then I felt a tiny hand on mine. Burrow was there with me running her hands along the length of my arm as she guided the revolver away from my temple and helped me point it toward her. She placed her forehead gently on the barrel, then looked down the side.

"Burrow's," she said. Her voice sounded so small in the enormity of what was happening.

I laughed. "Yeah…Burrow's."

"Burrow's…" she said one more time.

The Beaumont-Adams was hers, and if you looked just down the barrel, toward the cylinder you'd see her name carved on it - given you cleaned it up some of course. Maybe squint your eyes a little. It wasn't perfect, but she was a child when she carved it.

She held both of her hands on mine and guided the Beaumont-Adams toward the Stone of San'ctu. More specifically, one of the chains holding the massive rock. She tapped the revolver and made a *boom* sound, silently with her mouth.

That's when Reach's mouth-less head did something that at the time seemed completely unreasonable. It opened. A yawning maw opened like a grave toward me.

I pulled the trigger.

The crack of the bullet hitting the chain rang through the cavern. It snapped and the Stone of San'ctu broke free, swinging to one side before smashing into a column.

The cold, dark water of the Basin above us came like holy water to wash us free.

And then, my world went black.

CHAPTER FORTY-SEVEN

Out

"She's here!" I heard a familiar voice cry out.

Strong hands grabbed under my arms and tried yanking me free of whatever held my legs.

I coughed up dust and thick black water.

Sunlight warmed my eyelids.

I tried to open them, then felt a cloth wiping my face.

"Fool," I heard another voice. The voice was coming from the large man pulling at my legs. "Don't know how you survived that."

I sat up with the man's help and opened my eyes.

"Fuckin' Folks Emery," I whispered. Even my voice hurt. "I ain't owing you shit." I'd never been more thankful to hear his loud, dumb voice over me.

"Don't move," Folks said, kneeling down to my level. "That arm ain't right, that's for sure. Or that leg. If you weren't half ate by whatever the hell this is, you'd be good and buried. Saw your arm poking out…well first we saw this…*thing* wash up on the side of the river, thought to go look at it see what all the commotion was, then we saw your arm. Didn't know it was actually your arm. Just an arm. Sallow thought to pull you out when your finger wiggled." Folks was rambling, he was nervous, or holding back tears. I couldn't quite figure yet.

Sallow crouched next to Folks, cutting away at what I assumed was Reach's mouth with a long parring knife. When he was through the fat, bulbous part of the lip, he dragged me out. A bile covered, lump of person.

"The Cistern collapsed. And everything around it all the way up to Washmaid one way. All the Undergrowth. Half the Breige. All gone," Sallow said.

Folks and Sallow worked together to get me cleaned off, then lay me on a rock. I held still feeling completely broken. We were far from Charleston sitting on a rocky bend by the Kanawha River. A massive black lake now sat where a good portion of the city used to be.

Sallow handed me Worry'd and for a moment I wondered how lucky it washed out of the cavern with me. "S'was inside that creature with you. You were holding on to it still when we dragged your upper half out," he said.

"It was gross," Sallow added as he sat down next to me.

"I wonder if Truet made it out?" I coughed.

"Who?" Folks asked.

"I-", I started, then looked at Folks and Sallow and started to cry. "I'm sorry," I said, as best I could.

"For what?" Folks asked.

"For all of this," I vaguely pointed toward the black lake. The city of Charleston was no more. Their home. All of it. Everyone they knew. No one would have survived that.

"Now," Folks said. "Can we talk about what ever the hell this thing you were inside is."

I rested my forehead on Folks' shoulder and threw up.

CHAPTER FORTY-EIGHT
Hobbled

I hobbled - best I could - up a small, mountain trail through a low valley. Charleston was far behind me now. Colorful flags stood in a line along the trail; red, yellow, blue, greens, clapping in the wind. At the end of the trail was a small log cabin.

Charleston was lost. Catastrophically.

Nine months had passed and I still felt broken. Turns out I'd broken my other arm - the one not torn with a bullet hole. Broke my leg too. And several ribs. Lot of my blood got mixed down there with dust on the floor of the cavern and in the guts of Reach, that bastard devil from the ground. It took everything I had to make it up this trail, but I did the walk every day. I had to keep moving.

I didn't know if I'd ever really feel whole again.

Something was lost other than a home.

I got what I wanted in the end.

The Cistern was vanished under the collapsed section of the city, along with everything around as Folks had initially assessed. Couldn't really be said at what loss of life there was. A lot.

The Deluge in Charleston were as buried as the Cistern, what remained headed out of town before the dust even settled. Says a lot about them I'd say.

It was the regulars of Harklow Down, the workers and tradesmen, whores and get-abouts that stuck around, hoping to salvage Charleston enough to keep it worth living around the now so named Black Reach Lake. Charleston wouldn't prosper long around those dark shores, but the good people were up to trying.

My part was through. I got rid of the Deluge Chapter in Charleston and hopefully gave the people a proper way to start living as they always wanted. Away from the eyes of Low the Kind and his damned Deluge.

Reach was cut further into pieces and burned after a bout of convincing and double bribing, just to be sure it was dead, seeing as how it came from the belly of Hell, seemed the proper thing to do. Sallow complained every inch of cutting the beast apart as Folks Emery and I sat on a rock and watched.

Fair Nathaniel was never found. It was as if he were never even there. He vanished just as Truet and Samyel did, forever somewhere under that dark water I reckon.

I finally reached the cabin at the end of the trail and knocked on the door.

"I don't know why you knock," a girl's voice came from inside.

I opened the door and Keefie sat at a table tucked into the corner of a small kitchen. The scars from her wounds were glaringly obvious under her loosely tied blouse and skirt, which I know she felt self-conscious about by the way she pulled the skirt closed as I walked in. She grimaced.

"Still hurts?" I asked.

"Only as a reminder I suppose," she answered.

"I already told you, nothing new to me if you walked around here naked until you feel better. Nobody around but us hens you know," I said. I sat down at the table with her and stared for a moment. "Nothing I haven't seen anyway."

"Bah, I know," she said. "Just feels different. Can't explain it."

"Me either," I added.

"We could probably still get Foxmaiden going. Head to Boston or maybe out West in another month or two." she said. "Think I could still get work looking like this?"

"Looking like this?" I sort of laughed. "Keefie, just because you have a few extra bullet holes now doesn't mean you can't find work. Might be tougher to flex over halfway, but all the same. You'll heal soon enough and be right as ready to start earning some coin again. Just give it time."

"I don't want to go down to Charleston ever again," she admitted.

"Me either," I said.

"What'll we do then? Can't just stay up here in the mountains like this. I love you to death, but I'm getting sick of you."

I laughed.

Keefie flicked a bread crumb off the table. "Where did Folks and the lads head after we left the city? I never got to toss Tapper a proper thanks for dragging me out of Hawker Square."

"Don't know. West I think like he used to talk about, away from the mountains. Nevada maybe. Good place to be these days. I'm sure you get a chance to thank Tapper someday, though I bet he'd only say your word is enough."

Keefie continued, "He had something magic about him I never really noticed until I looked up and he was carrying me out of Charleston. He carried me all the way up to this cabin, took care of me you know? Cleaned me up, sewed me up, made sure I was okay. Kind of handsome. In a way."

I let her trail off.

I took a long inhale, then let it go. I stood up and went back to the cabin's door and looked out at the gaming trail going back down the mountain, low into the valley.

I had to walk it again.

"Good morning dear," I whispered.

"You're here to kill me," Henrold said. He hushed his voice, not daring to raise it for fear of Sparrow dragging across his neck, which I held tight against his throat.

I was lying next to him, snuggled up against his back in

a bigger spoon kind of fashion, my Sparrow holding hand draped over his waist and snaked up through his arms, ending at his neck. My breast drew rogue shapes along his bare back as we both breathed our breaths slowly, in and out, waiting for the other to move.

"Henrold Nanibold Merigold," I said, propping myself up on one elbow to get a better look at the man. "You betrayed me."

I felt him growing stiff from having me pressed in next to him. I moved one leg over his body, then I moved my knife from his neck to his cock.

"Tell me, were you with the Deluge the whole time? That speech you gave, the night we met, you didn't mean any of it." I let Sparrow explore the man's undercarriage as he rolled to his back and I moved to be on top of him. I was a tease, but a man thinks less, opening up more when the blood leaves his top half.

"I see you found your blade," he said, trying to turn around to steal a glance at me.

"I found it while I was digging through your stuff. So thank you for bringing it along in your attempt to relocate. Now, I do have to apologize for my appearance, but well, I thought it would be funnier this way. I also thought to conclude the flirtation we'd started the night we met, but then I thought, maybe he forgot or maybe I was wrong to assume. Plus, try climbing sneakily into a lad's bed while wearing a bustle and you'd understand," I said. "I managed to get out of it behind your tent, which is quite difficult in the moonlight. You get it. Best night of sleep I've had in a while.

You snore like a drowning duck by the way. Took me a while to figure out where you were camping. Took me a while, but didn't take much coin. Lot of people willing to give you up these days. But, back to my question." I waited as he squirmed.

"The Deluge left us alone in the Breige - " Henrold started.

"I already know you've sold out," I growled. "You owe me more of an explanation than that, but unfortunately I'm in a hurry this morning."

"I survived and I kept the Deluge out of the Breige. It's all business."

"You've done more than that."

"I would call my men in, but I'm growing quite fond of our position. Why are you here? Truthfully."

"Because you owe me a payment, and I'm collecting," I said. "But I'm feeling slightly generous considering your betrayal. I'll spare you and your little prick, if you give me one thing."

"And what's that?"

"Burrow, you're devilishly good looking, I would hate to kill you and upset that all, you're a rare man Henrold Nanibold Merigold," I said. I shifted my hips back and forth on top of him as he lay excitedly still waiting to see how far I'd take this, then said, 'Pynes' location. The real Pynes. Got a feeling a man like you actually does know where he is and I got a feeling a girl like me is willing to do anything to get that information out of you."

"And that's it? What about?" He nodded down.

"I'm not much for bedding those who betray me," I said. "When no coin's involved at least, but I'll be honest, I thought about it. One last toss before I leave. I was awfully close to waking you up last night when I rolled in, but you know, sometimes a nice sleep sounds just so much better. I decided heeding you a warning instead would benefit us both equally. When I leave here, you leave too. Don't pack, don't take anything with you. Just go. Who knows, maybe in another life, we could have been more than just business associates constantly betraying one another." I let him slide inside me once, but held him from moving beyond that.

"There is always time, Conley Mahren," he tried to remind me, smiling his wicked good grin as tried to shift. I wasn't allowing it.

"Pynes' location please."

Henrold shoved me aside, then rolled out of bed taking a pillow to cover himself.

"Pillow stays," I said. Humiliation was the least I could do. Henrold had betrayed me, but I wasn't the one for the petty death-dealing type of revenge and besides I was determined to let this man prove to be useful.

Henrold moved across his tent as buck as the day he was born to a deep chest and returned with an ocher hat knit of yarn. He tossed it to me.

"You should know, that's Pynes' real hat. It's not a replica. Kor brought it back with him before Pynes left for the Cistern. Kor couldn't tell me much of what happened there, he was already broken. It really is a lovely hat."

I shimmied myself to the edge of Henrold's bed, then

folded the hat on top of my lap. "It's nice to have back, thank you, but I'm after the man not his clothes."

He didn't say much after that as if he were thinking. "You know. I feel when a man such as myself is in this predicament baring all in front of a girl such as yourself, the only thing I'm left with is to be honest. About all of it."

"About all of it," I agreed. I already knew where he was going with this. It was a moment for him to bare all. Unburden himself. A man like Henrold didn't have this occasion much, but I'd let him have one this time. "You wanted the seal in the Cairns broken. You knew who was in there. What was beyond that gate."

He nodded. "I knew."

"Doesn't upset me. I'm used to being used. And, I've thought about it. I think even for the right amount of coin, I'd have done it without you lying to me. Can't reckon why you'd want anything to do with Fair Nathaniel though."

"I'm merely a pawn in this as well. A well paid one. Maybe have words with that young First Chancil of yours. She's insane."

"Truet? You're not - "

"I'm not saying anything. But, everything that's happened to you, everywhere you've been, every strap on your dress cut, pushing you to leave to go on a hunt for your Pynes."

"That's a bit specific," I said.

"Well it worked. Got you out the door. Err, window. I just wish it had been my idea."

"All Truet?" I asked.

"There's a reason she never killed you."

He paused. I let his eyes wander over me. Until you've stood bare in front of a man as you find out everything you've done in the past year was orchestrated by someone else - you lose all sense of self decorum, let alone proper conversation etiquette.

"I didn't know about what was under the Cistern. That was a misfortune. I didn't think-"

"What I think is that between you and our First Chancil you both thought you had me all figured out."

"That's absolutely true. If Conley is anything, it's that she's easy to figure out. Easy to push."

"The hell does that mean?"

"Point you in a direction, and that direction you will go," he said. It wasn't hurtful, and in fact I suppose it was true looking back. I was hardly the master of my own direction. Merely a passenger.

He shoulders dropped, "Listen, I couldn't tell you much about Pynes other than rumors and I cherish my manhood too much to lead you on another fox hunt. There was a rumor floating around the weeds of a devil in the South, lingering around Louisiana parts. Rumors that sounded a lot like what happened to Everett. A man full piss and rage. Might be worth a look."

I took a moment to consider, then said, "Take it all in," as I stood, "it's the last you'll likely be seeing of me."

"Your hair's longer," he said. Henrold watched me only a moment, went back inside his deep chest - all the way to the bottom - and returned with a pair of breeches. He tossed them to me. "What's next for Miss Mahren?"

We made a little bit more small talk after that as we got dressed, but I never really answered the man's question about what was next. Because I didn't really know myself.

On my eventual way out of West Virginia I stopped by the horse stables where our journey north initially started and found Robert McGee had, in fact, stolen our horses and brought them home. And, I was glad for that. Sarah Roy nuzzled into me as Robert approached.

"Didn't want the Moon-eyed to get 'em," was all he said.

As far as Pynes was concerned - the real Pynes anyway -

Maybe I'd get around to that eventually.

ACKNOWLEDGMENTS

This wouldn't have been written if not for the patient ears of my wife Annie. I'd fight a werewoof for you.

And, the very imaginative and active minds of my three sons. You keep me young and filled with stories.

To Bria and Kaeli for letting me talk hours about this book and never once telling me to stop talking.

And, finally to Ronnie. Whose ideas are as sharp and hilarious as anyone I know.

ABOUT THE AUTHOR

Dave currently lives in Ohio with his wife Annie and their three sons.

His grandfather let him drink coffee while watching westerns and his parents didn't cover his eyes while watching horror movies. He was probably too young. But, it didn't kill him.

Low, In The Valley is his first novel.